THE LAST DAYS OF HOLLY HAYES

HOLLY'S STORY

SANDRA J. PAUL

HAMLEY books

THE LAST DAYS OF HOLLY HAYES
First published: October 8th, 2024

Cover design by Sleepy Fox Cover Designs
Interior design by Design by Lotte
ISBN 9789464945782
NUR 285
Theme Code: YFCB 15+

Hamley Books Publishing prints its books on FSC© labeled paper. That way, we can help to preserve old and valuable forests. Take a look at our sustainability charter here: www.hamleybooks.be.

www.hamleybooks.be

THE LAST DAYS OF HOLLY HAYES

SANDRA J. PAUL

NOTE FROM THE AUTHOR TO THE READER,

This book is an Amazon exclusive interactive book that is available worldwide. You, the reader, can decide in what order you want to read about Holly and Dylan.

After every major section, you will get the option to choose. Make sure to read the instructions properly!

Maybe you will have discovered through social media that there is another version of The Last Days of Holly Hayes, a so-called flip over version.

This version is exclusively available in Belgium, The Netherlands and through Amazon Germany. It is also available on the website of Hamley Books Belgium.

Due to technical restrictions however, it is impossible to have this flip over version on Amazon, but this interactive version promises you the same experience.

I hope you enjoy the reading experience!

Sandra J. Paul
October 2024

TRIGGER WARNINGS

The Last Days of Holly Hayes holds mentions of the following:

- Graphic scenes of a possible end-of-the-world scenario as described by the characters in this book
- Mentions of paranormal and spiritual beliefs
- Mentions of doomsday prepping
- A few romantic love scenes between the main characters
- Use of curse words.

This story will deal with these topics in a subtle way. It is not the intent of the author to shock or harm the reader. If any of this is not your cup of tea, please refrain from reading this book. Conversations that may seem hurtful do not reflect the opinion of the author.

If any of these topics may upset or trigger you in any way, please be warned. If you need any help on any of these themes, please find help near you.

HOW TO READ THIS BOOK

Dear reader,

As this is an interactive book, you can choose where to start reading.

From this point on, choose what you want to read first.

1. Read Holly's story. In that case, continue reading.
2. Read Dylan's story. In that case, go to page 180 of the book.

If you choose Dylan first, you can come back later to this section of the book.

One way or the other, whatever you choose, you must read both storylines to get a complete picture of what happened.

HOLLY'S STORY

one

They always said that life was defined by nature and nurture. You were created by two people with a certain character or a set of character traits that they partially—or completely—transferred to you. Nature.

You're hopefully raised by those same people too, but in many cases, other people would get involved somehow, whether through loss, adoption, divorce, or whatever. Even more people, family members, played a part in the process, all of them leaving their mark. Nurture.

In both cases, as a child, you often didn't get to choose who those people were, where they came from, and what kind of character traits they brought with them. You didn't get to choose anything. And often, that meant that you acquired what they passed on to you, whether it was by nature or nurture.

I was one of the lucky ones. Born and raised in a loving family, from people who never once cheated on each other and stuck together, no matter what. My extended family was just as kind. Everyone cared about each other. Everyone got to be involved in whatever important decisions needed to be made.

My mom and dad were normal, hardworking, kind people, who hardly encountered any difficulties in their lives, except for the part where they wanted more than one child and my mom almost died to fulfill that wish. Her second pregnancy was one from hell, but she always said later on that it was worth it.

My sister, Emma, and I differed four years in age, but we had always been extremely close. I remembered what it was like to see my mom lying in bed for months in a row, too scared to get up in case she would lose her unborn child. That fear transferred to me, and I remembered very clearly, growing up, that I couldn't shake it off. Emma became my protégé.

I was too young to remember every detail but still old enough to realize that it wasn't normal for a mother to spend day and night in bed like that. I remembered the fear and anxiety, the constant care and the concern my dad radiated while looking out for her and me. I remembered my grandparents from both sides coming by constantly. I remembered weeks away with my grandma, to give my mom some rest.

In the end, though, my sister was born, and I doted on her from day one, even though I didn't remember those details either. Even now, I was still that big sister in every way, caring for her and about her, wanting to keep her safe from harm. Which hadn't always been easy. Just like everyone else in our family, I'd been overbearing, while there was nothing physically wrong with her. She'd been pretty mad about that in the past, so I tried to ignore my feelings.

"I'm not made of porcelain," she said one night, when she came home from meeting a friend. She'd gotten soaked through and through, and my mom and I rushed to hand her the biggest towel we could find. She was annoyed.

"Sorry that I care," I muttered.

"You care too much."

She did have a point there. I tried to do better since.

My dad owned a real estate agency in the area where we lived and did really well for himself. He bought and sold more houses in the area than anyone else.

My stay-at-home mom took care of us. After Emma was born, she never went back to work. Once Emma went to school, she didn't try to find another job but preferred to do charity instead. She could easily combine it with our care, and since Dad earned more than enough, there was no question whether they could afford that.

Dad was extremely proud of her. She ran most of the fundraisers for a lot of charities in the vicinity, and she did an amazing job too. Everyone knew and liked my parents.

Not once did they neglect me while loving Emma. I heard stories sometimes about kids suffering due to favoritism toward the other, but that never happened to me. I got everything I ever wanted and more.

When we moved to a gorgeous lake house that my dad had fixed up all by himself, everything just came together. Before the move, we lived in a beautiful house in downtown Beau, our hometown, but we were happy to leave it behind to move closer to the lake. Every day felt like a vacation after that.

We were one big happy family. My parents were my idols, and I vowed to become like them someday. I would find a man who would respect me as I would respect him. Someone who held the same values, who loved children, who wanted to be the best person he could be. I wanted someone I could trust blindly, who wouldn't lie to me.

I thought that Daniel was the one.

Daniel, eighteen years old just like I was. We met in our final high school year, about six months before the end of our senior year. He wasn't a typical high school student. He wasn't a jock, even though he had the physique. He wasn't one of the nerds, even though he had the brains. He was just a regular guy, walking around school, trying to make the best of things on the challenging road to college.

SATs defined my senior year. I had a goal and a purpose in life, and I was determined to get to where I was headed.

Ever since I was a kid, I had one major passion: to help people and animals medically. I soon discovered that the medical profession was not for me. I didn't have the patience or stamina for it, let alone the intelligence to work seven years or more to get a medical degree.

Of course, as I would discover much later, becoming a vet was just as challenging in many ways, and in others even more. Working with animals meant working with creatures who couldn't express themselves, who were often helpless and could not tell you where it hurt.

As a child, I used to play vet for our adopted stray cats. As a teenager, I had chosen my life's goal. Animals instead of humans. The helpless, the weak, and the caged.

I had a particular preference for wild animals, mostly the larger species. I spent hours at the zoo, just watching all those magnificent animals while feeling sorry for them too. I loved our local zoo because it was brand-new and huge. They had plenty of space for all the animals, and they did their best to make their lives as comfortable as possible.

Most of all, I loved the safari we went on when I was in my teens. My mom and dad surprised Emma and me for my sweet sixteenth birthday. They had arranged a two-week safari in South Africa, and I loved every single second of it. It was absolutely incredible.

I knew without a doubt that I wanted to study to become a

vet, so when the time came to write down my college choices, I kept two things in the back of my mind.

One: I wanted to be close to my parents and sister so I could travel home easily by car, bus, or train in case of an emergency. And I wanted to go home as much as I could during breaks.

Two: I wanted to learn how to take care of wildlife. Minneapolis was the only place I had set my heart on, so when I got in, I was the happiest person in the world. I had written a heartfelt letter explaining why I was so enthusiastic about their university, expounding with passion about their specialty course on wildlife. I told them I would do anything I could to become the best in my field.

So when I graduated from high school with honors, I was over the moon. I had a long summer ahead of me without a single worry, and I would enjoy every single second of it. With Daniel.

Or so I thought. Because Daniel did not get into any of his colleges of choice. Daniel didn't get his grades up high enough, despite the fact that he was intelligent enough. He was hooked on gaming, something he hadn't told me when we became something of an item, and that messed up his SATs.

He got his high school degree, but not with flying colors and definitely not with the kind of grades needed to get into the bigger universities. He didn't know what to do.

I remember that conversation all too well. Daniel came over to my house on graduation day because my dad had invited him to have a celebration dinner with us. Daniel's mom—she was divorced, and his dad was out of the picture—wasn't planning to do anything, so it made sense that he would come over.

When he arrived, he was moody and gloomy. He was not the boy I knew. Before that day, he had been nice and polite, always in a good mood, always cheerful. That time, he was in such a bad mood that my mom took me aside and inquired about what was going on.

"Did you have a fight?" she asked.

"No, we haven't fought once," I said. "But I do get why he's upset. He's angry that he didn't get in."

"I'm sorry, honey, but that is not your fault," Mom said. "If he's only here to mess things up for you, then he'd better go."

"Do you want him to go?" I asked.

"That is your choice to make. What do you want to do?"

"I'd like him to stay," I said after a short contemplation. "But only if he perks up a bit. I hope he does."

"Do you want me to talk to him?"

"No, I'll do it," I said.

Daniel and I had been the typical high school sweethearts up until that point. Just hanging around, holding hands, kissing, going to first base, making out on several occasions. It wasn't that big of a deal. I wasn't even sure if I liked him enough to keep him around once I moved to Minnesota.

Long-distance relationships never really worked out, especially when you lived in different states. I just wanted to have fun with him over the summer, maybe even sleep with him too, even though I wasn't sure about that yet. I was still a virgin. I didn't believe in casual sex; it had to mean something to me.

With Daniel, I wasn't sure yet if he was the person I wanted to be with for my first time.

I returned to the living room and found him sitting on the couch with his legs crossed. He was still in a foul mood. Dad was trying to get through to him, talk to him, find out what was going on. When I walked in, Dad jumped up and smiled.

"Shall we go? I'm starving."

"Can I just have a quick word with Daniel?" I asked.

"Sure, honey."

Dad kissed me on the forehead, hugged me quickly, and said he'd be in the kitchen if we needed him. I smiled and sat down on the coffee table in front of Daniel.

"Are you okay?" I asked, trying to get him to look at me. He didn't react.

I sighed and thought about the joy I had felt just a few hours ago. Why did he have to go and ruin the night?

"Look," I said, "my dad booked a table at this fancy restaurant, and you are still welcome to come with us, but not like this."

He looked at me indifferently.

"What do you mean?"

"You know what I mean. You're angry and upset. I don't like it."

"Why wouldn't I be angry?" he said, mimicking me. "Look at you, the golden child. You get everything you ever wanted, and I'm stuck in limbo as always."

"I'm sorry, Daniel, but that's not true. I worked hard to get this opportunity."

"Don't you think I worked just as hard?" he snapped.

I looked away.

"Holly?"

"No," I said after a painful silence where he looked at me as if I had just sprouted horns. "To be honest, I don't think you did."

He snorted. "That's rich. Never took you for such a cold-hearted bitch. You're not even trying to console me, are you?"

"I'm not a bitch," I said, taken aback. "How can you say that?"

"I didn't deserve that hurtful remark."

"And I'm sorry if it sounded hurtful, but it is the truth. You've said so yourself. You thought that you'd wiggle it, but you didn't."

He shrugged.

"And besides that, you didn't even think to congratulate me," I added. "You walked in, were in a foul mood from the start, and now you're trying to ruin my day. That's not very fair to me, is it?"

That was too much for him. He got up, reached for his jacket, and walked away.

"Fuck you," he said before slamming the door on his way out.

Later that night, he sent me several text messages, apologizing for his behavior. I ignored them all. During the following night, they became worse. Hurtful, angry, damaging, gaslighting. I blocked him. But somehow, while I tried to pretend that I was fine, I already knew that this would not be the last of it.

I was right. He never stopped texting me all summer. He used other people's phones to do so, mostly his mom's, who had no clue what he was doing.

He showed up at the lake house. He followed me around town. He became this terrible, angry jerk who stalked me until I cried my eyes out.

We took out a restraining order. He kept his physical distance, but he always found ways to taunt me.

Daniel ruined my last summer at home.

two

After I left for Minnesota, it felt as if I was free, but then again, I wasn't. Even though I was supposed to focus on my new life as a college student, I couldn't shake the fear he would follow me to Minneapolis.

He didn't.

He got tired of it, which was more than okay with me. I just wanted to move on from that terrible experience and forget all about it.

Besides, I didn't care about guys right now. All I wanted was to study. That's what I was here for.

Two days before my first year started, my parents drove me to Minneapolis, where I settled down quickly in a small building with only ten girls. My roommate, Anya, and I got the basement, which was one of the two dorm rooms available at the time. The other one was in the attic. Another two freshmen students moved in there.

I loved the room. It was huge, with lots of space and a separate bathroom Anya and I got to share. I also discovered quite quickly that she was totally different than I was, crazy in many ways but hilarious in many others. She was loud and often rude, and she loved sex.

During those first months, I'd seen about five guys walking around on campus with her. Fortunately, she had the decency to have sex outside of our room, something I didn't even have to ask her about.

We became close friends, shared food and drinks, music and books. We went to the movies a lot, often with other girls from our building or people I'd met in class, and we just had a great time. Life was good, with its small ups and downs, but mostly ups.

The one downside to it all was that I missed my family terribly. With me gone, there was this whole new dynamic in our family. I called or texted Emma daily, which was great, but it was not the same. I could tell she was bothered by it too.

In the end, though, by Thanksgiving, everyone had settled down into this new routine. I was studying hard, had great friends and a fantastic roommate, loved my courses, and I'd found a job at the local vet, where I could help out with some chores and basic things.

When Christmas arrived, I took the train home. Mom and Dad picked me up while Emma was at home decorating the house. It was amazing to be back there with them.

Unfortunately, Daniel was there too. Somehow, he had gotten wind of me arriving and showed up at the train station. He just stood across the street without doing anything, but it was enough to bring back that same feeling of terror he had inflicted upon me back in the summer.

This time, though, I fought back. I had grown a spine, had gained some self-confidence, and I wasn't prepared to let this asshole ruin my Christmas. My dad saw him too. He sighed, balled his fists, and moved away from our car.

My parents and Emma knew about all of this. We had

discussed it many times. They had told me that Daniel was studying at a local college and still lived with his parents. He was doing a major in accounting. They said he had a girlfriend, so they believed he wouldn't bother me anymore.

But there he was.

"No, Dad," I said, stopping him before he could move. "I'll handle this."

Dad wanted to stop me, but Mom held him back.

"She needs to do this," she said.

And that was true. I marched over to him as he casually leaned against a wall, pretending he wasn't there for me while keeping an eye on me at the same time.

"Well, well, Holly Hayes," he said. "You're looking good. Wanna hang out together this Christmas?"

"No, Daniel," I said, staying as calm as I could. "I don't. In fact, I think I'm going to pay your girlfriend a visit and tell her about the fucker you are and the restraining order you have just violated. See how she reacts to that."

"I didn't. You walked over to me," he said.

"Actually, you did. You didn't keep your distance to begin with, *and* you should have walked away. I can walk wherever I can, but you can't. So I'll be calling the police now. What do you say, huh? I should talk to your mom too, tell her what you've been up to."

"Don't you dare," he said, turning pale.

"Oh, but why not? You fucked up my summer, and you're obviously planning on fucking up Christmas too, so why should I consider your feelings?"

"Still stuck-up, I see," he said. "You haven't changed a bit."

"Still the biggest asshole in the world," I retorted. "But you know what? I don't care anymore. You're done."

I took out my phone. He got nervous.

"Look, you've got it all wrong, Holly. I came to apologize for my behavior. That kid was stupid, okay? He was jealous and humiliated when you told him to go away. I've changed."

"You were the one who left," I reminded him. "You did that, not me. I never harmed you in any way."

I took out my phone and tapped in 911.

"No. Please stop, okay?" he said, moving toward me. I stepped backward. "I'm sorry. I didn't—okay, I fucked up, I admit it. But I didn't want to hurt you this time."

"You have a great way of showing that," I said. "I pity your girlfriend, you know that? Does she even know that you're a stalker?"

He turned red. "I'm not."

"Then walk away and never come back. Respect the restraining order. Respect that girl. If I ever catch you doing this to anyone else, I'll call the police and tell them that you violated the rules."

"What evidence do you have?" he said angrily.

I pointed at my mom.

"She filmed everything."

Daniel deflated like a burst balloon. Gone was the bravado, the arrogance, the bully act, and terrible remarks. He looked like the old Daniel for a moment, before I remembered what he had done to me.

"I just miss you, okay? I've been missing you since the day we broke up."

"The day you walked away," I corrected him.

"Whatever. I fucked up. I want to try to make it work again."

I was stunned. Then I started laughing.

"What?"

"If you really think I'll allow you within one foot of me ever again, you've got it wrong, asshole. You're a horrible human being."

I turned around and walked back to my dad's car. Daniel never realized how much I was shaking and how terrible I felt doing that. I had to stop myself from turning around to apologize for my harsh words. But then I remembered that he had been putting the blame on me for his own behavior and that he would never change.

When I got into the car, he was gone. That was the last time I ever saw him. Months later, I heard from my dad that he had applied for a college transfer and was now studying in South Carolina. His mom moved with him, his girlfriend didn't. He never came back.

After Christmas, I felt liberated, and Anya noticed it too. Before the confrontation, I had been quite wary about dating, because of my horrible experience with Daniel, so I had brushed off any invitations that might have led to something more. But now, it felt like it was time to start living.

Some guys had shown interest, I couldn't deny that. I wasn't a photo model like Anya was or the gorgeous TikTok/Instagram/influencer girl that got so much attention—according to Anya, mostly to get laid quickly and dumped even quicker—but I had my fair share of guys wanting to go out on a date.

I went out for coffee with a few, had dinner with a couple, and went to parties with friends, where I kissed a couple of guys. None of them really felt like *this is it*, but it was fun, and I liked hanging out with them.

Anya helped me to choose carefully. She had a sixth sense when it came to the weirdos, which helped to ease the experience of dating.

By the end of the first year, a guy in most of my classes, called Simon, asked me out for a date. It turned out to be great. He was fun and kind and treated me with the respect that I needed to feel with guys.

We went out a couple of times, and about a week before finals started, we had sex. Simon knew I was a virgin and took his time making sure that I enjoyed the experience.

We continued to date for a while and had sex a couple of times, but neither of us felt enough of a spark to continue seeing each other during the summer. In the fall, at the start of our second year, we both silently decided that it had been fun while it lasted. We never officially broke up. It just happened. I was okay with that.

I realized all too well that it wasn't normal for someone not to long for the person they were supposed to be with during a long period of time, so mentally I had already said goodbye to him.

We met up for coffee, talked about it, and agreed to let each other go. I was happy that he taught me that sex was great. It had been a wonderful and beautiful experience, and I would cherish it forever, but that was it.

"I liked being with you," he said, "but it isn't enough for me. It doesn't feel like we are the perfect fit. Does that make sense?"

"In every way," I said. "But please, let us be friends."

Strangely enough, that's what we did. Simon became one of my best friends on campus. For months, our relationship grew into something I could describe as besties. It was great.

I helped him with biology, he helped me with math. We saw a bunch of movies together, hung out together, and just liked being around each other. We never had sex again.

He told me he would start dating again, I said I wanted to take it easy for a while and concentrate on my studies. He called me a bookworm, I said he should be careful that someone new wouldn't mess up his schedule. He laughed it away.

A couple of months later, Simon introduced me to his new girlfriend, Amanda. They had been dating for a few weeks by then.

Within five seconds, I knew she was the possessive, controlling type, and she didn't like me at all. One, I had dated her boyfriend. Two, we still hung out as friends. Three, he talked about me all the time.

Within the hour, I knew he was smitten with her and that I would hardly see him again from that point on.

I was right.

Simon stopped hanging out with me. No more movie dates, no more studying together. No more banter and fun moments. It broke my heart a lot more than Daniel's rudeness had ever done. It also made me wonder what was wrong with me. There had to be something wrong, right?

Simon dropped out of college and ended up marrying Amanda when she got pregnant. She was a classic Bridezilla.

Our third year. Time flew when you were having fun.

After a tranquil summer with my parents, I returned to college and focused on my studies. The goodbyes were a routine now, and I was a lot more at ease around my sister, no longer fearing for her constantly.

I didn't actively date anymore, despite Anya's insistence that I should. After Simon, I had seen a couple of other guys, but none of them really appealed to me, so I had decided to let it go. If someone came my way, fine. If not, that was fine too.

The first semester went really well. I had a lot of fun with a lot of people, enjoying my freedom. I made new friends, studied hard, and enjoyed hanging around with the girls from the dorm.

Christmas came and went. Another amazing vacation, spent with my closest family. January and February flew by quickly. Every year went faster than the previous one.

Until that one day in March.

Anya and I were at this coffeehouse we loved. It was a campus hotspot, the place to be to find out any and all gossip. It was crowded as always, but not in such a way that it felt overwhelming.

Anya prodded me.

"Did you see that guy? The cute one?"

I got shaken out of the brilliant world of veterinary medicine and looked up, confused.

"What guy?"

"The barista. Look at him. Why didn't I notice before that he's so cute? Damn."

The man she was talking about moved behind the counter as if he were used to being there. I remembered having seen him before, but usually I just came in for coffee and walked out quickly. This time, we were sitting here having our coffees because I had a test in an hour, and I needed to double-check some things. Since it was pouring outside, takeout coffee was a no-go this time around.

I looked at the baristas behind the counter, who were chatting amicably with each other and their customers. Everyone was always chitchatting about random stuff like football or baseball or something like that. Even in a medical college, sports dominated most of the conversations between the male students, and undoubtedly between a few of the female students as well, but for different reasons.

The other barista was attractive, but the one Anya pointed out, with the cute haircut and the glorious eyes, was the one that stood out to me the most. I felt an instant attraction. A twinge that I hadn't felt often before. I just didn't have the time right now to think about it.

"Not interested," I said, going back to my laptop.

"Come on, Hol. What, are you blind? Take a closer look."

I looked up, annoyed. "Why? I'm not looking for anyone."

"Not for you. For me."

"Oh."

I looked at my best friend and felt a sting of disappointment rush through me, realizing that she had set her eyes on this guy before I did, meaning that our rule of 'first come, first served' was valid. We had made that agreement a long time ago to avoid any arguments about guys.

"He's cute," she said. "Don't you think?"

"Yeah, he is," I reluctantly agreed, when all I really wanted to say was, *don't touch him, he could be mine someday.*

Anya seemed satisfied with my response. She got up.

"Hey, what are you doing?" I said.

"Why, I'm going to talk to him of course."

"Now? I have a test in an hour. I don't have time for this now," I protested, knowing that, if she got her way, she would forget everything else and just go for it.

"I don't have a test," she remarked. "I'm not even in your classes."

I reacted irritated. "Then stay here and do your mojo, but I'm leaving in ten minutes, and I want to pass that goddamn test, so if you'll excuse me, I'll focus on my book again."

Anya sighed. "You're boring."

"Good. I'll be a boring vet someday if you leave me the fuck alone right now. I'm trying to focus here."

"Nobody ever focuses in a coffee shop."

"I do all the time if the people around me would just shut the hell up. Will you just do your thing? Otherwise, sit down and leave me alone for a while."

She sat down and sipped her coffee. She was quiet for about thirty seconds before she started talking again.

"He's very cute. Look at that beautiful long hair. It's been a while since I saw anyone who could carry his hair that way and look damned good."

Long hair? Wait, what?

I looked up, catching a glimpse of the barista.

"Oh, you mean the guy on the right?" I said with relief I couldn't disguise.

"Yeah, who else? Oh…" She stopped and grinned. "You like the one on the left, don't you?"

I shrugged and looked away, but she caught me like a fly in her web.

"Holly Hayes, are you telling me you're finally crazy about someone? You, the college ice queen?"

"I'm not an ice queen," I protested fiercely.

"Yeah, you are. You're the only one in college who hasn't had sex the entire two years she's been here."

"I've had sex…"

"Oh? Who with?"

Fuck. I'd never told her about Simon because we had kept it low-key. I thought long and hard to come up with a convincing lie. I wouldn't hear the end of it otherwise.

"Okay. There was this one guy at a party and I had sex with another guy a few nights later."

"The one at the party stuck his tongue in your mouth and was too drunk to feel you up. I was there, remember? He fell asleep on the couch five minutes later. Who was the other guy? You never told me about him."

I became painfully aware of the fact it was eerily quiet around us at the coffeehouse. I looked up and found a number of college students looking at us, amused. God. Great first impression.

I looked embarrassed at the baristas, but to my relief, the cute one was gone. The other one was still there, and he couldn't stop staring at Anya.

"Gotta go," she said and got up.

Everyone around us kept staring at her.

"What?" she said, throwing evil glances around. "Never heard adult women talk about sex? Pathetic."

Everyone laughed, shrugged, and went about their business. Anya stood in front of the counter and looked the long-haired guy up and down.

"I wouldn't mind talking about sex with you," he said.

"I don't like talking," she replied.

I quickly packed up my things and hurried out of the coffeehouse as fast as I could.

A couple of hours later, Anya was waiting for me outside the main building. She looked flushed, like she always did when she'd just had sex.

"Seriously?" I said. "No, never mind, spare me the details."

"Did you know that coffee place has a great backroom with a comfy couch?" she said.

"God, gross."

"It wasn't gross. It was freaking hot. That guy has

amazing hands."

"Seriously, Anya, I don't want to know, okay?"

"Sorry. How did the test go?"

"It was fine."

"That sounds bad."

"It wasn't bad. Just fine." I sighed.

I tried to rub away the headache that had been bothering me for a few hours. I'd had a late-night shift at the veterinary clinic downtown with two emergencies.

Now that I was in my third year, they let me help more often, which meant I was also given a lot more responsibility. Even though I loved my job, it was exhausting to combine it with my studies, so I was actually considering getting a job without any responsibility at all.

We took the main path across campus, and Anya kept very close to me, which was odd. We weren't that touchy-feely with each other.

"What are you doing?" I said when she started increasing our pace.

"I'm helping you out."

"Huh? What?"

"Look in front of you, idiot."

I was confused. Until I saw him, the guy from the coffeehouse. The cute one, not the long-haired one who'd fucked her. He was coming from the other direction and walking straight toward us while glancing at his phone.

"What? Not now," I said. "I want to head to the dorm, drop this ridiculously heavy stack of books, take a shower, and get dinner."

"Excuses, Holly Hayes. If you don't want him, I'll take him."

"What? No!" I said before I could stop myself.

My reaction made her grin. God, I wanted to wipe that smug look off her face. She let go and picked up her pace even more. Before I could stop myself, I rushed forward, panting.

"You could help me, you know," I said.

"Why? You can manage. Come on."

Just like in a movie, he was heading toward us, as we were walking in his direction. But he had no clue who I was or what Anya was planning. He was just doing his thing, minding his own business. No lightning strikes, no extraordinary events happened when we reached each other.

He saw us coming, I could tell, and he took a step aside just in time. The moment he did, Anya shoved me in his direction. The next moment, I crashed into him and dropped my books. I could almost hear Anya snigger when I reached up and touched the guy's arm.

"Oh God, I'm so sorry. Are you okay?"

"Yeah," he said, "all good. It's fine. No harm done."

He tried to get away, obviously not willing to lose any time. For a second, I thought it would be over before it even started, but on impulse, I stopped him again.

"Are you sure?"

He seemed confused.

"Yeah, of course I am. Are you?"

I couldn't help smiling. It was so damn hard to conceal my joy when he reacted as I had hoped. God, I sucked at this. Why was I even doing this to myself?

"I am," I blurted out.

He smiled lightly. "Oh. Well, all's good then."

He moved. I stopped him again. *What the hell are you thinking, Hol? Stop embarrassing yourself!*

"I'm Holly Hayes," I said hastily and offered him my hand.

He studied my hand while he accepted it. Anya sniggered again.

"Nice name," he said.

"Thanks. And you are?"

He seemed stunned. "Excuse me?"

"Your name. What is it?"

"Oh. Dylan," he muttered.

"Dylan who?"

"Excuse me?"

I smiled patiently. "Your full name."

"Oh. Sorry. Dylan Blair. Nice to meet you."

"You have a nice name too," I blurted out. "It already sounds like a doctor's. Doctor Blair, please come to the desk right now."

He laughed, revealing his beautiful teeth. Yeah, I had it bad alright. He was just so charmingly, innocently perfect, and I liked him already.

"Does it now?" he spoke slowly.

"Yep, it does."

"Well, that's good to know. But I assume that you'll be a doctor one day too?"

My books still lay scattered around us, but I didn't care. All that mattered was his soft touch on mine. It felt electric, eternal. He'd stopped trying to get away. He was genuinely interested in me now.

God, what was I doing to myself? Why did Anya put me in this position? I reluctantly let go of his hand.

"Yeah, I will be, but I don't think my patients will be calling for me like yours will," I said, mentally kicking myself for being such an idiot.

"Why not?" he asked, not getting it, of course.

"I'm a future veterinarian. So unless a cat suddenly starts talking, it'll be someone else calling my name."

He smiled. "Oh. Well, at least your patients won't have a whole list of demands ready."

"Hm, I don't know about that. They might ask for special treats. Or extra pats."

He relaxed. "I'm sure you'll be happily fulfilling those demands. There are worse things than handing out extra pats on a cat's furry back."

"I'm sure there are," I said, laughing. He laughed with me. Anya openly mocked me.

I resisted kicking her in the chin.

A silence followed between us, but it wasn't uncomfortable. It was warm, fuzzy, cozy. He was just perfect. Too good to be true.

Daniel came to mind. Not Simon. This guy didn't even look like Daniel, but he acted the same. Would he turn into an asshole too? I didn't want this, not really, but at the same time, I did. Third time really was the charm.

"Nice to meet you, Holly Hayes," he said after a while. He hesitated. "Want to get a coffee with me sometime soon? I know a good place. Kind of work there too."

"I know. I've seen you around," I said hastily, again kicking myself mentally for being so obvious, but there she was, the idiot in me, who just couldn't shut up. "And yes, I would love to have a coffee with you when you're off work."

"Deal."

He picked up my books and handed them over to me.

"If you want, I can walk you back to your dorm. Those things seem pretty heavy."

"That's okay. You were heading in the other direction, and Anya here can help me. Right?"

"Right," Anya said, even though she didn't make a single

attempt to do so.

"Okay then. But I will see you around, right?" he asked nervously, as if he were scared I would disappear.

"You will, I promise. Here, give me your phone."

He seemed taken aback by my request. His hands wandered off to his pockets. I'd swear I could see more than one phone tucked away, or maybe he was a smoker. It was a bit odd.

He dug out the phone in his right-hand pocket, unlocked it, opened up his Contacts app, and gave it to me. I typed in my name and phone number, then sent a message to myself. It chimed on my phone.

"There, don't lose me now," I said.

"I won't," he promised. "But I do really have to go now. I'm late for a shift."

"Another one?" Anya said. He looked at her in surprise. "Sorry, it's just that we—I—saw you there this morning too."

"Ah, so you know the place?"

"Everyone knows the place."

He narrowed his eyes and looked at her before returning his gaze to me.

"You're not stalking me, I hope?"

Anya laughed. "No. I fucked the guy working with you earlier, so you don't have to worry."

He was taken aback. So was I.

"What guy?"

"Long-haired, sexy guy."

"What, Tom?"

"Yep."

"He's my boss. He's married."

Anya's mouth fell open.

"He's your boss? He looks like a freaking college student."

"He's not. He's thirty. Got married last summer."

"Fuck."

"Yep, that's what he does," Dylan reacted dryly. "He fucks around. It doesn't matter who; he likes all genders."

For the first time since we met, Anya was lost for words. She seemed sick, and I knew why. She never fucked married—and older—men. Thirty in our books was old. Dylan seemed shocked by her reaction.

"Oh, I'm so sorry. I thought you knew. Everyone knows. He's the biggest slut in town."

"And your boss. Should you even be talking about him like that?" she remarked dryly.

Dylan shrugged. "Everyone does. But anyhow, I really have to go. I'm so sorry." He turned to me. "So I will see you around?"

"You can bet on it."

He smiled and walked away. I looked after him. He stopped after a few steps and turned around, smiling even more broadly when he noticed I was still around.

"See you soon."

"See you," I said.

Anya turned to me. "That guy's an asshole."

"Who, Dylan?"

"No, his boss."

"Well, it's a good thing you know now instead of later," I said, placing my free arm over her shoulder. "Come on, these books are killing me."

She finally took over a couple of books and walked back with me to the dorm. Freed from my things, I plunked down on the bed and thought about the strange encounter with Dylan Blair. When I took out my phone, I noticed he had sent me a message.

Thanks for bumping into me. Nice meeting you.—Dyl

I sent one back.

You're welcome. Hope to bump into you again soon.—Hol

From that moment on, I was hopelessly lost. I was never going to date in college again? Yeah right.

three

I never thought that life could get this good, but it did. From the moment I saw Dylan, and the second we started talking on that warm spring day on campus, I knew that my instincts hadn't betrayed me about him.

I couldn't even begin to explain why, but I just knew that he was the person I was meant to be with. He wasn't like Daniel, who had always had two sides about him. Nor was he like Simon, who had been a friend more than a romantic partner.

I was drawn to Dylan like a moth to a flame. There was something different about this guy. He wasn't like the others. Where most male students seemed pretty confident, pretending they had everything under control and acting cool while struggling to keep up in class, trying to make sense of all the medical mumbo jumbo we got thrown at us, Dylan Blair looked the part of a serious medical student with only one focus in mind: to succeed in every way.

He wasn't a nerd, not even close. He wasn't a geek or a guy walking around in a suit with a briefcase. No, he wore tattered jeans, worn-down shirts, and sneakers that had seen their best days five years or so ago. It was just that look on his face, that determination not to fail, as if he were planning to save the world one day.

If someone had told me he was a scientist, I would have believed it too. His whole demeanor felt so mysterious, as if he carried a heavy burden that no one else could carry for him. It was odd.

I noticed this on the first real talk we had at the coffeehouse where he worked. He had sent me a text to invite me for coffee after his shift ended. I happily obliged without telling Anya, who would take matchmaking credit for sure.

When we sat down, I started rambling about my personal life and college. I got that way when I was nervous. I talked about Beau, my parents, and my sister. He told me he was an only child and lived in Montana, with the mountains in his backyard. It sounded impressive.

"Tell me more about your family," I said. "What are they like?"

"Busy, hardworking people. They are devoted to our community. I want to be like that, too, someday."

In the days that followed, I tried to figure out who Dylan Blair was. We immediately started seeing other a lot. I didn't even know who instigated it, but it just happened.

We connected in so many ways. We were both ambitious and hardworking, we both wanted to work and study, we wanted to experience college life to the fullest, without the casual sex. We spoke openly about it, even on that first date.

"Look," I said at some point, remembering Anya's encounter with Tom. "I just want you to know I'm not my roommate. I don't go around sleeping with people casually. I don't do one-night stands. I don't suck up to guys in hopes they'll fuck me against a wall or something. I'm not like that at all. I'm not even sure if I'm ready for a relationship right now. It's something I need to discover."

"In other words, you want to take it slowly."

"Yeah, I do. Is that okay?"

The smile on his face said it all.

"God, yeah," he said, releasing a sigh. "The thing is, I don't sleep around either. I've had one relationship on campus, and it wasn't even a real one. It was just this girl that I liked, but she wasn't it for me. I've had a high school sweetheart, and that's about it. I haven't been seeing anyone for the past year or so, and to be honest, I…"

"You weren't really looking for it."

"Yeah." He looked at his coffee. "Please don't take this the wrong way. I do like you."

"No, I totally get what you mean," I said quickly. "I feel the same way. Honestly, it was Anya's idea to run into you. I didn't even know she was planning to get your attention that way."

"I'm glad she did," Dylan said. "You are extraordinary, Holly Hayes. Where did you even come from?"

"Beau."

"Haha."

That first encounter in his coffeehouse was just the best moment I'd had so far on campus, and I never wanted it to end. I wanted to stay with him, but in the end, we said goodbye and promised to catch up the next day.

We went out for breakfast. We had lunch and dinner together. We spent time together, studied together, and talked. It just happened and felt completely natural, as if it were normal to want to be with someone from the moment you met them.

As it turned out, in the weeks and months that followed, life only got better. The more I got to know Dylan, the more I fell in love with who he was. He was everything I looked for in a partner, and somehow, he didn't even realize.

He was *the one*, I just knew it. Anya had known it too. The one who fitted me perfectly, the guy without a shred of arrogance, anger, or jealousy in him. The one who didn't care that I went out with male friends on occasion or needed some time alone now and then.

We had a lot in common, which made our lives so much easier. We could talk for hours about books and movies. He had a weak spot for art movies but secretly preferred superhero movies, liked to debate for hours on political topics, and detested the injustices in our country. I agreed with him on a lot, but not on everything. Some of our views were so different that we agreed to disagree, but we still loved to debate about it.

We were also very different in many ways. Our choice of food, what songs we liked. He loved soccer, I loved football. He liked jazz, I could bear it but only just. I loved opera—I know, a thing my mom taught me. He could barely stomach it. He loved ambient music to study with, I couldn't bear a single sound in the room when I was throwing myself into my books.

My greatest fear when we met had been that he might be casually seeing someone else. I mean, why wouldn't he be? He would have fitted into anyone's life. He was the type of guy you befriended, got to know, and took home to your parents without feeling ashamed about specific tics or quirky tendencies. Guys like him were trustworthy and normal and had no serial-killer character traits. They were just perfect.

Everyone who knew him felt the same way. Everyone who knew me congratulated me on finding that one person many would call their soulmate. I didn't believe in soulmates, but I was certain that, if such a person existed for me, they would bear Dylan's name.

The more we got to know each other and hung out together,

the more our lives became entwined. We kept our rooms of course, but we spent more time at mine than his because Dylan's roommate Harry and Anya somehow became friends with benefits, meaning fuck buddies.

By summer, Dylan and I had become "Holly and Dylan," and I'd gotten him to open up about himself, not only to me but to other people too. He'd gotten to know my friends and I, in turn, met the few he had. Our relationship was going strong. There wasn't a single moment that I'd regretted having bumped into him. We had our small differences, but not a single argument during the entire time we were together.

The one thing we did *not* have in common, though, were our families. I talked about mine all the time, he hardly ever spoke about his. At first, I only briefly wondered why, but after a while, I began to worry that something was amiss.

He was always very apprehensive and cautious when the subject of his family came up. He didn't really like to talk about his life at Midstone, his high school years, or his high school sweetheart, a girl named Allison. He told me about her but brushed it off as something unimportant, just like he didn't feel my relationships before I met him were a big deal.

"Let bygones be bygones," he said. "I don't care about past boyfriends, as long as they don't come around stalking you."

"You don't have to worry about that," I replied, laughing. "And I suppose you don't have a secret child with Allison?"

"God no."

There was one other thing that got me rattled on occasion, but it was difficult to discuss with him without bursting into tears. It reminded me too much of Daniel, and it scared me too.

When we were dating for about a month and we practically spent every spare moment together, after making sure we were working the same shifts and everything, he let down his guard around me. Before, he had always kept his guard up, even while we were talking. Just like the subject of his hometown and family was avoided as much as possible, he also didn't want to discuss why he carried multiple phones with him.

I asked him about it at some point. He was shocked that I had noticed. I saw him with different phones all the time, but somehow, he didn't seem to know I was aware of that.

"Why all these phones?" I said casually one night, when we were lying in bed. "You're not secretly married or anything, are you?"

"Married?" he repeated, as if he couldn't get why I would ask such a question.

"Yeah. Men who have multiple wives and lovers do that."

"I'm a college student, Hol, as you obviously know." He sounded irritated, almost angry, as if I were asking the most ridiculous thing ever.

"Lighten up, Dyl," I said. "It was a joke."

But still.

He became quiet after that, shifted into one of those odd moods of his where he was thinking about stuff that wasn't important enough to share.

"You're right," he said. "I do have three phones."

"But not three wives, I hope?" I said, trying to lighten the mood.

He smiled. "No. Life is complicated enough with just one wife."

"Hey!"

"Sorry. But you're right. I should give you an explanation. It's odd when you come to think of it."

"Dyl, don't," I said, stopping him before he could continue.

"You don't owe me any explanation at all. It was just silly banter. I was curious, but I have no right to be."

"Actually, if we are continuing this relationship, which I hope we are, you should know a bit more about me."

"Okay?"

He dug into his pockets and fished out three phones. The one he used the most was the biggest one. My number was in there. The other two were smaller and older. All three were active.

"I know you're going to think that this is silly, but this is my main phone, the one I use all the time."

"Right."

"My dad gave me the other two."

"Oh? Why?"

"Back home, it's hard to get a decent connection in the mountains, especially on these new devices. It's like the more expensive they get, the less you can do with them."

"Oh yeah, I know," I said.

"Connection back home is always crooked, so my dad, my mom, and I all walk around with one major phone and two spares. He calls them our emergency phones. It's a family thing. It comes from having to deal with emergencies on a daily basis. My mom, as you know by now, works as a mountain ranger. She's specialized in aiding and assisting tourists, usually when they get lost."

"But because the mountains are so difficult in terms of connection, your dad gave her two spare phones," I said, filling in the blanks.

"Exactly."

"But why give you two as well?"

"That's who he is," Dylan explained, smiling lightly. "For

some reason, it makes him feel at ease, I guess. I don't really know why, but he seems more relaxed knowing I have these phones on me at all times."

"I see," I said. "Now I get it."

"Everyone there, living nearby or working in the mountains, has two phones. That's just how it is."

"Everyone?" I said.

"Yep."

"That's crazy."

He seemed taken aback and defensive.

"That's how it goes in the mountains. You don't know what it's like over there. If you didn't grow up there, it would be hard to understand."

His reaction unnerved me. I had already noticed how his moods often got the better of him. He could change from outgoing and extroverted into this extremely private person. Sometimes, he would gaze at one of the other phones and—so I guessed—he would get some information or news that he didn't like. And he would act completely different. When it was really bad, he would head to his dorm and be on his own.

This was a point of concern to me, but not in such a way that I feared he was hiding stuff from me or trying to drive me away. Whatever happened, he never lashed out at me or sent me away.

I already knew that I was in love with him.

The next step was taking our relationship to the next level. And so we did.

On a hot May evening, I invited Dylan to my dorm room, knowing Anya wouldn't be there for the night. I was initially hesitant about taking him there, not because I was ashamed of having him over, but because it felt like the next level.

Dylan was perfect to me, except for the secrecy. That scared me more than I cared to admit. I wasn't ignorant nor stupid. There was more going on with those phones than he cared to share, but I brushed it off. I was not prepared to let my wild thoughts get the better of me.

He was not Daniel. That was all I needed to know.

I had come prepared. Fresh sheets on the bed, a light dress I loved to wear, sexy but decent lingerie, my favorite perfume. I wore sandals instead of sneakers and had even painted my toenails. As if he would care.

He was wearing a light T-shirt and jeans. He wore the perfume I had given him for his birthday recently. We had celebrated with a bunch of his friends. Burgers and fries, which was all we could afford.

We both wanted it to happen tonight. We'd been putting it off for various reasons, but in the end, I firmly believed that we both wanted to make sure that this was not going to mess up our relationship. We wanted it to count for something.

When we walked through the building, one of his phones buzzed. He frowned, and I knew why. It was one of the other ones, what he called the emergency phone.

He tried to ignore it at first, but then he took it out of his pocket to read the message. That troubled him even more.

"Is something wrong?" I asked, worried. "Do you need to go?"

He tucked away the phone and smiled weakly.

"No, not at all! It's—well, it's my dad. He keeps me up to speed on what's happening at home."

"Wait, did something happen in Midstone? Is your mom okay?" I asked, alarmed.

"No, no, it's not my mom. It's just things at home, you know? It's not important. I just need to figure out some stuff, that's all. It's fine, don't worry about it. It can wait until later."

It wasn't the first time this had happened, far from it. I had figured out by now that this particular phone was the one his dad used the most, and whatever he told Dylan was enough to shake him to the core. To be honest, I was starting to believe that his dad was manipulating him, using him, forcing him to deal with things he shouldn't be dealing with at all.

Dylan had told me he had a complicated family, but he never elaborated further on the subject, and I didn't ask. I didn't want to know.

"Are you okay?" I asked. "We can postpone."

"No. I want this." He smiled, took my hand, pulled me against him, and kissed me. I could feel his hard-on pressing against me. "God, you smell so good."

"Please fuck me tonight," I whispered.

His cock grew even bigger. It pushed against the fabric of his jeans and up against my leg.

"Oh yeah," he said. "God, yes."

When we entered the room, he was shocked to see Anya's side of it. Her area was dark, damp, and cluttered, with books, clothes, and shoes scattered everywhere. When we first moved in together, I had bought a big bookshelf and placed it between our two areas so I wouldn't have to deal with her mess.

The benefit of having the basement was that it was much bigger than the other rooms and had a private bathroom, which was a luxury for a college student.

We spoke briefly about Anya and Harry and their odd relationship, but to be honest, that was not what I wanted to discuss at all. All I wanted to do was fuck him. Which I didn't tell him.

I did tell him my big news. Anya was moving to London soon, which had been a surprise to me. Her parents were moving there permanently and wanted her to go with them and transfer colleges. Anya had agreed.

"So you'll get a new roommate?" he asked.

"Nope.

"Why not?"

"I'm moving too."

His eyes went wide with shock, which really pleased me.

"Don't worry, I will still be here," I reassured him, continuing with the second part of my big news. "It's just that my dad bought a tiny apartment for me downtown. He said it was a good investment, especially since I'm planning on specializing in larger animals, which means I'll be here for at least three to four more years."

"Oh. I thought you'd be working with cats," he said, sounding confused.

"On the side. I want to work with zoo animals. I'd like to combine both."

I had not told him that yet. It sounded too far off to become reality. I could only start thinking about that in a few years. He seemed in awe.

"That's amazing, Holly."

"And you know the best part, Dylan?"

"No?"

I took a bold step right there and then. Enough talking, let's do this. I tugged at his shirt.

"You'll be here for a long time too. That means you and me will have plenty of time and space to do the dirty."

"That sounds great," he said hoarsely.

I looked at his chest. It had some hair on it, but not too much. Just a bit around the navel, which I liked. He worked out a couple of times per week, and it showed. He wasn't one of those bulkier fitness guys, but he had just the right amount of muscle that I liked to see on a man. God, I wanted to feel him inside of me so badly.

"It'll be great too, I promise," I said.

"I have no doubt," he whispered as he pulled me closer.

We kissed fiercely. He panted. I wanted to get this dress off. I wanted to feel his fingers on me, in me. I moved my hands to his abdomen, down to his jeans, and unbuttoned it. He took off my dress.

Our hands were everywhere, our tongues entwined. I took him to bed, where we shed the rest of our clothes. When we lay down on the bed, both naked, I started shaking.

I opened the drawer and took out a condom, but my fingers wouldn't cooperate, and I couldn't get the wrapping to open.

"Sorry, I'm just so nervous."

He stopped me, sounding surprised.

"Why? I'm the one who should be nervous."

"Why?" I retorted, just as surprised.

"You need to ask me why? You're the most gorgeous woman I have ever seen, Holly. And you chose me."

His words changed everything for me. He thought he was the lucky one? No, I was. I really was. That moment defined the foundation of our relationship for me. He wasn't Daniel at all. He was Dylan. He was nervous because he really wanted to be with me.

I calmed down at once.

"I'm not gorgeous," I said firmly. "You are."

Dylan leaned into me, kissed me, and removed the condom

from its wrapping. We both prepared him, and by the time he entered me, I was soaking wet. It was the best feeling I had ever experienced.

We moved together as if our bodies were made for each other. I closed my eyes and let him ride me. My body did the rest. It was an automatic reaction to the way he treated me. I'd never had sex like this before. Simon had been sweet and gentle, but Dylan was firmer, stronger, and harder.

Once he set the pace and rhythm, passion replaced thought. I came hard. I heard myself gasp and held on to him while he drove himself into me. He came too, and I put my legs around him, so he pushed himself even deeper inside of me.

"Fuck," I said, wanting to savor this feeling forever.

He stayed inside of me for a long time.

When he pulled out, both of us satisfied, I couldn't help but look at him, desperately wanting him to feel the same way about what we just did. I was so scared that he hadn't liked it, but his face was flustered, and he had this look in his eyes that betrayed his emotions. He was touched.

"You are amazing," I whispered.

"No, *you* are," he said, and he kissed me.

Dylan rolled to his side and drifted off into sleep, but I stopped him. I didn't feel satisfied just yet. My body wanted more of this. It yearned for it. I leaned down and touched his dick.

"Oh no, you don't. We're not done yet, sir. Not by far."

His eyes flew open when his dick responded at once. I rolled on top of him, squeezing his member gently. I was so wet. I wanted him inside of me again. This time, I took the lead as I sat on top of him.

"You're insatiable," he said.

"I work out," I replied.

The second time was slower, gentler, but just as good. When it was over, I lay in his arms, satisfied for now. And I couldn't help but say the words that would change everything.

"I think I love you, Dylan Blair."

His reply came instantly. "That's funny, Holly Hayes. I love you too."

I already knew that, but it was damn amazing to hear.

That night was the beginning of pure happiness and sexual bliss. I can't even begin to explain how it felt to have someone in my life who changed everything for me.

Because that's what he did. Dylan changed my life. He gave me more purpose, more insight in what love could be. He made me see that I was worthy of happiness with a man, that the past could be forgotten at long last. My bad luck streak with men was over and out. This was a new beginning.

The first thing I did was call my mom and dad. In between spending time together, working out together, studying together, having sex and sleeping together, either in my dorm or his, that is.

Because from that moment on, we were an item, thick as thieves, obsessed with each other, always trying to find ways of doing stuff that shouldn't even happen on campus.

The fun and relaxing moments were when we spent time together at the coffeehouse or when I waited for him to get off work so we could walk home together, get dinner, have sex, and shower together before falling asleep. Since Anya and Harry were still going on strong, despite her determination to leave for London, we were either in my dorm or his.

I didn't see much of Anya during those days, which was fine. She had her hands full with Harry and was already preparing the move to London. We had already figured out together that it would be hard to keep in close touch once she moved.

It sounded harsh saying it that way, but the time zones and the work would really narrow down our conversations to a limited set amount of superficial conversations.

Losing Anya slowly but surely made me realize that I was arriving in that stage of life that everyone went through. It was the end of my youth and the beginning of adulthood. Being with Dylan was the best thing that could happen to me right now, as it made that transition easier.

As it turned out, Dylan and I had this thing for sex in strange places. We didn't have sex in the backroom of the coffeehouse, where his boss, Tom, took his girls, but we did do it in various places on campus that were notorious within the close-lipped student body.

There was this whole list of spots that they called the *Fuck-me List*, which was extremely popular. I had heard of that list but had never used it before. I never had the opportunity or interest to do so. With Dylan, it was different. So I asked Anya about it.

Dylan was apprehensive at first, convinced we would get caught one way or the other, but he felt that same urgency to have sex as much as possible, as if one day without would mean the end of the world.

So we took that list and went our way with it. It was amazing. I never thought of myself as being overtly sexual, but that all changed with Dylan. I discovered a side of myself I had never experienced before, and it was great.

I told Emma about him. Emma told my parents. I talked to Mom, texted Dad, spoke to Dad, texted Mom. I showed them photos of Dylan and told them about the things we did together. The decent ones.

"He sounds great," Mom said. "And he's normal?"

I laughed. "Yeah, he is."

"No tantrums or bizarre behavior?"

I tried to ignore the weird moods, which, by the way, were happening less by the day. He even forgot to take all his phones with him these days.

"He's normal. He's fine. He's nice."

"Good."

"Did you sleep with him yet?" my sister asked.

"That's none of your business," I said.

"So you did."

"Yeah, I did."

"Was it good?"

"Emma!"

"Sorry, just curious. It's not like I want to know what it's like. Just, you know."

"It was better than good."

"He doesn't have any weird things going on?"

"None at all. He's just a regular guy," I reassured her.

"Good. Well, then I'm happy for you. When do we get to see him?"

I thought about that. We were together for about four months now, which didn't seem that long, but it felt long enough to meet the parents. I wanted to take him home to see my family, but he had his own and they lived in a different state. I wasn't sure how that was going to work.

We didn't go home for the short Easter break. He said he had too much work, and I needed the time to study for my finals, so I had stuck around campus too like a lot of students did.

But summer was a whole different ballgame. We would have

plenty of time. We never got around to discussing it, though. Every bit of time we had left right now was consumed by studying, working, and love.

And to be fair, I feared what would happen during this long break, with him in one place and me in another. The last time I was seeing someone, our relationship had fallen apart during summer, and I was terrified this would happen again, even if it had been totally different with Simon. I hadn't told Dylan. He knew I had dated Simon, but he believed we had broken up before the summer.

We studied together for our finals. He helped me struggle through some materials I had a hard time with, and I absorbed all the tips he gave me. He made sure I passed every test, for which I would be eternally grateful.

"What are your plans?" I asked casually one evening as we lay in each other's arms. "Are you going home?"

He was surprised. "I don't know yet. I'm thinking about taking a summer course and heading home, but I don't want to go for too long. You?"

"I'm going home. My parents have this trip booked to LA, so that's a given, but we're only leaving half of the month. So… I was wondering if you'd like to come with me?"

He rose up and looked at me, stunned.

"Go with you?"

"Yeah."

"To Beau?"

"Yeah."

"To meet your parents?"

"And Emma."

"Hol… Are you serious?"

"Why wouldn't I be?" I said, surprised by his shocked

reaction. "I mean, this feels right, so why not stay together, if only for a little while?"

"I don't know. I've never met a girl's parents before, if you don't count the fact that I knew Allison's folks back home of course. That was more a normal Midstone thing, not really a boyfriend thing."

I smiled. "I've never met a boy's parents either."

"Not even the parents of your high school sweetheart?"

"Nope."

"Oh."

"Why are you so surprised?" I asked.

"I don't know. I figured that would have been normal in a small town like Beau."

"Not for me. Daniel came by our house three times before we broke up, that's all, and usually just to pick me up. He never really got to know my parents, and I certainly didn't know his."

"So you're saying this is the first time you're introducing someone to your family?" he asked.

"Yeah."

"And you're serious about this? You really want me to go?"

"I do," I said. "I can't imagine being without you for weeks in a row. I want to spend as much time with you as I can."

He smiled. "So do I."

"Maybe I can come home with you too? Just for a little bit?"

His face fell. I realized at once that he hadn't even considered that. It wasn't just the surprise of my question, more the realization that his parents weren't ready to meet me yet.

"Too soon?" I asked.

He nodded, looking embarrassed.

"I'm sorry, Dyl. It wasn't my intention to make you feel bad. I just thought that, if you would want me to, I could come home with you for a while?"

He grabbed my hand and cupped my face.

"I really want you to get to know my folks, but not just yet," he said. "They are old school. And they are expecting me to date and marry a local girl."

I was shaken. "Are you serious?"

"I'm afraid so."

"This is the twenty-first century, not the Middle Ages. What are they thinking?"

"It's not that they want to arrange a marriage for me or anything, Hol. It's just that they don't seem to realize that not everyone wants to marry inside their own community."

I didn't know what to say. It felt so weird to hear him speak like that. Something dawned on me that I hadn't asked him yet and I wasn't sure if I wanted to, but the thought had crossed my mind before and now it wouldn't go away.

He was in a cult.

His dad had to be part of some weird cult that allowed their children to study elsewhere but demanded they come home afterward and do whatever their parents wanted. That's why he was so keen on becoming a doctor. Cult members took care of their own. If he went back home to be his father's successor, he would become the cult's assigned medical doctor. That must be why he was acting weird at times. Why his phones were so important to him.

That had to be it.

"You really want me to come with you?" he repeated.

"Yes," I said.

He smiled. "I think we can arrange that."

four

At the end of our third year in college, at the start of a long summer, Dylan and I left for Beau, with the permission of my parents and Emma. I had wanted to make sure that she was okay with it too, seeing as we were used to spending a lot of time together. Emma was the first one to say that she was happy to meet him.

"I don't know why, but I have this feeling that he might be the one for you," she said one night, days before we left.

"How could you know? You have never even met him."

"I've spoken to him."

"Two seconds or so."

"So what? It feels like I've known him forever."

Her words made me happy because I felt the same. It felt as if he had always been part of our world, which was an odd thing to think, but there it was. It was that familiarity of him, the fact that he felt like a piece of home.

He would be staying with us for about two weeks, which actually scared me. I didn't know how that was going to work in case my parents didn't like him, but he had already considered that.

"If it gets to be too much too soon, I'll just leave," he had said when we discussed our summer plans. "I won't get in the way, I promise. I don't want them to think of me as an intruder."

"You're not an intruder, and you won't get in the way. The house is big enough for ten people, and you can always go down to the lake in case you want to have some time to your own."

"That's great, Hol. I want to help out, just so you know. I'm not used to being a guest somewhere; I prefer to help."

"Like, by doing the dishes?"

"That, or cooking. Cleaning. Whatever needs to be done."

"You can cook?" I blurted out.

He looked at me, slightly shocked.

"You do realize that all the times you have come by to eat, you were served a homemade dinner?"

I bit my lip.

"Don't tell me you didn't notice I made that pasta from scratch, Hol. Seriously?"

"I thought you bought it from that nice caterer around the corner. The one with all the eclectic food."

"You mean *you* always buy your food there," he said, mocking me slightly.

"Uh-huh."

He laughed. "Okay, so the first thing you'll need to learn is how to make home-cooked meals. Bought pasta. Seriously? I'm offended."

"Actually, you shouldn't be. This only means that I find your food just as good as the caterer's. That's a huge compliment."

He thought about my remark and then smiled.

"You're right. It is. I'll still teach you how to cook, though. You can't live off your boyfriend."

I moved to him and ran my fingernails over his spine. He changed posture and smiled lightly.

"Maybe you can eat off your boyfriend?"

"That'll taste better than any pasta."

When we left for Beau, I sat next to Dylan and looked out the window, gazing at the pouring rain. That didn't seem to bother him at all. It was not the main reason for his nerves. Because he was scared, I could tell, so I chose his favorite music. It didn't help.

"Stop fretting so much," I said when he started chewing his fingernails. "You're going to be okay. My dad doesn't bite, you know."

"Maybe your mom does," he remarked.

"She'll love you. They all will."

I took his free hand in mine and tried to soothe him, which helped.

"Don't worry about the weather," I said. "It'll clear up soon, trust me. It always does."

"I'll always trust you," he said.

We stopped at a diner on the way to have a bite to eat. We had a small breakfast earlier this morning, so we were both starving, which was clear by the way we rushed from the parking lot through the pouring rain into the diner. Even from that short distance, I was soaked through.

"You okay?" he asked.

"I'm great," I said. "Come on, let's sit in that corner over there."

We slid into a booth. Before long, a waitress walked over to the table and handed us a couple of menus.

"How are you kids doing today?" she said, as if we were teenagers.

"Great," I said.

"Do you want to hear the specials?"

"Actually, I'll have the homemade burger," I said. "Dyl?"

"I'm going to do the same," he said, without really looking at the menu.

"With curly fries?"

"Sure," I said when he wouldn't answer.

"Drinks?"

"Just tap water, please," I said because neither of us drank soda.

"Sure. I'll be right back."

She left without noticing that he wasn't really talkative, and I frowned. We had been chatting in the car once his nerves had calmed down, but now he was back there again, stuck in his mind.

"Hey," I said, placing my hand on his. "Are you okay?"

"Yeah, I'm fine," he muttered, but I could tell something was wrong. "Excuse me."

He got up and hurried to the bathroom, leaving me alone and stunned. I didn't understand what was going on. He just took off as if he were feeling sick or something.

I sighed and dug out my phone to send a message to my parents, hoping that he'd come back soon. The waitress returned with a can of tap water and two glasses, placed some ketchup on the table, and left again. Five minutes later, Dylan still hadn't returned.

A thought popped up in my head. What if he had left without telling me? What if, for some reason, he had gotten out the back of the diner, walked to his car, and left me to rot at the diner?

I shook my head forcefully, reprimanding myself for that ridiculous thought. This was Dylan. He was a good guy. He would never do this to me. But then where the hell was he?

Suddenly he was back. He slipped into the booth and sat down as if nothing had happened, as if he hadn't been gone for ten minutes.

"Are you okay?" I said. "What happened?"

"Sorry," he said, smiling as if he was totally fine. "I had to go to the restroom and started reading on my phone. I totally forgot the time."

Suddenly I couldn't help it. I started laughing and smacked him.

"What?" he said.

"You idiot."

"What did I do?"

"I thought something had happened to you. Do you even realize how long you were gone for?"

"I don't know. A couple of minutes?"

"Make that ten."

He looked shocked. "No way."

"Yes way. What the hell were you reading? *The New York Times*?"

He smiled and turned serious all of a sudden, as if someone had flipped a switch and changed him into a different person again.

"Sorry, Holly. I didn't mean to scare you."

"You did. I got worried. But I was stupid," I said, surprised he took it so seriously. "I know you love to read your phone when you're in the bathroom. I just didn't think you would do it here."

"I'm so embarrassed," he said, looking at his hands. "I took out my phone before I sat down, and the screen just popped up and, well, it was interesting."

"So I gather," I said. "Oh good, our food is here."

Two huge burgers were placed on the table in front of us. I stared at the massive amount of food and wondered how in the world I was supposed to eat all that, until I realized that Dylan ate for two. He would finish off the rest.

Dylan tucked in and started eating as if his life depended on it. Sometimes I wondered if he took time in between bites to breathe. I took my time and ate at a much slower pace. By the time I was halfway through my meal, he had finished.

"Good," I said. "You can help me finish this."

I cut the remaining half of the burger in two, gave him half of my fries, and smiled when he dove in again, finishing before I did.

"You're a monster," I said. "Do you even know what you're eating?"

"One of the best burgers ever," he said, licking his fingers. "That was delicious."

"Glad you liked it."

He leaned back and patted his belly.

"I'll probably have to go back to the loo."

"You do that," I said. "Take your time. But don't read this time. I want to leave in ten."

"Yes, ma'am," he said and got up, placing his phone on the table.

I laughed when he moved to the restrooms again. I looked at his phone when something struck me. He only carried one phone with him. Just one. For the first time since I'd met him, he only had the one phone. The others were nowhere to be seen.

When he got back, I studied his pants. My heart fell a bit. The other phones were still there. I could see the outlines. Damn.

"Ready to go?" he said.

I nodded. One step at a time, I guessed.

The rest of the trip, I tried to make sense of this man sitting next to me. So self-assured at times, so scared otherwise. Still clinging on to the phones that his dad had forced upon him.

There was no doubt in my mind that he had lied earlier. Whatever he had read, it had taken him a long time to recover from. It troubled me.

Hours later, when we finally reached Beau, the sun broke through the clouds. Gone was the rain, in came the sunshine, as if it were meant to be. I loved my hometown so much. Life was always beautiful here.

When we drove through the town's main street, I took in the small changes that were typical for a town like this. A couple of new stores, some houses that had been changed, adaptations to the town hall. Every year something seemed to be different, which was great. My town was modernizing, and I liked it.

Dylan followed my directions to the lake house, which lay two miles out of town. The lake itself was gorgeous. It was surrounded by various houses, woods, and a large public park. When he parked the car, I saw Dylan's eyes open wide. He hadn't expected the house to be this big, I could tell.

"I love it," he said.

"Told you," I said, happy that it so overwhelmed him. That happened to everyone who first came here, to my dad's delight. He had spent a lot of time fixing up this place, and he was always happy when new visitors acknowledged his efforts.

My dad was the first one to head out of the house after we parked the car. He came over to us with big steps and hugged me tight against him.

"You've grown," he said.

I laughed. "Dad, I stopped growing three years ago."

"You're wearing high heels then."

He looked down at my feet, seeing the white sneakers that I wore.

"Maybe you've shrunk a bit," I said. "Must be your age."

"You're a terribly rude creature, Holly Hayes." He let go of me and turned toward Dylan. "So you're the man who made sure my daughter barely calls me anymore these days."

Dylan opened his mouth to say something that would make sense in this situation but was stopped by Dad's loud laughter.

"Sorry, kid, it was just a joke. Don't look so shocked." He patted him on the back. "Come on, let's get you inside. You must be hungry. Do you like to watch baseball?"

"I love baseball," Dylan said.

"Great, there's a game on, come with me."

"Hey, what about me?" Mom said, standing in the doorway. "Don't I get to say hi?"

"I'm sorry, ma'am…" Dylan began.

"Hey, none of that sir and ma'am stuff," Dad said. "Call me Dan."

"And I'm Susan," Mom added before hugging Dylan. "I'll have dinner ready in half an hour. Do you want something to drink in the meantime?"

"I'll get it," Dad said, and he walked Dylan inside the house without looking back once.

"Great," I said, "I bring home a guy, and Dad just forgets I even exist." But I smiled and left the suitcases in Dylan's trunk. Mom wrapped her arm around my shoulders.

"You know what he's like," Mom said. "He's probably telling Dylan right now how glad he is that he's no longer the only man in the house."

"True," I said. "Where's Emma?"

"She's with some friends, but she'll be home in a few moments. She said she'd be home for dinner. How was your trip?"

"Good. Relaxing."

Mom studied me. "You don't sound relaxed. What's going on?"

"Nothing, Mom. Everything's fine."

"Are you sure?"

"Positive."

"Holly…"

"We'll talk about it later," I said.

"No, we'll talk about it now. Come on."

We sat down on the porch, where I told her about Dylan's occasionally odd behavior. She frowned before thinking for a while. She took her time responding to my story.

"From what I hear, it sounds like Dylan is suffering from childhood traumas, honey. I mean, if he's walking around carrying three phones in case of an emergency, which is odd on its own, he might have grown up in a world of fear or something. Have you ever asked him if something happened to him as a child?"

"No, mom. He won't open up about his past at all. His parents are never spoken of; he barely mentions them or Midstone. It's like he's ignoring the subject as much as possible. When I bring it up, he shuts down, so I prefer not to mention it at all, just in case it brings back some trauma that I don't know anything about."

"That's not okay, Holly. You know that you need to deal with past situations. What are you going to do if you continue with him? Ignore this for the rest of your life?"

"No. But for now, I don't have to bring up anything. What would the point be? He's obviously not ready to share, and we've only been together for four months. I'll hurt him by forcing him to talk about it."

"But what do you think happened to him then?" Mom asked. That was the million-dollar question, wasn't it?

"I don't know. His dad might have mistreated him or something."

"Or abused?"

"The thought has crossed my mind," I admitted. "The way he refuses to speak about his parents, it feels off somehow."

"And he doesn't have anyone around to talk to? Like friends in college? Family members, maybe?"

I shook my head. Dylan did have his share of friends, but I doubted they even had a clue about the phones. As far as I knew, he had never mentioned them to anyone.

"He needs time to talk about it. And when he does, I'll be right here for him," I said. "Right now though, I want to enjoy this vacation as much as possible. I want to be carefree, to live life to the fullest. I know that sounds corny, but it's been so busy that I just want to enjoy things as they come right now."

"You're absolutely right," Mom said. "Come on, your sister will be home soon, so I should finish dinner. Why don't you help me? We'll get your bags after dinner."

"Sounds good."

We got up, and Mom hugged me.

"I love you so much," she said. "And I'm so proud of you."

"Proud of me? For what?"

"You're allowing your boyfriend to deal with his issues on his own terms without prodding and poking about the ongoing situation. That takes courage. Most girls would harass him to find out what the truth is, but not you. It's amazing how you manage this."

"I love him, Mom."

She was surprised. "You do?"

"Yeah. I can see myself moving forward with him. He's everything I ever wanted in a guy. He's just—He completes me."

"Despite his strange behavior at times?"

"Yeah, and you know why?"

"Tell me."

"His behavior has nothing to do with me. He's not hiding another girlfriend from me or pretending to be someone that he's not. Whatever his secret is, it's related to where he came from, and that is something we can deal with. He needs time, and when he's ready to share, I'll be there for him."

"You amaze me," Mom said.

"Maybe you raised me to be like you," I said.

"If that is the case, I'm honored to be your mom."

I smiled and walked inside the house with Mom, where we found Dad and Dylan sitting brotherly on the couch, both of them with a beer in hand and feet up. I had not seen Dylan this laid-back in weeks.

"Hey," he said, getting up. "I missed you."

"I missed you too," I said as I walked over to kiss him.

He took me in his arms and hugged me as if he hadn't seen me for ages. I leaned into him, forgetting for one moment where we were.

"Hey, lovebirds," a voice said.

I turned around and saw my sister Emma, all grown up, walking into the living room. I released Dylan and gave her a hug.

"So this is the famous Dylan Blair," Emma said as she walked over to Dylan and gave him a hug. "Welcome to the family."

Those words made Dylan radiate with pride and joy. Emma was right, though. Just like that, this easily, Dylan became part of our family.

Those days at the Lakehouse were some of the best days of my life. Dylan stayed for two weeks as part of our family, and it felt as if he'd never done anything else.

Every single day I saw him relax more. Every hour of every day, he became this totally different person than he was on campus, and even there, he had been a great guy to be with.

Slowly but surely, he opened up to my family. Where he had been nervous and a bit distant at first, especially around my dad, who seemed to want to know everything about him despite my mom's warnings that he should cut him some slack, Dylan became this beacon of light and fun at the house.

Emma in particular grew very fond of him. She didn't have a crush on him or anything since he wasn't her type at all. They became really good friends. Whenever he wasn't around me, he was hanging out with her. They played games, had fun, joked around, had fierce arguments about music, movies and television series, and they kept on teasing each other. If I hadn't realized yet that my sister liked girls more than boys, I would have been jealous as hell. But now, seeing them banter together, it just warmed my heart.

I loved Dylan for liking my sister. For having lengthy talks with my dad about the sports he adored so much. For helping my mom around the house. He even offered to make his infamous pasta, recounting the story of me not having recognized the food as a home-cooked meal instead of catering-produced, which cracked up my sister.

"Holly doesn't have any taste buds at all," she commented

after dinner, where everyone had devoured Dylan's pasta as if there were no tomorrow.

"I don't," I admitted. "It's true."

Everyone started laughing. Dad patted Dylan on the back and congratulated him on an excellent meal. Mom hugged Dylan and asked him to do more of the cooking, even though he admitted he could just make this one pasta and that was it. And Emma ate everything until there was nothing left.

"I've got to go lie down," she said after finishing.

We had a lot of sex during those days. Beneath the bedsheets in my room—of course he was sleeping there; Mom didn't even consider offering one of the spare bedrooms—sex was an almost daily thing, and it never got boring.

We would do it quietly, slowly, and gently. He would use his fingers first, until I silently cried for him to fuck me. He would do it gently but firmly, like I was used to from him. We didn't dare to do it with the lights on or on top of the bed, fearing that one of them might sneak in, which was great in its own way. I felt like a teenager again, even though I had never had sex with anyone in this room before.

Every morning, Emma would look me up and down with this smug grin on her face, but without commenting on anything.

"I'm tired," I said at some point.

"I'll bet," she said. Mom raised an eyebrow.

Damn my sister.

A couple of days later, we went out for a walk in the woods. I had this thing in my mind about having sex against a tree. We'd never done that before, and it felt crazily hot to even consider it.

I convinced Dylan that we had to try it, even though he was apprehensive about it.

"This is your hometown, Hol. What if someone catches us? Can you imagine what they'll tell your parents?"

"They won't catch us."

"How do you know?"

"I know these woods. I know the spots."

He sighed, smiled, and let himself be persuaded easily. We went out there, as eager as a couple of teenagers.

Not even ten minutes later, he had me up against a tree. It wasn't rough sex, nor controlling or demanding. It was one of the sweetest things we had ever done, as if we both wanted to savor what was left of our time together here in Beau.

This amazing vacation was coming to an end.

As we sat down by that tree, relishing what we had just done, Dylan sighed. "We have to go back."

I was leaning against him, not wanting to let go just yet. He felt warm, strong, and so gentle. I never wanted this feeling to stop.

"I know," I said. And I blurted out the thing I wasn't going to say. I regretted it at once. "Please stay."

His shoulders drooped. That thing we hadn't discussed yet lingered between us. He was going to leave in a couple of days, and I wouldn't see him until September.

"I can't," he said. "I've got that summer class, and then there's my parents. I have to go home at some point, even if it is for a short while."

His reaction puzzled me. He got dressed and helped me with my clothes. We sat down by the tree, and he placed his arm over my shoulders so I could lean into him.

"Why?" I said. "Why do you need to go back there when it's so obvious you don't want to?"

"There's a difference between wanting to do something and

needing to," he said.

"Okay. So why do you need to go?"

"It's what's expected of me."

"Because…?"

"My mom and dad miss me."

"Hm."

"Hm?"

I moved a bit so I could see him.

"Why haven't they called you when you were out here?"

"What are you talking about? Of course they did."

"Oh yeah? When?"

"All the time."

"That's not true, Dyl," I said, getting up.

"Holly…"

"Why won't you tell me what's going on with your parents?" I said. "I know Dad had a talk with you about them the other day when you were working on the boat. He told me. He said he asked you if you had an issue with your dad because you're so weird about them. You told him you didn't, but is that true?"

"It is true," he said. "I swear they're good people. It's just that I don't really want to go back home, Hol. I really want to stay here with you, go to LA with your family, come back here and spend the rest of the summer with you guys. But I can't because I need to see my folks and reconnect with home."

"Then take me with you."

"No. Not yet."

"Why not?"

"I haven't told them about you yet."

I got up, surprised.

"Are you kidding me?"

"Don't look at me like that, Hol. You know why I haven't

told them yet," he said, trying to avoid my gaze. "Please don't turn this into a bigger deal than it has to be. It's just that I'm not ready to get all the slack, not just yet. I want to spend my time loving you, being with you, without the dark clouds hanging over me when they will find out about you. I'll save that for later."

"So you think they're going to hate me?" I said, feeling hurt.

"No, not hate. They just won't understand."

"Why not? What's there to understand about their son having a girlfriend?"

"I told you, Hol. They want me to choose someone from our own town."

His vague explanation didn't sit well with me. For the first time, I felt annoyed. I tried to hold on to what Mom had said before about my patience.

"I know," I said sadly. "I get it. And you're right. This isn't the right time yet, but I won't stop bugging you about this. You need to face your future, Dylan, and that future is with me, whether they like it or not. I don't want to make you choose between your parents and me. I want to be part of their lives too, and I'll do whatever it takes to make that happen."

He looked at me, stunned.

"Are you serious?"

"Yeah."

"You won't ask me to make a choice?"

"Never."

"Why not?"

"Choices of love never work out. Your parents will understand once you tell them. You're an adult. You have every right to be happy with the person of your choice. You just need to see that."

"It's difficult, Hol. They are not the easiest people to deal with."

"But you love them."

"I do, yeah."

"Then tell them when you're good and ready. It doesn't have to be now, or even tomorrow, but at some point, you'll feel it, trust me."

He smiled and touched my face.

"Why is it so easy to be with you, Holly Hayes?"

"Maybe because I don't want to make life so complicated," I said.

"Life *is* complicated."

"No, it's not, Dyl. Life's not about complications and issues and trouble at all. Life's about love."

He sighed. "I wish I had known you all my life. It would have made things so much easier."

"What things?" I asked curiously.

He was silent for a long time, but then he smiled.

"It doesn't matter. Things from the past that you fortunately don't have to deal with. Come on, let's get back before your sister sends out a search party."

"Emma knows we were going to have sex. She won't come here, trust me," I said.

He plucked some twigs from my hair and smiled.

"I really wish I could stay," he said. "But I have to go back, and you have to be with your family without me for a while. You've barely spoken to them separately, and that's not okay. You need to be with them."

"Dad asked if you could come to LA with us."

"That's really sweet of him, but no. I really have to go, and you guys need to make a family vacation out of this."

I kissed him. "When will I see you again?"

"By the end of the summer, but you know it isn't that long. We'll be back before you know it and make up for lost time."

"Dylan?"

"Yeah?"

"Promise me you won't leave me?"

He was surprised. "Why would I leave you?"

"I don't know. I'm scared. I love you so much."

"And I love you. I won't leave you, I swear. You mean the world to me, and I'll miss you so much in the next few weeks, but we'll have all the time in the world afterward," he said, kissing me.

"I know," I said, leaning into him. "It'll be normal life soon enough."

"Life is never normal, Holly Hayes."

"It is when I'm with you."

That pleased him. We walked back quietly to the lake house, where we showered together and stayed on the deck for the rest of the day, just doing nothing but reading, sleeping, and eating.

My parents were gone for the day, and Emma was meeting with friends, so we had the house to ourselves. I loved them for these stolen moments. They knew that Dylan was going to leave us soon, and they wanted me to enjoy it.

I did. Every single second of it.

When Dylan left a couple of days later, it felt like a goodbye but not a farewell. I was calm about it. This felt okay. I knew we would see each other again soon.

Emma stood next to me when we waved our goodbyes until we could no longer see his car. I knew I radiated sadness; I could tell by the way she hugged me, as if I were the younger sister and she was my older protector.

"It's only a month, sis," she said when I started crying, despite knowing I'd see him again in a videocall later today.

"I know," I said. "It still feels like forever."

"Then why didn't you go back with him? Mom and Dad would have understood if you had preferred to stay with him."

"We talked about it, but he didn't want me to. He's got that summer class, so I wouldn't see him that much anyhow, and I'd be spending my days waiting for him to come back. Plus, he's going to his parents afterward, and I'm not going with him."

"Why not?" Emma asked, surprised. "You're his girlfriend. What's the big deal?"

I avoided answering.

"Holly?"

"I don't want to talk about it," I said.

"Come on, it's me."

I sighed and wiped at my face before confessing what had been bugging me for so long.

"They don't know about me yet."

Emma stared at me.

"Don't do that," I said.

"Do what?"

"You're shocked."

"Yeah, I am. What exactly are you saying right now? That his parents aren't aware that he has a serious girlfriend?"

"Yeah."

"Holly, are you freaking kidding me right now? That guy spent two weeks at our house. He slept in your room, was part of our family in an instant, and became a great friend in the blink of an eye. But he didn't even tell his family about you? Why the hell not?"

Emma's reaction brought up all the red flags that I had been avoiding for months. The dam broke; I finally had enough of all the secrecy. For weeks I hadn't told my family about Dylan's reluctance to take me to Midstone, so I just blurted it all out. Emma was shocked, to say the least.

"That's not okay, Holly."

"I know."

"Why would he do that?"

"I don't know."

"Is there something to hide? I know that there have been all these crazy rumors about the area where he comes from for years. That's why I was so surprised he was so normal. Is that what this is about?"

"Rumors? What are you talking about?" I said.

Emma looked at me as if I had lost my mind.

"Don't tell me that you have never googled Midstone?"

"No, I haven't. Why?"

Emma and I settled down on the porch. She went into the house, got a couple glasses of homemade iced tea, and came back out. I used that opportunity to google Midstone, but all I could find was the usual info about any typical American town. The population rate, some photos of the most important buildings, and amazing pictures of the mountains and this famous hiking trail he told me about. I placed my phone on the table.

"I don't get it," I said. "What am I looking for exactly?"

"What do you know about where he comes from?" Emma asked.

"It's a small town called Midstone. It's at the foot of one of the largest Montana mountains. It's famous because it's at the beginning of this hiking trail that thousands of people do annually. It has a bit of tourism going on, but not that much."

"Okay, and what else? What do you know about his family and the community?"

"Just that they are a tight-knit community, that everyone knows everyone, and that they keep to themselves, but it's not like they're Amish or anything."

"Just a small-town community with a small-town spirit," Emma commented.

"Yeah, exactly. So what's the issue? You're not saying that they are like the Amish, are you? Or that there's some religious cult thing going on?"

"And what if there is?" Emma said. "Have you ever thought about the fact that they could be conspiracy theorists?"

"They're—what?" I asked.

"You know, like those people preparing for the end of the world. Doomsday preppers. I found a couple of websites about it when I googled Midstone, so I figured that could be his secret."

Emma took her drink and looked away, giving me time to think about what she said. I started to laugh.

"You're crazy, Em. No way. He's not a conspiracy theorist, let alone a prepper. He hardly ever talks about politics or climate change or whatever. He would have told me. This is ridiculous. No, that's not it, I'm sure of it."

"Then what is it that he's hiding from you?"

I thought long and hard about my answer while sipping my iced tea until I said what I had been thinking for a long time now.

"His parents have this girl lined up for him. Someone from their circle of friends or something. Like I said, they are a close community. They have a number of friends that have been part of their lives forever. They want to keep the love and care within that closed circle. That's what he told me too. What if his parents have chosen his bride already?"

"His bride? As in an arranged marriage?" Emma asked. "Do you know how you sound right now?"

"Yeah. I don't know." I sighed. "You know, I don't want to talk or think about it anymore. All I know for sure is that we love each other and he's going to be back on campus in September. That's what matters the most. So I don't want to spend these upcoming weeks thinking about this. I want to give him the space to tell his parents when he's ready."

Emma smiled and hugged me fiercely.

"There's no doubt in my min that he'll be there," Emma said. "He's crazy about you. But keep him crazy too."

"How so?"

"Just make sure he doesn't lose sight of who you are to him." She winked. "There are ways to do that, you know."

I burst out laughing. "I'm not going to send him any nude pictures of me. I'm not crazy."

"I never said you should. You can keep him on his toes by sending innuendos and stuff. And make sure you see him daily. That'll remind him of what he's coming back to."

I punched my sister on the arm.

"You are evil."

"Look who's talking. Come on, I feel like ice cream. Wanna drive into town?"

"Yeah."

We got up, changed, and drove into town for amazing ice cream.

Emma did her best to keep my mind off things.

I did my best pretending I wasn't thinking about this odd conversation anymore.

We both failed.

I couldn't help but listen to that voice inside my head, warning me that things were not as they seemed with Dylan. I tried to ignore the red flags. Somehow, I managed to do so too. And after a couple of days of phone calls, video calls, and millions of text messages, I had blocked my weary thoughts from my mind.

Every time I spoke to Dylan while he was on campus and I was in LA with my family, having a great time, he sounded normal, acted normal, and told me constantly how terribly he missed me.

Every night I went to bed thinking about him. Instead of this time apart making us grow apart too, it just increased the yearning and the hunger for each other. He was with me in LA. I was with him on campus; I was sure of it. There was no doubt in my mind that I was constantly in his thoughts.

That was the moment I realized how much I already loved him. Dylan Blair was the real deal.

When we got back to Beau for the last part of my summer vacation, time flew by. My dad was on the phone all the time, preparing to get everything ready for the apartment back in Minnesota.

He had hired someone to take care of things there. There was a handyman at work, a painter, and the furniture was delivered.

"I'm okay with going back sooner, Dad," I had said, but he insisted that I didn't have to.

"I want you to relax a bit before the start of the new academic year," he said. "I know how hard it is to study all the time, so just make the best of it. The weather is amazing; you should enjoy it."

I did. This was my last week at home, and I wouldn't see my family again for a long time, which always took away part of the enjoyment of being back home. Mom always got melancholy at the end of summer break before going into this frenzied state where she started preparing everything.

We decided that my parents would go back to Minnesota with me for a couple of days to get everything ready for the big move. Emma would stay here since her final year would start around the same time.

I was thinking about all the stuff I had to take back with me when my phone rang. It was Dylan, who was staying with his parents. He would drive back in two days, he told me, before adding how much he was looking forward to seeing me again.

I froze.

What if this was the call I hadn't been waiting for? What if this was the moment he would tell me he had a change of heart and we were done?

I didn't want to answer it.

But I had to.

five

Two days ago, Dylan had spoken to me on the phone as well. A regular, ordinary conversation.

"I can't wait to be with you again. I'm getting restless," he said.

"I know," I said. "I can feel it too."

"I'm so glad the summer is over. It's been way too long."

"You're not enjoying your time at home?"

"Mom is working all the time, and Dad has never had it busier in his practice either, so I'm usually alone during the daytime. The nights are okay though, loads of dinners and meeting up with old friends."

"So, what do you do during the day?"

"Just hang out, get some work done. I'm doing this online course that's not that hard and will get me some extra credits. I went on a few walks downtown, and up to the mountain." He sounded evasive.

"You mean, like, take the hiking trail?" I prodded.

"Yeah, something like that. Or help my dad. There's always stuff to do around here."

"Are you allowed to do that?" I asked, surprised.

"Yeah, as long as it's not really treating patients, I'm

good. Dad always needs help, and his assistant is away on vacation right now."

"But not all the time?"

He laughed. "No, he told me I need my time off too. Anyway, gotta go. Mom's calling for me. Talk soon."

He broke off that call quickly, which proved to me that he still hadn't told them about me. But that was fine. I had decided not to ask about it until he was ready to share.

I had barely heard from him yesterday, so when he called, I was surprised. He had told me he would be spending today with some friends.

"Dyl?" I said. "What's wrong?"

"Hol. Why would there be anything wrong?" he asked, dismayed.

"You wouldn't call me out of the blue if there wasn't a problem."

He was silent for a while.

"Dyl?"

"Why does there have to be something wrong for me to call you?" he finally said, sounding a bit offended.

"Oh, I'm sorry, I didn't mean it the way it sounded. It's just that you said you would be out all day."

"Oh." Silence. "You're right, I did. No, I've changed my plans. I kind of didn't want to go out today."

"Oh?"

"Yeah, It's—"

Silence.

"Dylan?"

"I'm sorry, Holly. I just needed to hear you."

Silence.

I didn't know what to say or do.

"Dyl?"

"I just wanted to let you know that I love you."

I smiled.

"Hol?"

"Yeah, I'm still here."

"I love you."

"I know. You told me."

"Yeah, I guess I did."

"Dyl?"

"Yeah?"

"I love you too."

"I know."

"But if you don't tell me right now what the hell is going on, I'll hang up the phone."

Silence. Followed by nervous laughter.

"I told them."

My heart made a leap.

"I told them all about you, and I'm so glad that it's out in the open now. It felt so goddamn good to tell them that I love you and I want to be with you all the time."

"You do?" I said.

"Yeah, what else? I can't exist without you. These past few months have made that painfully clear to me."

"Oh. That is so sweet," I said, trying to hold back my emotions. "I feel the exact same way about you."

"Yeah, I know."

Silence.

"Are we crazy, Hol?"

"Crazy? In what way?"

"We barely know each other, and somehow it feels as if we've been together forever. It's like I can't even remember what my life was like before I met you. I can't recall whatever it is that I did before you."

"I know," I said. "I've spent this last month thinking about you a lot, feeling guilty too that you weren't here with me. I've wanted you to come back so many times."

"I miss Beau," he said. "And your parents. They are so uncomplicated. It's so easy. And your sister Emma, she's just really cool."

"She likes you too," I reassured him. "She's still talking about you all the time."

"We're texting now and then, about ridiculous stuff, you know. Just funny memes and things."

"I know, she told me," I said.

"Even your dad has sent me a message."

"He did?" This surprised me.

"Yeah, he told me there would always be a place in your house for me. How sweet is that?"

"Totally sweet."

Dylan sighed deeply.

"Are you sure you're okay?"

"Yeah, I am. I'm leaving earlier. Tomorrow, instead of in three days. I want to go back and clean up the dorm, get my books, get ready for the new year, make sure I haven't forgotten anything. Maybe work a bit. It's time."

"We'll be there in two days," I said. "Only two days, Dyl. And then I'll have the apartment, and we can do whatever we want."

"Anything?" he said, sounding huskier.

"Anything."

"Well, that's something I'm looking forward to already then."

"Lots and lots of anything."

"You're a tease, Holly Hayes."

"Like you didn't think of all the possibilities of having an entire place to ourselves," I said, laughing.

"This is going to be quite an interesting year, I can already tell."

"One that we'll have to be careful about."

"Oh? How so?"

"With all this lots and lots of anything things going on, we might get too distracted. Lose focus of what's really important."

Silence.

"You're right," he said after a while. "We should set boundaries and time slots."

"Time slots?"

"Uh-huh."

"Meaning we can only have sex during ten p.m. and midnight? Something like that?" I said.

"What, just two hours per day?"

"*Between* those two hours."

"That's a bit sad, isn't it?"

"What, you want more time slots?"

"Uh-huh."

"Okay," I said, smiling. "Why don't you make a proposal? A spreadsheet or something. I'll make sure my working and studying hours will revolve around your schedule."

"That sounds good," he said. "Is it okay if I have four slots per day?"

"Isn't that a bit much?"

"We don't have to use them all; they could be placeholders."

"And what if they fall right in the middle of class?"

"Then we'll both have to excuse ourselves."

God. He was going to kill me this year; I knew it. I got horny just thinking about it.

"Deal," I said, imagining us having sex everywhere on campus. I was turning into Anya.

He laughed. "I'll get right to it."

"Great."

"Hol?"

"Yeah?"

"My mom and dad want to meet you. I told them that Thanksgiving could be a possibility, but maybe your parents wouldn't want that? I can imagine them wanting you back home."

"I'll take care of it," I spoke quickly. "Don't worry about it. I'll talk to them, explain, and we can meet up with your parents. In future, we'll have to split our time in two all the time anyway."

He didn't say anything, but it didn't feel like an uncomfortable silence somehow.

"What?" I asked after a while.

"You're talking about a future together. No one has ever done that before."

I realized what I had just said.

"I don't want to be with anyone but you," I said. "Not ever. We are meant to be together. There isn't a single doubt in my mind about that. You and me, Dylan Blair."

He grew silent again. God, had I misread him? Scared him off?

"You are so goddamn perfect, Holly Hayes," he said at last, emotion clear in his voice.

"No, I'm not."

"Yes, you are. I'll do anything to be with you for the rest of my life, I swear. This is forever, Holly. I'll never hurt you. I won't let you down. I'll change for you. No more secrecy, just you and me."

"I don't want you to change. You have to stay who you are.

I love you."

"I love you. Listen, I have to go. I'll give you a call before I leave, okay? And we'll see each other again in two days."

"Can't wait," I said.

He disconnected, leaving me sitting on my bed with the biggest smile on my face. When I walked into the living room, my mom looked up from her book. I didn't even need to explain.

"I'm so happy for you, honey."

"I'm happy for me too," I said.

And in a couple of months, I would finally get to meet his parents. That would undoubtedly be the most important moment of the year.

The college year started differently due to various reasons.

One) Anya was gone. She had left for London with her parents, just like she had said. Gone was my bestie, and she left a hole in my heart that I had underestimated.

Even though I had plenty of other friends, Anya had always held a special place in my life. Her loud rudeness had often made me cringe, but it had suited her. All those who knew her could agree to that.

Fortunately, I had decided to move out of the dorm in spring, so I was spared the fear of having to share the basement dorm room with a new roommate, which could have turned out for the best or the worst.

Anya and I still texted and spoke on occasion, but it wasn't that much. The long distance, the time zone difference, and the fact she was now leading a totally different life didn't make connecting with each other easy.

Two) My move from the basement room to a small apartment of my own was just crazy. I didn't have to deal with my friends' wishes anymore. I could come in and walk out as I pleased. I didn't have the party noise or the messy kitchen area to deal with anymore. I was my own person now, and I loved it.

Mom and Dad had come with me to Minnesota to get the apartment ready for my move. The painting had been done, bits and pieces had been fixed, so all we had to do now was get all the furniture in place and move my stuff from the basement to the apartment.

We went out shopping for framed pictures and posters and bought all these little things that would add to the coziness of the apartment.

It was a two-bedroom apartment. The second room would become a study, so I could keep the living area free from clutter. There was a small kitchen that I really liked, which had all the appliances that I needed. The entire living area had wooden floors that were easy to maintain. It was perfect.

Below me lived an elderly couple, and the apartment above me was occupied by a young widow in her late forties. She had a fifteen-year-old daughter that I connected with straight away. The place was isolated enough that we didn't disturb each other, even if the volume of my sound system was turned up a notch.

The best thing about this new year was change number three, though.

Three) Dylan. He was there the moment we arrived back in Minnesota. He hugged my mom and dad fiercely, as if they were old friends, and never left my side from that moment on. We picked up where we left off, without those weeks in between.

As long as my parents were around, we behaved. My parents had booked us into a hotel since I had to clear out the basement dorm room for the new occupants. Dylan didn't stay with us. He still had his own room that he shared with Harry, but he hadn't returned there yet.

He helped us with the apartment, never intervened or commented on the stuff I bought, even though I insisted that he should have his say, while he kept insisting it was my place and I should decorate it the way I saw fit.

"It's your home," he said. "I'm just a visitor. You should put your stamp on it."

So I did, but I still thought about what he would like too, convinced he would be spending more time here than in his dorm room.

I asked my dad if we could get a second desk for the living room, without explaining why, but he already knew.

"Great idea," he said. "You kids will need your own space to study. That's what you're mostly here for, right?" He winked when he said that. I got embarrassed.

Once the apartment was decorated, the beginning of the year was upon us. Mom and Dad said their goodbyes. Dylan bought a huge box of chocolates for them as a thank-you for the great time he had in Beau. My mom was very pleased with this gesture.

"You take care of yourself now," she said. "And take care of Holly too."

"I will," he said. "Thank you for your trust."

"You're a great guy, Dylan," Dad said. "Your heart is in the right place. We like having you around. If you ever need anything, call us, okay?"

"I will."

I hugged Mom and Dad goodbye, and as we waved them off, it felt different than it had the past two years. This time, I had Dylan by my side.

I took him by the hand and led him back up the stairs, into

the apartment.

"Fuck me," I whispered huskily. "I've been waiting so long for this."

"Me too," he said, pulling me up the stairs so fast that we both tripped.

He gently lowered me onto the queen-size bed, undressing me while kissing me so fiercely it almost hurt. His hands were all over me; mine were all over him. His fingers roomed everywhere.

"God, Hol, what the fuck are you doing to me?" he said as he entered me and defined the rhythm we both craved so badly.

The moment he filled me, I knew I was complete again. This man, this crazy, beautiful, gorgeous man, was what I had missed the most during the summer.

"Don't stop," I whispered as he increased the speed.

We came within seconds of each other. He panted as he lowered himself on top of me, holding me gently.

"I want more," I whispered as I nibbled on his earlobe. "Don't you dare stop now."

He laughed, sounding exhausted.

"I wouldn't even think about it."

He flipped us over.

Days, weeks, then months passed in a crazy frenzy of classes, work—I had found a new, less demanding job at a local flower shop—studying, spending time together, and having sex.

We had set our boundaries and had made agreements. We argued sometimes, but never about anything serious. There was never a fierce quarrel or a fight. He started to forget his phones. Didn't talk about his parents or his past at all. We lived a normal life, like every other college student.

I made new friends, and they fit in well with my old friends.

I still spoke to Anya, but it was rare these days. I enjoyed my studies, loved what I was doing. We worked hard, played hard.

Life was so good that I often feared it could only go downhill from here. That thought scared me. And, of course, there was the upcoming Thanksgiving weekend. My parents were all for me going to Midstone with Dylan. They knew we had to get this out of the way, that I needed to meet these mysterious people he barely spoke of. The people who defined that alternate side of him, which seemed to regain its grip on him the more we neared Thanksgiving weekend.

On Wednesday morning, we left for Midstone. While packing, I couldn't help but wonder if this was the right thing to do.

Dear reader,

You have now met Holly.

From this point on, choose what you want to read next.

1. Continue reading Holly's version of events on the mountain. In that case, keep on reading.
2. Read Dylan's story. In that case, go to page 180 of the book.
3. Finished Dylan's story already and want to read his version of events on the mountain? Go to page 266.

One way or the other, whatever you choose, you must read both storylines to get a complete picture of what happened.

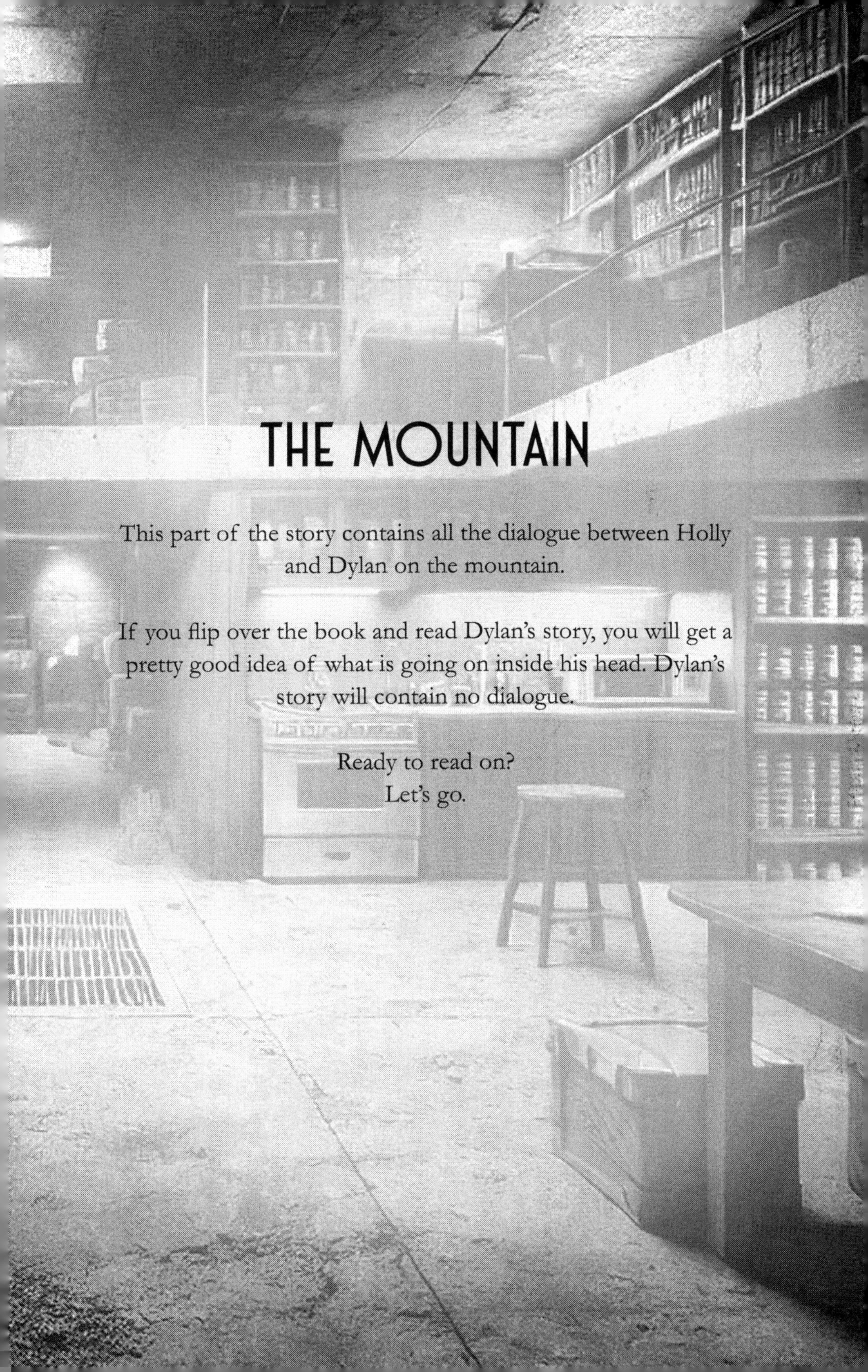

THE MOUNTAIN

This part of the story contains all the dialogue between Holly and Dylan on the mountain.

If you flip over the book and read Dylan's story, you will get a pretty good idea of what is going on inside his head. Dylan's story will contain no dialogue.

Ready to read on?
Let's go.

ONE

I loved Dylan. I always have.

From the very first moment I heard his voice, I knew he was the one. I never doubted that for a single moment. Not once. Not even during his strange moods or the moments he pulled away from me, to protect me or to hide whatever it was that he considered necessary to hide.

My sister Emma had told me about Midstone and the Montana community. I had brushed it off, even when she made some jokes about it when we spoke over the phone.

"It's such a shame you won't come over for Thanksgiving," she said, "but I do get why you want to go to his parents' house. Just don't end up as their Thanksgiving dinner, okay?"

"You're insane, Em. Stop it. I'm nervous enough as it is."

"About meeting them? Or about the secrecy he's been throwing around?"

"He's not the one acting secretively. You are."

She shrugged. "Okay, I'm sorry. I'm just curious, I guess."

"As am I, but it'll be fine. You'll see, they'll be these regular, boring people with normal jobs, leading a simple life. We're making this into something that isn't there."

"I know. It was just a joke. I'm so sorry."

"It's okay."

"Just call us when you get there, okay? And let me know if you need anything."

"I'm with Dylan. I won't need anything."

"Except for a good bed."

"Oh, shut up, sis," I said, smiling.

I wasn't too sure we would even sleep in the same bed. Who knew how old school his parents were? They might cling to the belief that we hadn't had sex yet.

Dylan and I had gotten so serious over the past month that I just knew he would be my partner for life. I had no doubt that I wanted to spend the rest of my life with him. I had told my mother so, even when I was afraid she would say it was too soon. She didn't.

"Your dad and I met when I was fourteen, and we have never stopped being together since," she said. "First as friends, later as a couple. I know the feeling, Holly. When you feel it, you can't ignore it. Enjoy it because it's the best thing you'll ever experience in your life."

"You really don't mind us going to Midstone for Thanksgiving?"

"I really don't. This is an important moment for both of you. Spend the weekend at his parents' house. You know your dad and I will come up for the weekend soon, so we can catch up then. And Holly?"

"Yeah?"

"They'll love you."

"Thanks, Mom."

When we packed up our things, Dylan unexpectedly started talking about his parents.

"I can't wait to see them again," he said. "To have them

meet you. I'm scared, though."

"About what?"

"I'm just hoping they'll like you."

"What would stop them from doing so?" I asked.

"I don't know. They're just a bit strange in that way. You know, with our whole community and such."

I didn't look at Dylan while I continued packing, wondering why he radiated such stress all of a sudden.

"You really don't like to talk about them, do you?" I said. "What was it like growing up with them?"

"Lonely."

I stopped packing and looked at him, silently encouraging him to continue.

"When I was a kid, I didn't see my parents all that much, Hol. It wasn't like it was with you. They were always working, even though they were close by. That didn't even matter because I didn't get to see them at all. They were always off somewhere, taking care of things. They're that kind of people, you know? The ones that others go to when they're in need."

"So they helped others but forgot about you?"

"I guess," he said, sitting down on the bed. "You know, sometimes I would go with them, but most of the time I would be home alone or in bed, waiting patiently for them to come home."

"That's sad, Dylan."

"It isn't, not really. It was what it was. When they were home, I got all of their attention, so that kind of made up for the loneliness."

"What about your friends?"

"Oh, I had plenty of those, even though we're all scattered around these days, so I barely have any contact with them. Some of them are attending college like me, but they're also planning on coming back. It's rare that someone leaves forever."

"And the other people living there? The adults?"

"They're very introverted and protective. Tourists are always treated with care, but they're happy when they leave too. It's like they can only tolerate them for a while."

I sat down on the bed beside him, feeling my heart sink deeper in my chest. The things he said sounded so dark and sad that it made me wonder if we would even have a future together.

The one thing I was most concerned about was our future together. Even though I had told Dylan that I would seriously consider moving to Midstone with him so he could take over his dad's practice, as was expected of him. He had made that very clear from the start—brutally clear even, that he had no choice in the matter. So if I wanted to be with him, I'd have to move to Midstone too.

Which was another reason why this Thanksgiving visit was so important. I'd only get one chance to make a good impression, meaning that I would have to deal with his parents, one way or the other. If they hated me, I would have to do my best to get them to like me. If they liked me from the start, I might stand a better chance of getting accepted into the Midstone community.

"It'll be fine," Dylan said, more for his own benefit than mine.

"Are you a member of a cult?" I blurted out.

He looked up in shock, releasing my hand at once.

"What? A cult?"

"Yeah, because it sounds like a cult sometimes when you talk about Midstone. Like some sort of closed community that you need to apply to. Emma actually wondered about it too."

He laughed, but was it me or did it sound nervous?

"No, Hol, we're not a cult. There's no guru ruling our universe or some asshole marrying eighty girls. We're not Mormons or members of any weird church, trust me. We're just very close-knit, that's all. Is that so weird?"

"Just a bit," I said.

"Why?"

"Because people usually prefer to get away from where they were raised. Kids often choose another location because they've already seen it all in their own town. Going to college also means getting a taste of a different life, you know."

"Not for us," Dylan reacted vehemently.

"Then why are you so adamant about taking over your dad's practice?"

"Because that's what's expected of me. He needs me to."

"What about your own needs? Don't you get any say in your future? I mean, you would make one hell of a surgeon. What if you were offered a scholarship or a grant to become a heart surgeon or something? Wouldn't you take it?"

"No, not right now."

He looked at his hands, not at me. A silence fell over us. What if I had pushed the subject too hard?

He looked up.

"It isn't necessarily my personal desire to take over the practice, but there's no one else and Midstone needs a doctor. My dad is holding down the fort while I'm here, but one day, he'll want to retire, and then I'll be there. This means everything to me, and if you want to be with me, you must accept this as a potential future for the two of us. And that's the whole problem, isn't it? I'm not sure if that is going to be enough for you."

He sat there, all serious and nervous and vocal about our future, and I knew that I would do anything for him, even move to the other side of the world, if that meant keeping him close to me.

"I get where you're coming from, Dyl," I said. "I would go to the end of the world for you because I love you. Whatever the future has in store for us, we can handle it. We can set up a dual practice. Towns always need vets, so I'm okay with being a regular vet and not focusing on wild animals if that's what it takes. I'll always follow my passion. It doesn't matter to me where that will be."

The smile on his face said it all.

"There's a wild animal preservation nearby," he said. "Only an hour's drive or so. You could try your luck there."

"There is? That's amazing!"

"It's a great place too. I love it. It'll feel like home to you."

Like home.

That's what I kept in the back of my mind as we drove to Midstone. I didn't tell Dylan how nervous I was since I could tell he was just as agitated too. Which increased my own nerves. If he was already so wary and cautious about me meeting his parents, what was I supposed to think?

I tried to make small talk, but in the end, we did end up discussing them again.

"We'll be fine, Dyl," I said at some point. "Stop worrying. I'll love them, and they'll love me. I'll be on my best behavior, I promise."

"It's not you I'm worried about," he reacted.

His words increased my worry but also the fierceness I had been building up as a shield in case things went wrong. If that were to happen, things would go downhill between us. No one wanted to deal with a mother-in-law from hell or a father-in-law who wanted to define their children's future, no matter what happened.

If that were the case and they would make him choose, I would have to take a stand. But we weren't there yet. And if we did get to that point? Then I would fight for him.

"If they act like assholes, that's fine too. It won't make me love you any less," I added.

I placed my hand on his in a reassuring gesture that—so I hoped—would tell him that I wouldn't just give up, no matter what.

Hours later, after a short break at a diner for a late second breakfast and some shopping at a gas station where we picked up sandwiches for our hike up the mountain, we arrived at Dylan's paternal home.

Midstone was gorgeous. It was a quaint small town with a nice church and a town hall that obviously dated from the 1800s. It had everything a typical American town needed, from several small and large grocery stores to a library, a couple of schools and even a museum. It lay in the shadow of an immense mountain, and it was just perfect.

Midstone and Beau had a lot in common. Both towns had the typical quaint setting, a close-knit local population, and seasonal tourism. But where Beau lay in a vast lake area, Midstone was defined by the mountains. The mountain range was overwhelmingly beautiful too.

"This is a beautiful town," I said. "I'd seen the pictures online, but they don't do it justice. My God, it's gorgeous, Dyl."

He seemed quite pleased with my remarks.

I could imagine myself living there, in this gorgeous

town with its beautiful houses, enjoying a view that was millions of years old. The mountain range was one of the oldest in the world, and it stood proudly facing the horizon, basking in the sun.

Suddenly my nerves were gone completely. If this strange calm that surrounded Midstone also radiated through its townsfolk, then I had nothing to fear. My anxiety diminished even more when I spotted people waving at Dylan as we drove slowly through town. They recognized him and greeted him as old friends. I let out a small sigh of relief.

He left the center of the town and took a road that led to a small area with about ten houses, all big, bigger and biggest. He stopped at a large wood-and-brick stand-alone home on a huge property with gated fences. The gate swung open when we approached it. He drove up to a three-story-building that was double the size of the lake house.

When we got out, Dylan stood for a brief moment, watching my reaction. I looked around and studied the house, whistling softly.

"This place is huge, Dyl. You never told me you guys had so much space. And that view of the mountains is gorgeous! It must have been amazing growing up here," I said, totally in awe.

"It was," he said, obviously pleased with me. "Part of it is my dad's garage in the back and his practice, so our living area is a lot smaller than it seems."

He walked over to the side of the floorboards and dug up a spare key.

"I never take my key with me," he explained while opening the front door.

Inside, he had to tap in a safety code to turn off the alarm system and then he let me in while he fetched the bags from the trunk of the car. He gave me mine.

"Come on, I'll show you your room."

"Isn't your room my room as well?" I quipped.

"I'm not sure yet," he said. "I have to check with my mom. We haven't spoken about the house rules yet."

"A spare bedroom is fine, as long as it's near you," I said, not wanting to hurt his feelings.

I dropped my things on the large bed in the cozy spare bedroom. It was nice, spacy, and beautifully decorated. I liked it.

Dylan opened the window and showed me his room. It was a typical high school teenager room with posters on the wall, a large bed, a huge desk, and a comfortable gaming chair. There was no computer or laptop on the desk, though. The room was cleaned and felt a bit sterile; it was obvious he hadn't stayed here for ages.

I was in awe of the house, which I told him. It was impossible not to admire and like this place. It had everything a person needed for the rest of his life.

"One day it'll be mine," he said, explaining how this was the family home and how it was customary for parents to move out once someone started a family.

So one day this could be our house? I couldn't even consider that possibility right now, as it seemed impossible for two young people to own a place like this.

"Come on, I'll show you the rest of the house," he said, "then we should get a move on if we still want to go up the mountain."

"Great," I said.

When we were in the kitchen, my eye fell on the backyard,

which was beautifully kept. Dylan explained that his parents hired a gardener to keep the garden since they didn't have time for it.

The garden itself was like most gardens. It had loads of bushes and large patches of grass, but there was one thing that caught my eye. In the middle of the garden stood a small concrete shed. What struck me was the steel door.

"What's that?" I asked.

Dylan shrugged.

"It's just an old shed," he said, before adding in a rush, "come on, let's get ready for our hike. It'll be good to stretch our legs."

He hugged me and turned me around so I wouldn't see the shed anymore. Why would anyone have a concrete building in their backyard? The nagging suspicion that he still wasn't telling me everything returned.

I wanted to address it, but this was not the right time, I could tell. Dylan obviously felt the same way.

"Love you," he said, before taking me into his arms.

He kissed me, exploring my mouth with his tongue, taking his time to get me turned on.

"I would love to fuck you right now," he said, "but we need to get going, or it'll be too late soon."

"I'd love to fuck you too," I said. "But you're right."

"I can still spare a few minutes if you can?"

I smiled, touching his stubbled chin.

"Hm. I suppose, but we'd need to shower and that would take time."

His hand traveled to my lower body, resting softly between my legs. I was wearing jeans, but even then, the touch felt exhilarating.

"Just hands and a quick wash then?" he said teasingly, already unbuttoning my jeans. His hand slid downward. His fingers brushed over my panties and then past them, sliding in easily.

"Fuck," I whispered, closing my eyes as the sensation of his fingers touching me there overwhelmed me. Standing up, resting against the kitchen table, with his fingers inside of me while he kissed me deeply, had me coming in a few moments. I shivered as I rested against him.

"You're insane," I said.

"No, I'm hard."

He pulled his fingers out of me and dragged me to his bedroom, where we got rid of his jeans quickly. I used my hands to bring him to orgasm while he lay down on the bed and enjoyed the moment.

"Fuck, Holly," he sighed, pulling me on the bed next to him.

"Let's keep that for tonight, unless your parents sleep in the room next door and won't allow us to stay in one bed?" I quipped.

"We'll do it in secret then. I seriously can't go five days without you. That's simply impossible."

"Me neither," I said. "I'm going to wash up and change, or we'll never get on that mountain."

He sighed. "Right. I'll come with you."

We quickly washed up and got changed into the right clothing for a hike up the mountain. I felt horny yet satisfied. Well, at least for the moment.

Dylan took his time getting his things. His mind was obviously elsewhere.

"All set?" I said, dragging him from whatever cloud he was drifting on.

"Yep. Let's go."

We left the house. Dylan locked up and put the key back where it belonged. He reached for my hand and squeezed my fingers. I kissed him.

"We're not going to do the whole hike," he said as we walked over the foot of the mountain. "It would take way too long, and it's already past noon. What we'll do is go up for about two hours and come back. There are some gorgeous sceneries to admire, so you'll love it."

"Will we do the whole hike some other day?" I said.

"For sure, but it'll have to wait until spring. Right now, it's just too risky. The weather could change too quickly."

We walked over to the start of the hike, where a security guy greeted us. I was surprised until I saw a sign explaining his role. He was here to make sure that people went up the mountain fully prepared and to stop wacky tourists who believed it would be a walk in the park instead of a serious hike.

The man greeted Dylan. I took in the sights while they chatted. How fantastic would it be to hike all the way up there in spring? It would be something to remember forever.

"It's been a rough month so far," the security guard said, which drew my attention.

"The mountain's been unrestful for a while, but the geologists have no clue why. They're talking minor quakes. If you ask me, it's the underground volcano that's getting restless," he said.

"The volcano? After tens of thousands of years?" Dylan said in disbelief. "No way."

"Afraid so. There are multiple volcanoes worldwide in dire straits. Didn't you hear about the one near Naples?"

"The Vesuvius?" I blurted out, which caused the guard to look at me.

"No," he said, "there's another one. Have we met? Lewis, nice to meet you."

"Holly."

"She's my girlfriend," Dylan said quickly. "From out of town."

He went on to explain that I was an experienced hiker. Well, maybe not as experienced as he led the man to believe, but good enough to hold my own. My parents took us hiking several times a year, but it had been a while. We hadn't gone on a nature walk since I went to college.

The security guard asked for my phone number, which Dylan gave him. It flattered me that he knew my phone number by heart.

"No later than five p.m., okay?" he warned Dylan, who confirmed that was the plan.

I turned to the mountain and missed a part of the conversation until I heard the security guard say, "A new member of the club, eh?"

Dylan took me by the arm and walked us past the guard, who waved us goodbye.

"What club was he talking about?" I asked.

"Oh, it's just a running joke in our town," he quickly explained. "We don't get that many new people here, so we refer to ourselves as 'the club.' Don't worry about it."

"Oh. Okay."

Dylan's tension was back as we walked up the mountain. I could feel it. He seemed nervous, but once he got into explanatory mode, he started to relax a bit.

"There are a few steep areas that will take us higher immediately. There are resting points in between and some amazing views, so it's worth it. If you need to take a break, let me know."

"I'm all good," I said. "Let's go."

We walked a couple of yards before reaching the bottom of the first steep challenge he was referring to. He went up first and gazed back over his shoulder to make sure I was okay.

"I'm fine," I said. "I'll call out if you're going too fast."

He didn't. Dylan took his time walking up the mountain. He never rushed once, nor did he want to make a contest out of it. He turned around a couple of times, seemingly satisfied with my tempo.

Once we reached the first scenic overlook, I caught my breath while admiring the panoramic view. It was absolutely stunning, and I told Dylan so, feeling invigorated and ready for the next part.

"Let's continue," I said, taking the lead this time.

Dylan followed my pace. I could hear him right behind me. This part was easier, and when we stopped again, I couldn't help but admire what was in front of us. The higher we went, the more beautiful the viewpoints became. It was so gorgeous that I could hardly grasp the beauty of it.

"Stunning," I said. "Gorgeous. Beautiful. Amazing."

I seemed to repeat myself at every vista point, but that was how I felt.

We walked for a long time, only taking breaks at viewing points or to have a quick bite to eat. I quickly went through two protein bars, while Dylan munched on bananas. It was obvious that he felt quite at ease up the mountain. He shared information about random stuff, showed me beautiful viewpoints, and recalled some funny stories about the trail.

But as soon as we reached a certain point on the mountain he grew quiet and started walking slower, as if he wanted to extend the journey to wherever it was that we were going.

The weather changed while we were hiking, but all in all, it wasn't too bad. A few drops of rain promised a wet evening, but we were dressed for the occasion, having prepared for the forecasted weather.

"I need to tell you something," he said when we walked next to each other on an easy slope. "When we reach the point I want you to see, I will need to tell you more about it."

"Sure," I said. "That's what we came here for."

"Yeah, I know. It's just that—well, there are some things on the mountain that might seem a bit weird, you know?"

"Weird, how?"

"Just weird."

I poked him playfully, trying to break the sudden tension.

"You are not making any sense, Mr. Blair."

"I know," he said. "I'm sorry."

He bit his fingernails. I stopped him.

"Stop fretting. It's fine. Whatever it is that you want to tell me, just make sure it doesn't have anything to do with ghosts, okay? You know I'm afraid of them, so please don't tell me how people plunged to their deaths on the mountain, or I'm out of here."

He laughed. "It's not about ghosts."

"Good. Then it can't be that bad."

"I hope so." He hugged me. "Let's go. Last part."

We walked next to each other before going up on the next steep area. Not so long after, the weather became pretty bad. Clouds were gathering at a rapid pace; drops of rain fell from the sky. His secret was important enough to him that he would risk taking me up on the mountain in bad weather, so I didn't ask to go back down, desperately wanting to know why he was being so evasive.

Ten minutes, he said, no longer. Then we would head back down. I could feel the tension radiate from him, which—again—troubled me. What was going on?

I wanted to ask him if everything was okay but didn't get the chance. His phone rang. Dylan froze. I was confused because it wasn't the regular sound I was used to.

He stood still without answering the call, and I knew why. I had heard that sound only once before, at the beginning of our relationship. He had taken his emergency phones with him. Fuck.

I knew from the second it rang, that something was wrong. Dylan's expression was a telltale sign. He took out his phone reluctantly. The moment he saw who was calling, he froze and changed into this weird version of himself that I hardly recognized.

It was the eyes. They changed into something dark and brooding, like he was back to being that introverted person I had met months ago. The man who lived a solitary life, who sometimes retreated in his dorm by himself to protect me from whatever secrets it was that he kept hidden so well.

It frightened me because we were in a strange place, and I didn't really want to find out what would happen if he freaked out on me high up on this mountain.

"Dylan, your phone's ringing," I said.

He didn't react.

"Dylan."

"Dyl?"

"Your phone, Dyl. It might be your mom or your dad. Pick up."

He finally picked up the phone. He put his father on speaker because I wouldn't move. I was as nervous as he was.

"Dad," he said.

"Dylan," his father's warm voice said. "Thank God. Listen, are you still up on *Dead Man's Walk* with her? Are you on the hike?"

"Yeah, we are," Dylan said.

"How far up the mountain are you?"

"Almost to where we need to go."

"The shelter?"

"Yeah."

Shelter?

"Good. Listen to me. We have a problem. The situation is dire," his dad said.

Dylan obviously didn't know what to say. His eyes were fixed on me.

"Dylan, can you hear me?" his dad asked.

"Yeah," he said, sounding hoarse. "How dire?"

"Is she with you?"

"Yeah, she is. She's listening."

His dad scraped his throat.

"The worst we've ever seen."

Excuse me—*what*?! What the hell was he talking about?

Dylan didn't react at first, but when he did, his voice sounded rough and hurt.

"Dad, please stop this bullshit. It's not true."

"It *is* true, son. Head for the shelter. The mountain's rumbling. The volcano is active. You need to go *now*, before it's too late. Stay there. You know the rules. Be safe."

"Dad…"

"Dylan, can you still hear me? Dylan, go n—"

The call got cut off. Dylan started yelling into the phone,

calling out his dad's name because the connection was so bad. Still, I had heard enough. Something bad was about to happen, or so he'd said. But that was nonsense, right?

Some of the things that he said didn't make any sense at all. And then the mountain rumbled, and it felt as if everything shook beneath our feet, as if we were going through an earthquake. This was not normal.

God.

Why did we go up by ourselves when even the security guard warned us that the mountain had been acting up for the past month? Why would Dylan have even taken that risk?

He had been so insistent on showing me whatever it was he wanted to talk about, and now we might get stuck here, on this very mountain, in grave danger.

"What was that?" I said, but Dylan didn't hear. He was trying to reach his dad again. He looked at the device as if he couldn't believe what was happening.

"Dylan!"

He still wouldn't pay attention. His mind was so far gone that it scared the hell out of me.

"I'm going back," I muttered, but somehow my legs wouldn't move. I couldn't leave.

The way down wasn't so hard. There were a couple of dangerous points, like those steep slopes that would make it difficult to just run down, but if I took my time and still made haste, I could be back by the house in about an hour.

The mountain rumbled again. It was a horrible, dark, and dangerous sound.

"Did you hear that?" I said shakily.

Dylan hurried over to me.

"Yeah, I heard and felt it. It's the mountain. Something's

going on. We have to go right now, Holly. Come with me, you'll be safe with me."

Again, the world shook. I stumbled on my feet. I held on to Dylan tight.

"We have to go," he said.

I was shaken to the core.

"I don't understand," I uttered.

"Listen to me, Holly! There's a problem on the mountain. They're afraid something bad is going to happen. We have to get to safety."

"They? Who's they?"

He increased his pace. "I don't have time to explain now, but you have to come with me. Trust me, Holly, this is the only way."

This was still that dark Dylan, the one I didn't like.

"I trust you, but that's not enough right now. Where are we going?"

"The shelter."

"What shelter?" I asked, puzzled. *What the hell?*

"I'll explain later. Come on."

I didn't move. Dylan picked up his backpack. Another tremble.

"Come on, let's go!"

What was happening? His dad must have called to warn him that we had to head back down the mountain *fast.* But that was not what he did. To my bewilderment, he walked further up the mountain instead of going down.

Wait, *what?*

This had to be a mistake, right? I was *not* going up the mountain when the logical way was down. So I turned and walked down the mountain, stopping only when he called out to me, shouting that we had to go *up.* What kind of crazy person would walk further up a mountain when disaster struck?

He grabbed on to me so tight that the mark of his fingers would probably leave a lasting imprint for days He stopped talking and started dragging me with him.

I fought with everything I had. I yelled, screamed, pulled, and shoved. I tried to free myself, refused to give up that easily. But nothing stopped him. He acted like a crazed man. He kept pulling me by the sleeve, refusing to let me go as the world trembled around us. He was much stronger than I was. I didn't stand a chance.

"Stop it, you freak!" I screamed. "You're crazy!"

He didn't even listen. Like an obsessed asshole, he pulled me with him, not letting go for even a split second. There was no stopping him. I had all these terrible ideas running through my mind, wondering what he was going to do to me.

Was this what he had been waiting for? Were these his true colors?

I fell hard on my back. He didn't even stop to apologize as he pulled me up and continued dragging me up the mountain.

For the first time since we met, I was scared of him. I was so scared.

My instincts sprang into action again. I kicked and screamed and used everything I had in me to get him to stop. He snapped.

"I'm trying to save your fucking life! Stop fighting, or I'll knock you out, dammit!"

I tried to kick him. He never gave in. He pulled me away from the main path, onto a smaller one that was barely noticeable. Bushes covered the path; it looked unused.

We stopped in front of a mountain wall. It somehow seemed slicker and different than the rocks we had come across going up, as if it were some kind of trail marker, without being too obvious.

Dylan knew exactly what to look for. Fear became my second nature. Was this the special place he had been talking about before? But how could this be it? This wasn't a viewpoint, no special spot that tourists just had to see to make their difficult journey worthwhile. It was nothing like that at all.

In fact, I'd bet my life on the fact that no tourists knew about this place. It was too out of sight, a hidden spot that would only be accessible for the select few. It would never stand out to hikers either, not even to those who knew the mountain by heart. On this side of the mountain, there were big old trees, most centuries old. It was an area where no one ever came. Unless you knew it was there.

Dylan turned around and glanced over the edge of the mountain while standing very still, as if listening. I thought for a second he was going to push me over, but then the trees would have caught me for sure. I realized he was making sure there was no one else in sight. There wasn't.

The fog was getting denser, and the trees were covered in semi-darkness, making it nearly impossible to see anything. If someone had been near us, we would have heard but not seen them.

Only when he'd made sure it was safe, did he pull me through this small path that was hidden behind the stone wall. The entrance to that path was broader than I'd first thought, taking us behind the outer stone wall that hid it from the world.

The path took us deeper into the mountain, into a carved stone tunnel with a big steel door, which was also very hard to see thanks to the natural darkness that hid it from sight.

Dylan took out his phone and used the flashlight to illuminate a steel box that was embedded into the wall next to the door. He had to use a lock to open the box, which then revealed a keypad.

He made sure I couldn't see the code he tapped in. He turned me around so I was away from the keypad, using his strength at the same time to still keep me close to him.

Once the door slid open, he pushed me inside a dark cave. The door slid shut behind us. We walked to another door, about three yards away, with another keypad attached to it. Again he typed in a code. Again, I couldn't see what he did under the beam of his phone's flashlight.

I had stopped fighting back, knowing there was no point trying to free myself from him now that the outer door was shut, so I let it happen. Only when the second door opened and shut and revealed what was behind it, did I start panicking again.

For a long time, I had believed that Dylan was taking me here for a reason, most likely to keep us safe. He had said that he would take me to safety, and as the world rumbled around us, I had honestly wanted to believe that was the case.

Now, I wasn't so sure anymore.

Whoever this person was, he was not my boyfriend.

He stood there in darkness.

I believed for a fact that he was a stranger.

"Okay," he whispered. "You're okay."

But I wasn't okay.

"Safe."

I was so scared.

"Dad."

He tried his phone. Nothing.

"Come on."

Silence.

"Come on, Dad."

I was lost for words. Panic overwhelmed me.

His phone was useless. All three of them.

"Dad, fuck."

He didn't even see me anymore. He just stood there in darkness, mumbling to himself.

"Come on, Dad."

When he turned to me, I saw a darkness in his eyes that was unfamiliar to me.

I ran to the steel door and banged on it. It was cold and hard.

"We're okay," Dylan muttered.

I banged on the door again.

He reached for my wrist and held on tight, stopping me from banging the door again.

"Stop it, Holly. We're fine. We're safe. We're okay. Nothing can hurt you now."

But we weren't fine, safe, or okay. We weren't out there in the real world. We were locked in.

This place was a prison.

I had landed in a freaking nightmare.

TWO

I stood in the darkness with Dylan holding me tight. His hand still gripped my wrist, keeping me so close to him I thought he was going to throw me on the floor and have his way with me next.

And why not? Why wouldn't he show his true colors after all this time? There were plenty of movies, television shows, and stories out there about men grooming women into believing that they meant to do right by them.

I knew what toxic men were like. He couldn't be one of them. There would always be people abusing other people. Men who preyed on innocent girls and vulnerable women. There were wolves out there with no respect for anyone. There would always be serial killers and rapists. Social media, hidden camcorders, sexting,… There seemed to be no boundaries these days. Didn't people say that real life often surpassed made-up stories?

I had believed without a doubt that Dylan wasn't like that. He didn't have a bad bone in his body. I knew him, I knew what made him tick and what drove his eagerness to do well. He'd never been this controlling or dominating. He always had this regard for me, a respect we had both shared from the start.

It felt good to be with him. There was no shame or anything bizarre about our lovemaking. He had never once given me any of the signals that hinted at a toxic personality, not once. He was just a regular, average guy who liked to be with his girlfriend.

Sure, he liked sex, but so did I. And yeah, we did it a lot, but it was always vanilla stuff, nothing too crazy, nothing too daring. No bondage or handcuffs, no abnormal fetishes or things that seemed too out there. I had trusted him with my body and mind, and I hadn't regretted it once.

But right here and now, trapped behind these two steel doors, I couldn't help but wonder if I had been wrong all this time. This would explain his moody episodes. His bizarre reactions to phone calls, his secrets. Didn't Bundy appear to be this nice, regular guy too, until he went on a killing spree?

There had to be a reason Dylan was doing this to me. Had he been grooming me for months, knowing all along that he would abduct me as soon as we came to Midstone, where he would hold me captive without anyone ever finding out? And stupid me, I fell for it with my eyes wide open.

Was this whole scheme something he had planned from the very moment we met? But to what end? Why turn me into a prisoner when I was already in love with him and ready to share my life with him? I had gone up the mountain with him without a single hesitation, trusting him to show me his secret. I would have walked into this cave willingly; he didn't need to use force on me.

It was the phone call that triggered this strange behavior, no question about it, the weird, nonsensical things his dad had said to him. The moment that phone rang, Dylan had changed. His dad had the obvious power to turn him from a self-assured, calm man into a stranger. Like a switch flipped inside his head.

And this wasn't the first time it had happened either.

I was exhausted after screaming and struggling to free myself.

This place, whatever it was, resembled a secret prison. It was big enough to keep many people locked in. It seemed to be created in a natural cave that had probably been formed thousands of years ago. But alterations had been made to the cave to make it inhabitable.

I didn't need the flashlight on Dylan's phone to know that he had that odd look in his eyes again. There was a franticness about him, like he was being haunted or chased. It felt extremely eerie. He barely seemed to notice me. Still, he had brought me here for a reason.

This *place* existed for a purpose. I just needed to figure out what that was.

Dylan released my wrist, but that didn't take away my anxiety or fear. He only let go because the door was closed and locked, and he knew I couldn't get out. This seemed to calm him down.

He walked around, flipping light switches wherever he went. The place lit up, and I could see it was much bigger than I had expected. I was surprised at the size of it. This cave had to run deep into the mountain.

It was cold to the point of freezing. I could see my own breath. I kept my hands in their warm gloves and was glad that I still wore my coat.

"Are you okay?" he asked when he returned to me, sounding like himself again.

"It's cold," I muttered.

"I know, I'll get right on it."

He walked to an unlit area where he opened a door, and I could hear him do something that created a loud clicking noise.

A deep, dark, brimming sound soon filled through the room. He came back out and closed the door behind him.

"I've just turned up the generator, so it'll get warm soon. I'm sorry about the cold. It takes a while before it gets comfortable. Why don't you keep your coat on for a while?"

"The generator?" I asked, surprised.

"Yeah."

"Why does this place have a generator?"

"Why do you think?" he said, not understanding my confusion. "Everything's fine, Hol. We're good for now. You're safe now, you don't have to worry. I'll take care of everything."

He tried to hug me. I slapped him in the face with my gloved hand. The smack echoed so loud against the stone walls that it shocked us both.

His hand flew up to his face. He looked at me with such shock that it made me feel guilty, if only for a second.

"What the hell was that for?"

"What do you think?" I snapped. "Do you even realize what you just did to me?"

"I didn't do anything wrong."

"Oh, really? You kidnapped me!"

My words made him cringe. It finally seemed to dawn on him.

"Fuck. You still don't realize what's going on, do you? I'm so sorry, Holly. I'm sorry I had to put you through this."

He confused me. He sounded genuinely apologetic. I wouldn't have any of it.

"Sorry. Is that all you can say?" I snarled.

"What more do you want me to say?"

"I'd like an explanation."

"Yeah, of course," he muttered, still holding his hand against his face. "I'll tell you everything, but are we going to just stand here? I can make some coffee. We have cookies."

Coffee and cookies. Seriously?

"You just kidnapped me. I don't want any fucking coffee, let alone cookies," I snapped.

He blinked. Froze. Looked hurt.

"I didn't kidnap you. Again, I'm terribly sorry, but you don't seem to understand why I did this, do you?"

"No, I don't."

"I don't know how to even begin to explain this."

"Try me."

He sighed while he removed his coat.

"I know what it looks like, Hol, but I couldn't risk your safety. You were going to head down the mountain, which would have been a death sentence. I didn't have the time to explain and you barely listened to me anyhow, so I made the decision for you. I'm really sorry about this whole mess, but know that I saved your life."

"Saved me?!" I yelled, losing my temper. "You locked me up in some dingy, dark mountain cave. Is that what you call saving?"

"You're not a prisoner, Holly. Just calm down, okay? I'm still the same person you used to know."

"Are you? Or did you just turn into some crazy-ass Ted Bundy?"

"No."

"How can I know for sure?"

"If I wanted you dead, you would be by now."

He sounded calm and composed, and he did have a point. He wasn't Bundy. Maybe I should try to trust him again.

I knew Dylan. I had always trusted him. Despite what he was doing now, a big part of me still did. I didn't understand this blind trust, but there it was and I couldn't ignore it.

Ever since that door closed, he hadn't touched me or threatened me. He even left me alone while he went to switch on the generator. But of course, he had used a code to lock those doors.

Dylan sighed. He seemed weary.

"Look," he said, "we have a lot of things to discuss, but that can wait until later. I tell you what, why don't you get an idea of this place first, and then we'll talk. Just promise me you'll stay calm and won't do anything stupid."

"I *am* calm."

"That's good. Now please, go take a look around, and I'll explain everything to you, I promise."

"Okay. Fine. But you stay where you are while I look around. And if you dare to leave me alone in here, I swear I'll hunt you down and kill you slowly."

"I won't move an inch," he promised.

To his credit, he didn't. He stayed put while I looked around hesitantly. Once my vision had adjusted to the dim lights that shone through the damp, cold, rocky cave, I got a closer look at my surroundings while keeping an eye on him too.

We were in a quarry of some cave that consisted of cold stone walls and floors that had been evened out. There was no way they could have gotten this perfect by themselves. This wasn't a natural cave or quarry. It had definitely been created by humans.

The cave was big enough for most people, unless you were a giant of a man. I could imagine the tallest basketball player hitting his skull on the roof or missing it by an inch. The generator provided a buzzing sound that was audible throughout the room.

What struck me was how big this place was. The large, central space held a couple of large wooden tables with ten chairs around each table. There was a kitchen area located in the back of the room. It was obviously well equipped, including a number of appliances.

On the right-hand side, giant racks from floor to ceiling took over the entire wall, as if it was one giant storage facility. Every single one of them was filled with cans, jars, bowls, and huge bags of flower, salt, sugar, and whatever other supplies that could be stored for a long time. There were bottles of water and juices of all kinds, there was a lot of rice and pasta, and there were cans and cans of tomato sauce, beans, pickles, carrots, and peas. I even spotted astronaut food.

All the chosen food was suited for long preservation, as if someone expected to be cooped up in here for weeks, even months. There were no fresh foods and vegetables, nor was there anything that could rot in a matter of days. No fresh meals, no dairy, except for cans of long-preserving milk that tasted terrible.

Everything was set up for people who were to stay here for a long, long time. It reminded me of that one movie I'd seen once about this girl who was locked up in a cellar, surrounded by food, captured and held prisoner by a man who told her that she would be safe as long as she stayed with him. That man had set up a bunker to protect him from anything bad happening on the outside.

In fact, this whole place reminded me of disaster movies where people would gather when the end of the world was near, whether it was brought on by alien attacks or natural disasters. Usually the government would select people to survive and ship them off to caves that were hidden behind steel doors, where they would survive with the help of a ton of supplies.

But there was no army here, and there were no alien attacks or natural disasters. Which could only mean one thing.

My conversation with Emma last summer popped up in the back of my mind. It had never really left my thoughts, but I had brushed it off as nonsense.

I knew what this place was. Who Dylan was. Which meant that his parents would be the same. Which would also explain his secretive second nature. I finally understood who and what I was dating.

"You're a doomsday prepper, aren't you?"

Dylan cringed as if I had hit him in the face again, this time with my fist. He was so nervous that sweat trickled down his face. He didn't dare to look me in the eye, as if he were ashamed.

"Look at me, Dylan."

He looked up. "Yeah, I'm part of a preppers community. Well, my parents are, which means that I automatically am too."

"For real?"

"Yeah. Always prepared for the worst-case scenario," he said, trying to make a joke out of it.

But it wasn't a joke. I had never spoken to preppers before, let alone had any idea of how they lived. To me, they were regular people with a tendency toward the fanatic, always looking for the next disaster to strike, never *not* cautious or carefree. I hadn't judged them because I didn't know them. But this explained everything.

"That's why you were always so nervous. Why you would act so strangely when your dad called you or sent you text messages. The three phones. They were backups in case something happened."

"Yeah. I'm sorry I didn't tell you before, but it's not

something that you share just like that. We are a closed community, and there aren't many people out there who know where our shelters are. We don't show them to just anyone."

"Should I be flattered?" I said, sounding sarcastic.

He shrugged. "As long as you're not scared of me now. There's nothing to be afraid of, Hol. I'm still the same person I always was."

"But you lied to me."

"I didn't lie. I just didn't tell you."

That was technically true.

"You're right," I said. "I can't really say that you lied to me, but I am hurt you didn't trust me enough to confide in me."

"I tried to on several occasions, but it isn't something you just drop on someone. I didn't want you to run away screaming."

I got that too. Dylan's behavior made total sense to me now. My anger died down to the level of upset, verging on understanding.

"I don't know anything about how preppers think and live," I said. "I do know that they are always looking out for dramatic events to happen, right?"

"That's right. There are several sites and apps that predict natural disasters. And of course there is the news, which will update us about whatever war is going on."

"So this is a lair? Like a place you guys would run to when shit hits the fan?"

"It's a *shelter*," he corrected me. "We have plenty of places like this, but only a few this high up in the mountains."

"Why here? Wouldn't that make it more difficult to go to when something happens?"

"It actually has a lot of benefits. For one, it's a safe haven when a tsunami hits," he explained.

"Is this cave man-made then?"

"Yes and no. The area is millions of years old, and these mountains have survived several natural disasters. They've even seen dinosaurs. This whole area is a hotspot for dino skeletons. There are a lot of paleontology digs going on in the broader area. The rocks we are standing in are so thick that they will withstand anything, except a volcano eruption in the center of the earth, but that would mean the end of everything anyhow."

"Okay," I said. "I get all that. It's a safe place, and you brought me here to help me, according to your own words. So are you telling me that right now, a disaster is happening out there? That is what your dad was referring to?"

"Yes, there is."

"What kind?"

"I don't know. An earthquake or a volcano eruption perhaps, or something worse. It could be any of those things, but I don't know which one. As you heard for yourself, Dad didn't have the time to tell me the details, just that it was bad and that we had to head over here fast before the call got cut off."

"Do you believe him?" I asked.

"Why wouldn't I?"

"He could have exaggerated the whole situation."

"He wouldn't. We never make light of these things," Dylan said, fiercely defending his father.

"So if this is real, then where is your dad right now? And what happened to your mom? Shouldn't she be here too?"

"They were in town. They'll have taken shelter elsewhere."

Ah. "Let me guess, the garden shed that isn't a shed at all but a bunker?" I asked.

"Yeah."

"Okay. But things aren't adding up," I said. "By your own

definition, there's a disaster going on right now and this is the safest place in the area, but your parents aren't here. If you guys really are doomsday preppers, shouldn't you have seen this coming? Don't you have, like, radars and stuff to watch what's out there? And you have all these emergency phones to warn each other. A natural disaster like this should have been predictable."

Dylan was obviously uncomfortable.

"Or maybe I just don't know anything about it," I said.

He sighed and frowned. "Look, Holly. It's not that simple, okay? We have everything at our disposal, but sometimes nature catches us unawares and hits us by surprise. It's not a perfect science; things still happen. We have tools for survival, but there's never a guarantee that they'll warn us in time. There is a certain level of unpredictability here."

"Then your science is useless. Your whole policy of survival against all odds sucks big time."

I looked at the empty, barren space that could hold so many people. I tried to imagine strangers in here, with us, in a cave room that would quickly start to feel suffocating and too small with too many people occupying it. But right now, it felt too large and useless.

"Holly, you have to understand," Dylan attempted again, "it's not that easy. It's a complex situation, and I wish you weren't thrown into it like that."

"It's ridiculous, that's what it is," I interrupted him. "I mean, even if something was going on right now, what point would there be to surviving in this terrible shelter? Who would want to live like this? Why would you even want to survive a disaster if everything out there is gone? What's there to look forward to then after you get out? No thanks."

"You're kidding, right?"

"No, I'm not," I said.

"Why the hell would you *not* want to live, Holly?"

I smiled sadly. "Because survival alone isn't enough. It needs to have a purpose. A goal. A future."

"You are my future, Holly. If you aren't in here with me, what point is there to my life?"

THREE

My fear for him dissipated. He sounded so sad and genuine it broke my heart. He truly believed every single word he said. Yes, he had locked me up, but I was starting to see why. He really believed that he was doing the right thing. That what he did was to save me in some twisted way.

He would never harm me; I knew that now. He hadn't touched me, hadn't tied me down, hadn't forced me on the ground, hadn't chained me against one of those racks even though he had plenty of opportunity to do so. Whatever else I wanted to believe, I needed to trust in the person he was before we hiked up the mountain.

He was ashamed. He looked away from me and walked over to the racks of food, reading labels as if he were seeing those cans and jars for the first time. He was muttering to himself, ignoring me while trying to figure out what to do next. I felt sorry for him.

"Dylan, please look at me."

He didn't turn around.

I walked over to him and touched his shoulder, but he still wouldn't turn around. He shook slightly. Around us, the rumbling sound had returned, but it seemed to quiet down. I wasn't scared anymore.

"I'm sorry if I hurt your feelings, but I need to understand where you're coming from. I have no experience with doomsday preppers or how you think and feel. Can we please start over, as if none of this happened?"

He hesitated.

"Please?"

He didn't move.

"Dylan, come on. Look at me."

He turned around.

"Thank you," I said, releasing a sigh of relief. "Now then, can we just talk about this?"

"Okay."

"Great. Because I need you to hear this. This isn't your fault; I know that now. You acted on your beliefs and love for me. I'm sorry if I hurt your feelings."

He was genuinely surprised by my reaction. Hope flared, I could tell. His eyes lit up, and his whole demeanor changed. He smiled lightly.

"Thank you, Holly. Thank you so much."

I smiled back and reached for his hand. He was cold. I was worried about him. This whole situation had put stress on him, as it had done on me.

"Come, sit down with me," I said.

We settled down at the kitchen table. He didn't dare to look me in the eye.

"Please look at me, Dylan."

He lifted his face. "Sorry."

"It's alright. Can we just go back to the beginning? Before your dad called? Is this place what you were going to show me earlier?" I asked.

"Yeah." Dylan swallowed and sighed. "Okay, so basically, I was going to tell you today about my family and who we are. I figured it would be easier if I showed you the shelter, so it would be clearer from the start. I needed you to understand where I'm coming from and what this lifestyle means to my family and friends. Outsiders don't get it, unless they become a part of us. Even then, it would take a while to understand."

"You thought I wouldn't get it?" I said.

"Yeah. It's normal to not understand our way of thinking at first. I mean, there are so many stories about us out there that are over-the-top and exaggerated, so I figured it would be best to explain on-site."

"I get that," I said.

"But do you know what we are about?" he asked.

"I'm trying to, Dyl. I really am. I want to make sense of why you would want to exist here if something should happen. I guess I don't see it that way."

"Why not?" he asked fiercely. "Survival is all that matters when the end comes. It's what we are supposed to do. If not for ourselves, then for others."

"Who is *we*?"

"All those who get to live, no matter who it is or where they're from. It's mankind's duty to survive when the end comes. Preserving our species is absolutely necessary, so those who end up here at the shelter will have to take on that task. Billions of others won't be that lucky. We owe it to them to make it at all costs."

"Perhaps the ones that die out there when disaster hits will be luckier," I said softly.

Dylan didn't say anything. He was distracted when the

ground beneath our feet rocked gently. I could feel it too, like a small wave that would hit when standing barefoot in the ocean. It was barely noticeable, but it was there and it scared him. I had never seen him like this before. He returned to his agitated state of mind and shed off his fake self-assured posture in the blink of an eye.

He glanced over at the slightly shaking racks. Some of the canisters trembled slightly, but nothing toppled over. The shaking stopped within a few seconds. I could only imagine this happening all the time. A mountain was a living thing. It moved with the surface it was on.

"Damn," Dylan said. "This is not okay. The shelter shouldn't be shaking like this. This has never happened before."

"It's barely a tremor. It's nothing," I said. "We're inside a mountain, Dyl. Isn't this normal behavior?"

"No, it isn't."

"Okay then," I said, seizing the opportunity. "If this isn't a safe place for us to stay, we have to head outside right now and go down the mountain. Staying here couldn't be much better."

I got up, walked to the steel door, and touched it. I tried to open it manually and pushed and shoved at it, believing there might be some sort of hidden lock or door handle, but of course it wouldn't budge.

"Don't bother," Dylan said behind me, pointing at a keypad to the left of the door. "You can't get it to open. It needs the code. It's pointless to try."

"Then give me the code."

"I can't."

"Why not?"

He frowned. "No matter how you feel about it, it's safer in here than it is out there. You'll have to trust me on that. We can't get out for at least a month, maybe longer. It'll depend on the tremors of the mountain."

"A month?! Are you insane?"

"Listen," he said, "I know everything there is to know about this stuff. I know what I'm doing, Holly. We can't get out until it's safe out there."

"How will you know when that will be?"

"We won't, or at least not for certain for a while. If the mountain remains calm, I could go out to check how the world is doing. If the mountain continues to shake, then we have a problem. But we won't know for certain. We'll have to head outside not knowing what we'll find, so a month is the minimum we'll have to wait, as per our orders."

"Orders?"

"Yeah, we have instructions. Survival rules."

"Fuck the rules. You'd rather wait inside this stone prison than take your chances out there?" I said, feeling my anger flare again. "That's just great, Dylan. And what about me? What say do I get in this?"

"None. Like I said, this is my area of expertise, not yours," he said.

His words upset me. All the anger and fear I had felt when he dragged me up here returned, infuriating me.

"How can you stay so calm under these circumstances? How dare you imprison me against my will? I *want* to take the risk. I'm not scared of going out there, no matter what. This is not your choice to make!"

"It is."

"Why?"

"I'm the responsible one here, Holly. The one with the experience. The world is coming to an end, don't you get it? I won't let you go out and find certain death. You need to stay here, with me."

"And then what?"

"We'll figure that out as we go."

"You're full of shit, Dyl. If there's one thing I'm certain of, it's that there's nothing going on out there. I would feel it, know it in my heart."

"How can you? You didn't even consider that we could die today, Hol. You have no idea what it's like to live like this!"

"Then tell me," I demanded. "Tell me why you are so adamant about your beliefs."

"Because I live this life every single day. There's this constant fear that something terrible is going to happen. It's like this shadow hanging over you day and night, coloring everything in an undeniable darkness."

I tried to reason with him.

"If you really lived with these convictions, then you have to accept that many of us out there don't. I don't believe in end-of-the-world scenarios or doomsday prospects, Dyl, and even if I did, there would have been warning signs from the government or something. But there was nothing. There was no foreboding of something bad happening. The mountain wasn't splitting open; there were no fireballs dropping from the skies. So how can this be the real thing?"

"My dad told me so."

"And you're saying he has never made a mistake in his life?"

Dylan gaped at me, stunned.

"That's what I thought."

"He called to warn me. He never does that unless it's serious, Hol. And unlike you, I *do* have that sense of dread and urgency. It's real."

"Okay then, I'll prove it to you," I said. "I'm willing to take the risk and go out there if you just give me the codes."

He looked at me sadly.

"Sorry, Holly. I won't."

"Give me the codes, Dylan. Please."

"I won't."

I lost it. All my feelings for him, my sympathy for his situation, and my trust that he really thought he was doing the right thing, evaporated. No matter what he believed in, this was going too far. I needed to get out of here.

"Give me the codes," I repeated.

"No."

"Give me the goddamn codes!"

"Stop asking me, Holly. I won't give them to you."

"I insist," I said through gritted teeth.

"So do I."

I balled my fists, resisting the urge to hit him.

"Can't you see I'm trying to protect you?" he said.

"I don't need protection. I need to get out of here, and I will, one way or the other. Give me the codes!"

He didn't answer. My anger dissipated into an unwilling anxiety. If he really planned on keeping me here, there was no way I would ever escape.

"You can't keep me in here against my will, Dylan. This is kidnapping. Do you even realize what you're doing?"

"It's not when I'm trying to protect you. Besides, who's going to arrest me when they're all gone?" he said miserably. "The world is coming to an end, Holly. Right here, right now, out there, behind those doors, there is nothing left. That's the reality you need to accept. And you will at some point, I know it."

I started crying.

"I need to see my parents, Dylan."

"No."

"You can't keep me from them."

"I can and I will."

"Please, Dylan."

"I said no!!!!!!"

His voice echoed hard through the shelter. He balled his fists and towered over me. I noticed for the first time how big and tall he was. He was strong enough to slap me to the ground if he wanted to. There was no way I could win this fight, so I backed away in fear. When he saw my reaction, he calmed down instantly.

"Sorry, Hol. I'm really so, so sorry. I didn't mean to shout like that. It's just that I feel so hopeless and frustrated. Why won't you listen to me?"

I wiped away my tears.

"Because you won't listen either. You can't force me to stay."

"Do you honestly believe I would hurt you?"

"No," I said, "I don't. But you're taking away my choices. You're deciding my future for me."

"Because there is no choice to make." He sighed. "What will it take for me to convince you of the truth?"

"And what if your truth is a reality?" I said, finally starting to get it. "You said we'd have to stay for a month, but you're really talking months and years, aren't you? Are you seriously going to keep me here for that long?"

"It will depend on what is out there, but yeah, I am."

I tried to wrap my head around the fact that Dylan would keep me captive here without remorse, believing with all his heart that it would protect me.

"My dad—and my family—have created this shelter so that

we can survive here for years," he explained. "They created this clever wiring system, which leads to the generator buried deep inside the mountain, so we don't have to cower in the dark using the lights of flickering candles. We can lead a decent life in here, with enough food to survive for ages."

"You're burying us alive," I said bitterly.

"I'm sorry if that's what you want to believe, Holly. I really am."

I took a deep breath. "Even if you are right and the world is coming to an end, I would still not want to spend my remaining time here with you. I would take you away with me, to be with our parents and Emma. I would use whatever was left of my time to tell the people who mattered to me how much I cared about them. But I would not want to spend my last days cowering in this fucking cave like a bat, too scared to even exist."

I could tell by his reaction that he would never believe that my convictions were the right ones. He had been brainwashed by his parents and his community his entire life. Seek shelter and survive, no matter the consequence or mental cost. Whatever I said, he would abide by those rules. There was no point arguing with him.

"I'm sorry, Holly."

I felt defeated, but I refused to give up hope. My only chance of getting out of here was to show him that survival didn't matter without meaning or purpose. Without love.

"Dylan, come on," I said, touching his hand. "I have to go! My parents will be so worried about me, and Emma won't understand why I've disappeared. *Please!*"

"They won't even know," he said quietly.

My heart fell. "Why not?"

"They're already dead."

Silence fell in the shelter. I should have been angry, but I wasn't. I was numb. He might as well have knocked me out. I pulled away my hand and recoiled.

"I'm sorry, Holly. I shouldn't have said that."

"Fuck you."

"Please, Hol. I hope it happened quickly, that they barely knew. I pray they'll have found their peace."

"Stop it!" I yelled. "This is your belief, not mine. My family is alive and well because the world is *not* ending right now. I would have *felt* them slip away from me. I would know it."

He looked at me sadly.

"It's so much easier to believe, isn't it, Holly?"

"Fuck you, Dyl. Go to hell. I don't care if the entire mountain crumbles down on us. I refuse to live in this cage with you even if that means survival."

"You don't mean that."

"I do. Let me go!"

I backed away and sat down with my back against a rack of food, desperate to get a grip on the situation. He was stubborn and determined, two character traits I had always admired but loathed right now. He knelt down in front of me. His voice sounded eerily calm.

"I know what you are thinking, Holly. You want me to ignore the rules that were laid out a long time ago. I won't. Never."

"Let me go."

"You have to adapt, Holly, just like I am doing right now. I've been spending my entire life preparing for it. Now that it's here and you're here with me, I see it as a sign that this was meant to be. It's no coincidence that this happened on the day you came to the mountain for the first time."

"I want to leave."

He pointed at the doors.

"There's only one way out of here, and I'm the only one with the codes, which I'll never give to you. So you might as well get used to living in here. Trust me, it isn't as bad as you think."

"You're an asshole."

"I'm a realist."

"You don't respect me."

"I do. I always have. I love you. But right now, I need you to love me too."

I looked at him, hurt.

"If we were here in different circumstances, Hol, you would have wanted to find out more about our beliefs, I'm sure of it. You would have understood, maybe even have considered joining us."

I couldn't say that. It fascinated me, that was true, but right now, their beliefs were the exact reason why I was locked up in here. Pity was written all over his face, as if he was tutoring a child.

"The world has existed for hundreds of millions of years, Holly. And it will continue to exist for hundreds of millions of years more, unless the sun explodes or something. But it will not be the way it has been. Things will change, humanity will suffer. But we'll also survive, because that's what we do. That's really all there is to it. And that is exactly why we are here."

No matter the consequences, right?

FOUR

I took off my jacket and threw it on the floor, feeling hot all of a sudden. Or perhaps that was due to the generator doing its job.

"Come on," he said. "You can't sit here all day. Let me help you find your way around the shelter."

He offered me his hand. I allowed him to pull me up. We didn't speak. I moved to the racks of supplies, touching the jars and cans as I went.

Maybe I needed to bide my time. As soon as anyone out there belonging to the preppers community figured out nothing was going on, they would come and find us up here and inform us.

But a terrible thought crept up. What if everyone in said community was hiding in other shelters too? What if they didn't figure out for days or weeks that it was a false alarm? That would mean that we would be stuck here for that time too. Would they even know where we were?

I would be off the grid for a long time without a clue to my whereabouts. My parents would go out of their minds. They would assume I was hurt or dead, but they would have no idea where to start searching for me until someone in Midstone figured out what was happening.

This would take a couple of days at least. They would assume I was too busy during Thanksgiving weekend to call them, even though I texted my mom daily and Emma at least twice a day.

They had no clue about any of this. They didn't even know where exactly Dylan's parents lived or how to contact them. They would start calling me first, then Dylan. Then they would call the police, and after a while, those cops would hopefully contact the Midstone police. All of that would take a long time. I was an adult, so they wouldn't immediately treat this as a missing person's case, unless there was valid evidence.

Did the police even realize that the preppers had received these warning signs and were hiding in their shelters? Would that take a while too for them to figure out? Or were they used to this sort of alarms? Were members of the police squad also part of the preppers community? I had no clue.

And what if they were somehow finally able to either reach the Midstone cops or to get here on their own account? They would still not know where I was. The only ones who knew were Dylan's dad and Dylan.

God, my parents would go out of their minds with worry. Emma would be devastated.

And what if something happened to me in here? What if that rumbling of the mountain wasn't so innocent at all?

Or the worst-case scenario: what if Dylan was right after all? What would I do then?

No, everything but that.

"Okay," I said. "I'll stay."

He was shocked. "You will?"

"Yes. But you will need to tell me the codes. What if something happens to you? I won't make it out on my own."

He smiled and shook his head lightly.

"Sorry, Holly. Nothing will happen to me. You'll be fine."

"You could die."

"Are you going to kill me?"

"No, you idiot. But you could get hurt or have a heart attack or something. And then what?"

"I'm too young to have a heart attack."

"Young people have heart attacks too."

"Holly, you'll be fine. Stop worrying. But thank you."

"For what?" I said, surprised.

"You're putting faith in me. That's more than I could ever ask for, seeing the circumstances."

He sounded like his old self again. Maybe that was the key to everything.

"I'll go take a look at the generator to see if it's functioning properly," he said. "Why don't you take a look around? You've only seen a small part of it."

I didn't know what to do or where to go.

He pointed to the right, where a door led to another area I hadn't seen yet.

"You can put your coat on that rack and your shoes on one of the shelves by the door. There are warm slippers available, but the floor isn't that cold, so you can walk around in socks too if you'd like. If you want to change, you can go to the sleeping area. We have wall-to-wall shelves with tons of clothes, so don't hesitate to pick out anything you'd like. We've got them in all sizes and shapes, but nothing too fancy. Everything's functional and warm. Why don't you make yourself comfortable? I'll be right back."

Dylan turned around, but when he did, the cave walls started shaking. The racks with canisters trembled. Everything seemed to shiver. Some cans fell over, but again the rumbling stopped within seconds. He looked scared and confused, but he relaxed when it was over.

"That was intense," he said, "but we're okay. The shelter's equipped for this."

"Are you freaking kidding me?" I snapped. "Don't you get it? We have to get out of here *right now*. If you believe that something's happening out there, that means it's also happening inside the mountain. We'll be buried alive in here!"

He didn't reply.

Frustrated and angry, I stomped back to my fallen backpack. All the food we had picked up at the gas station fell out. It felt like a lifetime ago. My head felt heavy; I was stiff and sore, but I ignored the warning signs that I should eat and get some rest.

Of course my phone didn't get a signal, as I had long presumed once we got in here. There had hardly been any signal on the mountain either. Dylan's other phone, the one I didn't even know he had, was different than a regular smartphone, but he kept it close to him and he hadn't used it once, which probably meant that it was useless in here as well.

The walls were too thick. The steel doors kept all signals out. I had no idea how deep we were inside the mountain, but I was pretty sure no signal would be allowed to enter or go out. That worried me immensely.

"Do you have a radio?" I said, turning toward him. "You must have a radio or a walkie-talkie or something, right? Do you need to stay connected with those other shelters you were talking about? You would want to contact your parents, right? Then why don't you do just that and find out what is going on out there?"

He shook his head.

"We tried to install radio-systems and walkie-talkies for years, but nothing protrudes these walls. We experimented with everything from radio waves to morse code. Unfortunately, communication was the one thing we still haven't been able to resolve in the mountain shelters. We knew that, when a disaster happened, we would be on our own, or at least those surviving in the mountain shelters. The atomic shelters are able to connect with each other."

"Atomic shelters?"

"Like the one my dad has in his backyard."

"Ah. That strange door."

He nodded. "Those shelters were built during the Cold War, not long after Hiroshima and Nagasaki. My grandparents and other people living in the area around that time believed that the bomb changed everything. Oppenheimer created a monster. Therefore, it would only be a matter of time before it was unleashed again on the world. That was the start of everything for us."

"You mean that your grandparents and all those people around here believed that we would get killed by an atomic bomb?"

"They weren't the only ones," Dylan continues animatedly. "There were people all over the world back then who believed that it would happen, up until today. I mean, look at the war between Russia and Ukraine. One false move, and it'll turn into a global disaster. Unfortunately, Hiroshima changed the game. A nuclear bomb would forever change our landscape, our way of living, nature. Natural disasters are rare events, but they can happen, like comets. We are worried about what will happen once the ozone layer is breached."

Dylan took a deep breath before continuing rapidly,

releasing everything he had held inside for all those months. I never thought he would be that fanatic about anything. He never was during his studies, even though he worked hard to succeed. This version of him surprised me a lot.

"I mean, look at our planet, Holly. It's never been in more danger. We're talking solar flares now, and climate change, and all those natural events that are endangering mankind and animal life. We're talking about a planet with too many people on it. Our natural resources are exhaustive. We can't go on like this. Mother Nature always takes revenge. When something's not right, it'll send a virus into this world or make sure that an earthquake or tsunami kills hundreds of thousands, and there is nothing anyone can do about it. That's what I'm talking about here. I'm not a conspiracy theorist, not even close. I don't believe that viruses are man-made and sent to us on purpose. I do believe that new viruses are meant to eradicate life partially so that our planet can breathe again."

"Are your parents into conspiracies?" I said wearily. "Is their doomsday belief just a ruse for conspiracy theories?"

He laughed. "My parents? Not at all. They are firm in their beliefs; that's what they fight for every single day. They see, feel, and experience everything that happens around here, and they are in touch with those in every corner of our world who do too. Their work was important and lifesaving, but every single day, we all hoped and prayed that we would never have to use the shelters."

"I thought you were agnostic," I said.

He smiled. "I don't pray to a God. I pray to our planet."

He made a good point there.

"Why didn't you tell me before?"

"I was afraid to. Most people mock us. They believe that

we're a bunch of idiots."

"I don't believe you're an idiot," I said. "You're an asshole for doing this to me, though."

"I know, and I will regret that for the rest of my life. I never meant to scare you, Holly, but I was afraid to tell you the truth. Midstone is a closed community, and those who become part of it are expected to believe in our ways as well. I was—and still am—scared that you never will."

I got that. I understood. I remained silent, sighing in defeat. Did I love him enough to accept this new reality? Was that what I needed to figure out?

"I don't know," I said after a while. "This place isn't exactly inviting, is it? It could do with some couches and blankets and rugs on the floor to brighten it up a bit. And some color on the walls, that sort of thing?"

He laughed. His genuine smile returned, showing me he was still the old Dylan I loved.

"I know you hate me right now, but can I please show you everything? You'll understand then," he pleaded with me.

"Okay," I said.

"Thank you. That means a lot to me, Hol."

I followed Dylan through the open space to the far back, where a closed door lead to yet another area. I was stunned to find a wide living area with couches and fluffy blankets but no rugs on the floor. How big was this place? It must have cost years and a fortune to build.

"It took us fifty years to get it like it is today," he said. "This shelter, and five others, were created as backup plans in case a flood hits us. In the best-case scenario, we can harbor about fifty people in each shelter, but that's cutting back our survival supplies by a year."

He walked into another kitchen area that was even bigger. This one came well equipped with pots and pans, even more racks of more food, cupboards with dishes, jars, and glasses. He took a bottle of water from the rack closest to him and opened it, filling two glasses. He slid one toward me. I drank eagerly.

"You still trust me," he said, smiling.

"What makes you think that?" I said, surprised.

"You didn't hesitate once to drink that water."

I smiled.

"I never said I didn't trust you."

"You actually did. A couple of times. You had every right to. I messed up big time, Holly. I really did. I should have told you from the start."

"I would probably have run off screaming and never turned back," I admitted.

"That's what I was afraid of."

He drank his water and refilled the glass.

"It's not easy for me either, you know," he confessed. "It's been hard living a double life. It's hard now too. Everything I've ever worked for in these past years is gone. My studies, my life in Minneapolis, my future, my relationship with you. But all that matters right now is keeping you safe. This is the easy part, Holly. What comes after, with the level of destruction that we were facing, is going to be so damned hard."

"Why are you so sure it's so destructive? It might 'just' be an earthquake," I said, raising my fingers to make air quotes.

"I pray it's only that," he spoke quietly. "That would mean the world gets another chance, or at least for now."

"You're really convinced of these doomsday scenarios, aren't you?" I said quietly.

"I don't want to be, but yeah, I've seen so much evidence

of past events that it has made me aware of the ticking time bomb this planet is."

He looked at his hands. I drank my water, wanting him to continue. My desire to get out of here was temporarily replaced by my eagerness to get to know him better.

"I'm sorry. I'm scaring you again," he finally said. "I should stop doing that."

He got up.

"You know," I said, "I always thought that a nuclear bomb would be the easy way out. Just get it over with, destroy everything before anyone even realizes what was going on. That sounds like the best choice for mass destruction, don't you think?"

He turned to me. "Seriously?"

"Yeah. I mean, if we have to go, just do it already, you know? I don't want to spend my time thinking about what will come next, and I certainly don't want to die a slow and painful death from radiation poisoning."

"Hm."

"I mean, you are obviously intent on surviving, but you've never really considered what that would be like, am I right? You haven't seen the real fallout of such an event, and hopefully you never will. None of your community has. All of you are about preserving our species and I get that, but have you ever considered what life after an extinction event would be like?"

"No," he confessed. "But I do know how to deal with grave situations. That's what I've been training for. I can treat severe medical injuries. If need be, I can even perform surgery under the right conditions. I know exactly how to exist inside this shelter of stone. I know how many cans and pots and bowls were stacked in here and their due dates. I know how much I could eat per day. There's enough rice to feed an army and pasta that will last a couple of years. There are clothes and blankets and shoes and small heating devices that can be used for a couple of hours per day. There's a ventilation system that's connected to the generator, which is connected to the pipes and wires that lead into the outside world. I know how to fix everything, from the smallest issue to the biggest one."

"But in the end, all of this isn't enough, is it?"

"What do you mean?"

"It doesn't take away the fear."

He shook his head. "No, it doesn't."

Something struck me.

"Is this the first time that you're in here on your own? Or were you trained for that too?"

He looked uncomfortable. "No. We've had practice, but always with other people around. This is the first time. It's not that easy."

"You miss your dad, don't you?" I spoke softly.

"Yeah, I do. I miss them both so much. My parents would be a lot better at answering all of your questions. And they would be able to deal with whatever goes wrong."

His words frightened me.

"Like what?" I said.

"There could always be something wrong that I'm not equipped to manage. That's my greatest fear right now. What if I fuck things up and kill us by accident?"

I placed my hand on top of his.

"That won't happen. And if it does, we'll get through it together."

He looked at my hand. "You're not afraid of me."

"No," I said. "I'm not. I get you now."

"How? Why?" he said, puzzled.

"I've loved you from the moment I first met you, and I'm doing my best to understand this part of you. I want to get to know you completely."

"You won't try to run away?"

"No."

"Do you mean it?"

"I do."

I got up and took him in my arms. He shivered against me. I kissed him gently. He relaxed against me. His arms wrapped around me tightly, holding me firmly as if trying to get some heat from me into him.

"You are amazing, Holly Hayes," he said.

"So are you," I said. "Thank you for trying to keep me safe. Now then, why don't you show me the rest of the shelter?"

"I love you so much," he whispered.

"I love you too," I said, and I meant it.

FIVE

We had dinner, if you could call our meal dinner, that is. We had the leftovers of the food we had brought with us and combined this with shelter food as Dylan called it. He opened a can of tuna while I cooked up rice. We stirred both in a frying pan, using a ton of herbs to get it to taste like something. It was terrible.

"It's great," he said, "you're an amazing cook."

"If that's what you call cooking," I muttered, trying to get used to the bland taste of rice and tuna. The meal was dry and tasteless, but it was enough to fill our stomachs.

The mountain shook repeatedly during dinner, making it difficult for me to focus. As much as Dylan was convinced it was the right thing to do to keep us here, I worried this only proved we needed to escape.

After dinner, he took me on a tour of the shelter, and I had to admit I was pretty impressed by what I saw. The separate bedrooms were small but decent, with a double bed and a closet standing in each room. Dylan explained that years ago, they had taken all the furniture up here by trucks, using the road that reached halfway up the hill. From there, it took only about twenty minutes on the hiking path to reach the shelter.

"I wasn't there when all of this was done," he explained. "This was long before me. As you can see, the furniture is old and the mattresses have never been used before, so it's not like this place has ever been occupied before. It's all brand-new."

He pointed at the sleeping cubicles.

"You can choose to sleep anywhere you want, wherever makes you feel the most comfortable."

He opened several closets in various cubicles and showed me the clothes he had mentioned before.

"Take whatever you need."

"I'm fine with what I have right now," I said. "Is there an option to shower or wash up anywhere?"

"Follow me."

He showed me a couple of bathrooms that consisted of a rudimentary shower system and a sink.

"No baths, I'm afraid. Water is pretty scarce, so you'll have to take quick showers."

"I'm surprised we can even shower. Where does it come from?"

"My granddad installed this filtering system that leads from a natural source to the shelter. There's plenty of rain in this area, so we never run out of water, which flows from the mountain to a reserve, but it's not endless and it needs time to refill."

"That's okay," I said. "I'm just happy to be able to shower."

"It's a very soft stream, so don't expect a luxury rain shower, but it's enough. There are towels over there. Make sure to only use one per week since it needs to dry in the air. All our clothes are to be washed manually as well, as a washing machine and dryer would take up a lot of our scarce energy. We prefer to keep that for the lights and the kitchen appliances."

"You guys have really thought about everything," I remarked.

"Everyone who ever worked on the shelter fortunately had plenty of time to think things through."

"What was your job?"

"I helped with the supplies mostly. My dad did most of the work. He came up with a lot of innovative ideas, like the triple generator system. The biggest one and two spares."

"What if the generator system were to fail at some point? Would that mean we're trapped in here?" I said.

"Why would we be?" he asked, puzzled.

"Don't the doors run on the same system?"

"No, they don't. This guy from our community created a failsafe system to get us in and out, even if the generators would give up the ghost. Whatever happens, we can always get out."

"That's good to know."

He looked at me inquisitively.

"You really are worried, aren't you?"

"Yeah, well, it's not that I'm quite handy or anything, so if something were to happen to you, I would be stuck in here without any knowledge of these generators and stuff. So yeah, that worries me."

"Why do you keep saying 'if something were to happen to me'?" he asked.

"I have to keep that in mind, don't I? I mean, you're the one with all the knowledge, while I'm the newbie. Of course that worries me."

He cocked his head a little.

"Is this your way of trying to get the codes, Holly?"

"No, I swear," I said quickly. "I know you don't want to share them, so I won't ask for them again. It's just that I want to know what I need to do in case of a technical failure. We are dependent on those generators, right?"

"Yeah."

"Then teach me how to fix them. I mean, I've got plenty of time on my hands, so why not?"

The brief tension was gone again. He tried to figure out if I meant what I said, and honestly, I did. If I was going to be stuck in here, I might as well make myself useful. What else was there to do?

"You really want to help?"

I nodded. A smile broke out on his face. He looked so relieved I felt guilty over making his life miserable before.

"God, Holly, I really thought I would be spending our time together feeling guilty as hell over doing this to you. I imagined you locking yourself up in one of those cubicles, hating me for eternity."

"I do hate you," I said, but I smiled. "Come on, let's clean up the kitchen and get started. It's early in the evening, and I want to do something."

"You don't want to shower now?"

"Later," I said.

And maybe not alone, but I didn't tell him that. I couldn't even explain it to myself, but I wasn't angry anymore. The anguish, the upset, and the fear were gone.

This version of Dylan, pleading with me silently to forgive him, was the man I had loved before we walked up the mountain, and he was still the person I loved right now. You couldn't just switch off love like that. That didn't mean I wasn't eager to get my hands on those codes.

Dylan took me to the generator area, standing behind a thick door that held back all noise and heat. He showed me how it worked. He switched the main generator on and off and explained the details of the panel system attached to the circuit.

"I honestly don't know yet how warm or cold it's going to get in here," he said. "The community did several tests, but we've never had a real-life situation before, so there's no telling what will happen if fire and heat hit the mountain walls. We'll have to figure that out in the next couple of days and adjust accordingly."

It was comfortably warm inside the shelter right now, even a bit too warm, so we decided together to turn the temperature down a bit. He then showed me the water system and an array of manuals that explained the details. In the largest kitchen, we went over all the supplies and gear, and he explained the food system.

"We don't have any livestock of course, so there won't be any meat or eggs, but there's a lot of protein-rich food to compensate. Rice and pasta fill the stomach nicely, and canned salmon and tuna are rich in fat. You'll lose some weight, but that's normal. Eat plenty of canned vegetables and fruits, like peach and pineapple."

We looked over the food schedule and figured out what to eat first. As he spoke, I caught myself really getting into this. Sometimes I had to remind myself that it probably wouldn't be necessary to eat this stuff for long, but I still went over the lists with him and got into the rhythm of setting up our schedule.

At one point, I realized it was after ten p.m., and we were still stuck in here, with no one coming to save us. That was when I understood that there were no heroes about to barge in and rescue us. His mom and dad, and whoever was still out there, had not come up the mountain. They were most likely still stuck in their atomic bomb shelters, believing this doomsday scenario as much as Dylan did.

I shivered.

"Are you okay?" he said. "It's getting late. You should shower first and go to bed."

I looked at him, contemplating my options.

"Where do I sleep?"

"Plenty of rooms to choose from," he said with a wave of his hand. "You can pick whichever one you like, as far away from me as you'd like."

His words startled me. I saw the anxiety in his eyes. He seemed to accept that I had stopped loving him in a heartbeat. I felt sorry for him.

"You're right," I said. "We should shower. Come on." I took him by the hand.

"Together?" he asked softly.

"We have to save some water, right?" I quipped.

"Holly—"

"I insist. Please, Dyl. I don't want to be alone right now."

He walked with me to the bathing area. In silence, I stripped him until he stood in front of me in his boxers. He took his time stripping me to my underwear. It was cold in the room without any clothes on. I shivered.

"Are you okay?" he asked worriedly.

I nodded. "I don't want sex tonight; I'm not ready for that just yet. I just want companionship. To feel your warmth against me."

"Are you sure?" he asked, puzzled. "I can wait outside until you finish your shower. I know you must hate me right now."

I shook my head.

"I don't hate you, Dylan. I love you."

"You do?"

"How could I not love you when you're trying to

protect me?"

He cupped my chin and kissed me softly, lovingly.

"I'm going to make you a promise right here and now, Holly. Give me a week. Seven days from now, I'll open those doors to see what's out there. But please grant me those seven days. In return, I will give you the codes in the morning."

I was in shock. "Are you serious? You'll trust me with the codes?"

"I will, as long as I can trust you to trust me to do the right thing."

"Okay," I said. "Agreed. You get one week, I get the codes. We have a deal."

He kissed me. "Thank you."

I removed my underwear. He turned on the shower. The water rained down on us in a soft, caressing pace. He took a new bar of soap and a washcloth and washed me from head to toe, back and front, lingering around my breasts, buttocks, and between my legs. The water felt like soft summer rain, tickling and sweet. It washed away the soap through a draining system. Us being here together gave me new hope that everything would be okay.

"Come on," he said, turning off the shower and handing me a big, warm towel. "Let's go find a sleeping space."

We chose a cubicle right in the middle, where we slid into bed naked. I turned to him while he lay on his back, with his hands folded behind his head.

I moved closer, resting my head on his chest. My left hand roamed lower, until I felt him. Slowly, I began stroking him. He hummed and sighed.

"If you continue this, I won't be able to stop myself," he whispered.

"Maybe I don't want you to," I said.

He turned to the side and placed his hand between my legs.

"You definitely don't want me to." He smiled.

Early in the morning, I sat at the kitchen table in sweatpants, a T-shirt and a sweater, when Dylan walked in with a blanket wrapped around his shoulders. His hair was sticking out, and he yawned as he took a seat. I poured him a cup of coffee. He looked pale.

"Happy Thanksgiving morning," I said. "Did you sleep well? You don't look well."

"I think I'm catching a cold or something. I've got a splitting headache. I think I'm running a fever too."

I got up and placed my hand on his forehead.

"You're warm."

"We've got plenty of medication; I'll take something later," he said, placing his head between his hands as he leaned on the table.

"Why don't you go lie down for a while longer? I'll get you some breakfast and medication. You need to eat first, or you'll ruin your stomach."

"Thanks," he said. "I'm sorry."

"What for? It's probably just a cold. You'll be fine soon enough."

He smiled and leaned against me.

"You're the best, Holly Hayes."

"I know," I teased. "Now then, according to our food schedule, we can have protein pancakes with protein egg replacement goo. How does that sound?"

"Terrible, but doable."

"I can make fake egg-tuna too if you'd like."

"Nah, let's do the pancakes," he said, pulling a face. "How did you sleep?"

"Pretty good, despite my many concerns. Last night was good, though. Sex definitely takes the mind off things."

"I swear, you are insatiable, Holly Hayes, even when the world is coming to an end. You can really wear a man down."

I punched him gently.

"Hey, you weren't complaining last night, so don't put the blame on me. It's cold in here. Maybe you're coming down with something."

"Probably."

"I'll heat something up," I said. "You go lie down."

Dylan slowly walked over to the living area, where he lay down on one of the couches, pulling three blankets over him. He was definitely feeling sick.

I focused on the pancakes, following the clear instructions. Only when the pans started heating and I had the first batch of batter ready, did I look at him again. He was asleep.

When I got breakfast ready, I put everything on two plates and walked over, placing the food on the table in front of the couch. He was shivering and sweating at the same time, which concerned me.

Last night, he had shown me where I could find the medication, so I went and got Tylenol and water. I shook him awake. He blearily opened his eyes and blinked.

"I'm sorry I had to wake you up," I said, "but you need to eat and take medication. Can you sit up?"

"I'm not hungry," he muttered.

"Just a bit. It'll help get your strength up, and you need it before you take this Tylenol."

Dylan reluctantly sat up. I placed the plate on his lap

and watched as he took a few bites. He took the medication without complaining, drank some water, and lay down again, closing his eyes.

"I'm sorry about this," he said.

"Don't worry about it." I sat down on the other couch and ate while watching him. He stayed awake this time.

"Talk to me," he muttered.

"About what?"

"Anything. I just want to hear your voice."

He still sounded off, but I ignored it.

"Last night was amazing, Dyl. If you're right and there is no tomorrow, then I'm glad that I got to spend my last hours here with you."

He pried open one eye.

"We're not going to die. That's the whole purpose of this shelter."

"Just figuratively speaking."

"So I'm forgiven?"

"I already forgave you last night. I love you, and I am convinced that we will spend the rest of our lives together, no matter what that life might be."

He moved to his side so he could see me better. He was sweating profusely. I put my plate down and moved to his side.

"Your fever is spiking."

I pulled away the blankets, but he stopped me.

"I'm cold."

"Your temperature is too high. You need to cool down. Come on."

"Where are we going?" he muttered.

"The showers."

"I don't want to shower again."

"You have to, Dyl. Work with me."

I pulled him up and held on to him, walking him to the showers, where I stripped him down to his boxer shorts. He remained standing while I turned on the shower before stripping down to my underwear too.

"That's it," I said, holding him as the soft water rained down on us.

Dylan shook and shivered, but as the water poured down on us, he seemed to cool off. He stood beneath the water beam with his eyes closed while I held him.

"Feeling better?" I said after turning off the water.

"A bit. I think the Tylenol's working."

"Good. Come on."

I pulled his towel off the rack and dried him off. He sat down on a chair while I did the same. I took him to the bed we had slept in last night and pulled a thick blanket off the bed, leaving only a thin one and a bedsheet.

"Lie down," I said.

He rested his head on the soft pillows and closed his eyes, then sighed in contentment and reached for my hand. I sat down on the bed and watched him fall asleep.

I left the door ajar and walked back to the living area where I cleaned up the remainder of breakfast, taking the time to check every cupboard in every room. With Dylan asleep, I had plenty of time to scout the place.

With nothing to do, I took a book from the extensive library cabinet in the living area, sat down on the couch, and tried to read, but my mind wandered off the entire time.

I contemplated trying to search for the codes, but I knew it would be pointless. He'd sounded so certain about me not finding them that I just knew they wouldn't be written down anywhere. All I could do was wait for him to wake up and tell me.

And then what?

Part of me contemplated breaking my promise and escaping immediately, but I already knew I wouldn't do that. Dylan had made a promise to me, and he would keep it. If I wanted to stay a part of his life after this, which I did, I would have to respect that. I wanted us to survive as a couple and not let this get in our way.

And I was scared too. A small part of me was afraid he might be right about the world's end. The mountain had been shaking all night. I could feel it lying in bed. It felt as if we were asleep next to a train track, with heavy trains moving past us at the speed of light.

Dylan had fallen asleep quickly after we had sex and slept like a log. Maybe that had been his illness settling in already because he didn't wake up once.

A scream shook me from my thoughts. I threw the book on the table and rushed back to the cubicle, where Dylan lay in bed with his eyes wide open. Something must have startled him. His hands grabbed the bedsheet and pulled at the fabric.

"Holly?" he cried out. "Holly!"

"I'm here," I said, touching his hand and forehead. He was burning up. His skin felt hot and dry. "Shit."

"My head," he cried out.

"Dyl, do you have a headache again?"

He didn't answer but closed his eyes again and passed out.

"God."

I ran to the medicine cabinet and retrieved everything I could find that could help stop the fever. I took his temperature—104°F.

"Dylan, can you hear me?"

I shook him gently, but he was completely out of it. I panicked since there was no way I could understand what this was. It could be anything. If our roles were reversed, he probably would have figured this out instantly, but I was used to working with animals, not people.

I needed to get Advil into his system, but how would I do that if he couldn't keep it down? There was no way of getting an IV into him. All I had to work with was medication and water.

I shook him until he finally blinked and opened his eyes again.

"What's going on?" he muttered.

"You're very sick. I need you to take medication right now. And then I need to get you to a doctor."

"You're a doctor," he whispered.

"Not the kind you need. Can you sit up?"

"Hm."

I pulled him up into a sitting position. His head slumped. He closed his eyes and fell back.

"Dyl, wake up!" I screamed, shaking him roughly.

"Hmm." He responded. I could have cried.

"Good, now stay awake so you can take the Advil."

"I'm fine," he slurred.

I pulled him back up and practically shoved the pills down his throat and forced him to drink water. He swallowed most of it. His eyes remained closed all the time. I lowered him back on the pillow.

"Good. Now I need you to do one other thing, Dyl. You need to give me the codes."

"I can't…"

"You have to."

"Can't remember them," he whispered.

Fuck.

I watched him fall asleep again. I was no longer able to hold back my fears. A raging panic attack threatened to take over and consume me.

I fled from the room, ran to the bathroom, and closed the door. My legs could no longer hold me, my whole body shook.

This was going to be the death of us; I could *feel* it. This would be our end.

Hours later, I sat by Dylan's side and read a book. His fever was down, he was no longer shivering, and he seemed to be doing better overall. I had managed to get another Advil into him and plenty of water.

I was so enthralled by my book I didn't even realize he was watching me.

"You are right," he spoke with a hoarse voice, nearly making me jump out of my skin.

I dropped the book, slid out of the chair, and practically ran to the bed.

"You scared the hell out of me," I said, kissing his hand. "How are you feeling?"

"Terrible. What time is it?"

"Way past noon. What was I right about?"

He reached for my hand and held it against his face.

"It's just as dangerous being in here as it is surviving out there. I never realized that. I'm so sorry."

"You don't have to be. All that matters is that nothing happened, and we're both fine."

"I love you so much, Hol."

"I love you too," I said, "and I'm so glad you're okay. Do you think you can eat something?"

"Yeah."

"I'll go get something. I found some toast. Let me get some."

Before he could say anything, I was out of the room and in the kitchen. My whole body shook with relief and happiness. It was going to be fine. Everything was going to be just fine now.

We were going to get out of here.

I returned with toast and water. Dylan sat up in bed, looking a lot better. His fever had broken.

"Thank you," he said, eagerly eating the toast.

I sat down on the bed.

"So what do we do?" I said. "I know you're not going to give up your conviction that the world out there is gone."

"I don't know what to think, Holly. I had the strangest dream while sleeping."

"About?"

"There was this thing coming right at us. A huge ball of fire, like a comet. It was enormous, and there was nothing anyone could do."

"But what brought us here was not a comet," I said, confused.

"No, it wasn't." He shrugged. "I guess it was the fever taking over. Everything seemed so muddled."

"I was scared, Dyl. What if you were seriously ill? I couldn't have gotten out to get you help."

"I know. I'm so sorry. I realize now that this was wrong," he said, sounding ashamed as he rubbed his face. "I told you last night I was going to give you the codes, and I meant what I said. One way or the other, you need to be able to choose."

"And what if the world out there is gone?" I asked.

"Then we'll deal with that. But if it's not, you can leave."

"Only if you're coming with me," I said.

He looked at me worriedly.

"Do you still want me to?"

"More than ever."

He smiled. "Thank you."

I sat down on the bed and pulled his head on my belly, stroking his hair.

"So what do we do next?" I asked. "I know you'll never be able to travel down the mountain, so I was thinking I should do it alone, or at least until I get a connection on my phone to call for help."

He lifted himself up. "No way."

"Yes way. You're too sick to do the hike. I'll go."

Dylan reacted forcefully.

"I'm not going to let you wander off that mountain all by yourself, Holly. You don't know the path as well as I do. Just give me a couple of hours, and we'll go together. I'll be fine by then. Assuming the world is fine."

"Are you ready to accept my theory?" I inquired.

"No. But I have to verify it for myself. And I can't be responsible for your choices."

"Lie down, Dyl. Get some rest. I'll wait for you to feel better, and we'll decide our next steps then."

He nodded. His eyes drooped.

"I'm so tired, Hol."

"I know; that's why you need to rest. Just relax for now, and we'll talk about it later."

He sank down on the bed again, looking at me until his eyes shut and he was out like a light. I moved from the bed and left him alone in the cubicle, feeling sick to my stomach.

I had been denying it since Dylan walked into the kitchen this morning looking like hell, but there was something terribly wrong with him. Something so wrong that it could threaten his life. I could feel it in my bones.

This was not just a fever. It was a lot worse than that.

Another couple of hours later, I was terrified. Dylan was in between states of awareness and oblivion. He muttered in his sleep, was running a high fever again, and was totally out of it one minute and lucid the next.

No matter what type of medication I gave him or what I did, nothing seemed to work. I had given him oral antibiotics and more Advil, but by now he couldn't keep anything down. He threw up whatever I gave him.

I was convinced he had meningitis. All the symptoms seemed to match. He was complaining about the aches in his body, mostly his neck, threw up a couple of times, felt drowsy, and complained about light, even though I had made sure all the lights, except for one, were turned off.

I couldn't do anything but give him fever medication and keep him comfortable, but I knew enough about the disease to know he would die if I didn't get him treated straight away.

"Dyl. Honey, you need to give me the codes," I whispered whenever he was lucid enough. "The codes, please."

He looked at me without recognizing me before sinking away again. He had to go to a hospital, to be treated by a proper doctor. If there were still doctors out there.

I shook my head, refusing to allow Dylan's beliefs to mess with my head. Of course everything was fine with the world. They would all still be out there living their lives without any idea of what was going on in here.

But without the codes, how was I going to contact people who could help *and* get Dylan off the mountain? He wouldn't make it if I had to drag him down, but I couldn't leave him here either. That would almost certainly mean the end of him. I was the only one who could give him medication and water, even if it was the only real thing I could do.

He needed a hospital.

My head spun from the various choices that all seemed worse than the other. In the end, the only good decision I could make was to find a way out of this place somehow and risk leaving him here.

I estimated it would take me about twenty minutes to find a spot on the mountain where my phone would work and another half an hour back to the shelter. And only if I took my time and made sure I didn't risk my own life. If I fell and broke my leg or worse, he would be here by himself for God knows how long.

Of course, heading off the mountain was only possible if I got the codes, which was a major problem right now. Nothing had changed since he wasn't physically and mentally able to give me the codes.

My heart sank while I watched him. I had contemplated this scenario for hours, and it was slowly killing me. What if he never woke up at all? I couldn't even fathom it. I would go insane here if he died, which was a very real possibility right now.

What would happen if Dylan died today and he had been right all along? I would be in here with him—with his body. No. The thought was too gruesome to contemplate.

"You've got to wake up now," I said, moving back to the bed. "Come on, you need to come back to me now, Dyl. Don't do this to me, okay? You have to remember that I need you. You're the only one who can get us out of here."

He remained silent.

"Without you, there's no tomorrow for me either. If you're gone, I'm gone too. Don't do that to us, okay? Wake up, for me."

He wouldn't. He didn't stir, didn't talk, didn't move, didn't respond. He just mumbled and went through his feverish dreams.

His phones. They *had* to work here. Why didn't I think of that earlier? I ran to his backpack and searched through it, but they weren't there. I remembered him keeping the phones on him last night. They were still in the trousers he wore yesterday.

I dug them out, but they were coded. They were useless. They were old-school phones too, without visual or fingerprint action. Damn it!

I should have forced him to open those doors last night. I should have asked for the codes then, but he wouldn't have given them to me just yet. I knew that. My anger grew.

"Dylan, wake up," I said. "Come on. Stop being so goddamn stubborn. I can't do this on my own, you know that. I hate you, do you know that? I hate that you didn't listen to me. You should have listened to me!"

I looked up when the shelter's rocky walls started shaking again. It wasn't as severe this time, but it was still happening, serving as a reminder of where we were. The rumbling made me contemplate and rethink my position. I took my hand away from Dylan's sweaty jaw and looked at the medication available to me.

Wouldn't it be better to be trapped in an unconscious state without the possibility of waking up than to face a certain death? Dying could be the best thing for him right now. I shouldn't hope for him to wake up and realize he would drift in and out of consciousness while suffering.

If I couldn't get us out of here, dying in his sleep would be easier for him.

But I would still suffer. I would *watch* him die and know that I couldn't have done a damned thing to save him because I hadn't pushed him hard enough. I was desperately trying to hold on to my sanity as I sat on the bed with my hand on Dylan's chest, feeling him breathe for as long as I could.

Suddenly the entire shelter started to shake again, but it was different than before. This time, it felt as if we were standing on a road that got split open by an earthquake. As if a giant was taking the top of the mountain between his hands and shaking it like a toy. This was *not* like before. This was a lot worse.

Everything shook. This had to be what he was talking about: the end of the world. A volcano eruption or a severe earthquake or that catastrophe his dad warned him about. Whatever it was, it was bad.

I gasped. Fuck.

All this time, during all our arguments, he had been right, and I had been so wrong. This was the real deal. This was the end.

The bed shook; the closet was ripped from the wall and dropped forward. Its contents spilled on the floor. The shaking increased so much that I felt my head spin. I threw myself on top of Dylan, protecting his unconscious form against the effects of the quake, fearing that the stone ceiling would break into large chunks of stone and drop on top of us.

It took forever, and I endured it with my eyes closed while Dylan breathed beneath me. He held on for dear life. I didn't really want to open my eyes and see it unfold in front of us. I didn't want to face this new reality, the end of the world as we knew it.

It stopped abruptly.

I organized my thoughts, remembering every detail without having lost a single memory. I looked down at Dylan, fighting the panic attack that could render me unconscious. He stirred lightly.

I was so glad he hadn't experienced this.

The rumbling, albeit gentler this time, came and went for a while, but it wasn't as bad as the first one. It felt like an aftermath, but each rumble persuaded me that there was no life anymore out there. It was over. He was right, and I had been wrong all this time.

Which meant that my parents were probably already dead. Which meant that I, too, had nothing to live for anymore. What point was there to finding a way out of here now? It was over.

My heart broke for everyone I had known in my lifetime. I cried. I envied Dylan for being unconscious and not experiencing this heartbreak. I tried to jump into survival mode, but it was pointless even trying.

This was it, our end.

Help wouldn't come.

The lights flickered. I looked up. Something was terribly wrong; I could feel it. Dizziness overwhelmed me. The temperature in the cubicle rose; it felt terribly uncomfortable in here. More dizziness.

Oh God.

I left Dylan on the bed and ran to the generator room, praying that everything was fine and running smoothly, but already suspecting that it wasn't.

I was greeted by a huge amount of heat and steam that instantly grabbed me by the throat, making me cough and choke. The headache and dizziness I had been experiencing increased. I had trouble breathing. The room was unbearably hot.

Feeling sick, I kept my hand on my mouth and hurried to the main generator. Its panel flickered as an array of red lights.

Steam and heat escaped from the broken generator.

The second one made odd hiccupping sounds. Two lines that ran in and out were broken off. The entire setup was malfunctioning.

The only generator still working was the third and smallest one, which was the backup of the backup. The panel went wild as it tried to keep the other machines and itself going.

Fuck.

The whole system was malfunctioning, and it quickly became obvious that it was beyond fixing. Everywhere were scattered pieces of rock that had broken off. A huge crack in the wall showed that this side of the mountain had suffered serious damage due to the quake. The result of that damage had caused these broken generators.

I nearly passed out because of the thick air that was no longer being ventilated. Sick from the heat, I ran out of the room and shut the door. I sank to my knees, battling against the overwhelming dizziness.

The earthquake had done some serious damage to the system that was supposed to keep us alive for years. That plan had now failed, and there was no backup left.

I had no idea how long it would take before the generators gave up the ghost, but once they did, we would die within hours, or even less. The cooling systems would shut down, making it as hot in the rest of the shelter as it was in there. The ventilation system would stop working. The air was already being poisoned. We would suffocate.

It was quite simple really. We were doomed, and it wouldn't take too long for our end to come. Dylan's would come sooner than mine. He was already so sick.

I forced myself to stay awake as I lay down on the bed. The

one comfort I had was that it wouldn't take too long.

I moved his face against my chest.

"You're a jerk, you know that?"

Silence.

"We're going to die," I said. "Aren't we?"

No answer.

"I wish you could disagree."

He remained still.

"I'm sorry that I put you through all this. I'm sorry I didn't believe you. I'm sorry I couldn't save your life."

The nausea was overwhelming. I felt sick to the bone. Warm to the touch. Dizzy. Exhausted. Sleepy.

"We should get some sleep," I whispered against Dylan's hair. "It'll be over soon."

I held Dylan's hand while I felt myself falling into oblivion. At least the end would come soon. That was the only comfort I had.

Dear reader,

You have now read Holly's story and her version of events on the mountain.

From this point on, choose what you want to read next.

1. Read Dylan's story. In that case, go to page 179 of the book.
2. Finished Dylan's story already and want to read his version of events on the mountain? Go to page 266.
3. Finished Dylan's story and his version of events on the mountain? Go to page 315 to read what happens next.

One way or the other, whatever you choose, you must read both storylines to get a complete picture of what happened.

DYLAN'S STORY

one

When someone goes to college, there is always a reason for it. Getting a good education. Getting a degree. Getting a great job that you like. Finding a significant other too, if you're one of the lucky ones. Having a great time. Getting laid. Doing stupid shit and not getting busted. Doing whatever the hell it is that makes you tick. Having the time of your life. Messing around. Having fun. Not giving a fuck about other people.

That wasn't me. None of it. I couldn't give a rat's ass about all of the above. All I'd come here for was something I needed badly so I could continue the rest of my life back home.

I wasn't an idiot that hung around campus and got bullied because I stood out the wrong way. I wasn't a nerd, wasn't a jock, wasn't one of the top class students. I wasn't popular with the girls and didn't really care about the boys. I blended in perfectly. I was the perfect prototype of the boy-next-door as they were portrayed in movies and television shows. The one that people hardly remembered seeing but still noticed around.

My goals were totally different than those of my fellow students from the start. The plan was quite simple: go to college, get a medical degree as fast as possible, and get the hell out of there. I didn't want to waste too much time fooling around or having sex. There was no room in my life for drama. All I wanted was to focus on the work and get that degree as fast as humanly possible so I could go back home to my family.

The University of Minneapolis seemed like the right fit for what I needed. It offered one of the best medical programs in the country, with a focus on various specialties. It was close enough to home in case something terrible happened, but far enough not to be bothered by my family all the time, which, truth be told, also felt like a relief.

And it was affordable too, which was important to my dad, who spent most of his money preparing for the end, with nothing to spare for extras. Every month, he put a significant amount of money aside for supplies, meaning that he didn't want to spend too much on me either. I didn't hold that against him. My entire family did exactly the same thing.

The college grounds were big, so I wouldn't stand out in the crowd. And anonymous enough that not too many people would know me. I applied for a scholarship and got it, so that took care of the money side of things. Minneapolis ticked off all the boxes, and I was happy to attend.

I turned twenty last month and had never been further than a day's travel from home. I'd never been on a plane, had never traveled by car to either the East Coast or the West. My entire world centered around Montana, and that was just fine. I lived and breathed Montana, felt it course through my veins with every heartbeat.

The choice of studying at Harvard had never been on the table, and neither was heading down to UCLA, even though I had been offered scholarships to both, which made me consider both options for a split second before calculating on

Google Maps how long it would take me to travel from here to there without the use of a plane. In the back of my mind played the amount of obstacles I would have to overcome in case the world was ending and I needed to hurry back home. The conclusion was that I wouldn't reach my parents before it was too late. So I'd passed.

Princeton seemed like a whole different planet to me, so I never even considered them when they asked me to apply. Too far away, too complex to return home, no preppers on campus, and certainly no one to lean on if serious events would take place. I didn't like their recruitment videos much. They weren't prepared for a Montana Prepper like me.

Ignoring all the big colleges meant that I had deliberately chosen the life my parents wanted me to live, and that was okay. I didn't want to head in any other direction anyway. Their way of thinking had become mine, and we all accepted it for what it was. When one is part of such a life, it becomes a mantra. A vision. A prayer.

As a kid, I spent my weekends prepping. I believe I was about three or four when I was taken out on my first excursion, as I call them. I don't have any recollections of my grandparents, who all died at a very young age, but I do remember carrying a large bag with canned supplies into a gloomy shelter. I had been scared shitless, but a part of me also loved it from the first moment I was part of it. It felt as if my parents were indoctrinating me into their world and as if I had become part of some sacred mission that no one else would understand.

I remember seeing some of my family members there, my dad's cousins, who had kids my age. The other kids and I'd looked at each other, and we all had this shit-eating grin on our faces, as if we knew how important this was.

That was the first of a zillion visits to the shelters. I had no idea back then, I was sure, that this would become exhausting and often devastating. Thinking this way ate at your soul. It became such a big part of your life that you were constantly looking at the skies, wondering if anything would happen that day.

I didn't always think to feel that way. Those dark thoughts entered my mind when I was about fifteen or sixteen. Before that time, I was happy. I felt special. I was part of a big gang of people who loved to come together to take care of themselves and their offspring.

Hiking into the mountains to check the shelters had been my favorite pastime throughout my first years, and I'd had a good time doing so. It meant being close to my parents, aunts, uncles, and cousins, who were all part of the same Montana mountains community of Midstone, where I was born and raised. No one questioned us; not a soul mocked us. We rarely saw any strangers in our knack of the woods, and we liked it that way.

"No one would get it," my dad would say. "They don't belong here. Only those who are a part of our community can understand how we feel."

"But to become a part of our community, you need years of patience and a lot of goodwill," my mom would add.

In other words, outsiders rarely got in, and if they did, they would spend years trying to convince our band of brothers that they really wanted this way of life. It was hard living it, breathing it, existing in it. It was tough believing that the world could come to an end in a heartbeat. It weighed on all of us, even on those who were the fiercest of believers. But it was our way of life, and I wouldn't change it for the world.

I did have to face facts, though. I had changed, and that bothered me. Over the past two years, I had become a slightly different person than I was when I'd moved to Minnesota.

Coming to Minnesota had opened up a whole new world to me, one where my fellow college students were not checking various websites every day for natural disasters or nuclear threats and where sunshine seemed to replace fear. The longer I spent here, the more I came to realize that for them, life wasn't the same as it was for me. In the past, that had never even crossed my mind.

I met one other prepper on campus in my first year, a guy named Roland, who came from Montana as well and was living in a small town close to Midstone. We met a couple of times during preppers conventions, but that was it. I barely knew him and wouldn't have recognized him if he had walked by me on campus. Still, my dad had told me to look him up, and I did.

Roland was in his fourth year and looked exactly like all the other college students. So did I, for that matter, with the one exception that I carried three phones with me. He only had one. That felt off to me. It unnerved me. It was the first red flag that he wasn't the kid I used to know.

"Sooooo," he said, sounding bored as we sat down at a diner he frequented. It was a typical college-town diner. Bad food, cheap prices. Perfect for our budgets. "I remember you vaguely. You're one of us, huh?"

I didn't like how he said it. *One of us* made it sound like we were part of some secret conspiracy or something, which was probably true in a way. Still, it sounded troubling and dangerous, just like all the threats our planet was facing.

I shrugged. "I guess."

"What do you want to know?"

"What do you mean?"

"You looked me up for a reason, didn't you?"

"I really don't know," I said. "My dad told me to look you up, but I don't really understand why. Maybe it would be nice to know what life is like here? And how do you manage to keep track of all that's happening at home?"

"I don't," he blurted out, looking away.

"You don't?"

"Nope."

"What does that mean?"

"Just what I'm saying, man. I don't keep track anymore. I got rid of my phones, don't check sites anymore, don't care about that stuff anymore. It's crazy shit anyway."

"Crazy shit?" I repeated, disturbed.

"Yeah, dude. Come on, who does that? Who goes around carrying three phones as if he's part of some drug cartel thing, checking disaster websites as if that's a normal thing to do? It's not, you know."

"Not normal?" I repeated, like I was some kind of idiot.

"Hell no. Have you ever read what they say about us? About the craziness of it all? They mock people like us. We're a laughingstock, a bunch of crazy conspiracy idiots who believe in alien abductions and crazy doomsday prophecies like the one the Mayans made. And you know what? Everyone else is right too. This life that you lead? It's a setup, a game. A way to keep us all calm, like meek sheep."

Roland shocked me like no one had ever done before. I knew that our way of life wasn't accepted by those who didn't care to understand. I knew that people mocked us. Plenty of them out there put us together with those idiots who believed the Earth was flat and that aliens had been among us since

Roswell, 1947.

That was also the main reason why I never told anyone the truth about me or my family. Whenever I spoke to someone outside of our community, I kept those things to myself, even though at times it'd been hard. But this was the very first time that someone from our own community bashed our way of life, and it hurt like hell.

I wanted to escape, but part of me was so eager to find out more about his new beliefs, despite the hurt it would bring me, that I stayed.

"Why did you quit the life?" I asked Roland.

"Because it's ridiculous, kid," he said, without even using my name. "It's stupid to believe that the world is going to end when it's been here for millions of years already. I mean, why bother living like this when no one else does? No one can keep this up, unless you're insane."

"Did you tell your family?"

He drank his coffee and suddenly looked sad.

"I haven't seen my folks in over two years," he said. "And as long as they hold on to their beliefs, I'll never see them again."

"God…"

"God has nothing to do with this. I'm just fed up feeling afraid, okay? I need to do this, need to find a future where I'm *me* and not *them*. I didn't ask for this, and neither did you. Besides, I'm not the only one."

"There are others?"

"Hell yeah, plenty of us out there. You just need to find them. I did. And I'll tell you what, kid. If you find the strength to pull out of that life, give me a call. I'll help you, I promise."

"Did you get help?"

"Oh yeah."

"From whom?"

"People like me. People that were you before they grew up. And I promise you that, when you put your mind to it, you'll find the light at the end of the dark tunnel as well."

"I don't know what..." *What you mean*, I wanted to say, but I stopped before I could. It was obvious that he and I were on a whole different level now. We both felt it.

Roland got up, dropped some money on the table, and smiled at me with something I could only describe as pity. It made me feel uncomfortable, and it felt denigrating.

"One day, we'll see each other again, kid. Mark my words. And then you'll feel it too. But I just wanted to give you one last piece of advice, if you want to hear it?"

"Sure."

"If the day comes that you have to choose between love and your old life, don't hesitate. Chose love. Trust me, I know what it's like to give up everything, one way or the other. It'll hurt, but you'll be all the better for it."

He left me at the diner, stunned.

That was the one and only time I saw Roland in college, even though we messaged each other on rare occasions. He graduated the same year, at once moved to New York, and got married to his college sweetheart. He sent me a photo of himself and his wife, both smiling happily, with a message attached to it.

This is what being free looks like.

two

In my first year of college, my dad would send me urgent messages almost daily. Sometimes I tried to ignore them, other times they freaked me out. Every message was the same, no matter the content. Fortunately, I was used to living with the knowledge that our planet was in constant dire straits.

Be careful. Watch out. Go into hiding.

Storm A or typhoon B would be coming my way. A freak storm, an earthquake or whatever poisonous cloud would be heading to Minnesota.

Sometimes he would write a lengthy mail about how bad things were going between various countries, like with the whole Russia thing. He would comment on the presidents that ruled the world, including the trigger-happy ones. He would say that North Korea was planning a coup or a nuclear war.

He tried to tell me that the Chinese were playing around with AI-driven machine guns or the Japanese were planning a hostile takeover. Apart from the whole range of natural disasters, World War III was at the top of the threat list that he kept on referring to.

In those messages, apart from informing me about the

imminent dangers, he would also send detailed information on what to do if something were to happen. I had received clear instructions when I left home, and these were repeated on a weekly basis, as if I hadn't already memorized them.

There's a shelter about twenty miles from campus. Worst case, if you don't make it back home, you can head over there. I know the guy who runs it. He will give me the access code.

You'll be safe there. Don't forget: one way or the other, we will always find each other. Don't ever give up hope. Don't do anything stupid or rash. Make sure you are safe.

These types of messages popped up daily during my first year until I called home and told my dad I wasn't able to concentrate on my work due to the sheer volume of the messages.

"I have to make sure that you are cautious at all times, son, even when you're studying," he said. "My dad did this too, even in times the internet didn't even exist yet. He sent me letters and text messages. He called me constantly. This is the way it works. You'll do the same with your kids someday."

"But, Dad. It's just too much," I tried to tell him. He was so mad at me that he ranted on for an hour.

"Things do not change because you're in a different state, son. Don't you get it? You'll never be safe anywhere. You *have* to stay alert. You can't afford to lose time when something bad happens. Just remember, this thing won't go away. The world is dangerous everywhere, and you have to be better than the ignoramuses who live and breathe around you. Just remember, when push comes to shove, you don't care about the people around you. Convincing them would cost you precious time that you can't afford to lose."

"Are you saying I should just let them die?" I had asked,

stunned. "I'm a medical student, Dad. I can't do that."

"No, son. I'm saying that you need to take care of your own. You won't be able to save everyone."

He was right. It still hurt.

That first year was hell for me. I couldn't focus at all. My mind wandered off to whatever danger was out there, making it hard for me to stay. There were so many times I just wanted to run away. But I persevered.

What I remembered mostly for that time was looking out the window in class, wondering what kind of disaster would end us all and how much time I would get to make it to the shelter. I would look at my fellow students and wonder what they would do when the bomb dropped.

I started realizing that I needed to compartmentalize my thinking. That was the only way to divide the ideology from the work. I started making my own plans in case of emergency, like creating an extensive list of known shelters.

In my spare time, I connected with the local preppers community. During the weekends, I often went to one of their meetings to discuss the status updates on the shelters.

Once I gained their trust, we became friends. I told them about the way things were done in Montana and gave them tips in return for friendship. The Minnesota community was different than the Montana one. Different people meant different mindsets, and I had to adjust to their requirements.

We got along pretty well, and it gave me extra reassurance that I would be okay in case of disaster. I didn't tell my roommate nor the scarce group of friends on campus of course. They would obviously freak out if they knew what was happening.

That connection to that other part of me helped me to find

enough peace of mind to focus on my studies. And as an added bonus, I got my dad off my back. He settled down once he knew I would be safe.

I only went home on three occasions: Thanksgiving weekend, Christmas, and Easter. My stays were short. I barely saw anyone except for my mom and dad. We hung out, had a great time, and I was off again.

That first year flew by quickly once I got into my routine. I passed my exams with flying colors and drove home for the summer, feeling quite happy about how things were going.

But what I hadn't realized was how hard it would be to reconnect with my own community. By the time I got readjusted to life in Montana, it was time to return to the Minnesota campus.

I left for my second year with the knowledge that I had changed during my first year and would probably change even more by the time I came back from my second year.

The second year flew by even faster. I had my routine down to the final detail by now. I still connected with the local community, but my visits became less frequent due to my study-work balance.

I had found a steady job at a local coffee shop, where I worked as many hours as I could to earn enough money to survive. Even though Dad was giving me a bigger allowance than before, it still wasn't all that much and life was expensive.

I had the good fortune of being smart enough to combine a job with my studies, but there were times when I would fall asleep over my books. After a while, I got used to the lack of sleep. Or maybe my body didn't care all that much anymore about the lack thereof. Whichever way, a few hours of sleep a day had become part of my routine.

My dad still sent me his warnings, but not as frequent as they used to be. They were reduced to three to four times per week. He would use all three phones I had at my disposal, as if testing me. I still carried them with me all the time.

I didn't go home for Thanksgiving weekend that year, but I went back for Christmas (five days) and Easter (three days).

By the time I had to go back for summer break, I realized that I didn't really want to go back just yet. I didn't want to spend over a month in the gloomy darkness of danger, even if I was still afraid of it. I had reconnected with the Minnesota group and told my dad I would stay longer for a summer class on emergency first aid before coming home. He encouraged me to take it.

In the end, I spent two weeks at home. During that time, Dad tried to send me out on dates with three local girls, all in college too, spread across the country. I went out on two dates, knowing that I wasn't ready for that sort of commitment yet, so I politely told them that. The girls were relieved. One said she had a boyfriend in college (UCLA), and that she hadn't told her parents about him yet. The other told me she was gay but was afraid to tell her folks. She had a girlfriend back in New York. They had met online. I encouraged her to tell her parents, but when I left, she hadn't done so yet. We became good friends and continued texting weekly.

The third one never showed up, which was fine by me. It was my last night in town, and I couldn't wait to head back.

I had turned twenty in late August, right before I left, and my dad had a heart-to-heart with me on the subject of love, as he called it. It was pretty embarrassing, to be honest.

"Listen, son," he said. "I know you probably had sex already, and that's just fine. But remember that you can't give your heart to anyone. You can fool around, have fun, enjoy yourself. But when it comes to love, marriage, a family, you have to find all of that back home."

"Dad, please," I said. "What are you even talking about? I'm not interested. I just want to study and come back home. That's my goal. I don't care about any of that other stuff."

"Good, because I want you to be careful."

"You're afraid I'll meet someone outside of our community, aren't you?" I said.

"Maybe."

"What if it's one of the Minnesota preppers?"

"That's pretty much the same, even if it's the lesser of two evils. You'd still have gone outside of our community."

"They're nice, Dad."

He looked at me curiously.

"Is this your way of telling me you already have a girlfriend?"

"No, Dad. It's just hypothetically speaking. I'm not seeing anyone, I promise."

"Good. Because I don't want you to."

His message was loud and clear, and I abided by it. For months after I got back for my third year, I focused on nothing but my studies and work. Thanksgiving came, but I didn't go back. Christmas came, and I went back for three days only, saying I would be better off studying at the dorm. It would be quiet on campus for Christmas. There wouldn't be anyone around. It would be good for me.

My parents reluctantly agreed. I went back to campus, to the place I now considered home, and studied hard. I loved the peace and quiet, loved how empty the campus was. It was a nice contrast to the crowds that hung around at the coffee shop, where Christmas music would blare out of the speakers and people came together in droves to spend at least a couple of hours together, in between studying.

I took part in everything. I acted as if I loved Christmas. I even ignored my phones for a while. During those moments, between those crowds and being with my friends, I couldn't believe that there really could be assholes out there that would fuck up this world of ours on purpose. Or that a snowstorm could rampage over our city and take it all away.

Soon after Christmas and exams though, life turned back to its old, often boring self. Every day was pretty much the same. I studied hard, kept to myself, never skipped class, went through the motions, went to the preppers meetings, and worked weekends and sometimes night shifts at the coffee shop for extra cash. I often fell asleep over my books, but I nonetheless always passed every test.

This third year looked exactly the same as the last ones, or so I'd thought. How wrong I was. Because one March afternoon, I bumped into the girl who would change my life.

I *literally* bumped into her. Not fall, not walk. Bump. As if fate itself had thrown us together to make my life even more complex than it already was.

I had never seen her before, of that I was sure. I would remember this creature if I had spoken to her on campus. I couldn't even recall seeing her at the coffeehouse, even though she probably hung around there on occasion with the rest of them.

This radiant, lively woman was talking to a girl her age, who moved at the same pace as she did, heading toward me from the largest building on campus. I was heading in the opposite direction, using the main path that brought me from the medical center to the science building.

I had one of my three phones in hand, the one I used for daily stuff, and was scrolling through some messages about classes being shifted, but I still saw the two girls in time. I moved aside instinctively to give way to them. At the last moment, the one who'd caught my eye stepped sidewards and just sort of crashed into me, dropping her books and crash-landing them hard on the concrete path. Fortunately, they didn't hit my feet.

Crashing is overstating it. It felt more like a gentle shove. It didn't make me drop anything or even sway on my feet. I stood sturdily with my phone in hand, wondering what the hell she was up to since there was more than enough space for the three of us to move past each other.

"Oh God," she said, reaching for my arm as if I was hurt. "I'm so sorry. Are you okay?"

"Yeah," I said, trying to hide my laughter. "All good. It's fine. No harm done."

I was in a hurry since I was running late for a shift at the coffee house, so I started moving away, but she stopped me again. This time her hand would not let go of my arm. The touch felt soft, even on top of my jacket.

"Are you sure?" she said.

I looked at her, puzzled.

"Yeah, of course I am. Are you?"

I added the question because it seemed polite to inquire if she was alright, and a smile suddenly radiated on her face as if that was what she had been waiting for.

Ah. The obviousness of it was endearing.

"I am," she said emphatically.

"Oh. Well, all's good then," I said.

I still had to go. Time was ticking, yadda yadda.

Again, I moved forward. Again, she stopped me.

"I'm Holly Hayes," she said, offering me her hand.

I looked at her slim fingers and automatically accepted it. How could I not? Those sparkling eyes of her held me captivated.

Her skin felt warm to the touch. I instantly became physically aware of her presence. Of her as a person. *God, not now,* my inner voice screamed at me. *You're late. Get a fucking move on.*

I didn't. Couldn't. Not when I was smitten by this too-perfect creature.

You're such an idiot. Don't do this. Don't fall into that trap.

It wasn't the first time a girl on campus had started up a conversation. I had gotten used to their boldness by now, especially because in this day and age everyone spoke their mind and girls just wanted to find the right guys on their own terms and conditions.

It was the first time someone caught my attention enough to stay put. I had never experienced anything like it before. It was fucking mind-blowing.

Her friend sniggered audibly. I probably blinked. Maybe I started breathing again somewhere down the line too. Fuck.

Holly Hayes. That almost sounded like a song. *The Ballad of Holly Hayes.* I loved it already.

"Nice name," I said because it was all I could manage to utter.

"Thanks," she said with a broad smile. "And you are?"

"Excuse me?"

"Your name. What is it?"

"Oh. Dylan."

"Dylan what?"

"Excuse me?"

"Your full name."

"Oh. Sorry. Dylan Blair. Nice to meet you."

"You have a nice name too. It already sounds like a doctor's. Doctor Blair, please come to the desk right now."

I laughed. "Does it now?"

"Yep, it does."

"Well, that's good to know. But I assume that you'll be a doctor one day too?"

"Yeah, I will be, but I don't think my patients will be calling for me like yours will."

"Why not?" I asked, confused.

"I'm a future veterinarian. So unless a cat suddenly starts talking, it'll be someone else calling my name."

"Oh. Well, at least your patients won't have a whole list of demands ready," I retorted.

"Hm, I don't know about that. They might ask for special treats. Or extra pats."

I smiled. "I'm sure you'll be happily fulfilling those demands. There are worse things than handing out extra pats on a cat's furry back."

"I'm sure there are." Holly laughed. So did I. Her friend snorted audibly. Again.

Holly's books were still on the ground between us, and I was still running terribly late for my shift at the coffee house, but somehow, none of that mattered anymore.

The moment she'd offered me her hand and I caught it, captured by that radiant smile on her face, everything else seemed to become unimportant. Holly Hayes was by far the most beautiful creature I had ever seen, and she'd caught me in her web, devouring me without even blinking her eyes.

Her hand was still in mine. She didn't pull free, but then neither did I. It was fucking awesome.

I was painfully aware of the three phones in my possession and the little voice inside my head that represented my dad. I shrugged lightly.

"Nice to meet you, Holly Hayes," I blurted out.

She waited. I laughed.

"Want to get a coffee with me sometime soon? I know a good place. Kind of work there too."

"I know. I've seen you around," she said. "And yes, I would love to have a coffee with you when you're off work."

Her friend sniggered again.

That moment was one of the best of my life. Things just couldn't get better.

Only later, while working my shift, did I come to realize the reality of it all. That was the moment the raging panic attack started.

I remembered standing in front of the coffee machine, grabbing a coffee, turning around and imagining seeing her there, at one of the smaller tables, watching me with affection written all over her face.

I remembered setting down the coffee, yelling the customer's name, and looking out the window. I remembered envisioning a disaster heading our way. A twister, forming so unexpectedly that it just crushed our building.

I remembered imagining everyone inside the coffeehouse screaming as they were pulled away by the hurricane. But she remained seated. She just looked at me and smiled.

"It's okay, Dyl," she said. "Nothing can happen as long as we stick together."

But we didn't stick together.

I imagined running out of the coffeehouse and leaving her alone back there, as per my dad's strict orders.

"Run," he would scream inside my head. "Run, and never look back."

And so I ran and left her behind.

The next thing I knew, I was on the floor, panting. My friends and colleagues were gathering around me. My boss was kneeling by my side. He pushed a paper bag in front of my nose and mouth.

Some of the coffee shop's regulars looked curiously over the counter to see the drama. I blacked out for a couple of minutes and was sent home with one of my friends to help me.

The next day, I told my boss I hadn't eaten all day. He reprimanded me for not telling him. He was concerned. I thanked him.

I never thought that way again, but I knew all too well why I'd had that panic attack. It had been a warning, a foreboding of what would happen if Holly became a part of my life.

I wasn't mentally prepared for her. For this. For whatever love or care was. My dad had taught me well.

"Never care about anyone," he would say. "They don't know what's out there, but you do. When push comes to shove, you have to take care of your own."

I decided right there and then.

One part of me wanted to chase her away before this even became a thing. This whole world of mine could and would mess her up. I didn't want that for her or anyone else.

Another part of me wanted to find out what this thing we both felt could lead to. What it would feel like to be with someone who obviously experienced life in a totally different way than I did.

But a third part of me lied to me. It told me I could make this relationship work without telling her about my reality.

I chose to believe that part.

Holly and I exchanged numbers. Of course we did. After that whole setup—which I believed was part of her scheme to get me to talk to her, even though God knows why since there were plenty of perfect men strolling around campus as if they had the world in their pocket—I couldn't *not* give her my number.

Her friend, Anya, also her roommate, sniggered the whole time we exchanged glances, hands, and phone numbers. She also kept on glaring at me in a way that made me uncomfortable but was understandable. Her overprotectiveness was actually quite charming. She was looking out for her friend, even when said friend obviously picked me out of the crowd herself.

Not everyone on campus was nice, and I knew enough about the world and social media to understand how things worked these days. These were difficult and even exhausting times. My parents might have raised me differently than most people, but I wasn't stupid. I'd seen and heard enough from the guys I hung around with in my rare free moments to know what life was all about these days.

And of course there was my roommate Harry, who was my complete opposite and didn't give a fuck about college or working his ass off to get a medical degree. How he managed to pass every year was beyond me, seeing as he didn't give a rat's ass about assignments or finals, let alone study for them. Rumor had it that his dad bought his college degree by supporting the university financially, but I didn't believe that for a second. It made no sense at all. Harry just got damn lucky every time, and he knew it.

I didn't like to recall the many times I had seen Harry's bare ass as he fucked a girl in our room, with me still in my bed by the window, trying to ignore the sounds. At first he tried to muffle the sounds by throwing a blanket over them, but when they were at it, they seemed to forget everything else.

"Why don't you join us?" his last girl said at one point, which made me get up and leave the room to spend the rest of the night in the community living room.

"Fuck off," I'd muttered as I left the room.

I started either working more night shifts or bunking at someone else's dorm room, often sleeping on the floor. Male students were not supposed to share rooms with females, but everyone knew that this was not uncommon in college and no one really seemed to care. It frustrated me to no end.

When I'd talked to Harry about it, telling him I didn't like this whole situation and needed the room to sleep and study, he'd just shrugged and said he would let me know upfront when he was going to take a girl home so that I could spend the night elsewhere. As if it was so easy to switch places to both our benefits.

The last time we had an argument about it was two days ago, before I met Holly.

"Why don't you find some girl and bang her? Free bed and all."

"You're a pig, Harry."

"But you still love me," he said, laughing out loud and without a care in the world.

"I don't want to *bang* some random girl. I want it to have meaning," I started, but he shushed me with a shocked expression and raised his hands.

"Dylan Blair, seriously? Are you frigid?"

"No, I don't like it when you say things like that," I muttered, feeling extremely embarrassed. "I want to get to know a girl better before we do it. Don't be so rude."

"You don't like it when I use the word bang?" he said.

"No, I don't."

"Screw then. Sleep. Fuck. Have sex. Is that better?"

His words made me flush because I wasn't raised to talk about these things so openly. My parents had taught me to always respect people, no matter who they were or what they said or did. They had plenty of experience with being called names or being mocked, but not once had my dad lost his temper when someone told him he was fucking nuts.

"You can curse all you like," my dad always said to me, "just don't swear or talk about nasty stuff in front of other people. Always be respectful toward everyone, and the respect will come back to you."

Trust me, when you're part of college life, cursing and using crude words became second nature, but I always refrained from talking rudely myself. I wanted to give respect just as much as I wanted to earn it.

I guess that's why I stood out on campus in a way I hadn't expected or wanted. My peers called me the politest man on campus, but they had no clue that I, too, often cursed or thought the same things they did. I just didn't say them out loud.

Harry looked at me with narrowing eyes, triggered by my words.

"Dylan Blair, are you still a virgin?"

I wasn't, actually, but I didn't talk about the girls I'd dated with anyone. It wasn't Harry's or anyone else's business who I had been with or what I had done. And I sure as hell wasn't a virgin.

I was seventeen when I slept with a girl for the first time. Her name was Allison, a local girl from Midstone, where I grew up. We had both been virgins at the time, in our late teens.

Midstone was often called the gateway to the Montana mountains' wilderness, and it was situated at the start of a beautiful but dangerous trail called *Dead Man's Walk,* an inviting name to those who wanted a challenge in life. Hiking was part of our life.

It was one of the most beautiful areas in the world, and I was proud to be part of it. It was also a tiny area, felt secluded and often suffocating, and very much *not* what many people would be able to endure their entire lives. It could get pretty boring. The rural countryside had hardly anything to offer, except for the mountains and the lakes in front of them.

We had a local school, a couple of grocery stores, some large, some small, bakeries, shops, and ice-cream parlors. You name it, we had it, so it wasn't as if we lived on a different planet. But Midstone was very small. Everyone knew everyone, which could get pretty suffocating.

Locals lived off tourism but, at the same time, detested the droves of hikers that would come in summertime to take on the *Dead Man's Walk* challenge. From March to early November, hikers came by, but once the snow hit the mountains, it got too dangerous, and the trail would be closed off.

Allison and I had been friends since kindergarten. It wasn't until I turned seventeen that I realized I had feelings for her. We started dating in our senior year, but it never became anything too serious. We both knew it would be a temporary situation and that we would not remain a couple once I moved to Minnesota.

She didn't go to college. She was going to work at her dad's successful grocery store, which she would take over when he retired in a couple of years. He'd taught her everything she needed to know. She had a feeling for the business and made interesting choices that would often service the demanding flocks of tourists. She introduced vegetarian and vegan food, worked with protein-rich products, and made sure the tourists and locals had plenty of choice.

Allison and I had made vague plans to keep seeing each other, but of course we both knew that it wasn't going to happen. We slept together four times before I left, and we never did so again afterward. She wasn't my one and I wasn't hers.

The last time I went back home, which was during Christmas time, she was seeing Anthony, a nice guy who fitted perfectly with what Allison wanted from life. He had studied to become a mechanic and was combining two jobs, working at his dad's car body shop and helping out at the grocery store, meaning that he was serious about a future with her. I was happy for them. They were getting married soon. I was invited.

"I'm not a virgin," I said. "I just don't want to sleep around. Besides, that's my business and not yours, Harry. So why don't you buzz off and get a room whenever you want to have sex with some random girl, okay? This is also my dorm room, and I don't care to see you guys doing your thing."

"The lights are turned off when we do it. I use blankets. I tell the girls to be quiet."

"Yeah, and the moon definitely doesn't catch your bare ass when you're humping. It's embarrassing, man."

He laughed and patted me on the shoulder.

"You're a good guy, Dyl. You're right; I won't do it again. It's kind of embarrassing when the other guy in the room doesn't want to join in anyway. But seriously, the sooner you start sleeping around, the sooner our problem is fixed."

I thought about what he'd said and thought, no. I wasn't going to fuck around, just like I wasn't interested in dating girls.

Two days later, I met Holly.

three

A day after we bumped into each other, Holly came to the coffee house around the end of my shift. She smiled when she saw me. I threw aside the apron and walked to the front of the bar, smiling when I ordered two house specialties and a couple of brownies. My colleagues smiled broadly and made an extra effort with the foam heart they usually kept for girls they liked.

"Go get her tiger," Frank said before handing me the coffee and brownies.

"Fuck off, man," I retorted.

When we sat down by the window, she smiled at the heart before stirring the foam. She looked at me nervously, which relaxed me. So I wasn't the only one feeling these tingling nerves. That calmed me down.

I didn't know what to say. I just tried to make sense of the fact that she had chosen to get to know me instead of one of the many other guys that probably suited her needs better. Feeling like the eternal impostor, the odd one out, the student that didn't fit in, made me realize all too well that I should not even have considered inviting her, but I did. There was no way back now.

I was nervous, wondering what I could talk about without giving away my secrets. College life? My studies? My life away from home, when that home was different than most homes? How could I even steer her away from all of that when girls usually wanted to know everything about their love interests?

In the end, talking didn't pose a problem as Holly took the reins. She freely spoke about her life, both personal and at college. She was open and honest, and I liked it.

It was an amazing first coffee date, and many more would follow. I had no doubt about that.

If there is something like a lightning strike or some hunch that tells you that this might be the girl you'd want to spend the rest of your life with, I definitely got a sense of that. It instantly felt different than it did with my ex-girlfriend Allison, mostly because I had seen Allison grow up and remembered her as a toddler, a child, a teenager, and a young adult.

I knew Allison's ins and outs, her good and her bad, her tantrums and her amazing moments. We had great times, but when I left for college, we knew this thing we had wouldn't last and we were both okay with that.

With Holly, I knew absolutely nothing. She could tell me whatever she wanted about herself, and I would believe it because I had no reason not to. She had a younger sister, Emma. She used to have cats, but they had all passed away from old age, and her parents, who loved to travel, had decided not to get any more pets, seeing as Emma was going to go to college in the fall, which would give them more freedom to travel whenever they wanted to.

She was a normal girl growing up in a normal family. Her parents owned a house by the lake in a small town called Beau, which seemed to be as beautiful as the name suggested. They had their own dock and boat. The boat was small and old, so Holly said, and her dad had fixed it up himself, turning it into a hobby project, like he had done with the lake house years earlier.

"My dad's into real estate and often sells big development projects, which allows him to venture into side projects," she explained. "He'll buy old houses and fix them, often selling them at excellent prices after spending a lot of weekends working his ass off to get them ready for sale."

"That must be amazing though, to turn something old into something beautiful," I said.

"Yeah, it is," Holly said, showing her affection for her dad without holding back. "When he bought the lake house, he also intended on making it a sales project, but he fell in love with the location and the place itself, so he sold our old home and we moved in ourselves."

"Did you regret leaving your old home?"

"No, not at all. The lake house is just perfect. I always feel like I'm on vacation when I go back."

"Do you want to stay in Beau after graduation?" I asked, thinking about the unwritten pledge that I would return to Midstone to become a General Practitioner there. There was a huge lack of GPs everywhere, and I knew I could pick wherever I wanted to go, but my heart and soul belonged to Midstone.

"I don't know. It'll depend on the person I am going to share the rest of my life with."

The way she looked at me made me glow, albeit on the inside. Perhaps a bit on the outside too, but you'd have to ask someone else about that.

Holly, for whatever reason that still eluded me, had obviously chosen me to be that potential person. It unnerved me and excited me at the same time. Could this really become my future? Could I be so lucky as to share my life with a woman like her? Would she be able to accept me for who I was?

That was the catch, wasn't it? Thinking about that hidden part of my life, my heart sank. I knew this could never happen. Holly wasn't the right person for me, or at least not the one who would fit into the lifestyle I had chosen for myself. She was not the Rose to my Jack, which, come to think of it, would be the most terrible thing that could happen. I didn't want either of us to die for the other person, let alone perish in the heartbreaking, destructive manner that *Titanic* seemed to make so romantic. Nope, that was not for us.

Even though I felt something from that very first second, I didn't really want to spend too much time with her, but I couldn't help myself. We met again. And again. And again. And every time we spoke to each other, I grew more infatuated with her.

But every time I went back to my dorm, to my three phones and my preppers websites, I knew I couldn't risk getting her involved. I didn't really want to put her through that, knowing she would have to learn our way of life from scratch, which would be difficult for a non-prepper.

Prepper kids often married other prepper kids because they understood where all of this was coming from. They shared the same beliefs, felt the same fears. It was our way of life, and that was hard to explain to outsiders. My parents had warned me on several occasions not to get involved with a stranger, the way they were also taught by their parents, as if we were a cult of some sort. Which we probably were in many ways, but without the weird clothes or religion. My parents were atheists, and so was I.

Some time ago, my mom had inquired about my love life. That was before Holly. There was this girl I was vaguely interested in, but we never made it to second base. We just hung out together. It was fun. I made the mistake of telling my mom about her.

My mom's reaction said it all.

"Having fun is a good thing. You should do that. But don't let things get too serious with her. Once she knows what you believe in, she'll get out anyway. Newcomers rarely understand what we feel every single day. Relationships with outsiders are doomed to fail. It's better to avoid it now if you're not willing to go in that direction. If the girl's just a fling, then it's okay. But you're not the type of person to have flings, are you?"

I wasn't, and that was exactly the reason why I broke up with the other girl. I didn't want casual sex and then forget all about her. So I told her that I wasn't in the right state of mind to date. She shrugged, left, and fucked one of my classmates instead. I really didn't care.

But with Holly, I did. This was totally different in every way. I couldn't stop thinking about her. Couldn't go a day without seeing her. Pretty soon, we had a routine going on where we either met for breakfast, lunch, or dinner. My work schedule was adapted around her, as was hers around mine. She worked at a local vet. We managed to work the same hours as much as possible, so we could meet before or after, or on campus.

This was serious. I fucking loved her. She became my everything, and yeah, I was stuck between a rock and a hard place. I couldn't put off talking about my family. I couldn't avoid telling her some stuff.

I lay awake thinking about my predicament. Not just one night but many. Every morning, I convinced myself I would tell her the truth so she could decide for herself if this was what she wanted, but I always ended up telling her absolutely nothing. Whenever the moment came to tell her what was on my mind, I backed out.

"What is your family like?" she asked, two months into our relationship.

The question didn't come out of the blue. I had been avoiding the subject for too long, and she wasn't an idiot. She knew all too well that I was being evasive.

She stirred her coffee without looking at me, as if her question was taking us to the next level, despite the fact I already knew all about hers. This was my time. The moment I should grab with both hands.

"My family? They're okay, I guess," I said, shrugging slightly, as if it didn't mean anything to me to talk about them, even though my heart was racing a million miles per hour.

"Your parents are nice?"

"They're great. I love them to death."

"So you're close then?"

"Very," I said. "They're great."

That made her smile because family was very important to her. She had made that clear from the start. It was something we shared. It made me happy to realize that we weren't too different in many ways, but it still scared me that she had no clue about everything else.

"I'd love to meet them someday."

"You will," I said. "Someday."

"And you will meet mine."

"Yes, someday," I added.

She laughed. "Maybe even faster than you think. We could spend our next vacation together? I'd love to explore Midstone with you."

Fuck. What the hell was I going to do?

"Midstone isn't all that fancy," I quickly said. "It's just a typical American small town. We live near the foot of the mountain range, which is cool if you like that sort of thing."

"What does your dad do for a living?" she asked.

"He's a GP as well."

"Oh really? You didn't tell me that before," she said, obviously surprised.

"Midstone is a tiny little town, so it's not like his practice is huge," I said quickly. "That's why he has plenty of time to do other stuff as well. He's a fixer-upper in his spare time. He loves working with his hands. It gives him peace of mind. He's a great handyman."

Which is a necessity when being cooped up in a shelter with a dozen or so other people, trying to survive the apocalypse.

"And you're going to take over the practice when you return home?" Holly asked.

"That's the plan. My dad wasn't that young when I was born—he's almost sixty, and he's seeking to retire—so it would be great if I could take over."

"That's amazing, Dyl," she said in awe. "It's also very noble. Towns like that are often forgotten by doctors, especially with all these possibilities to go work anywhere you want."

She leaned forward. "Tell me more about your home."

"It's just a town, I guess. We live off tourism and forestry, basically. Those are our two greatest sources of income, and they're enough. We have a lot of older people. Younger people often tend to move away, even though these days there seems to be a good balance between the generations."

"What does your mom do?"

I smiled. "She's a mountain ranger."

Holly was amazed. "Oh, really?"

"Yeah. She's responsible for certain areas, warning hikers when they go off the trail or when a possible natural event is about to take place."

The moment I blurted it out, I knew I had made a mistake. Holly's curiosity was instantly peaked.

"Natural event? Like what? An earthquake or something? Or flooding?"

"Yeah," I said, recognizing it for the lie when I said it. "We can get some issues in the mountains, like rocks threatening to fall or a small earthquake. The lake at the bottom of the mountains can get flooded when there's too much rainfall or when the snow starts to melt after a harsh winter. A lot could go wrong."

"Sounds ominous," she said, not picking up on the lie.

"Yeah, but mostly things are just going fine," I reassured her. "It doesn't happen very often."

"It sounds important, though. Does she like her job?"

"She loves it."

I was an only child, which she already knew. I didn't tell her about my other family members. I didn't want to talk about my uncles and aunts and the cousins whose lives were all centered around the same thing we all were. I took a deep breath, trying to grab the momentum, but it had already passed. She placed her hand on my wrist.

"Anya is going on a date with your buddy, Harry, tonight," she said. "She kind of told me to make sure that you wouldn't be in your dorm room tonight. I don't want to know the rest."

"Me neither," I said. "Spare me the details."

"Trust me, we'll be busy too doing other things."

I smiled as Holly leaned forward, taking the lead by placing her hand on mine. One kiss was all it took to seal the deal forever. From now on, I was Holly's.

"I'm guessing I'll be going home with you then," I said.

"I guess so too," she said.

It was a warm evening in May when I walked Holly to the dorm room she shared with Anya. I couldn't keep my eyes off her.

For days now, it had been a lot hotter than was usual for this time of year, which made this moment even more special. There was a certain buzz in the air that seemed to affect a lot of us.

Holly wore a yellow dress; I was in a white T-shirt and blue jeans. Despite my secret still weighing heavily on me, I was horny as hell.

We walked into her building and straight to her basement room, where—according to her—it was cool in summer and warm in winter. She loved it here because it was the biggest room in the building, with two large windows that no one could peek through in the back and one in the front that was barely visible to people walking by.

The building was small, with only ten girls living there, which made them a cluster of very close friends. According to Holly, there was no drama or tension, just the freedom, quiet, and privacy that they all craved.

I was staying in a building that housed fifty students. It was always crowded and noisy. You could hear everything, and there was always someone around to meddle in your affairs. I was used to it by now, even though I loathed Thursday Party Night. I usually took a double shift then as the perfect excuse not to go.

Holly and Anya both had space for a double bed, while there was still plenty of room for their desks. The basement floor came with a private bathroom and toilet, giving it the feeling of a small, private apartment.

Holly's side of the room was decorated with a neutral pastel wallpaper, with just one beautiful frame of her parents' lake house hanging over her neat and clean desk. She had one picture of her parents and sister on the desk, a small sculpture of a black cat, and a quote that read, *Whatever you carry out today will become a bigger success tomorrow.*

The desk was as tidy as she was, as were her bed and closet. Anya's space was the exact opposite, with paper scattered around everywhere and cluttered on the floor and bed. Her wall was painted black, which kind of suited Anya's usual dress code. Not that Holly saw a lot of Anya's junk. She had placed a narrow but large bookshelf between the two beds, which gave her some privacy and probably a lot less stress.

"How she can sleep in that bed is beyond me," Holly said, shaking her head slightly. "I love Anya, but she's messy and sloppy. Other than that, she's awesome and incredibly funny."

"Sorry to hear that," I said. "Can't you switch roommates or something?"

"Not necessary. Anya's leaving in the fall."

"Oh?"

"She's moving overseas with her parents. They're headed for London for her dad's job, and she has already decided to go with them. She'll be finishing her studies in London. It's all been arranged."

"Oh," I said.

"Harry knows."

"Why would he need to know?" I asked, confused. "It's not like they're a couple."

Holly looked at me in surprise.

"Um yeah, they are."

"No, they're not. This is their first date. Isn't it?"

"Oh," Holly said. "He didn't tell you?"

"Tell me what?"

"They're kind of an item. This is their fifth date or something."

"But he just…"

"Had sex with someone else?"

"Yeah," I said, embarrassed.

"She did too."

"Really?"

Holly smiled. "Yep. It's not like this is an issue for them apparently, so I'm not making it mine either. It's their lives, so if they're happy, I'm cool with it."

"I seriously didn't know," I said. "Five times, huh? That's a record for Harry."

"For her too. But Harry's okay with her leaving, and so is she."

"Good for them then," I said and smiled. "Why are we talking about them again?"

"I have no clue," Holly said, laughing. "Truth be told, part of me is happy to get rid of her mess and her sex drive. I get tired of her taking guys here all the time."

"So you'll get a new roommate?"

"Nope.

"Why not?"

"I'm moving too."

My face fell, which made her laugh.

"Don't worry, I will still be here. It's just that my dad bought a tiny apartment for me downtown. He said it was a good investment, especially since I'm planning on specializing in larger animals, which means I'll be here for at least three to four more years."

"Oh. I thought you'd be working with cats."

"On the side. I want to work with zoo animals. I'd like to combine both."

I was impressed. "That's amazing, Holly."

"And you know the best part, Dylan?"

"No?"

She moved toward me and started pulling off my shirt. "You'll be here for a long time too. That means you and me will have plenty of time and space to do the dirty."

"That sounds great," I said, allowing her to take off my shirt. Her hands roamed softly over my chest, touching it from shoulders to navel while she allowed her fingers to scratch my skin gently.

"It'll be great too, I promise."

"I have no doubt," I whispered, leaning into her.

When my lips found hers and my tongue explored her mouth, her touch became fiercer. We were both panting, excited, horny as hell. Everything about her radiated sex as she stood there.

I couldn't believe my eyes, couldn't believe my luck. She was just perfect, a lot more so than I was. And now she was mine.

Holly wasn't a virgin; she'd dated a guy on campus before. She told me it was nice, a great first experience. She didn't elaborate further about him, nor did I ask. Something had happened between them, but she didn't clarify what and I didn't want to know. She also told me that this guy from high school had stalked her for a while, but that he had given up after a while. That was shocking to hear. She wouldn't elaborate on that either.

I had told her about Allison and the girl on campus that I

had blown off before having sex with her. She just smiled and said it was nice that I still had a good relationship with Allison.

Holly moved her hands to my abdomen as I took off her dress. Her fingers roamed down to my jeans, unbuttoning them. I couldn't help but wonder how I'd gotten to be so lucky to see this gorgeous creature standing in front of me.

It was only the second time I had seen a young woman standing so exposed in front of me, but it felt totally different than the first. She wasn't like Allison at all, both in behavior and body shape. There was no resemblance at all.

We touched each other gently, lovingly, eagerly. Our fingers moved everywhere. It was goddamn amazing. I couldn't believe my luck as we sank down on the bed. I was in a dream. This had to be unreal. It was too good to be true. How could she have chosen me from all the guys on campus that would kill to be with her tonight?

Holly opened the drawer and took out a condom, removing it from its package with shaky fingers.

"Sorry," she said. "I'm just so nervous."

I took her hands between mine.

"Why? I'm the one who should be nervous."

"Why?" she asked surprised.

"You need to ask me why? You're the most gorgeous woman I have ever seen, Holly. And you chose me."

She laughed nervously.

"I'm not gorgeous. You are."

I moved forward and kissed her gently before ripping the package apart to expose the condom. This eagerness to get inside of her was something I had never experienced before. It was the best sensation ever. The moment we were both ready to go, we felt the atmosphere change. Everything around us just swirled into something surreal. I felt like a virgin again.

She lay on the bed. I hovered over her before pushing myself inside of her. We moved gently in the same rhythm. She moaned; her eyes were closed. Her excitement was palpable. I could feel her enjoyment. It was the best feeling ever.

Holly cried out when she came, gasping as she pulled me against her and held on for dear life. She was so beautiful. I came at once after, lowering myself on top of her as she held me against her with her legs.

Afterward we lay down on the bed, just staring at each other. Holly smiled as she touched my face.

"You are amazing," she whispered.

"No, *you* are," I said, kissing her softly.

I closed my eyes as I rolled on my side to face her, wanting nothing more than sleep, so I could dream about her. I drifted off quickly, on a high that was incomparable with anything else.

"Oh no, you don't," Holly said, as her finger trailed down to my lower region, touching my dick. "We're not done yet, sir. Not by far."

Owkay.

She rolled on top of me. My dick responded at once, albeit slower this time. Her hand found me, touched me, excited me. I could feel her wetness. God, this woman was going to be the death of me.

"You're insatiable," I muttered.

"I work out," she said.

Much later, as she lay in my arms with her hands on my chest while dozing off contentedly, she whispered the sweetest words in my ear.

"I think I love you, Dylan Blair."

"That's funny, Holly Hayes," I said. "I think I love you too."

Damn. *Fuck.*

What was she doing to me? Who was this being that entered my life and took it over on every level? Me, the most sane/insane person on campus, who had always managed to keep his focus on whatever he was doing, had fallen head over heels.

I never really thought that people could be so attracted to each other that they would forget everything else, but hey, here we were. Holly Hayes had bewitched me. She had taken over my sanity, ripped it to pieces. I loved it.

She drove me nuts with her innuendos, her clothes, her gestures, her attitude, her hair, her eyes. That gorgeous body of hers was more than I could bear, more than anything I had ever seen or imagined. And she was all mine, in every sense of the word.

I knew she was crazy about me too. I saw it in her behavior, heard it in her words, in the way she talked. She couldn't stand not hearing from me every day. When I was working at the coffeehouse and she had some time off, she would come in for a coffee. Or four. She would sit at the same spot in the corner where we had our first date, just to watch me work.

My boss and colleagues teased me. I didn't care.

Whenever I was off from work or studies, she was there, and her presence was so physical I just wanted to rip off her clothes and have my way with her. I'd never considered sex to be mind-blowing. It had always been great with Allison, but it didn't feel to me as if it would alter my life in a way that would make me stop thinking about anything but that. Allison and I had been a good, decent pairing, but she hadn't lingered in my mind when I left for college, and I was pretty sure I hadn't lingered in hers.

With Holly, I had it all. The friend and the lover. It was just amazing. We hung out as much as we could, finding ways of fucking each other as if our lives depended on it.

Her dorm became mine in the weeks that followed, which was helped by the fact that Anya and Harry were fucking each other's brains out as well. Harry even talked about moving to London with her; he was that crazy about her. Harry and Anya were an item now too, going far beyond the whole friends-with-benefits thing that they'd started out with.

"I love that girl, man," he would tell me when we had lunch together. "Never thought that good sex could lead to a real relationship."

"Usually it's the other way around," I remarked.

"Yeah, yeah, I know, but in her case, it's the sex that led to other things. I really don't want to lose her. She's amazing."

"Then don't. Do what your heart tells you."

"But move to London with her? I don't know, man."

"Or ask her to stay here? Her life's here, her studies are here. Wouldn't it be easier if you guys shared a place together or something? She would be able to finish college in Minneapolis, and you can choose where to go afterward. It'll be years before you both graduate anyway, so what's there to lose?"

"Her parents won't like that."

"London's only a flight away, and she's used to college life," I pointed out. "I don't know, man, it seems like the most logical thing to do."

My words seemed to make sense to Harry, who smiled as he tried to puzzle the bits and pieces together.

"What about you?" he said. "What are your plans with Holly?"

"Oh, well, things are different with us. We don't have that

urgency that you guys feel, you know? We're taking it nice and quiet, and it's perfect as it is."

"I've heard you guys are fucking like bunnies."

I rolled my eyes. "Seriously?"

"Yep, that's what the gossip mill says. I heard you got caught in the back of the library and on lover's lane."

"Is there a lover's lane here?" I said, surprised.

He started laughing.

"What?"

"You just confirmed to me that you did fuck her at the library."

I flushed.

"You did, didn't you? You animal. Who would have thought that Dylan Blair, model student, would do naughty things like that?"

I thought about the one time I went down on her at the library, all the way in the back, in the section of the Polish and Rumanian books that the university library had for some bizarre reason, and I felt myself get hard again at the very thought of it.

We had shared plenty of moments like that by now. The movies, of course, with her hand feeling me up and rubbing me so fast that I came within a couple of minutes. My car, after we drove to the countryside and parked near a lake. Her on top of me so I could feel myself sinking deep inside of her.

Everything felt perfect and not at all awkward. Having sex with her was as normal as talking to her, loving her, caring for her.

We studied together, side by side, in her dorm room. I used Anya's space, which was as good as empty now that she had moved a lot of her stuff to my dorm.

It was June, the busiest month of the year, and I had to divide my time between thinking about Holly and studying for finals. In the end, somehow, I managed to get both done without going crazy.

I helped Holly out with her finals as well since she needed more time to absorb the material than me. Math had always been a struggle for her, so we went through the details, and I gave her tips, which she used.

There was one thing we didn't talk about at all, and that was the upcoming summer vacation. Even though we were so close and probably neither of us dared to imagine a summer away from each other, we didn't make any plans at all. I didn't want to take her home with me just yet, but I was also hesitant to meet her parents and her sister. What if they didn't like me or somehow saw through me? What if they disliked me from the start and would get her to break things off with me? I was afraid of what our future held and just wanted to enjoy the moment.

I knew it would come though, the question of what was going to be next for us. After the finals, we would have a lot of time off, a long break before a new school year would start. After the summer break, in which everything could change, there was a great possibility that I would come back to find my life changed. That Holly would find someone back home that suited her better.

Besides that, there was another issue that we hadn't spoken of yet. Holly would move into the apartment her parents had bought, and I would probably have to find another room *and* roommate, seeing as Harry and Anya were either going to move to the UK or moving into an apartment together. Whatever they'd decide, I couldn't imagine myself living with

Harry anymore. He had chosen her, which was perfectly fine.

I decided to talk about the situation with Harry over the phone with my dad, without telling him that I had met Holly. That would come later, but right now it wasn't the first thing I wanted to share. I wanted to tell him in person that I had met someone, even though I already dreaded that prospect.

"The dorm is pretty crowded and rowdy," I said. "I'm not sure if I'm even able to share with someone else, as my studies are getting harder every year, but I don't see any other solution right now."

"You can find a place to live on your own," he said. "Your mom and I can afford it. I know we asked you to work to support yourself, but that was mostly to give you more financial freedom. If you can continue to combine your studies with work, we can pitch in for the rest."

"I don't know, Dad," I said, hesitating.

"Think about it, you don't have to decide right now. The option is there, so if you want to get your own private space, we're happy to help."

"Thanks, Dad. I really appreciate it."

"Of course, son. By the way, are you coming home for the summer? We will get to see you, I hope?"

"I will come home, but I'm thinking about taking some summer classes. I want to get some extra specialties done, and they have a great program on medicine addiction, after that whole OxyContin disaster went down a couple of years ago."

"Oh, I see. Yeah, you should do that. It could be useful, I suppose. Just don't stay away all summer, okay? Your mom and I miss you."

"I won't, Dad, promise."

I knew I would go home. I also knew that, for now, I would

lie about Holly. Or at least simply not tell them about her. It felt like the right thing to do, considering I had no clue how to prepare them for her, and her for them.

My whole life, despite the fact I was still secretly checking all the sites and making sure I didn't miss any calls, had completely changed. I felt it, and they would feel it too once they saw me.

I didn't know if I was ready for that confrontation yet.

four

So, this is what happened. I didn't take summer classes, even though at first, it was my intention to do so.

Holly took me to Beau instead, to the lake house. She had told her parents, Dan and Susan, and her sister, Emma, about me, and they had invited me to come with her for a lakeside vacation.

I didn't want to go. I didn't want to get involved in their lives. Didn't want to risk them finding out about my parents. But I went anyway. How could I not? It was obvious by now that she wanted to be with me. To have me in her life in summer as well. I was no longer a college fling. I was her *boyfriend.*

All the way to Beau, with me driving the Volkswagen Golf my dad had given me for my eighteenth birthday and which he had fixed up himself, I felt agitated and nervous. Holly blamed it on me meeting her folks.

"Stop fretting so much," she said as I bit my fingernails. "You're going to be okay. My dad doesn't bite, you know."

"Maybe your mom does."

"She'll love you. They all will."

She entwined her hand with mine. If this were a movie, she would have leaned into me while we were sitting in a convertible, with the sun beaming down on us, making her hair and skin glow. In reality, it was pouring down all day as a reminder that we didn't live in Sunny California.

"Don't worry about the weather," she said as we reached Beau. "It'll clear out soon, trust me. It always does."

"I'll always trust you," I said.

As if she could predict the weather, the clouds started to clear out as soon as we reached Beau, and by the time we made it to the lake house, one single beam of sunlight had breached the clouds, making the world seem like a whole different place. It was absolutely gorgeous to see how the sun touched the water. The area was stunning. She hadn't exaggerated one bit.

"I love it," I spoke in awe.

"Told you," she said, beaming as much as the sun did.

As it turned out, her dad was one of the nicest guys I'd ever met. He greeted me like I was his son, patting me on the back and taking me inside the house, exclaiming how glad he was that he finally got to talk to a man instead of being overwhelmed by female chatter about clothes and makeup.

"Call me Dan," he instantly said when I addressed him as *sir*.

"And I'm Susan," her mom said.

Dan was down to earth and loved to talk football and baseball—two things I happened to like and follow too whenever I could. He also loved to talk about movies and music—not my cup of tea, but I tried for Holly's sake—and he was generally aware and critical about a lot of things that were happening in our world. He worked on boats and loved gardening and growing his own vegetables and fruits, which he succeeded in pretty well.

Susan was just as nice. She was slim, wore sweatpants and T-shirts around the house, had her hair up in a bun, and loved to cook and work with her hands. She had a shed out in the back where she worked on old furniture that she fixed up and sold again. She didn't have an ounce of arrogance in her, despite the fact that these people were obviously rich.

When we went out to dinner later in the evening, she cleaned up nicely, wearing a summer dress and high sandals. Her hair was just as long and flowy as Holly's, who was an obvious mix of her parents. I loved them. They were so easygoing and didn't talk about anything serious, like the everyday threats that were going on in the world.

But the person I liked the most was Holly's younger sister, Emma. She had just turned seventeen, and she was just the funniest person at the table. She made a lot of jokes, talked constantly about whatever was on her mind, and we bonded during talks about the most beautiful places we would want to see someday. She connected with me, and I thought of what it would be like to have a sibling that you could joke around with.

When I looked at Holly, she obviously liked the fact that I adored Emma. Holly was crazy about her sister, which was obvious in every way. They chatted constantly on the phone or WhatsApp. Not a single day went by without them hearing from each other one way or the other.

Later, Holly told me that Emma wasn't supposed to be born. Her mom's first pregnancy, when she had Holly, was quite complicated, and the doctors had recommended that her mom should not have another child. She stubbornly refused to listen and got pregnant again, although she had to rest in bed for seven months. Emma saw the light of day through a cesarean, but they were both fine and healthy. Emma was considered a miracle, and Holly bonded with her from the day she came into the world.

I remembered Holly telling me about her parents' offer to get her an apartment where she could be on her own. During our stay there, the details were arranged. I had decided to stay in the dorm for now, especially since Harry had called me a day earlier to let me know he had broken things off with Anya, who was moving to London in a few days.

"I don't see our relationship working in the long haul," he had said. "Her parents obviously don't like me, and I can't just give up everything here and move there. They are insisting that she move with them. They even said they would no longer pay for her college fees if she doesn't. So we've got no choice. It was fun as long as it lasted."

He sounded really sad and depressed, which made my decision to stay at the dorm final.

"I'll stay, but we need to set new boundaries," I said over the phone. "No more girls at night, no more sex when I'm there. Got it?"

"Got it." He stopped, and then he laughed.

"What?"

"You won't be there for much longer anyway. You'll be with her all the time."

That was true. Holly would have her own apartment, and even though her parents obviously wanted Emma to move in with her in a year, seeing as she would also go to Minneapolis to become a nurse, this upcoming year it would be hers alone. Which meant freedom to do whatever we wanted. Perfect.

I loved every minute of every hour of that vacation at the lake. It was amazing, beautiful, and relaxing. We did a lot of walking and hiking on various trails. Another thing we both loved was going for walks and nature. We took a three-day road trip by ourselves in my dad's Golf. When we got back, her parents and sister welcomed us again as if we were long-lost children.

All the time, I had my emergency phones with me, but I hardly checked them once. There were times I forgot to scan the websites. There were several hours where I managed to forget the continuous threats to our world.

We didn't watch any news—Dan refused to and called it too dark and depressing. He hated the fact that the media pushed us into believing that everything was grim and gloomy. We didn't read any newspapers (again, for the same reason), but the girls and their mom sang and danced on happy Spotify playlists. Even Dan often chimed in. He had this dark, deep voice that fitted Susan's voice perfectly.

"Come on, Dyl, sing," Holly ordered, when I sat and listened.

"I can't sing."

"Bullshit, everyone can sing."

So after a while, I sang. It was terrible. Nobody cared.

Dan was fixing up another boat and asked me to join in. Thanks to my life in Midstone, I'd grown up pretty handy. Of course I didn't tell him how I got to know so much about engines and working with mechanics.

"You're a natural at this," he said while showing me what he was working on. "Sure you want to become a doctor?"

"It's kind of the same, isn't it?" I said. "It's just fixing up people instead of machines."

He laughed. "That's true. So, tell me about your parents."

I'd known this question would come. I had mentally prepared myself for the inevitable inquisition. After all, which parent wouldn't want to know more about the family of the man their daughter was seeing?

"There's not much to say, really," I said. "My dad's a doctor, my mom's a mountain guide. I was born and raised in a small town with a lot of family around, as an only child."

"Alone but not spoiled rotten," he commented.

"I guess," I said. "I learned how to work hard at an early age. My dad felt it was important that I pitched in as soon as I could walk."

"Did you like it?"

"I did. I still do. It's important to know your way around things. Makes it a lot easier when it comes to the smaller obstacles in life, so you can prepare for the bigger ones."

The moment I said it, I knew I had made a mistake. Dan looked at me strangely and put down his tools, wiping his hands on an old rag.

"Sit down, Dylan."

I felt my heart churn. This was the moment he was going to tell me he knew I had things to hide. He had figured me out, googled me—even though I knew there was nothing to find since my life had been quite anonymous throughout my entire existence. Of course that didn't mean he couldn't have found out more about Midstone, which was known for its preppers community. If he had done that, his next question would be about my beliefs.

I sat down, trembling. He shoved a chair closer to me.

"Look," he said. "I know it's none of my business, but ever since you arrived here, I've noticed that you're pretty jumpy at times and always seem to be cautious about what you say and do. It's like you don't want to go past your own boundaries, as if you want to restrain yourself from having fun. Can you tell me about that?"

I was stunned. How could I have been so obvious when I honestly believed I had let go of many of my fears over the past week? I already felt different than when I was home, but it was clear to me now that I was still the odd one out.

"Holly mentioned it too. She said you are very introverted and closed off."

"I am," I said, not denying it. It was true.

"She also said you never talk about your family."

That was true too.

"I just don't have that close a bond with them," I said, shrugging a bit. "A lot of people don't."

"That's true," Dan said.

"You don't have to worry about me. I'm fine. I've always kept to myself. I'm just not the type of person to talk for hours, you know? I wasn't raised like that, and my parents were also so busy that I spent many hours home alone. I guess I'm used to not having people around to talk to about personal things."

"Hm." Dan frowned.

I knew it wasn't enough to satisfy his curiosity. I wanted to tell him so badly, but I just *couldn't*. If I told them the truth, they would keep Holly far away from me.

I swallowed, realizing that this moment could define my future relationship with Holly. These were good people. Good, decent, lovely people. I loved them already, couldn't imagine going back to Minneapolis without having their support.

"I need to ask, Dylan," Dan said, moving forward a bit. "The thing is, I've seen this kind of behavior before in my own circle of friends, and I know that it's rare to happen, but I can't just brush it aside. I hope that you're not offended by my question, but…were you hurt as a child? Did someone in your family do something to you?"

I looked him in the eye, realizing what he was saying.

"God no," I said. "Not at all. No one has ever touched me

or hurt me."

He didn't say much at first, but then he sighed in relief, running his hand over his face. My God, did he really think that I had been hurt and that this was the reason why I was so closed off?

"Dan," I said, leaning forward myself. "Thank you for looking out for me. I swear that nothing happened to me as a child." *Apart from being raised to live in fear, that is.* "I love my parents and my family and the town that I grew up in. I'm just me. This is who I am. I promise to be less jumpy and less cautious and to let go a bit more. I'm trying, for Holly. I guess I'm just not used to being with people who are so open about their feelings. It's new to me."

Dan smiled and patted me on the wrist.

"I know. It was obvious. Be true to yourself, Dylan. Holly loves you the way you are. God, she would kill me if I had asked something like this in front of her."

"I won't tell her," I said.

He smiled and got up, obviously relieved and satisfied with my replies. He seemed at ease, while I started realizing that I needed to adapt my behavior when I was with them. If they had known about the phones and my online search results, Dan would not have been put at ease so quickly.

"Now then," he said. "Let's work on this baby, or she'll never be ready before the end of summer. Such a shame that you have to leave in a couple of days."

"Yeah," I said. "I know. I love it here so much."

"You're always welcome here."

"Thanks, Dan."

I watched Holly's dad as he threw himself into the work, turning up the radio volume so he could whistle and hum as he worked. I already loved this man. How easy would my life have been if he had been my dad?

Holly and I had sex at her parents' house, but it was the quiet version, where we'd sneak under the blankets, feel each other up until we both were horny as hell, and then I'd slide inside of her, fucking her gently. She would muffle her moans and snigger beneath the blankets and sheets, and we would gaze into each other's eyes in the dark privacy of her childhood bedroom.

It was amazing and awkward at the same time, especially knowing that her sister was sleeping right next door and her parents were down the hall in their master bedroom. It still didn't hold us back from having sex; it was just a totally different kind. It was the best.

When I felt her fingers on my dick and sensed how she wanted to take it slow, I enjoyed it without the awkwardness that often came with a hand job. When I pushed my fingers inside of her, feeling the sleek wetness that I had grown so used to as a reaction to her excitement, it felt absolutely perfect. When I sank inside of her, always looking into her eyes as I did, even beneath the covers, I felt our bodies move in the same rhythm.

We didn't experiment with kinky sex, nor did we do anything to jeopardize the peace and quiet at the house. But every morning, I could feel Emma's gaze resting on Holly and me, obviously knowing exactly what we had been up to.

"I'm tired," Holly said at one point.

"I'll bet," Emma reacted.

Another morning, a couple of days later, Emma, Holly, and I were sitting at the breakfast table.

"Let's go for a walk by the lake," Holly proposed, looking at me but not at her sister while she smeared her toast. "I know this really nice path that goes into the woods. You haven't been there yet."

"I might actually go with you," Emma said, even though she obviously was not invited.

"Well, I wanted to go with Dylan," Holly said hesitantly. "I thought you had other plans?"

Emma started laughing.

"Of course you do. Well, gotta go. Have a good one, you guys. Don't do anything I wouldn't do."

"You're wicked," I whispered to Emma when she walked past my chair.

"Uh-huh," she said, laughing loudly as she left us alone in the kitchen.

"Soooo," I said. "A path into the woods, huh?"

"Yep. One that not too many people know about," Holly said, her voice husky and lower, a sure sign she wanted to get it on. I guessed she was tired of the bedroom sheets.

"I'd love to find out more," I said, growing aroused in a split second. Holly knew, of course. She could tell by the way I gazed at her and tried to focus on my toast. If I got up now, I would probably drag the table with me.

Her mom walked in.

"You guys doing okay?" she said, sitting down and pouring coffee for herself.

"More than okay," Holly said. "We're going for a walk now. See you later, Mom."

I dropped my last bit of toast on the plate, got up quickly, and rushed out of the kitchen, followed by Holly. Once outside, we hurried to the path Holly pointed out to me, which led us far from the lake house and into the wooded area on the right side of the lake.

Ten minutes later, I had her up against a tree, holding her as we made love. It was amazing.

When I left Holly and her family three days later, I cried behind the steering wheel of my car.

I had planned my summer vacation in three parts.

Part one: the vacation with Holly at the Beau lake house. I stayed for only two weeks because then she was leaving for Los Angeles with her folks and her sister. They always took a lengthy trip together, and I didn't feel it would be right to go with them, even though they'd offered. I thought about how I really wanted to visit the West Coast but still declined, telling them this was their time together and I didn't want to impose.

Part two: summer classes. The whole addiction class wasn't a lie, and I genuinely wanted to know more about the effects of pain medication on people. I had just lied about the length of it, which made it possible for me to spend nearly two weeks at Holly's parents' place.

When I returned to campus, I got swept away into the summer class routine. It was intriguing to find out what made pharmacists produce such crap and what made people, knowing that it was crap, continue taking those pills. Holly was in LA during those two weeks. We texted constantly.

Part three: going home for two weeks, which was the longest I could bear. I had changed, and I knew it, thanks to Holly and her family, but there was also a big part of me that was already returning to caution modus as soon as I started driving home. Holly would come back to campus by the end of the summer, so I wouldn't see her until then anyway. There was nothing keeping me there.

I needed to see my parents. Not going home was not an

option. It was something I needed to do and something that I used to love, until now. Just like I had been afraid that Dan and Susan would find out who I really was behind the blanket of trust, I was just as afraid that my parents would figure out I had been with people who didn't hold up to their standards.

Despite the fact that I felt like I was growing apart from my parents and family, I still wanted and needed their approval and love. I couldn't imagine being kicked out of our community, let alone being forced to spend my life away from them. It was just that their beliefs were no longer matching mine, which added to my increasingly growing reluctance to be an active part of the community. That feeling didn't start with Holly, but she amplified it unknowingly.

Every time I'd gone back home in the past two years—before Holly had entered my life—I had already realized that my views on life had changed quite a bit. I was no longer that same kid who used to do everything blindly, to listen without prejudice to whatever my peers and older family members said. Yet I was also still the kid who knew the codes by heart, who helped to restack the shelters and to check the supplies and the generators that would automatically jump into action whenever one of us went to a shelter.

This, however, would be the first time that I would see my parents and lie to them without batting an eyelash. They still didn't know about Holly, and I planned on keeping it that way for as long as I could. I would tell them eventually, but not this time. I wanted to spend the next two weeks in their presence, trying to figure out my goals in life.

Could I not be a regular kid with prepper parents who wanted more in life than fear and vigilance? Could I not tell them that I had met this girl who knew nothing about prepper life, whom I really, really liked and wanted to spend more time with? Could I not tell them that I wanted more peace of mind and maybe study something else, now that I was at it?

Driving home, I took my time to mentally prepare myself. My dad would ask about my studies and my life, my mom would inquire how Harry was doing, and maybe they would ask if I was seeing anyone at college, but they wouldn't care about the answer because I already knew that I was supposed to marry a local girl. They would most likely try to set me up with the daughter of one of our community friends.

When I arrived after a long drive, stopping a couple of times on the way to get a coffee or a bite to eat, our reunion was gentle and friendly. My dad shook my hand, and my mom kissed me on the cheek and commented on my appearance. We had spoken mostly over the phone, so they hadn't really seen me since spring break. Dad quickly left again because of a medical emergency that had someone rush over to the practice next to the house, but Mom stayed with me. She had taken the afternoon off, so she told me.

"You're slimmer," she said. "Love your new hair. You're looking well-rested, honey. Tanned. I didn't know that summer classes could be so relaxing."

I smiled briefly, thinking about the many hours I'd spent on the patio overlooking the lake.

"It was fun," I said. "I learned a lot. We had a good group. Took our time in between classes. It was all very relaxing and chill."

"And you didn't mind not having a real summer break until now?" she asked.

"I have one now, don't I?" I said. "If I didn't take up classes, I would have worked anyway, you know that. I'm not the type of person to spend months on the beach."

I looked away briefly, not wanting to show the lie in my eyes. I still missed the lake house. In fact, I had spent the entire trip over to Midstone wanting to return, especially when Holly texted me to let me know that she missed me so much already. *You can still come back to Beau*, she had sent. That almost sent me over the edge, but I decided against it. I needed to see my parents, to spend time with them. I needed to know they were still right about everything they believed in. This was my home after all, and one day I would return to it.

Mom placed her arm around my shoulder. Even though she was almost as tall as my dad, it took her effort to do so. When I was eighteen, I had my growth spurt. Since then, my length had been pretty much the same. I hit the gym quite a lot, working on my physique and strength, which my parents always pushed me to do.

"When the time comes, you will need to be strong," my dad always used to say after he started taking me to the gym at the age of fourteen, like most kids in our community did. "You need to get ready."

I had kept that motivation when I went to college, hitting the gym at least three times per week. Even at the lake house, I went out for a run every morning before dawn, enjoying the way the morning sun settled over the lake as I ran past it. Sometimes, Dan had come with me.

"So, what else is new?" Mom said.

She took me inside the house, settled me in the kitchen, and put on the kettle. We were herbal tea drinkers at home, which was much better than coffee, so I had been told at an early age. Herbs meant health, and health was a necessity.

I didn't drink herbal tea in college. In fact, I kind of hated the taste of it, but I never told my mom, who was an avid herbalist. At the diner, I drank coffee or hot chocolate, thinking that chocolate couldn't be that unhealthy when it was mixed with milk.

I shrugged. "Nothing much, really. Things never change in college. I'm glad another year has passed. How were things over here?"

"Well, we had quite a few scares," Mom said. "The mountains are rumbling abnormally, and we've even had a slight earthquake, summer storms, and harsh winds. It's going to be a rough winter. We've already had to help some tourists get off the mountain due to heavy rainfall and colliding, falling rocks. It's not looking good for the winter either. We think that we'll manage to allow people up the mountain until half of October, but then we'll have to shut off all the trails, unless the weather predictions change rapidly."

"That sounds ominous," I said.

"It is. It's going to be an early winter. Snowfall predictions are pretty serious. I'm worried."

There it was, the same fear that caught me at the heart, the one I never felt when I was at college. I regretted coming back, despite the fact I was so happy to see my mom again, who never traveled to Minneapolis. My parents never did, seeing their limited vacation days and busy, all-consuming jobs.

"So something's going on in the mountains?" I said, gazing outside the kitchen window at the mountain range that stood about a mile away and overlooked the area as if it were its protector and a threat at the same time.

"We think so," Mom said as the smell of herbal tea filled

the kitchen. "We're monitoring it very closely, so there's no need to worry."

She placed a mug in front of me and added some local homemade biscuits I really liked. When I sipped the tea, I realized I actually didn't mind it as much as I used to. It tasted like home.

Home. This was my home, and I needed to remember that, despite the fact I had trouble with some parts of it.

"Thanks, Mom," I said. "I've missed your tea."

She brightened up.

"Thanks, honey."

It suddenly became clear to me that my mom had been quite nervous when I arrived home, as if she was taking a stranger back into her house, which was partially true. This was my home, and these were my parents, but I had barely seen them for years. Of course she would be afraid that we had grown apart, just as I had been, driving over.

I read this quote once that said that, as soon as your kid went off to college, you lost a part of yourself. In a way this was true for most Americans, who would often part with their children for months in a row.

"So what about worldwide threats?" I said, trying to show as much interest as I could.

"Everything's fine. Well, if you can call it fine," my mom said, pulling a face. "Life's never really fine, is it? It hasn't been for years, and it just seems to be getting worse. I hate wars, Dylan. I really do. That continuous cat-and-mouse game between countries gets under all of our skins. It's like you constantly have to be cautious. It's never been this bad since the Cold War, and I haven't lived through that. The stories my parents told me were pretty much the same. It's horrendous how people keep on killing each other, making a mockery out of it."

"It is," I agreed.

Dad walked in and entered the kitchen, sipping from Mom's cup of herbal tea before hugging me and patting me on the back.

"It's really so good to have you back with us," he said. "I miss you around the house, kid."

"I know, Dad, I miss you too," I said. "But it's for a good cause, isn't it? It's only a couple more years."

He laughed. "What you call a couple. You'll be gone for a long time still, but hey, that's okay. It's what you need to do. I'm so proud of you for choosing medicine, son."

"Thanks, Dad."

"Do you still want to take over my practice?"

"I do, Dad."

He beamed. I felt guilty.

"Let's have dinner in town tonight," he said. "I'm not on call, so we have all the time in the world."

"Sounds good, Dad."

Dad walked over to Mom, hugged her, and kissed her on the cheek. They were so good together, so close. It was amazing to see them love each other so much after all these years. I had a flashback to the way that Dan and Susan had held on to each other. Both couples were pretty similar. They were nice, gentle, open, and affectionate with each other and the people around them. There was no denying that.

I got up, put my cup on the kitchen counter, and hugged the two of them together, holding on longer than I normally would have.

"Love you guys," I said.

They both seemed pleasantly surprised. I'd

surprised myself too.

Some things remained pretty predictable in Midstone, like the stores and the people. When we walked into town to have dinner together that night, all the way down, people greeted us and patted me on the back. It was obvious my parents had told their friends and relatives that I was coming over for a couple of weeks. It almost felt as if the whole town went out of their way to welcome back the prodigal son.

"Hey, Mrs. Smythe. Hi, Mr. Thomas. Yes, everything's fine. Yes, college is going well. Yes, still studying medicine. Yeah, I heard about the mountains. How are your kids doing?"

I found myself repeating the same words, but different names, over and over again, until my dad rolled his eyes and laughed.

"You're almost a celebrity, or so it seems. Come on, I'm starving."

We walked into Dad's favorite Italian restaurant and were greeted by Pietro, who showed us to our regular table. Dad always ordered the linguini, my mom was crazy about the vegetarian lasagna, and I always went for pizza. They were the best I'd ever had, or maybe I was just biased.

Pietro gave Dad a bottle of wine on the house and sat down with us to talk about my studies. Then he promised to get me the best pizza ever, and I knew he would give me the house special, which was a rich mozzarella-based pizza with all the fresh herbs one could possibly imagine. I was already salivating.

My phone buzzed, but I ignored it. It buzzed again. And again. This was my only phone of the evening, seeing as I was with my parents, who had their emergency phones with them. I had promised myself not to get too preoccupied with the frantic craziness of it all but to leave that up to my parents like I used to do when I was a kid, depending on them blindly for guidance.

This dinner would be amazing, I was sure of it. We ordered finger food while we waited, and the conversations were about anything but the mountains—something my parents obviously had discussed beforehand. We had the best of times.

Pietro came to tell us that there was a problem with the oven, so we would have to wait a little while longer, which I found odd, seeing as a lot of people around us were being served. My dad waved away the apology and said we had plenty of time.

Then, a befriended couple walked in before our food was even being served, followed by their daughter, Lisa. I went to school with her; she was one year younger than I was. I mostly knew her as a wild, spoiled brat who didn't really want to hang out with boys, but the person who walked into that restaurant was beautiful and self-assured. The last I had heard of her was that she was studying languages at the local university.

The moment she walked through that door and I saw my parents' reaction, I knew I had been set up. Of course.

"What a surprise!" Mom said as she hugged her friends. "Why don't you join us?"

Pietro was already moving the empty table next to us closer, and I just knew that there'd never been a problem with the oven. He had been ordered to wait with the food until the other guests arrived. Lisa came to sit next to me. I barely managed not to roll my eyes.

"Hey, Dylan," she said softly.

"Hey," I replied curtly, wanting to ignore her for the rest of the evening. So this was my homecoming dinner, huh? A setup by both our parents as if they were planning an arranged marriage.

I didn't care about Lisa at all. She was friendly enough, but she wasn't the person I saw myself sharing the rest of my life with. She was just one of the gang, a girl I had grown up with. She wasn't Holly.

While our parents all laughed and toasted, pretending a bit too hard that they had not set us up, Lisa and I just talked about random things, without once really looking at each other. She obviously didn't have any feelings for me either and was just as annoyed by all of this as I was.

I made it quite clear that I wasn't into her, talking only about our high school days, without once asking about her current interests. And she didn't even care. She told me in a whisper, without her parents listening in, that she wasn't looking for anyone, but she avoided telling me why.

"I'm not either," I whispered back. "To be honest, I hate it when they do something like this."

"Me too."

"Let's just stay friends then," I said, raising my glass.

She laughed. "Here's to friendship."

When we walked back home later that night, just my parents and me, I took a deep breath as I pushed my hands deep into the pockets of my jeans.

"Don't ever do that to me again," I said.

They didn't comment. I knew they *would* do it again and again and again.

"I have a girlfriend."

My dad stopped. My mom gasped. They both looked at me, stunned.

"Who?"

"Her name is Holly. She's a college student, and I'm

crazy about her."

"Why didn't you tell us?" Mom asked, obviously hurt.

"Because she's not from around here, Mom. She's not a prepper. She doesn't know anything about it."

"And you haven't told her," Dad said, sounding almost accusing.

"That's right."

"Why not? Are you ashamed?"

I looked away.

"You are. Well, that's rich, son," Dad said, sounding hurt. "I knew this day would come."

"Dad... It's not that I'm ashamed. I just don't know how to handle it, okay? It's like we're both part of totally different worlds. She has her life, I have mine. It just doesn't match yet. I need to figure out a way to tell her everything without driving her away, okay? Don't you understand that?"

"What I understand is that your mom and I warned you not to get involved with a girl outside of our community, Dylan. And yet you still did it anyway. What the hell's gotten into you?"

"I just like her, okay? She's really nice, and I want you to meet her."

"When?"

"Well, not right now obviously."

"Why didn't she come with you?"

My dad started firing question after question at me, and I knew I had made a mistake. I hadn't wanted to tell them like this, but the whole thing with Lisa had upset me.

"I want to define my own life, Dad. I don't want you to decide for me what is right and wrong. Just—Holly is great, okay? She's everything I want in a girl, and I love her."

"What do you know about love?" Dad snorted as if I had just told him a ridiculous joke. "You're twenty going on twenty-one, for God's sake. You're just a kid."

"I'm not a kid anymore, Dad. I'm grown up, and I know how I feel about her. So stop setting me up with girls; that's all I'm asking."

Dad turned angrier by the minute. Gone was the friendly banter between us. This was the man who could react extremely fiercely toward his peers whenever they lacked interest in checking the shelters. Who could drive people insane like no one I had ever seen. Who managed to get things done because no one dared to defy him. He was a gentle man too, but when he was angry, he turned into a volcano.

"You don't get to tell me what to do," he said. "Have you ever considered what you've caused, Dylan? Have you thought about the consequences for that girl when she comes to live with you here? Do you even realize how hard it is for newcomers to adjust to our way of life? Did you even consider what you're going to put her through before you 'fell in love'?"

The disdain in his voice was hard to bear.

"You know, Dad, you really have no clue about anything that goes on outside this little world of yours," I said. "Out there, life is pretty much normal. People don't walk around carrying emergency phones. They have fun, they enjoy every single day. Do you know how hard it is to return to all of this?"

We were still standing in the dark streets of our town, and I just knew that people were listening in on us, even though we hardly saw anyone. Our voices carried in the dark.

"I know it's hard, son," Dad said. "I know. I've been there too, believe me. I went to Minneapolis too, remember? I studied there, had a girlfriend there, had a great time there, and then I came back home and married your mom, which was, by the way, the best decision of my life. So yeah, I know it's hard. I know how you feel. But in the end, it's not about you, is it? It's about Holly, who has absolutely no clue what you're dragging her into. Think about that for a moment."

Dad turned and walked to the house, leaving me flabbergasted. Mom smiled gently, pulling me against her. I realized that my dad was right. It wasn't about me at all.

He had just confirmed what I had known all along. I couldn't bring Holly into my life.

Later that week, I saw Lisa around town, leaning awfully close into Anne, a girl who was a couple of years younger. I knew then that her interests lay somewhere else, and I was happy for her. I was also relieved. They were sitting in a coffeeshop, and I walked in on purpose, waving at Lisa as she noticed me. She turned red. When I walked over, Anne excused herself and went to the bathroom. I sat down with my coffee and looked Lisa in the eye, smiling.

"You and Anne, huh?"

She turned red.

"Come on, Lisa," I said softly. "We are living in the twenty-first century, you know. Why are you hiding your true feelings from your parents?"

"You know why," she answered softly.

I did know why, right at the moment she told me. If she was gay, she would not be able to have children, and that was considered mandatory in our community. Children meant the continuation of life. Children meant that mankind would continue to survive, no matter the urgencies or disasters. Not having children was *not* an option.

"Maybe you can have both," I said softly. "Get the girl, get the kid. Just find someone that will help you with the latter part."

She smiled and placed her hand on my wrist.

"You are so sweetly naive, Dylan. It's obvious you've been spending too much time in a different state. And by the way, when are you going to admit that you're in love with someone else?"

"Excuse me?"

"The whole town heard you the other day."

"Oh."

"You know what?" she said, smiling. "The day that you bring that girl here to live *our* life is the day that I'll tell the world that Anne and I love each other. How's that?"

I sat back and stared at my coffee.

Hell would probably have to freeze over first.

five

Things were quite strained between my parents and me after that first night, but we never spoke about Holly again. I knew that for them, she was just a fling. I would have fun with her, and then I would return after graduation and marry a local girl that I'd gone to high school with. After all, there were still many years to come, so why worry?

Life went on like it always did in Midstone. Dad worked hard at his practice, and Mom went into the mountains to protect tourists, who were taking advantage of the excellent weather to hike into the mountains but never seemed to realize how dangerous things could get in the blink of an eye.

I spent most days the same way: waking up early in the morning to head for the gym or to run my usual track, having breakfast, heading into town for whatever groceries were needed, meeting with some old friends from high school, just to hang out with them, making dinner—which I really loved doing, I actually used some of Susan's pasta recipes a few times—and hanging out with my parents at night. We went out to dinner on occasion, but mostly we ate on the patio, enjoying the view of the mountains.

All in all, it was a pretty peaceful vacation, and I felt glad that we didn't talk about Holly again. We texted and video-called multiple times, and I told her how much I missed her. She was having a great time at the lake house, taking walks on the beach and hanging out with her family, enjoying life like it should be enjoyed.

I still had to fight the urge to just hop into my car and head over there, but it would take far too long, and I was afraid of flying, so that was not an option. Besides, I knew my parents enjoyed having me around, so I didn't want to cut my vacation short.

Dad took me on one of the shelter trips during the second week. We hiked into the mountains, to the biggest shelter of them all, halfway on *Dead Man's Walk*, hidden behind a curtain of thick rocks that concealed a secret passageway and steel door that led into the shelter. There was a road leading up to the mountain that ended in a parking area with a small café that only opened when the weather was good enough for hiking, offering coffee and snacks.

Not a single tourist realized that they were near one of the biggest shelters the state had and that it was stashed with all the necessities to survive for at least three years, with a maximum capacity of twenty-five people, or thirty-five if need be.

Normally we would take the car up to the mountain and then walk to the shelter, but it was such a warm day that a hike felt like the best thing to do. We passed by several tourists, talked to some, and went on our way.

When we reached the shelter, Dad and I made sure that no one saw us before we headed through the passageway and up to the door that would one day become the barrier between danger and safety. This was my favorite shelter because it was so big and so well equipped. It was higher up, so floods couldn't reach it.

As a kid, I'd always thought it didn't feel suffocating at all. It felt large and spacious, with plenty of room for all those who would one day live here. It was totally different than the atom shelter in our backyard—which was my dad's second choice and fallback plan in case we wouldn't make it up the mountain—or the one in my uncle Udo's backyard, which was a bit larger but felt just as damp and narrow as my dad's.

Dad had taken a couple of days off in my second week at home, which wasn't that easy these days, seeing as how his practice was flourishing. I had offered to help out because I had nothing else to do and was bored out of my mind, but I wasn't yet officially allowed to practice medicine, so that would have been an issue.

These were our only days together and I wanted to make as much use of them as possible, so as we hiked up the mountain, I felt at peace. I watched him as he unlocked the door, using the code that only a select few knew. When we walked inside, a sense of dread overwhelmed me. The outer door slid shut, the inner door slid open, and there we were, standing in artificial light, gazing at the interior of the shelter.

It wasn't open and broad and welcoming at all. It was terrible. A dark place carved in rocks, with areas that were divided into smaller spaces that would give us some privacy but would ultimately still keep us locked inside.

Lights were added throughout the long, broad area that had taken my family forever to create. There were bedrooms in the back with four bunk beds each, two bathrooms, with a sign on the door, a room with books and games, a living area, and of course the storage facilities, which held food for a couple of years.

Every six months or so, we did a quality check on the food, including verifying the end dates and replacing them where necessary. The foods that were about to expire were taken home and divided among our community members.

Most of the food stayed perfectly containable for a couple of years, but it was always a painstaking exercise to replace whatever needed replacing. It was necessary, though. We couldn't afford anyone getting sick or running out of things to eat.

All of us preppers had received instructions on what to do in the days that followed after a doomsday scenario. This, alongside other detailed destructions, was part of what we were supposed to do:

- *Don't go outside for at least two months and only if you need to*
- *When you go outside, wear a mask*
- *Don't allow anyone to come inside*
- *Don't try to save animals*
- *Be sparing with the supplies*
- *Don't allow fights inside the shelter*
- *Take no risks*
- *Remain calm at all times*

These were the instructions that we were all drilled to follow, so when the time came, these would become our lifelines.

Dad went on with his list of things to check. The food, stored by expiration date, the ventilation system, the generator and the spare, the lights, and the rooms. It took him about an hour or two to do so, and I helped, going through the motions. When we were done, we sat down in the living area, where Dad wiped his brow and sighed.

"Another run done. Let's hope we get to do a million more."

I knew what he meant. Despite the fact that we were always prepared for the worst, none of us wanted to have the worst to happen. Ever since the fifties, since the start of the Cold War, or even after Hiroshima and Nagasaki, a lot of communities like ours had been preparing for a tragic event, but none of us had ever been forced to flee into the mountain.

"Let's cross our fingers and hope it'll never be necessary to make it to the mountain," I said.

"Cheers to that." Dad raised an imaginary glass and smiled. "I know you're questioning our lives, Dylan. It's been pretty obvious since you came back that you're struggling with everything. It's normal, you know. It's something we all have to go through. It'll calm down again, that turmoil inside your head. Trust me."

"I hope so, Dad," I said, thinking about the peaceful lake house where doomsday scenarios were as far away as I could possibly imagine.

"You should bring Holly with you next time."

Excuse me. What?

He laughed. "Don't look at me like that. Your mom and I are aware that you really like this girl. So we're just saying that, if you are serious about her, you should take her to Midstone, have her meet us and get to know our way of life, maybe take her up to the mountain. Show her the shelter, talk about the sites, the phones, and the continuous caution. See how she reacts. If she really loves you, she'll accept your way of life and your choices."

He did make sense. I had been postponing this for far too long. If she really wanted to get to know me and was serious about me, she had to know.

"Okay," I said, "I will. Under the condition that you stop trying to set me up with other girls."

"We only did it once," he protested.

"Still one time too many."

"If you had told us about Holly earlier, we would not have done that."

"Yeah, maybe," I said. "Or maybe you would have been even more persuasive about it."

He laughed. "Maybe." He patted me on the back.

I smiled. "Thanks, Dad."

"For what?"

"For not kicking me out of the house."

He smiled. "You're my son. I love you. Why would I kick you out? How could you ever even think that?"

"I sometimes do," I admitted.

Dad turned serious, realizing I meant what I said.

"Dylan, come on, son. You're one of us, no matter what you think or feel right now. You can't take away that part of who you are, and it's really okay to question everything. In the end, though, that doesn't change a damn thing. You'll always come home to us because that's who you are."

This was what I was afraid of. Exactly this. What if who I was right now was not the person I wanted to be in the future? What if I had already changed too much?

I thought about Roland. Happy, free Roland and what he had told me that one time we met. I still had his messages, thought about them on occasion.

"So when do we get to meet her?"

"What about Thanksgiving weekend?" I said.

Dad smiled. "That sounds good."

Another college year started, but there was one big difference this year, and that was Holly. When we saw each other again on campus, we picked up quickly where we had left off.

Dan and Susan came with her. They hugged me warmly. They brought things with them for the new apartment, which I helped to fix up and get ready in the few days before college started again. There was new furniture combined with things from Holly's dorm room, and we added framed pictures, a couple of framed posters, small knickknacks and things that Holly liked. It really was her place, but I loved it as much as she did.

We had lunch and dinner with her parents, and we talked about the upcoming year. We had a great time. I showed them photos of the mountains that I took on my walks, and they showed me photos of their trip to the West Coast. They left the day before classes started.

When college started, time flew by fast. One day blended into another, and life became this comfortable routine where things were predictable in a good way. We got our schedules, which were pretty much the same in terms of hours but brought us to different buildings on campus, as our majors were different.

Harry was right about one thing: I hardly spent any time in our dorm anymore. I slept at Holly's all the time. Most of my stuff was at her place, as well as my books and personal things. Harry had our room all to himself, but I did sleep there occasionally, mostly when I needed to study for a big test.

When I was with Holly, it was so easy to get distracted. We always ended up sleeping together, forever feeling that urgency of wanting to be as close to each other as we possibly could. Being together every night also meant having a lot of sex. We were both equally insatiable.

I couldn't get enough of her, and that feeling was obviously quite mutual. The more we got to know each other, the more the eagerness to feel each other up grew. We were in a sort of honeymoon stage where life consisted of a lot of love and sex. It was probably the best time of my life so far. It was also the most distracting one.

The main bedroom was hers and carried a queen-size bed that was big enough for the two of us. The second bedroom became her study area. We installed a second desk in the living room, where I would study whenever we stayed together, just to make sure we wouldn't end up staring at each other all the time.

We had set ground rules about our time together, making sure that we both had enough space to study and work on our assignments without bothering each other. We also agreed on moments where we would work separately. We had set up a timer system that worked perfectly.

I still worked at the coffeehouse, and Holly had found a new job at a flower store at the mall with better hours, where she would work evenings and part-time weekend hours. We tried to get our hours to be pretty much the same, but sometimes I worked the night shift and she would be alone at the apartment, or vice versa. She worked Sundays, when I would spend an afternoon working without distractions.

I paid for most of the food, which felt like the right thing to do, seeing as I was living here for free, so she wouldn't have to worry about that. Her parents paid for the utilities. My parents had no idea we were practically living together, and I wasn't sure that Dan and Susan knew, but they were obviously aware of the fact that we were together a lot.

Holly often went out with her friends, which I also insisted on. I didn't want to be this tight-knit couple that didn't allow others in their lives.

I hung out with Harry, who was now dating another girl, made new friends, and relaxed more. The times that I forgot to check my phones and sites increased rapidly. I still called my parents on occasion, but I always did so when Holly wasn't around.

As the weeks went by, this became our lives, and we were extremely happy. I honestly never wanted it to end. I could have easily lived this life forever. We didn't have much to worry about.

September and October had excellent weather, and the weather predictions for November were quite good too. My dad told me they were keeping the mountain trails open until the end of the month, an obvious hint that this might be the time to take Holly to Midstone.

My parents and I had been in touch all the time, and I had not lied to them anymore about Holly. It was obvious to them by now that we were very close, and they insisted on meeting her during Thanksgiving weekend, even though I felt guilty toward Holly since she wouldn't be able to see her parents then.

"Oh, that's okay," she said when we discussed it. "Mom, Dad, and Emma are going to come over the weekend after. Dad is meeting with some friends downtown, so Mom offered to take us shopping. We can have dinner and then on Sunday go do some family stuff."

"And they really don't mind that I want to take you home on Thanksgiving?" I said.

"Of course not. I told them that I haven't met your parents yet and that they invited us over, so they were perfectly okay with that. We'll be at the lake house for Christmas."

We decided to drive over on Wednesday, taking a scenic route instead of the busy highways like most people. We would be arriving around noon, meaning that we still had the afternoon to ourselves. I would use that moment to take Holly up the mountain and show her the shelter.

What would happen after that, I couldn't say. It made me nervous since I had no idea how she would react. I wasn't even sure if she would stick around for much longer. Worst-case scenario, she would flee and never look back. Best-case scenario, she would spend the whole weekend with us, so we could explain what our lives were like. I prayed for the latter but feared for the first.

"Look, Mom, Dad," I pleaded over the phone on Tuesday before we left, "I want to take Holly up the mountain first and show her what it's all about. Then we can use the rest of the weekend to talk about what it really means. But please, when we arrive, don't mention anything yet, okay?"

"Sure, son," Dad said before he fell silent.

"What is it?"

"Nothing, just keep your phones close at all times, okay?"

"I always do, Dad," I said.

He obviously wanted to say something more, but he didn't.

He left me with that nagging feeling that I had been trying to suppress for ages. The one that lingered in the back of my mind, telling me that I should not go. But Holly was insisting that we should, and she had her mind set on it.

"We'll have a wonderful time," she said. "A great Thanksgiving dinner with your parents, hiking up the mountain. I can't wait to see what all the fuss is about."

"You'll love it," I managed to say, but I was scared to death.

I knew I wouldn't be able to find the right excuse not to go, so I didn't bother trying to find one. We left on Wednesday morning to drive to Midstone for Thanksgiving weekend. I took my phones with me.

Dear reader,

You have now met Dylan.

From this point on, choose what you want to read next.

1. Continue reading Dylan's version of events on the mountain. In that case, keep on reading.
2. Read Holly's story. In that case, go back to the beginning of the book.
3. Finished Holly's story already and want to read her version of events on the mountain? Go to page 95.

One way or the other, whatever you choose, you must read both storylines to get a complete picture of what happened.

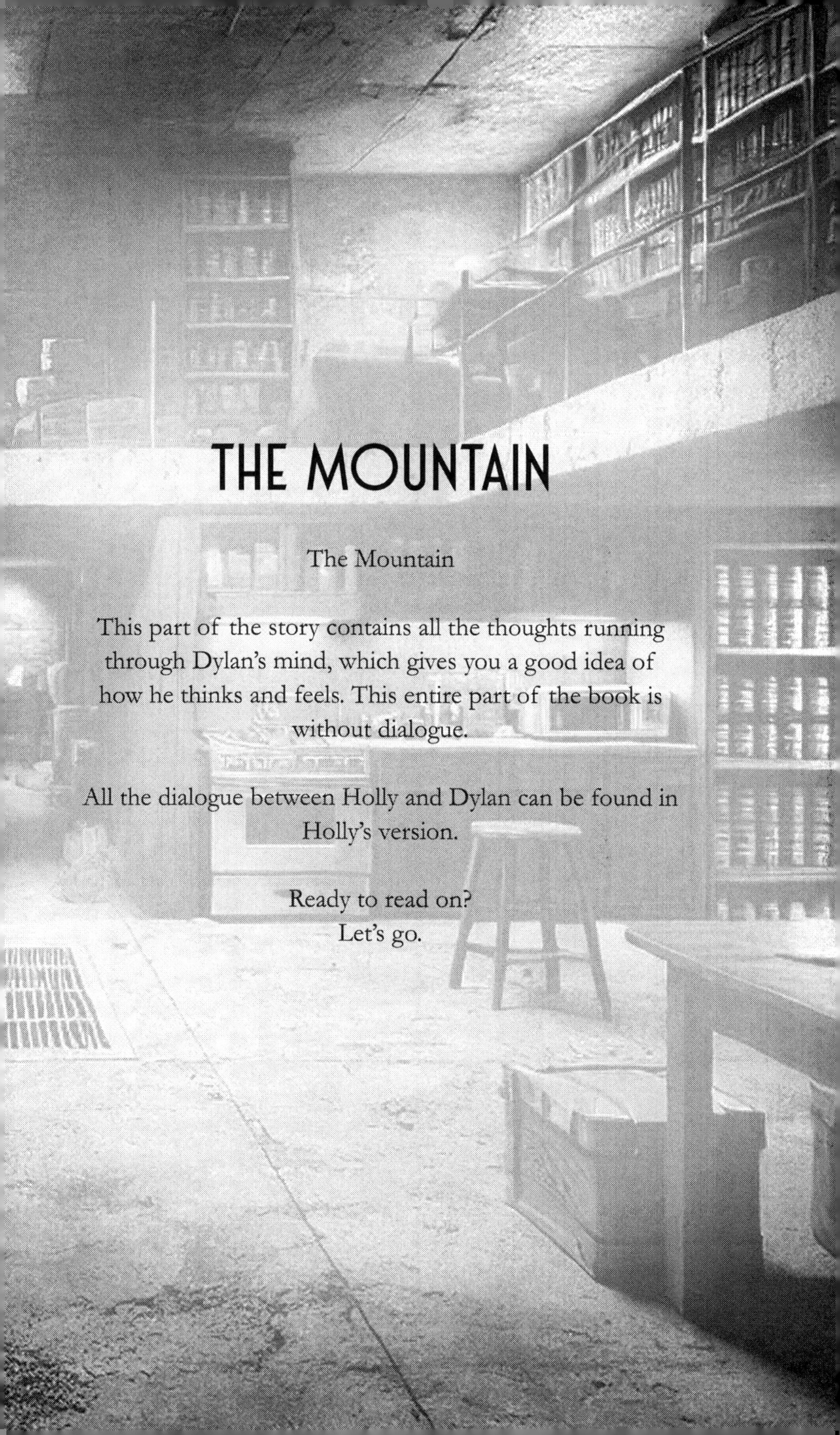

THE MOUNTAIN

The Mountain

This part of the story contains all the thoughts running through Dylan's mind, which gives you a good idea of how he thinks and feels. This entire part of the book is without dialogue.

All the dialogue between Holly and Dylan can be found in Holly's version.

Ready to read on?
Let's go.

ONE

During the drive to Midstone, it was hard for me to hide my nerves, so I didn't bother pretending that I was perfectly fine. Holly felt my anxiety. She treated me with respect and care.

This was it, the ultimate moment that would break or make our relationship. Today's events would define our future. The choices were hers to make.

Holly still didn't have a clue why I was so anxious. She ascribed it to her meeting my parents, which would be the obvious conclusion for her to draw. I felt guilty. Foremost, that was what got me this anxious right now. I should have told her sooner. I should have confided in her parents, who had sensed something was wrong when I came to stay at the lake house.

I'd had nine months to explain what my life was about, but I never did. Now I would be confronted with my selfish decision. Because selfish it was.

Had I told Holly sooner, she would have been able to decide for herself if I was the type of person she wanted to get involved with. She could have called it quits and moved on with her life, onto greener pastures with a normal guy.

Now we had come to the point where we couldn't breathe

or exist without each other. I couldn't even imagine spending the rest of my days without her. To be on campus knowing she was there too. I honestly didn't even know how I was going to survive without her. I couldn't even think about it.

For Holly, this was the first meeting with my parents. For me, this would define who I was going to be with for the rest of my life. Or who I was going to be as a person.

One thing remained as certain to me as life itself, though. I would not abandon my parents nor the future they envisioned for me. They were the people who taught me that life was about cautiousness, safety, and protection. And often about fear. They raised me to protect the ones I loved against all costs, and I would continue doing so for as long as I lived.

Holly told me to stop fretting when I started tapping my fingers on the steering wheel like I always did when I got nervous. Her words took me back to last summer when we had headed out to see her folks at the lake house. I had been nervous then too, even though I had known that I would get to meet these sweet and loving people and there had been nothing to worry about.

She didn't realize that my innate fear was much worse now. That I hadn't slept properly in days thinking about today. The future worried me so much it made an insomniac out of me. I was so goddamn scared I was going to lose the people I loved the most.

And what if my dad ordered me to choose between them? What if Holly couldn't understand our way of life? What if today ended in this big fight that would force me to choose? What was I to do then? Go back to the loner I was before all of this? I couldn't.

All that I could hope and pray for, was that Holly and my

parents would see eye to eye. That their love for me would be the glue that bound them together. That would be the best possible outcome.

My head hurt. It had been hurting for a couple of days now. I was exhausted, drained. The lack of sleep didn't do much good either. I hadn't told Holly any of this. It wouldn't have done much good without telling the rest of the story.

Holly's hand came to rest on mine. I stopped tapping and concentrated on the road, driving slower than usual, but still fast enough for her not to notice. She turned up the volume and hummed along with some cheesy song, obviously trying to release the tension in the car. We were both lousy singers.

My thoughts drifted to my dad. He wasn't that easy to get along with. He had this tendency to ask harsh, direct, and often hurtful questions.

My mom was sweet on the outside but tough on the inside. She was outspoken and candid, but she always addressed things with a certain respect.

I had learned to address things respectfully while balancing my opinion and voicing it whenever it was needed. I always tried to put things on the table in such a way that it would never feel hurtful or denigrating. I could be quiet for days but turn extrovert in the blink of an eye.

I never spoke about my life with anyone. The reasons for that were obvious. It still felt like lies of omission to me. Holly's reaction today would change everything. She would either accept it or call me insane. I was betting on the second.

We would go up the mountain first. I had planned it that way. In the trunk of my car lay all the equipment and clothes that we needed for the hike up the mountain. We had packed two small suitcases filled with clothes that were suitable for any occasion. I had two extra pairs of shoes with me, including the ones needed for the hike.

That hike was the most important walk I'd ever go on in my life. The second would be the one going down the mountain to meet my parents. *If* she still wanted to do that, that is.

We were avoiding all the busy highways, but there was still plenty of activity around us due to Thanksgiving. Thousands of people were heading to their families. I had to remain cautious on the road.

We pulled over at a stop in the next small town we passed, where I filled up the tank. I parked the car. We walked to the crowded diner next door, where we slipped into a booth and ordered a late breakfast. While waiting, I calculated how much longer it would take us to get to Midstone. Two hours, maybe a bit longer.

Holly looked around before taking out her phone and tapping a message to her sister Emma, who treated me like her new brother whenever we spoke on the phone or sent messages to one another. She was really cool. I actually contemplated telling her first, but I never dared to.

Assuming she would stay with me after learning about the shelter, Holly would meet my parents. I imagined my dad's first reaction. He wouldn't comment on her attractiveness, but he would immediately get down to business in his typical way. He would welcome her warmly in his house and ask her random stuff about her life and the things she enjoyed most. He would talk about her studies and her future, and then he would ask her how I was treating her because he cared about how we, as a family, treated others. I'd seen him do it to some of my cousins when they brought back their girlfriends.

Then he would start digging deeper. Not at once, but as soon as she was at ease in my parents' house and unaware that the interrogation had only just begun.

Dad would talk about the preppers community and their doomsday beliefs. He would ask her how she felt about it and if she saw herself stocking up supplies in the shelter. He would prod and poke until he was sure she would be a) capable of living the life and b) believed enough in our just cause to gain the trust of our community, for she would have to fight her way in.

Then the tests would start. He would find ways to trick her and see how she would react. He would ask her to go to community meetings and monitor her reactions closely. That would be the hardest part.

He'd chased away a couple of my cousins' girlfriends by asking in-depth questions or telling some misplaced anecdotes that would get them to see their future in a very graphical way.

That was my dad for you. I loved him dearly. Besides being a pain in the ass, he was the best mentor and father I could have wished for. Without him, I wouldn't know what to do. What he said went. But whenever he was present in the room, there was no argument possible. I had no doubt about the power he held over the people he loved the most.

I spoke to my mom on the phone yesterday evening, when I was back at the dorm packing some things for the trip. Holly was at the apartment, so she didn't hear the conversation. I was surprised to hear from her, since my dad was usually the one doing the talking.

She told me that the mountain was showing odd behavior and to take my emergency phones with me. She wasn't too happy about my plan to take Holly up the mountain, but I brushed off her warnings. There was always something going on, some days more than others. That's just how it went.

When I didn't take her warning the way she wanted me to, she told me to drive Holly up to the parking lot near the shelter instead of going up the mountain. I declined that offer too. Then she said to head back down immediately at the first warning sign of trouble. I promised her I would.

She sighed and remained quiet for a while, obviously debating what to say or do. I knew she didn't want me to bring Holly to Midstone at all. She had practically confided in me about that weeks ago. Girls like Holly don't belong here, so she had stated, reminding me of what my duties were.

It had pissed me off. Even after all these months, she still couldn't be happy for me. I'd told her curtly we'd be fine and hung up the phone, but her words stuck with me and worried me. Dad had never once said that I shouldn't bring Holly up the mountain, but the one thing he shared with my mom was his reluctance toward my relationship. They had both assumed Holly was just a fling. She wasn't. I loved her and I wanted to be with her for the rest of my life, even if the most important people in my life didn't seem to like it.

For one moment I contemplated not going. Maybe it would be easier to divide these two parts of my life indefinitely. Holly didn't really need to meet my parents, and I didn't need their approval. But then what? There would come a time when I'd be expected to return home and take over my dad's practice. What would I do then?

Maybe it was too early, a little voice inside my head insisted. Maybe I should not go just yet. I could use the mountain's unrest as an excuse, but Holly would know and start asking more questions about my parents, which would cause another form of unrest. She would know I was backing down. And that would be the truth.

So off we went. And in came the stress, resulting in that nagging headache that just wouldn't leave me alone anymore. I was tired by the time we got to the house.

Fortunately, Holly was distracted by the size of my parents' property. I had never told her how big their house was. They were wealthy, but not like hers were, and it didn't really matter to me since they didn't share much of their wealth with me. I was working my way through college because they felt I should know how to earn a living and respect the money earned through hard work.

Holy stood on the porch looking out over the mountain range, whistling softly when she studied it. She loved this area immediately, that was pretty clear to me, and I was happy and relieved. Not everyone takes to the mountains; some called the area threatening. I got that. During the night, the mountains could feel like living creatures hovering over us all. There was something unique to them that could not be explained to people who hadn't seen them in real life.

I took the spare key hidden beneath the floorboards of the porch, opened the front door, and let Holly in. With our bags in hand, I took her to the spare bedroom, where she dropped off her things. My old room was next door.

My parents slept on the other side of the hallway, where they had an ensuite that gave them plenty of privacy. There were more spare rooms upstairs in the attic, next to the room where my dad worked out. The house had more space than two people really needed, but they still managed to use most rooms.

It was the family's custom that the house and doctor's practice would belong to the next in line. My grandfather had moved to a smaller house after his retirement and so would my dad at some point in time.

Following Holly around the house was an eye-opener to me. She went around complimenting things in such a way I began to realize how unique the property was. Not only that, in my mind's eye I pictured her ten years older, a mother with three kids chasing each other through the rooms.

I could see a couple of dogs and a few cats. I imagined animals in the backyard, horses and alpacas, donkeys and sheep on the meadows behind the house. She would love to have her own little private animal farm. Our kids would inherit her love for animals.

This was the first time that something clicked inside my mind, like a vision of our future. Maybe she could really be happy out here with me. She could have her own private practice and do the work she so loved. We could be so happy together. I should have told her the truth sooner.

She walked over to the kitchen window and pointed at the small concrete shed and its steel door standing in the backyard, which led to the atomic shelter, and asked me what it was. I knew I should tell her now, but I couldn't. Not yet. Instead, I told her it was an old shed. She didn't really buy it, I could tell.

Before she could ask more questions, I kissed her passionately. The tension and heat inside her grew as I had expected. I took advantage of that moment to fuck her with my fingers right there, in my parents' kitchen. It was one of the hottest things I'd ever done. She moaned deeply and forgot all but her own drive to climax. She also forgot about the shed. For a moment I felt so blissfully content I almost forgot why we were here. But then reality returned.

Afterward, we filled our backpacks with the food we had

bought at the gas station, extra clothes, water, and protein bars. While packing, I remembered and rehearsed the practicalities in my head since this was the first time I would be going up there alone. Usually there was always someone with me.

The shelter had two steel doors, and each one had a separate lock and code. Those codes were only handed out to the shelter's insiders. I'd known them since I was a toddler. It was the first sequence of numbers my dad ever taught me, the one he made me repeat at any given moment, as a random test.

5—3—9—8—6 was the code for the outer door.

4—1—0—7—2 was the code for the inner door.

When I was a kid, I asked my dad why I had to remember them, when I could just as well write them down on paper?

He told me that people were unpredictable. That some of the preppers would try to get out in a panic. Once trapped in a devastating situation, all sorts of crazy things could happen, even wanting to escape the one thing that could save one's life, because people lost their common sense in times of stress. So if those codes would be lying around somewhere, someone would surely find them and use them, either to escape or to let strangers in who would be trying to seek shelter. That, too, is a valid risk that all preppers were wary of.

Dad had warned me multiple times that the world was a terrible and harsh place, and when it came to survival, people were the worst. It was our duty as doctors to help mankind for as long as we were physically able to do so. But when it came down to Doomsday, to choosing between family and friends or a group of total strangers, there was no choice to make at all. Only the prepared would be able to survive.

If mankind were to survive, it meant choosing the right people for the job. Survival of our species was imperative, no matter the cost. That is why we did what we did in the first place. Being back here reminded me of that. My faith in the greater good held firm.

We walked to the starting point of *Dead Man's Walk*, the infamous trail that thousands of people tried to conquer annually. Around this time of year, only the locals did it, as the tourist season was coming to an end.

If you wanted to do the whole trail to the top of the mountain, you would need about six to eight hours. But that was not my plan. The shelter lay about a two hours' walk up, halfway on the mountain, close to a road that would swirl around the mountain and was used mostly by tourist buses, mountain rangers, and locals. Tourists were not allowed to take their vehicles up the mountain on their own. It was just too dangerous to drive the narrow road.

At the trail's entrance, there were always security guards to monitor who was going up the mountain. They took down telephone numbers and emergency contact numbers, just in case something would happen. Visitors would also be warned that night fell quickly on the mountain and that they had to be back by five in winter and seven in summer. There were plenty of hikers who lost track of time and had to spend the night on the mountain.

When the hiker seemed too inexperienced, the security guards would recommend that they book a group hike and come back the next day. If they came prepared, they were allowed to go by themselves.

I was known in the area, just like my folks. Today, a guard named Lewis was on duty. He greeted me warmly. He told us how the mountain had been quite restless for a while and that the local geologists were investigating the cause. He blamed it on the volcano beneath the mountain, even though that had been dormant for tens of thousands of years. He was curious about Holly, whom I introduced as my girlfriend, before starting our hike.

The walk went smoothly. Once we were past the first steep area, we reached a point with some amazing views. Holly was in excellent condition and didn't stop to rest once, not even when the second steep part loomed in front of us. She was in better shape than I was.

I was so glad I had taken her up the mountain, just to see her reaction to the beauty and magnificence of this area. I saw my home through an outsider's eyes for the first time in my life, which was extraordinary. Growing up here, it was hard to recognize its beauty for what it was. It felt normal to me, hiking up the mountain without ever taking enough time to admire the gorgeous views. This particular area, known for its centuries-old pine trees, made me realize how small we were in the bigger scheme of things.

As we made our way up, the views became even more impressive, but it bothered me that the fog increased so quickly, which made it a lot colder on the mountain. I was worried about the fog, but when Holly insisted it was fine, we kept on going.

In ten minutes we would reach the shelter. The old familiar sense of urgency and nervousness returned in full force. My stress-induced headache returned in full force. I felt nauseated and weak, shivering at the thought that Holly would soon find out the truth.

This was it, the end of the line, the final test. There was no way back now. In a few minutes I would show her the passageway and the door leading to our shelter and monitor her reaction to both.

This was it. Accept or run. Never look back.

Or stay.

In my pocket, the emergency phone rang. Before we left, I had turned it on, remembering my mom's warnings. It was a sound I hadn't heard since that one time a year ago, when Dad called me out of the blue to warn me about something that wasn't that important at all. For minor stuff or regular chats, he would call me on my normal phone.

This was the most unwelcome sound ever.

I stood stunned, unable to move an inch. The phone lay in my hand as if it were a weapon. *Fuck.*

Holly turned around.

I didn't react. I couldn't pick it up. I just *couldn't.*

Holly walked over to me and tried to get my attention. I still wouldn't pick it up.

The sound stopped, only to start again. Holly frowned. She wanted to take the phone from my hand, but she didn't.

I looked at the trees covering the mountain, cast in fog. The weather was changing rapidly now, a lot quicker than I had imagined. I chided myself for not paying more attention to the changes. Something was very, very wrong.

A shiver ran down my spine, like an omen predicting something terrible was going to descend upon us. Something was on its way that could threaten our very lives. My first instinct was to run back down the mountain; my second one was to finally pick up that damned phone.

So I did.

Dad let out a sigh of relief. I put him on speaker, so that Holly could listen in. Dad was talking loud enough for her to hear anyhow.

The line cracked while he spoke. I could barely hear what he was saying. This had to be some kind of joke, a prank he was pulling on me. A test. He knew I was taking Holly up the mountain, so he invented some crazy-ass test to scare her off. This was just what he would do, his way of *helping me out.* But then why was he talking so urgently? I'd only ever heard him speak this way when it was really bad.

Dad's voice was hard to understand. I heard words here and there. *Shelter. Go. Safety.* The connection was so bad that I could hardly make sense of what he was saying. But I did hear the most important things. *The mountain's rumbling. The volcano is active. Shelter.*

Dad's voice was cut off; the connection was dead. Fuck, what was going on? This couldn't be happening. It just *couldn't* be true. Dad had to be making a mistake.

But it wasn't a mistake at all.

A rumbling sound surrounded us, echoing against the mountain walls. I had never heard anything like it before. It came from the heart of the mountain, as if giant dwarfs that came straight out of *The Lord of the Rings* were digging into the stone walls with their axes.

Holly looked at me with this horrified look on her face, proving to me that she had felt it too. This was not my imagination. This was very much real.

We had to do something. *I* had to take the lead on this one. Mom and Dad weren't here, and there was no one to guide me in this decision-making process. There was only one choice to make, and in my heart, I felt it was the right one. I had to save Holly.

Something clicked inside my head.

This was what I had been practicing for. My mind went

into this bizarre state of focus. I could feel a sense of urgency take over. Everything else became pointless. I had two options.

1) Taking Holly off the mountain would be the most logical choice to make, but also the riskiest one. It would take us forever to get to safety. Who knew what could happen in an hour and a half? We could get stuck or covered by lava, if the volcano was to blame.

2) Taking her to the shelter could mean a certain survival, as I had been taught for years. The shelter was sturdy, well equipped, and could survive any event unless the mountain would collapse onto itself, which would take an E.L.E. And even then, it might outlive that disaster, as we all hoped. Only a real-life situation would test that theory.

Maybe we were facing an *Extinction Level Event.* Maybe it was a volcano eruption. It could be an earthquake, or a series of them. It could be local or global. Whatever it was, it was not a drill this time.

Option number two it was.

The mountain rumbled again. Holly grabbed me tight as the ground shook beneath us. It stopped within a few seconds, but it was enough to send my thoughts reeling. I told Holly we had to go and started walking up the hiking trail to the shelter's pathway.

The blue air had slowly but surely turned into something sinister and gray. Clouds had formed, and rain was slowly falling from above us. The ground beneath us trembled again. It was scary as hell.

She didn't come after me. She just stood there, watching me as if I'd turned into a stranger. Then she turned around and walked back to where we came from at a steady and fast pace. I ran back to her, yelling that I was trying to save her life. She looked at me like I was a total stranger.

The ground beneath our feet trembled again, which made her sway on her feet. She screamed. I pulled her with me, but she was panicking by now. When I flipped her around, she tripped and fell, landing hard on her back. She gasped as her gloved hands scratched the surface of the rocks beneath her. She sat dazed, confused, and scared out of her mind. Her eyes betrayed how her good mood had turned into cold fear in a matter of seconds.

Words were pointless; time was running out. The world started rumbling, the clouds turned darker, a storm was breaking. The rocks trembled. Every instinct told me to head down the mountain too, to follow Holly. But I didn't. My dad had told me to head to the shelter, and I always did what I was told.

I pulled Holly roughly on her feet and dragged her up the hiking trail. She fought back. She kicked, screamed, hollered, and struggled. I treated her badly, but what choice did I have?

I dragged her to the shelter, pushed her through the hidden passageway to the steel door that lead to the shelter and opened the keypad attached to the door.

The reality of our situation pushed me into a state of calm frenzy. I needed to be careful now. I had three attempts to unlock the door before it went into safety mode and I wouldn't be able to get us in at all.

I tapped in the right code without a single hesitation. The heavy steel door slid open. Despite her protests, I dragged Holly inside. The door closed; an emergency light flickered on. I opened the second door in the exact same way.

When it slid open, I gave Holly a push. She fell forward, on her hands. The door closed behind us.

We were safe.

TWO

I stood heaving in the darkness of the shelter, with Holly somewhere next to me, my hand still around her wrist in a desperate attempt to keep her safe. My headache increased, I felt terrible now that the adrenaline rush wore off.

I couldn't let go of her, not yet. It was too dangerous to release her without knowing what she would do next. She couldn't be trusted to make the right decision just yet. Tension radiated off her.

She was scared. Of course she was.

She was upset.

She was devastated.

And I was angry at myself. Fuck, this was not the way it was supposed to happen. I messed up so badly.

She sniffled. Her anxiety turned her into one big mess. She was on the verge of a massive panic attack. This was not Holly Hayes anymore, but a shadow of the woman that I had fallen in love with. I knew I only had myself to blame. I felt the anger, the fear, the disbelief. She would never understand my actions.

But her sadness and shock didn't change anything. I still knew that I would never let her go. My actions would save her life, whether she accepted them or not. It was my duty to protect her from what was out there and right now I didn't care that she hated me for it.

If my dad hadn't called, things would have been totally different. I could have taken the time to explain everything to her, from the moment we reached the rocky slab, to the opening of the steel doors behind them. I would have told her about the codes that opened those doors and the way that things had been set up for years. I could have told her the history about this place, how my great-grandfather and his brothers had found the hollow cave and decided that this would be a great place to set up a tsunami-proof shelter.

I could have made her see that our way of life was a safe one and that it was okay to feel imminent threats hovering like a shadow over your existence every single day. That it was a good thing to know when to run or to feel afraid when some president threatened the world with nuclear bombs. It was all okay because we had the perfect backup plan. Meaning that nothing could ever happen to us.

Years ago, back in the late fifties, when the world was still recovering from one of the worst wars there had ever been and with the dangers of nuclear weapons upon us, a lot of people were suddenly creating these atomic shelters that would protect them against whatever would happen next. With the Russians becoming a threat post-war and the battle for nuclear warfare so imminently dominating the world's gloomy prospects, it seemed logical.

Only to realize it was not enough when a tragedy occurred in the early sixties and my great-grandfather was there to witness it. An unpredicted flood had washed away a town on the other side of the mountain. That flood was caused by an earthquake. Hundreds of people perished because they weren't equipped against this natural disaster. The shelters weren't enough.

If another flooding occurred, survivors would have to go higher up to be safe. So a number of men went up the mountains and started searching for these natural caves. My great-grandfather led the investigative party. They researched the mountain until they found a cave that was large enough for multiple families. The cave was rudimentary when they discovered it, but everyone saw the potential to turn it into a fully functional doomsday shelter.

The men worked hard to broaden the cave, so that it became big enough for about thirty people. Then they added interior walls and doors and made sure that it was stocked to the brim with supplies. But still, the cave remained very rudimentary and, frankly, difficult to survive in for days, let alone weeks, months, or years.

In the eighties, my grandfather's brother, who was a scientist, came up with all these cool ideas on how to create a functional shelter, including a generator. That became the first step toward something that could be seen as functional survival.

Twenty years ago, my dad and his cousins did the rest. The generator was connected to this intelligent wiring system that could use regular electricity, but since the mountain's wiring was unpredictable, gasoline was still needed at times.

A spare generator was added to take over in case the first one failed. A third, and smaller, generator could be used as additional backup. The wiring system was expanded, and the generators were adapted so that they became easier to use and scarcely needed gasoline.

From then on, things improved quickly. With all the new technology being developed, there were plenty of improvements to be made. Even the food supplies lasted longer now. Every year, some kind of improvement was added to the cave.

Today, it could be called modern, as if we were sitting in a government bunker that would protect those who needed to stay safe. The only thing we didn't have was the typical government computers and connections to the outside world. That remained a big issue. Once in here, there was no way to connect to the outside world. We would literally be cut off.

The cave lay embedded deep in the heart of the mountain, and the stone walls were too thick. That was the one thing we could never fix, not even with today's modern equipment. Behind the steel doors, not a single phone worked. There was no radio system that could penetrate the rocks. And since we were not a government institution, that would most likely never happen.

The rocks kept the cold out and the warmth in. It was actually pretty comfortable temperature wise. We had created it as a home for those who would want to stay here in case of emergency of their own free will. The one thing I had always been convinced of was that the people who came to live here needed to *want* to live here.

But what I didn't know was how someone would react if they were forced to stay here against their will. That had never happened before.

I couldn't tell Holly all of that now; she wouldn't understand. There were other things to deal with first. She would need time to process what had just happened, and I felt the urgent need to explain myself to her. It was normal to be afraid. Nothing about this cave was normal to begin with, so she had every right to be frightened.

But I would still keep her here.

A long time ago, Allison and I came up to the cave to count the supplies. It was in the middle of summer, and I was sixteen. We were kind of an item, but not officially yet. Both prepper kids, eager to continue the good work our parents had started.

One of our first dates, if you could call it that, was going to the shelter and making an inventory of all the stuff that was in here. It was something that needed to be done every year, and that year, it was our first time doing it.

We had this very long list of supplies with us and needed to check the expiry dates on every single can and wrapping. The ones that were about to expire would be brought down the mountain by others; the ones that were still okay, we kept in the shelter.

Most of the food here wasn't something you would eat every day. There were a lot of protein-rich foods, and a lot of conserved stuff such as black beans, peas, or carrots. There was tons of crackers, rice, and pasta, but no potatoes, because you couldn't keep them for long. There was dried and canned meat.

As a backup plan, there was also some astronaut food, but they always told us this would only be eaten if the rest was gone. Which, so they said, would probably not happen, as it would take years to run out of supplies.

As a kid, I had often imagined myself living here and eating nothing but this unhealthy stuff. I didn't want to know what it would be like to have no access to fresh fruit and vegetables, but that would be the prospect of someone living here.

Allison and I never spoke about it. We just went with the flow and did what we were asked to do. I had asked her once if she thought we would ever experience an *E.L.E.* She looked at me as if I had lost my mind. Then confessed she didn't know what an E.L.E. was, which was not totally illogical.

Allison came from a family that participated in the preppers community, but they weren't as actively involved as some of us. Her mom worked out of town, her dad couldn't work because he had a severe physical disability after an accident on the job. He couldn't function without heavy pain medication, so he was relieved of his job with a golden handshake that would support them for the rest of his life.

No one had ever told her in any detail what we could be facing in the near or distant future. I told her what my dad had explained a long time ago. How there were several possible disaster scenarios, like earthquakes or volcano eruptions or a nuclear attack. But the worst one is an *Extinction Level Event.* That one was a game changer, like the comet that eventually destroyed the dinosaurs.

But an E.L.E. could also be a massive earthquake or volcano eruption, possibly followed by a huge tsunami, like the one that happened years ago in Asia and killed hundreds of thousands of people. That was one of the worst ever. The tsunami wasn't caused by a meteorite but by an underground, oceanic earthquake. An event like that could wipe out several US states at the same time.

The thing about meteorites and volcanic outbursts and all was that they only partially destroyed the world when they happened. It was mostly the fallout of such an event that would cause the biggest destruction. And as mankind wasn't as physically strong as dinosaurs, the destruction wouldn't take as long either.

Aliens, by the way, were not part of our conviction. We left that to other conspiracy theorists.

We did get tested in different ways. Dad always said the

adults had to keep their kids on their toes. Alison told me she had been pulled out of bed on several occasions and that she didn't like it but endured it.

My dad never did this to me. He was always open about everything, and he had promised me he would never force me to do anything against my will. So when he called me, I always took it very seriously.

Like that one time, two years ago.

In my first year in college, he called me up in the middle of the night. He used the emergency phone, just like he had done now. It was the one and only time he ever did. I was in Minneapolis three weeks, if I remember correctly.

He started screaming that something was on its way to Minneapolis, and I needed to leave my dorm room at once. I was a kid, too young to take care of myself in an emergency situation, but there it was. That moment that would define my life.

I asked about my parents, holding back my anxiety so I could focus. A panic attack rose to the surface, but I fought back and got it under control. He said they were going to the mountain shelter. I admired the way my dad retained his cool. I almost lost mine when he told me to get the hell out of there.

I hadn't connected with anyone back in Minneapolis at that point. I wasn't part of the local community yet, and I hadn't spoken to anyone that could help me. Roland wasn't in my life yet either. I was all alone.

I didn't have anywhere to go because he hadn't told me, so I just put on some clothes, left the room, and drove miles into the countryside heading for Montana, only to realize about two hours later that a) I had forgotten all about Harry and 2) there was nothing going on. I was alone on the road, driving a hundred miles per hour, going out of my mind with fear. Until I discovered, once my thoughts reorganized themselves and my vision cleared, that the world was still there.

There were no fires from the skies descending on us, no earthquakes shattering the concrete slabs that we called roads, no tsunamis washing over us, no tornadoes tearing apart houses. The world was as it always was.

I parked the car on the side of the empty road in the middle of nowhere and allowed the panic attack that had been fighting its way to the surface to take over. It crashed over me so hard that I nearly passed out. I saw spots in front of my eyes, felt my heart beat so fast in my chest I thought I was going to die right there and then, and I felt my entire body cling together in this weird version of myself that I could not control.

I don't remember how long I was out for when darkness finally came for me, but it must have been at least half an hour to an hour. When I woke up, I was still out there in the darkness by myself, with no one to help me. The road I was on, and the area I was in, were that isolated.

Once I had calmed down enough to drive safely, which took at least another hour, I returned home, but I didn't feel safe at all. I drove believing with all my heart that at any given moment, something would open the ground below me and swallow me whole. But it never did and when I returned to Minnesota around five a.m., the city was asleep like it had been when I left. The only thing betraying its early morning awakening were the garbage trucks collecting yesterday's dumps.

Everything was just fine, and I cried as I drove to the campus parking lot. Around six a.m., I snuck into the dorm where Harry was still sound asleep.

I sat down on my bed, going through a second panic attack while muffling my mouth, until I was capable of lying down without feeling like I was going to die. This time, I didn't pass out.

I fell asleep believing that I would never wake up again and that I had made a terrible mistake by returning to Minneapolis. The buildings could collapse at any given moment, or the predicted firestorm would kill us all in the most gruesome and painful way possible.

For days on end after that incident, I woke up relieved that the world around us still existed and that I was still breathing. I had several panic attacks per day, fortunately not in class. Harry nor my friends on campus ever knew what had happened. Harry probably didn't even realize that I'd been gone. If he did, he never told me. Or maybe he thought I was having sex with someone.

I felt embarrassed and angry, the latter most of all. Once the panic attacks subsided and I was calm enough to talk to my dad, we spoke over the phone. The days before I had ghosted him, not able to speak with him without yelling at him. He had tried to call me several times, but I had denied him the privilege of talking to me until I was well enough to reply to whatever bullshit he was going to feed me.

He knew what had happened since I had left a long voice message telling him to go fuck himself, not in those words. My words were clear enough to express how I felt about my nightly trip.

When we finally spoke again, he apologized profusely and told me the signals had been read all wrong and how he hadn't expected me to panic in such a way. He ensured me it had not been a test because he had always promised not to do that to me. From then on, he continued sending me messages in case something would occur, but not before making sure that it was serious.

That moment defined my decision to connect with the local preppers community, so that I would at least know where the nearest shelters were. Dad had been so apologetic that there was no doubt in my mind he meant well. It was a simple misjudgment of the situation, and I couldn't stay upset.

Things quickly went back to normal. It never happened again, except for once, right at the beginning of my relationship with Holly, who had believed my story about always carrying emergency phones with us since we lived near the mountains. Dad called me to warn me, in one breath saying that the signs were unclear and it might as well be nothing, but how I should prepare myself in case it did become *something*.

The past three years, there were signals and small things, but nothing out of the ordinary and nothing that differed from the telltale signs we'd been seeing for years. There was never any indication to panic.

I had gotten lazy.

I had allowed myself to believe that I could lead a normal life, like anyone else.

I had assumed that being with Holly would chase away the demons somehow.

I had believed for a fact that my preppers future would be to check the shelter now and then, to make sure that everything was okay, and to continue living a relatively normal life.

I was wrong about everything.

Nothing would ever be normal for me. Never. That was the price one had to pay for being with me and I hated it. I detested it with a vengeance, but I still could not help it. I couldn't avoid it.

That defining phone call from my dad changed everything, and Holly and I both felt it. It brought me back to my true purpose in life and the reason why I was studying medicine in the first place. I had been preparing for this very moment my entire life. There wasn't a single doubt in my mind that this was not a drill.

THREE

As soon as I let go of her, Holly rushed to a corner of the room and sat slumped with her back against the racks of canned food, cowering away as if I had just beaten her up. She was scared while I was battling my own demons. I was not capable of helping her right now and I knew it.

Let her go, a small voice in the back of my head called out. *Let her go, it's what she wants.* But the mountain rumbled, and I knew I couldn't do it. I couldn't set her free.

Holly was too scared to be coherent, so I decided to get things started according to the preppers plan I knew by heart. Turn on the lights first because it makes people feel more comfortable knowing they won't be spending their days in the dark. Make sure everyone's okay. Avoid panic at all costs as this will cause more distress. Holly was the only one I needed to comfort, and that was a good thing. It allowed me to focus on her.

In the main area of our shelter were a couple of decent lights. They flickered, which slightly concerned me. The electrical wiring circuit still functioned, but maybe it wouldn't be enough to support the lights at some point, depending on what was going on out there and how much the wiring system was affected.

When I turned around, Holly stood with her gloved hands pressed against her chest. I could see her breath whenever she exhaled. She was freezing. It was a lot colder here than it was out there because the generators were only used when people came here to restock the shelter.

I opened the door to the generator room and started the main machine, which would produce the warmth we so desperately need. Back in the main living area, Holly glared at me. Her fear was replaced with anger.

She fired dozens of questions at me, so fast I barely had time to process them. She had every right to ask me anything, but my head spun and I could barely cope. Part of me didn't understand it either. I had assumed by now that she already knew what this place was. It seemed pretty obvious, but apparently it was not.

I told her that everything was fine and taken care of, but in truth I wanted to confess that I needed her comfort just as much as she needed mine. She would probably mock me for it.

I made an attempt to hug and comfort her, but she struck me in the face with her gloved hand. The slap echoed loudly and rattled me. It didn't hurt. She didn't even hit me that hard, but it shocked me so much that I stumbled backward.

Off she went, on an unstoppable tirade that proved I would never get her to see my point of view. It was just impossible to deal with her right now. She accused me of kidnapping her, threw all these horrible accusations my way. God. She wouldn't stop. Why wouldn't she stop? My head hurt.

She finally looked around the cave, taking in the large tables and chairs and the adjoined kitchen with all its basic necessities.

The area was large, spacious and had plenty of light. There were couches in a separate area and shelves stacked with books in different genres and for all ages. There were iPods with thousands of songs and enough batteries to keep them running for years. Everything had been foreseen to live a comfortable life, even if it meant having to eat canned food for years and not seeing the light of day for a long time.

There wasn't a single crack in the rocks to provide us with external sunlight, not one way to catch a glimpse of the outside world. That had always been a point of concern for my dad, who was worried about the survivors' eyes once they left the cave after a long period of being locked up. When someone wasn't used to staying indoors all the time with nothing but artificial light at their disposal, it would damage their eyes.

While Holly looked around, I tried to formulate an explanation in my head that would not shock her too much, but when she turned around, I could tell she had finally realized what was going on. She voiced her findings with such disdain it broke my heart. I couldn't help but cringe. She noticed that, but she didn't care. She was angry at the injustice of being locked up and me acting as her prison guard.

The whys, the hows and the whos came at me as if I was being shot at by a firing squad. And I was so tired. I just wanted to get some rest, to switch off that button inside my head that made it hard for me to focus.

I was scared. I needed my dad here with me. I needed his advice. His mentorship. I might have been an adult, but I wasn't mature enough to make it out here on my own. I never once believed that I would end up in this shelter by myself. In my mind's eye, he would always be here with me, taking charge of whatever needed to be done. Not a single moment had I considered that I would be the one taking the lead.

Holly's reaction, her contempt, sadness, and anger were a mirror for my soul. I sucked at leadership, just as I had failed the boyfriend test. *You should have told her,* that voice in my head said. *You could have avoided this whole mess.*

I should have. Could have. But I didn't. This whole mess was on me, and I was lost. Without my dad's advice, I was a nobody. Without my mom's support, I didn't know how to calm down Holly. I wasn't ready for this.

This morning, I was still a college student going home for the first time with his girlfriend, who, admittedly, was not accepted by his parents. But that had not persuaded me to *not* go.

I had feared Mom's reaction to Holly a lot more than my dad's. He always remained calm, no matter the subject he addressed. Yeah, he could be fierce in his tales but never sharp in his use of words. Mom, however, never was the easiest of mothers. She was set in her ways, clung to her own definitions of what life and love were all about. She was determined to make the best out of every crappy situation we found ourselves in and adamant about protecting those she cared about the most.

Working on the mountain had made her fierce and cynical. She would rage against those that didn't do as required. She would snap at the security guards if they slacked or didn't follow her set of rules. She would go off against lazy tourists who had no respect for the mountains. But she was also the sweetest and best mom whenever it was needed. Despite our different characters, she had accepted me for who I was. I was the shy boy, the quiet one, the kid that only needed a couple of friends and not a whole circle.

Whenever I got in trouble, which was rare, she didn't snap at me or tell me that I was a bad boy or a lousy kid. She always rewarded me when I did a good thing and gently reprimanded me when I did something bad.

Holly was a mix of my parents. She could be fierce and sharp when it was needed, sweet and gentle when it came to everything else. She knew what she wanted from life, and she worked hard to get it. I shared more with Holly than I had done with my parents. She and I were kind of the same, except for the fierce and sharp part, that is. When it came to arguments, I was the one who left the room because I didn't want to get into a fight. So I waited for her to calm down significantly, knowing that she would need some time to do so.

I was right. After a while, she finally settled down enough for me to explain to her what was going on. She looked at me as if I had suddenly sprouted horns when I explained about the possible disaster taking place right now. She brushed it off, mocked it, denied it. She reacted sarcastically. I'd lied to her, she said. I told her it wasn't technically a lie to withhold information.

I got distracted when the mountain shook and the floors, ceiling and walls trembled along with it. Even the cans stood shaking on their shelves. This had happened before, but not to such an extent. It frightened me, but I kept that to myself. No one had ever recounted stories about these tremors before. This was new, and it was scary.

Holly tried to persuade me on multiple occasions to let her go because I usually let her have her way. Not this time, though. Out there, the world was dangerous. In here, she would survive.

She tried to open the doors. She failed. She tried to persuade me to hand her the codes, but I refused. Never, I said. I wouldn't do it, despite her urgent insistence that I should.

She pushed my buttons, and I got so angry. So damned

angry. I yelled at her. She recoiled.

Fuck.

The moment I shouted, I already regretted it. My voice sounded hard through the empty room, echoing against the sturdy walls.

She turned into this small person, withdrawing in herself. I seemed to grow taller as I barked at her. She backed away. I apologized.

I told her that her parents were probably already dead, that she would never see her sister again. The look on her face was devastating.

I hated myself.

I hated who I had become.

But she still would not be able to get out, not as long as I lived.

I couldn't breathe. My anxiety grew to an unbearable level. I felt sick and trembled. If this was going to continue to happen, this would end up in tragedy.

And then something changed between us. I didn't even know how it happened exactly, but it did. Holly calmed down to the point she started listening to me. She didn't yell anymore, didn't beg to get out. She actually listened.

I think it started when I could finally get through to her. Her fear was gone, and her sympathy returned. I was ashamed of what I'd done to her, so I backed away to give her the space she needed. She came to me and asked me to talk about it.

We did.

She told me she loved me. That was the best moment of my life. I could suddenly breathe again, as if she had given me fresh oxygen to recover. Even with the shaking walls making it hard for me to focus, I was able to rejoice.

She promised me she would stop fighting, and she did. She calmed down so much that I was able to show her around the shelter for the first time and convince her that there were reasons why we were here right now. She seemed taken aback, but then she started listening to me.

Before long, she started asking the right questions. Hope flared. If I could convince her that there were valid reasons to keep us here, she would understand.

My fear turned into hope. Hope turned into a belief that our future together still stood a chance. She listened to my stories about our community, and I told her the ins and outs.

But she still wouldn't believe that something was happening out there, not even when the walls shook and the cave did not behave the way it should.

I wanted to believe her so badly. I really did. Part of me started questioning if I hadn't overreacted, if she wasn't right about the improbability of this being our new reality after millions of years. But the mountain shook and I couldn't risk killing her life by allowing her to go outside.

So we stayed.

And she adapted. We had a quiet, peaceful dinner using the supplies at hand and according to the preppers' rules. There was plenty of food, but we had to use it sparingly, so we ate what we'd taken with us, combined with a meal of rice and tuna.

She listened as I talked about my life before today, my parents, the fear that took over my existence so many times, and the ultimate anguish that had taken over my thoughts from the moment we got here.

I was scared of fucking things up. I was horrified that my wrongdoing could get her killed. I was sad that I had hurt her so much. My constant stress was making me physically sick, but I hid that part from her. I couldn't confide in her about the way my body seemed to battle against the constant anxiety and panic attacks that were lingering at the surface.

I didn't want to pass out in front of her, but I yearned for some peace, quiet and rest. Even in the quiet of the cave, this voice in my head screamed at me to calm the fuck down, to go lie down, to find solace in the silence of the cave. But I didn't tell her that, because the conversation we were having was too important to cut short.

This was the defining moment, and it could change everything. When she told me she still loved me, I could have wept from happiness. I was so exhausted.

I was supposed to keep Holly Hayes on her feet, to protect her against the world. Instead, she was protecting me in every way possible.

When she asked me to stay with her during the night, I happily obliged, even though my mind was trapped in an uneasy state of its own, until I made my decision.

I impulsively told her I would give her the codes. That I would grant her the freedom she so desired, if she would give me just one week. I had my reasons for asking for seven days. I figured that, if my dad discovered that the world was still okay, he would come up the mountain to get us out. We probably wouldn't have to stay here for a week. He could be here in a day or two at the most.

If a week passed and nothing happened, then it probably meant that I had been right all along and that we were going through a terrible event. In that case, Holly would have to see it with her own eyes. If I opened the door after a week and she witnessed it for herself, she would accept her new reality without protest and we could live here for a long time while the world out there recovered. Hopefully, once we got out, there would be other survivors and we could reconnect.

Holly was thrilled. She was so happy I could cry.

We went to bed together that night, which I had never dared hope would happen after everything that went down today. But when she quickly fell asleep, exhausted as she was, I lay awake for hours, wondering if I had done the right thing.

Holly made a valid point. I should at least check to make sure, but I was too scared to do so. If I opened those doors and something terrible was going on out there, we could be dead in seconds.

With a plan settling in my head, I managed to get some sleep.

FOUR

I woke up feeling like crap in an empty bed. Holly was gone; I heard her rummaging in the kitchen. I lay back in bed listening to her familiar sounds, not ready yet to get out and face another day in our harsh reality.

I was covered in sweat; my head was bursting. A splitting pain shot through me each time I tried to move. The aches increased every time I decided to get a move on, so I wound up staying in bed for a lot longer than I wanted to.

Finally, I managed to lift myself out of bed, but the cold crept through my system, making me ache even more. I didn't need to be a future doctor to realize I was coming down with something. Or maybe I had been sick for the past few days as well, which would explain my constant headaches.

My throat hurt, and I felt queasy. Great. This was the worst time ever to get sick, especially with Holly cooped up in here with me. If I infected her too, we would be two miserable people living in a terrible situation.

Holly welcomed me when I shuffled into the kitchen. Her cheerful hello changed into concern when I told her how awful I felt. She sprung into doctor mode at once and ordered me to go lie down. I complied, knowing there was nothing I could do right now but rest. As I lay down on the couch feeling awful, sleep overwhelmed me instantly.

I had this dream, and somehow I knew it wasn't real while I went through the motions.

We were no longer at the shelter but in my parents' home, sitting at the dinner table. My mom had cooked a wonderful Thanksgiving meal. She placed the food on the table while my dad, Holly, and I raved about her work. Mom sat down with a beatific smile on her face and told us to dig in.

But then, as we were eating, she said that this would be the last meal we'd ever have together because we had run out of supplies and the world was coming to an end in an hour.

I looked outside the window apprehensively, but there was nothing to see. The world was normal again, except that the mountains seemed to have grown in size and the skies turned dark while I watched them.

I was pulled out of the dream into real life again. I came to and found Holly shaking me awake to get medication in me. My heart was pounding in my chest; I felt as if a sledgehammer had knocked me over the head. It was the worst feeling ever.

When she ordered me to eat, I obliged. I wanted to get back to sleep, even with the prospect of weird dreams, but she wouldn't let me because my fever was spiking.

Standing in the shower with her as she rinsed me down in hopes of beating the fever, I focused on her to stay awake. Slowly, the Tylenol she had given me from our medicine cabinet started working a bit. She dried me off and helped me in bed. I couldn't help but sigh in relief before I fell asleep.

I was instantly back in my parents' house, with my mom serving her fantastic Thanksgiving dinner. More food was on the table this time, too much to choose from. There were other people too. My great-uncles, some cousins, a couple of friends. Allison. Everyone was having a fantastic time. We were all talking loudly and Holly held my hand in hers, so I could only eat with the other one.

Eat up, my mom said. It's time to die.

I looked at her in shock, but everyone else, even Holly, just smiled, nodded, and started shoveling food in their mouths. Soon enough, the entire table was cleared of food. All the plates were empty and the dishes gone.

Great, my mom said. We were right on time to see the end of the world. I got out of my chair and walked to the window. Holly came to stand beside me. I put my arm around her shoulders.

A huge fireball came straight at us. I looked aside to see everyone in the room evaporate. My parents were first, followed by our friends and family members. Holly and I were the last ones to go.

There was this bright flash that became an overwhelming fire that seemed to burn from within. It hurt like nothing else. The pain split my head, devoured my consciousness, took every part of me.

I woke up quivering, sick to the bone. I made it just in time to the bathroom, only to find Holly behind me, gently touching my back, before holding a washcloth against my forehead to cool me down.

I got back into bed somehow and slept.

More dreams.

In every possible dream, we all died. The next one had us standing on top of the mountain. Holly and I were there, watching the starry skies, until smoke and dark clouds came from the foot of the mountain and reached us way up where we were.

I looked down to find the mountain split open. I saw a huge sea of fire, as if we were facing the fires of Mordor, like Frodo and Sam had. We fell into the endless night, until the dormant volcano, which wasn't so dormant anymore, consumed us.

Every time I woke up startled, as if an electric shock had run through me. Every time I sank into crazy dreams again. It felt like this endless, unstoppable loop.

I couldn't think. Couldn't focus. Couldn't do anything but suffer. The pain was too awful to bear, and I felt myself slip away.

I was dying.

My mind was telling me through feverish, dark dreams that I was so sick I wouldn't survive whatever it was that had taken over my body in such a short period of time. This was more than just a headache, more than just being sick.

Meningitis.

I knew it, even in my feverish dreams. My brain was all muddled; my body could barely move anymore. This disease was pushing aside every rational thought.

Bacterial meningitis was lethal, unless treated urgently in a hospital. I didn't stand a chance in here, under these circumstances. I would be dead in a few days.

And that would leave Holly locked up in here, which was her worst fear. I had to make sure she got out. But then I fell asleep again, and when I dreamed, everything else faded away.

When I woke up in between dark dreams, I remembered what I had to do. I had to tell her the codes. But I couldn't remember them.

I was so sick they were gone from my mind.

I screamed and woke up.

Holly was there. She begged me for the codes. I couldn't give them to her. They were just gone.

More medication, more sleep. More nightmares.

I fell asleep wondering if I would ever wake up again.

It's the end of the world as we know it.

My mom sang the lyrics while she put dessert on the table. Ice cream with strawberries and whipped cream.

In this dream, we had made it past the main course. I was no longer choking on turkey or getting engulfed by fire while sitting at the table next to Holly.

My dad walked out of the kitchen carrying Baked Alaska. He started singing alongside Mom as he put her creation on the table.

She said she wanted to watch Independence Day. He said he preferred The Day After Tomorrow. Holly chimed in saying she preferred A Quiet Place. My uncle chose Deep Impact. Allison wanted to see Melancholia.

I said nothing.

I just got up and closed the drapes, so we wouldn't have to watch the world explode while eating dessert.

I did wake up.

I woke up feeling a lot better, which was the oddest feeling after all these weird dreams. It gave me hope that things would start to improve from now on. Holly was by my side reading a book. She didn't even realize I was awake, so I had time to watch her. I had never seen anything more beautiful.

When she looked up, spotting me watching her, she smiled the biggest smile I had ever seen. She was as relieved as I felt. I was doing better, which meant it was probably just some bug and not meningitis. It couldn't be.

The fog cluttering my brain was slowly lifting. Parts of the codes started coming back to me. I was even hungry, and when I told her that, she hurried to get some toast. I told her about my recurrent dream of a comet striking our very planet.

While I ate some toast, I confessed to her that one thing had become quite clear to me while dreaming. That it was useless staying here, when us being here was just as dangerous as facing the world out there. My sudden bout of illness had proved that. If I had died, she would have been trapped here with no way out. It was an unforgivable thought.

Holly said she wanted to open the doors, leave the shelter, and find a place to make an emergency call, assuming there still was a world out there. If there wasn't, we would have to deal with it. I didn't want her to go out on her own, but I was too sick to hike down the mountain with her. Even the conversation wore me down.

Unfortunately, my bout of lucidity didn't last long. While we talked, I could feel the brain fog reappearing. I had difficulty staying awake, as if someone had injected me with a sleeping aid and my body was struggling to stay awake.

I went out like a light.

A voice spoke to me.

You need to give me the codes.

Give me the codes.

Dyl, hon, give me the codes.

The codes. It's important that you give them to me.

Do you remember the codes?

Silence. Followed by that same voice.

You've got to wake up now.

Come on, you need to get back to me now, Dyl.

Don't do this to me, okay?

You have to remember that I need you.
You're the only one who can get us out of there.

Silence. Darkness. Followed by more pleading.

Without you, there's no tomorrow for me either.
If you're gone, I'm gone too.
Don't do that to us, okay?
Wake up for me.

I was trapped in the abyss between life and death, and death was slowly but surely winning. I lost all sense of time and being.

There was this cold darkness, followed by the strange awareness that maybe it would be better for me not to wake up ever again.

The voice spoke again.

Dylan, wake up.
Come on.
Stop being so goddamn stubborn.
I can't do this on my own, you know that.

Silence.

I hate you, do you know that?

I hate myself too.

I hate that you didn't listen to me. You should have listened to me!

Then the voice stopped talking. The sound faded away. I

felt a strange shaking, followed by a lot of noise. It was the oddest feeling.

There was a very long silence where I couldn't move at all. There were no dreams left. There was only this strange sense of abandonment.

The owner of the voice had left me, and I was all alone in this terrible, cold place where the souls of the dead were already standing in line, waiting for me to join them.

I couldn't move and was mute, so I couldn't tell them that I was afraid and didn't want to go yet. That I wanted to return to Holly and save her first. But I couldn't do anything.

It became more difficult to breathe, hard to resist the ultimate darkness. I just needed to make a few more steps forward, and then it would be over. But there was something near me that stopped me from going to the dark realm of the souls.

Someone was near me, lingering over me, touching me, stopping me from crossing that final line.

After a long while, the voice returned. I now recognized it as Holly's. She was close to me.

You're a jerk, you know that?

I couldn't answer.

We're going to die, aren't we?

Yes, we were.

I wish you could disagree.

I wish I could tell you that it didn't hurt to die.

I'm sorry that I put you through all this.
I'm sorry I didn't believe you.

Wait, what?

I'm sorry I couldn't save your life.

The strange sense of not being able to breathe anymore became overwhelming. There was something terribly wrong with Holly.

But there was nothing I could do for her.

We should get some sleep. It'll be over soon.

The voice faded away. Until I heard it behind me, in the abyss. I turned around to find Holly standing right there. I walked over to her and reached for her hands.

She was home.

Dear reader,

You have now read Dylan's story and his version of events on the mountain.

From this point on, choose what you want to read next.

1. Read Holly's story. In that case, go to the front of the book.
2. Finished Holly's story already and want to read her version of events on the mountain? Go to page 95.
3. Finished both storylines and want to find out what happens next? Keep on reading.

HOW TO SURVIVE
HOW TO SURVIVE

A BROKEN HEART

Holly

Was it a dream? Or was I in limbo, waiting for Death to pick me up and claim me as his next victim?

Everything was as jumbled as my existence in the shelter had been. I was confused when I walked through the darkness, trying to find a way forward. Or backward.

I wasn't alone at all. Dylan was there with me.

In fact, he had already been there when I started my descent into the silent darkness. He had been waiting for me.

But then he said the oddest thing.

"I know you want to be here with me, but it's too soon. You have to fight your way back. You have to hold on, Hol."

"Why?" I said. "Why should I fight when you're already here?"

"Because they're on their way. Dad's almost at the shelter, Hol. He'll find you and save you. You can't wait for him to come for you. You need to help him too."

"Neither can you," I insisted. "You have to hold on with me."

"It's too late for me. I'll be dead before they find us."

"You can't know that."

"I do know. Please let me go."

"No."

"Holly…"

"I said no! If you don't come back with me, I'll give up too."

He looked at me with sad eyes.

"It isn't that simple. I'm too sick. I'm dying."

"I don't care. You're stronger than this."

"Please, Holly."

"No. Fuck you, Dylan. If you think I'm going to spend the rest of my life mourning you, forget it. You are going back with me."

He hesitated. He turned around, staring in the dark abyss that was laid out in front of us. He was so sick, so weak. But he smiled when he looked back at me.

"Do you really think I stand a chance?"

"I know it."

"Then I'll hold on for you."

I woke up startled and with a headache so severe I thought it would send me straight back into the abyss. Everything around me seemed jumbled somehow. The room spun in front of my eyes; I had trouble thinking straight. Breathing properly seemed a privilege.

The generator. We were still here, at the shelter, trapped inside this clusterfuck. Nothing had changed, no miracles had happened. We were still in grave danger. The world out there might still be gone.

Miracles didn't happen.

Except for one. Dylan, still resting underneath me, had opened his eyes. He was as sick as a dog, still burning up from the fever that ravaged his body, but somehow, he was lucid.

"You held on," I whispered, which made him smile.

"For you," he said, smiling weakly, and he started moving. "We need to go."

I slipped off of him onto the ground, pulling myself back up to a sitting position. Dylan pushed himself up with everything he had until he was half-sitting on the bed. I knew he didn't have much strength in him. Every second counted.

"The codes," he whispered. "You need to get me to the doors."

I fought the nausea that wrecked my body and forced myself in a standing position to help Dylan get off the bed. I didn't know what miracle was holding him up right now, but I couldn't afford to ignore it.

With his arm leaning heavily over my shoulder, we shuffled to the living area, until he slipped to the floor and rested with his head against the wall, panting heavily. I left him there to make my way to the numeric panel attached to the door.

"The first code is 5—3… No, wait. That's not right."

Dylan swallowed heavily and closed his eyes.

"Dylan. Dyl!"

His eyes flew open.

"I'm awake," he muttered. "I'm here."

"Focus."

"Is okay," he slurred. "Got it."

I leaned my head against the door while trying to focus again.

"4—1—0—7—2," his voice droned, before repeating, "4—1—0—7—2."

"Four. One. Zero. Seven. Two." I said it out loud.

The door flung open. I wept with joy.

I shuffled back to him and pulled him up, forcing him into the dark tunnel between the two doors. The first door remained open. It didn't automatically close behind us.

I practically dragged Dylan to the second door, where

I sat him down on the floor, with his back against the stone wall. He sat close enough to the outer door to touch it. We both did. It was cold to the touch. There was no fire beating against the steel, no tornadoes pulling at its seams. It was just a goddamn door.

"Ready?" I said, moving to the panel.

My head started clearing already, now that we were out of the danger zone. The air was strangely fresh here, as if it wasn't a tunnel running partially through the mountain.

He nodded and looked at me when he spoke the magical numbers we needed to get out of here.

"5—3—9—8—6."

I tapped in the numbers and watched the outer door slide open.

Strong wind and fresh air washed over me. I allowed my tears to flow freely now. We were *free*. The world was just as normal as it had been before. My heart leaped; my thoughts went haywire. I breathed in deeply and allowed the air to clear my mind.

"We made it," I said, looking at Dylan. "We're free!"

He smiled weakly and slid to the side until his head rested on the stone floor. He had lost consciousness.

"Dyl. Dylan!" I screamed, making my way to him.

He lay on the ground, breathing so shallowly I could hardly detect it. He had sacrificed his last ounce of strength to save me. To get me out. In front of me, the world waited for me. All I had to do was get up and walk. But I knew he would die without me.

I didn't have enough time to run down the mountain and get help. There was nothing I could do now that would get someone here on time to save his life. He needed a medivac or an ambulance with all the necessary equipment to handle the situation immediately.

I sat on the cold floor with my back leaning against the wall and turned him around, so his head rested in my lap. He was nearly gone. I cried as I leaned forward, pressing kisses on his face, waiting for the end.

Waiting for a miracle.

And then it suddenly came in the form of four men appearing out of the blue in the tunnel. Four men, one of whom resembled Dylan so much that it couldn't be anyone but his dad. I'll never forget the look on his face when he saw us sitting there.

"Holly? Oh my God, Dylan!"

He ran to us, knelt in front of us, and pressed his fingers hard against Dylan's throat.

"He's still breathing," he said with the greatest sigh of relief. "What happened?"

"He's sick," I managed to get out. "He's been sick all day. I think it's meningitis."

"He's burning up," another man said, placing his hand on Dylan's forehead. "We need to get him to a hospital straight away. Holly, are you okay?"

I nodded, even though I wanted to puke my guts out and just pass out. I forced myself to stay awake so I could hold on to Dylan for as long as possible.

"We need to move him," Mr. Blair said. "Did you give him any medication?"

"Tylenol. Advil," I whispered. "Lots of water. Some food. It's too late."

"No, it's not," Mr. Blair spoke determinedly. "We took the car."

He pressed his fingers against my throat.

"Sluggish reaction, drowsiness, shallow breathing. Your pupils are dilated. What happened to you in the shelter?"

"The mountain shook. The generators failed," I whispered.

While Mr. Blair was checking me over, the other two men ran into the shelter and came back shortly after.

"The filtering system malfunctioned. They were being poisoned," one of them said.

"Damnit," Mr. Blair said. "Come on, we need to get them to the hospital right now."

Dylan was lifted from me by Mr. Blair and another man while the other men pulled me on my feet. Dylan was unconscious and couldn't move on his own. He was carried by his dad and his friend. One man stayed behind while I was picked up by the third man as if I was as light as a feather.

"It's okay now," he said, watching me struggle to stay awake. "You can sleep if you want to. We'll take care of you. You're going to be just fine."

That was enough for me to finally give up and slip into the darkness.

It was late in the evening when I woke up in the silence of a hospital ward. It didn't take me too long to figure out I was in the ICU. A nurse was standing by my bed. She smiled when she noticed I was awake.

"Welcome back," she said. "You had us worried for a while."

"Where am I?" I croaked.

My throat was parched, and I felt like I had just run a marathon. My body felt as if it had been pulled apart and reassembled. I was on oxygen; an IV was pushing fluids into my veins. This was the first time in my life I was in a hospital.

It was scary.

"You're in Great Falls Hospital," the nurse said, squeezing my hand. "Let me get a doctor."

She was gone before I could ask any questions and came back with a young female doctor, who smiled reassuringly while examining me. The nurse gave me a cup of water.

"What happened?" I said.

"Do you remember anything?"

"Yeah. The shelter's filtering system malfunctioned. We were being poisoned."

"That's correct, Holly. After you were found, we received a distress call about a medical emergency. A medivac brought you here from Midstone yesterday evening since the local hospital wasn't equipped for this kind of emergency. We've been pushing oxygen and proper medication into your system to counteract the effects of the poisoned air you'd been breathing in for hours."

"Am I going to be okay?" I asked.

"For sure. You have nothing to worry about. Your vitals have stabilized, but we're keeping you in the ICU for another night, just to make sure that you'll be fine. If all goes well, you'll be out of the hospital in a few days. Your parents and sister arrived this morning, and they have been waiting down the hall the whole day. We'll tell them you woke up so they can come in to see you."

I started to cry. The relief and happiness were almost unbearable. My parents were here? Emma too?

"Where's Dylan?" I asked, already dreading the answer I would receive. "He's dead, isn't he?"

"No, Holly. He's alive. In fact, he's right over there."

The doctor pointed at the ICU cubicle next to mine.

The nurse helped me to sit up so I could see him. He was unconscious or asleep, pale as a sheet, but still alive. Oh God. How was this even possible?

"He's very strong and very determined to make it," the doctor said. "He's not out of the woods yet, but he's getting there."

"He was sick."

"Yes, we know. Bacterial meningitis, like you told his dad when they found you. In fact, your diagnosis saved his life. Based on what you said, his father acted extremely quickly. As soon as they got the two of you from the mountain, he inserted an IV that pushed the right medication into him. If his dad hadn't done that, he wouldn't be here today. Those crucial moments helped save his life."

I cried again.

"How did you know?" the doctor said.

I looked at her.

"You're not a doctor, are you?"

"No."

"Then how?"

"I don't know," I whispered.

"Well, you saved his life, so you can be very proud of that," the doctor said. "If you're able to eat, we'll get you some food, and I'll have a word with your parents and sister. Unless you want to rest first?"

I shook my head.

"We'll be right back then."

The doctor left the glass cubicle while the nurse stayed with me and checked the IV and oxygen. She scraped her throat, obviously wanting to ask me some questions.

"Is it true that the two of you were trapped in a preppers'

mountain shelter?" she finally asked.

"Yes."

"How come?"

"It's a long story," I whispered.

"Some people say your boyfriend kidnapped you."

"He didn't," I snapped fiercely.

"The police came by earlier; I thought you should know. They want to question him once he's lucid enough to give a statement. They want to talk to you too."

I leaned back against the pillows, trying to wrap my head around it all. Did Dylan kidnap me, like *they* said? Yes, technically he did. But it wasn't his fault. He was acting on instinct.

"It's not true," I finally whispered.

The nurse obviously wanted me to say more, but then my parents and Emma rushed through the ICU department toward me. The next thing I knew, Mom flung her arms around me and held me so tight I thought I would suffocate again.

"Relax, honey," Dad said. "You're going to choke her."

Mom let go of me so Dad could give me a fierce, fatherly hug. Then Emma embraced me so gently it made me cry again. Why couldn't I stop crying?

"I'll leave you to it," the nurse said, obviously unhappy I hadn't told her anything else. "Ten minutes, that's all. Holly needs her rest."

She closed the glass door, granting us some privacy. Mom and Dad took chairs while Emma sat on the side of the bed, holding my hand. When she glanced sideways, she saw Dylan lying on the other bed.

"Is he alright?" she asked.

"Yeah, he's going to be."

"They said you saved his life."

I shrugged. "I don't know about that. He saved mine, though."

"After kidnapping you first?" Dad asked, but he didn't sound mad about it.

"It wasn't kidnapping, Dad."

"Then what was it?"

"I don't even know how to begin to explain this."

"Is it true they're preppers?" Emma asked.

"Yeah, it is."

"His dad spoke to us earlier. Said that he had received some sort of warning that something was about to happen on the mountain. He said that he told Dylan to take you to the shelter."

"That's all true."

"Then what happened?"

I glanced over at Dylan's cubicle. He seemed so lonely and abandoned, lying there. His parents weren't here, nor had there been any mention of them. He was just out here on his own, and I felt so sorry for him.

"It's a long story," I finally said, "but there's one thing you need to know before I tell you. It's not Dylan's fault. If there is anyone to blame, it's his parents. You have to trust me on that."

Dad smiled and reached for my other hand.

"Tell us everything," he said.

Dylan

I'm running through a lane with big old trees that seem hostile somehow. They're caught in a strong wind that waves them back and forth, back and forth.

I hear the pounding of paws behind me, and when I look around, I see a leopard running toward me. It's not growling, and it doesn't seem angry, but it's still there, chasing me.

The leopard is replaced by a black bear.

The bear is replaced by a tiger.

I can feel its pace increasing. It's coming for me. It growls and lunges at me, and I run up the mountain, using the hiking trail. It follows me, but its pace is slower than mine. Until it grabs me and holds me back. I can't get up the mountain anymore.

I scream, but not a sound escapes my throat. It's like my vocal cords are cut. I can't speak, I can't cry out for help, I can't fight back while the animal is pinning me to the ground. I can't breathe. I can't find air in my lungs. I'm choking, desperately heaving for air.

I hurry to the top of the mountain, desperate to reach it. A hand grabs my wrist and holds on tight. The next thing I know, I'm on the top of the mountain.

The tiger is gone. Instead, I see Holly. She's standing in front of me in a beautiful dress that brightens her eyes and hair. She reaches for my hand.

"It's okay," she says. "I'm here. You're fine. We're going to be just fine."

I believe her because when she's with me, nothing bad can happen. But is everything really alright?

Around us, the world is on fire, but it's different than in my other dreams. It's more realistic. Trees burn everywhere, and smoke fills the sky. The mountain seems to be on fire, as if someone has used a huge lighter to burn everything down. The world around us brightens when sparkles of light mix with the dark of the starry skies. It's absolutely gorgeous.

"We're going to be okay," Holly says before the mountain crumbles, and we sink together into oblivion.

This time, when I scream, I can hear my own voice.

Things felt odd around me.

For a long time, I could make heads nor tails of it. Everything happened in a blur.

I'd swear I heard voices, but I doubted that they were real. It'd been a while since I heard anyone but Holly talk to me, and I wondered if I was still in that odd dream or back in an unreal, almost hypnotic state of reality. It was hard to distinguish both.

The voices came from afar. They were unrecognizable at first, but then they changed into a certain familiarity, as if my mind was trying to tell me that they really weren't part of my dream but belonged to the world I had to go back to. I was reluctant to do so. Going back to the mountain shelter only meant fever, pain, and a certain death.

I heard my dad's voice, or maybe I was just imagining that. I heard Holly's too and that of my uncle, who was always checking the mountain shelter with my dad.

That was impossible. It couldn't be my dad. He was far away from here, in a shelter somewhere below ground, waiting for the post-doomsday moment he would be able to leave his safe haven. He couldn't possibly be here unless…the world was still okay?

I didn't dare get my hopes up. I didn't dare think about a positive ending to all this. Everything that had happened was one big clusterfuck, and I didn't dare think beyond that.

I had lost Holly. Deep down, I knew that.

I had lost Holly, my life, my parents. They were all gone. All that was left for me was a never-ending nightmare. I was still in the shelter, dreaming about things that didn't belong to me anymore. I was telling myself my dad was really here, while he was just a figment of my imagination.

One of my earlier dreams had been about a good life with Holly, one where we existed in a trouble-free world, where no one thought about doomsday scenarios and the world was running itself. I had seen our future together. We would have two kids and all the animals she wanted. We would live in a house somewhere by the lake, not too far from her parents. Midstone was a thing of the past.

My dreams gave me false hope. It was foolish to think that anything good would come out of any of this. I was still stuck in my dreamscape, deep inside the shelter, and my mind was playing tricks on me.

But then why did everything around me feel so real?

I slipped in and out of consciousness, barely able to distinguish where and when I was. I heard vague voices talking about me. Holly's voice was lost to me at some point.

My body was shaking as if I was in a car. I leaned against

someone. A person was holding me tight. The car drove fast but erratically. My head spun. I was in so much pain.

"We need a medivac right now," I heard my dad say. "Drive to the house. Hurry up!"

I was out of it again. My head seemed to explode whenever I was conscious, so I was grateful for the times I wasn't.

Then I was up in the air. There was something over my nose and mouth. Fluids were pushed into my arm. I was still alive and out of the shelter, that much I knew, but my brain just couldn't keep up with my new reality, so I slept again, until I was forcibly shaken.

An unknown female voice spoke to me.

"Dylan. Dylan, can you hear us? You're in the hospital. You're going to be just fine. Dylan, open your eyes. Can you do that? Can you open your eyes for me? You're safe, but we need you to talk to us. Please talk to us."

I couldn't respond at all. It hurt too much.

Then I heard my dad's voice.

"Come on, Dylan. Wake up, son. We're all here. You're in the hospital, and you're going to be just fine. It's over. You made it."

This time, I complied. I forced myself to respond. Dad was with me at the hospital, and there were all these other people with him. Seeing the relief in his eyes made me want to weep.

"That's it, kiddo. God, I'm so glad to see you awake. You scared the hell out of me."

He hugged me. I was too weak to hug him back.

Mom rushed into the room and came to me with big strides. She hugged me and cried. She turned to my dad and said something I couldn't make out. She was so upset.

I fell asleep again with her hand in mine.

It was only when I woke up again in the ICU, watching all

these people around me do their best to save me, that I realized Dad had lied.

Not everyone was here. Holly was missing. She was nowhere to be seen. And God, I was so scared that she had died on that mountain.

It was the one thought that haunted me in my feverish dreams while my body fought to survive the attack on my system.

Holly

I had never met Mr. Blair nor spoken to him. All I knew about him was what I learned from Dylan, who had always been quite sparse with information about his dad. I had figured out on my own that his father was a dominant figure but also someone with an obvious heart for the people in his life.

I was surprised to see him enter the private room I had been moved to after a second night in the ICU. When I was considered to be out of the woods, the ICU doctors and nursing staff had wished me well. I was to stay at the hospital for another day or so, depending on the speed of my recovery.

I had requested to see Dylan before I was moved, but he wasn't doing so well, so they wouldn't allow it. His fever had spiked again, and he was apparently hallucinating, which troubled me. No one would allow me to see him or talk to him.

"You'll see him after he's a bit better," Mom said. "I'll make sure they keep us posted."

In the end, it was my dad who pressed the doctors for more information on him, and they gave it to him freely, taking into account the circumstances that had brought us here. I wasn't sure, but I believed Dad had spoken to Mr. Blair about the whole thing. He got extremely upset, but he wouldn't tell me why.

Once they moved me to this room, Emma, Mom, and Dad took turns staying with me, but I slept a lot and barely remembered them being there. The day went by quickly, and every time I woke up, I felt better.

It was evening when Mr. Blair showed up. Mom was in the room with me while Dad and Emma had gone out for a walk and a bite to eat. I had insisted that Mom would go with them, but she had adamantly refused.

"I nearly lost you, so there's no chance in hell I'll leave you out of my sight for the next ten years or so."

"So you'll come live with me on campus then?" I quipped once Dad and Emma were gone.

"If needs be, yes."

"I'm fine, Mom. It's over."

"No, you're not and it's not. We need to discuss this when you're better, Holly. A lot of things happened out there we can't just ignore."

"We don't have to ignore it, but I don't want this to take over my life either."

Mom opened her mouth to say something, but then Mr. Blair walked in. He was an older version of his son. The same eyes, nose, and mouth, the same posture. It was like seeing Dylan's future. I could imagine why everyone in Midstone seemed to dote on him.

"Mrs. Hayes," he spoke politely, addressing my mom. "Could I speak with your daughter in private?"

"No," Mom reacted vehemently. "You can't."

He didn't walk away.

"I really would like to speak to your daughter alone."

"Why? So you can manipulate her into dropping the charges against you and your son?"

Charges?

"What charges?" I blurted out.

"The police is pressing charges against them," Mom explained. "That's what we need to talk about."

"Who asked them to do that?"

"We did, Holly. We nearly lost you."

"Mom, I don't want you to press charges against him," I protested. "This is ridiculous. Why did you do that?"

"They almost killed you. Do you realize that, Holly?"

"The mountain almost killed me, not them. It wasn't their fault," I snapped.

"Because they took you there."

Mr. Blair raised his hands.

"I'm sorry," he said. "I'm not here to ask you to drop anything. I just wanted to see how you were doing. Can I take a seat?"

Mom obviously wanted to send him on his way, but I was curious to find out what he wanted.

"Mom, can you please go have dinner with Dad and Emma? Please? I'll be fine."

She hesitated but finally shrugged. She got up and kissed me.

"I'll be right outside."

She glared at Mr. Blair, who pretended to ignore it as he sat down. Mom left us alone. I could hear some shuffling and imagined her sitting by the door as my guard.

I became awkwardly aware of my hospital gown and the vulnerable position I was in, lying in bed with an IV pushing fluids in my arm and an oxygen canula in my nose.

"How are you?" he asked.

"I'm doing okay."

"Anxious to see Dylan, I bet." He smiled lightly.

"How is he?"

"He's stable and awake. Confused and upset. Sad and feeling terribly guilty. He'll be in the ICU for another night, but the fever finally broke and he's doing much better. I'm sorry that you had to go through all that."

"Which part exactly are you sorry about?" I blurted out.

He shifted in his seat. "What do you mean?"

I looked at my hands, trying to find the politest way to say this, but I was beyond being polite. I was done with his crap.

"You sent your son in that shelter thinking the world was coming to an end. How could you make a mistake like that?"

He grimaced.

"Just like the weather cannot always be accurately predicted, neither can the signals we get from various sources, Miss Hayes. Since you don't know anything about our life, I can imagine it must be hard for you to accept the errors in our imperfect system. I'm sure Dylan explained the basics of our way of life."

"Did you lie to him to test him?"

He looked me square in the eye.

"No."

"So you really believed something was going on?"

"Yes."

"Where were you when all of this took place?"

"In our own shelter near the house."

"And you stayed there all this time?"

"I did. At least until we were certain the threat was over. We came up the mountain immediately once we were certain it wouldn't happen again."

"So what exactly did happen?" I asked.

"An earthquake."

"Is that what caused this whole mess? A simple earthquake?"

I asked in disbelief.

He smiled softly. "Miss Hayes, there's no such thing as a simple earthquake. Earthquakes always have consequences, no matter how big or small their fallout is."

"I see."

"We had no idea that the generator system would cause such a dangerous situation. This was the first time it failed on us. Our people are investigating, so it won't happen again. I truly apologize for this situation. We had no way of knowing the two of you would be in such grave danger."

That was true. It still pissed me off that we were put in that situation, but I didn't say so.

"It wasn't your fault," I said. "And I won't press charges against you or Dylan. He saved my life, and I love him."

He frowned at me.

"You love him?"

"Of course I do."

"Even after all of this?"

"More so than before."

He shifted uncomfortably in his chair. This was apparently the last thing he had expected from me. I plucked at the blanket.

"Can I ask you something, Miss Hayes?"

"Sure."

"You went through all of this, but have you considered what this will mean for you in the future?"

"What do you mean?"

"My son is a prepper, which has become clear in the past few days. You've experienced for yourself how that feels. Are you willing to do the same thing the next time an event occurs? Will you support him when an actual catastrophe takes place? When push comes to shove, will you take your children to that shelter?"

I didn't have an answer to that question. The truth was that I simply didn't know what I would do because I wasn't a mother yet. I did know, having been cooped up and terrified in that shelter, that I didn't want to go through that again myself. I had made up my mind about that, even if I hadn't discussed it with Dylan yet.

"I'll put it differently," he said. "Will you support my son and my family in the future, or will you ask him to give up everything he believes in?"

His question startled me. Not once had I asked Dylan to give up his goals in life. I would never do that. They were his beliefs, and I would respect them at all costs. This hadn't changed that.

"All I wanted during our time in the shelter was for him to realize that there wasn't a massive catastrophe happening and that he didn't have anything to fear."

"But what if it really happened?"

"Can't I ask you the same question? Will you support my choices if I decided *not* to go to the shelter while being married to Dylan?"

He got up.

"The thing is that when you marry into our community, you automatically become part of it. There's no other way, Miss Hayes. So if you love my son and you want to spend the rest of your life with him, this is a prerequisite you must accept."

"And what if I don't?"

"Then you cannot continue this relationship."

"With all due respect, but that's not up to you to decide, Mr. Blair."

He smiled lightly. "Miss Hayes, let me tell you one thing about my son. He is very loyal to his people. Why do you think he ran around carrying three phones during the past three years in college? You can't deny that fact, even if you want to."

"That sounds like a threat, sir," I said.

"No, Miss Hayes. I'm just stating the obvious. This whole event will not change my son, trust me. Knowing him, he'll be even more determined to improve our way of life. Goodbye, Miss Hayes. I wish you well."

I knew I would never see him again. Mr. Blair had made it quite clear that I was not to set foot inside his house ever again.

This was quickly turning into a battle, and I hated it. But if that was the battle I had to fight for Dylan's sake, I would accept the challenge.

Mom entered the room.

"What is it?" she said. "What happened?"

"I'm going to lose him, Mom," I said.

Dylan

I woke up sometime late in the evening. It was dark in the ICU. Everyone around me was asleep. At the nurse's station, a few people were walking around. I could see their shadows.

My mind was still quite foggy, but everything started coming back slowly. Holly was on my mind. I hadn't seen her since I was admitted to the hospital, and that worried me. In my dreams, she was always dead, even when the nurses told me she was fine and resting in a private room.

When the door to the ICU opened, I was surprised. A woman walked past the nurses' station and into my room. I had expected to see Holly, but it was her mom. When a nurse caught her, she quickly identified herself and asked for a couple of minutes with me.

Mom and Dad had just come by to have a talk with me. I'd been seeing them on and off ever since I woke up in this cubicle for the first time. Dad had apologized profusely about his mistake, explaining into the finest detail what had gone wrong.

"As you know, we had received several warning sounds about a big event happening soon, but we misjudged it. It wasn't the dormant volcano acting up. It was a massive earthquake beneath the mountain range. It was bad, but not mortal for us.

When we figured out everything was fine, life returned back to normal quickly. Well, as normal as could be expected."

"That's when we realized you didn't know nothing was wrong," Mom continued, "so I had your dad drive up the mountain to get you guys out. Imagine his shock when he found you the way he did."

"It was an accident, Dad," I said, reaching for his hand, but he wouldn't take it. "You're not to blame."

"That's right," Mom said. "It was our joint decision to call you and warn you. This wasn't anyone's fault."

It was obvious, though, Dad felt responsible and guilty. I tried to tell him it was okay and that we had made it out alive, but he barely responded to what I said. It would take some time for him to come to terms with this.

Mrs. Hayes stood in the doorway and gave me a troubled smile.

"Dylan, can I come in?"

"Of course," I said. "How's Holly?"

"She's fine. She's been asking to see you, but the doctors put her on bedrest until tomorrow."

"I am so sorry about everything," I said, barely able to look Mrs. Hayes in the eye. "This is all my fault."

"Dylan, stop. You two have been blaming yourself long enough. This isn't anyone's fault. The circumstances lead to this." She moved closer and squeezed my hand. "I came here to tell you that our family loves you and is not upset with you in any way."

"Do you mean that?" I asked in disbelief.

"Every word of it. You are family. Emma sends her love, and Dan wanted you to know that you'll always have a home with us."

"I fucked up big time, Mrs. Hayes. Shouldn't I be punished for that?" I blurted out.

"We all make mistakes, Dylan."

"Not you guys. Your family is just perfect."

Mrs. Hayes smiled. "No, we're not. Nobody is. There's no such thing as perfection."

"I don't know about that. Holly practically is."

"My daughter is a great person, Dylan, but she can be pretty damned stubborn too. You've probably noticed that before."

"Not at all," I said, deadpan.

She smiled.

"I came to tell you that you should focus on getting well, and I mean this in every way possible."

I was confused. "What are you saying exactly?"

"Holly told me how upset you were back in the shelter. We've heard the whole story, and it troubles us that you lost all sense of self-control and reality after you received that phone call. That's why her dad and I believe that you need help. Therapy. You went through quite a shock, and this will stay with you for the rest of your life. You need to deal with that."

"I'm not crazy, Mrs. Hayes."

"No one says you are, Dylan. Therapy isn't for people who are off the rails. It's for those who want to live their lives to the fullest. And you, Dylan, are someone who lives with such passion and conviction, that it might harm you until you find ways of dealing with it."

"You mean until I no longer pull Holly with me into the abyss. I've already made up my mind that it's best for us not to continue our relationship."

She smiled patiently.

"Dylan, Holly knows what is going on in your life now. She was directly affected by it, was hurt physically and mentally by the effects of you hiding this important part of your life from her. But she loves you more than ever. The first thing she said when she was lucid enough was that she didn't blame you and still wants to be with you. Are you now saying that you don't?"

I was stunned. This was the last thing I had expected. I smiled.

"I thought you were going to chew me out."

"Why would I do that, when I admire you so?"

"What?"

Mrs. Hayes still held on to my hand.

"Dylan, you were dying. You had contracted bacterial meningitis, which caused you to hallucinate and suffer physically in ways that no one should suffer. You went through hell. Add to that the toxic air you were breathing in, and well, you can imagine how close you were to death. But somehow, you fought back to the point where you were able to give Holly the codes she needed to open those doors. If you hadn't done that, your father would have found the two of you dead. I admire you for your relentless drive to save her at your own expense."

I didn't know what to say. I hardly had any recollections of those moments on the mountain. Others had filled in the blanks.

"Thank you," I said.

Mrs. Hayes got up. "You need to rest now. I'll make sure that you and Holly can see each other in the morning, once they've moved you to a private room. Try to get some sleep, Dylan. We'll talk again soon."

"I will," I said. "Mrs. Hayes?"

"Yes?"

"I'll find a way to deal with this, I promise."

"I know you will," she said. "Goodnight."

She left me alone in the peaceful, quiet darkness. I fell asleep knowing that I would see Holly again in the morning. That her family cared about me very much. It gave me hope that someday I would be able to forgive myself.

I was settled into a private room early in the morning after a long and peaceful night. The brain fog had lifted now that the antibiotics had run its course. I was doing much better. I felt more like myself again.

As soon as I was alone, Dad knocked on the door and came in before I could say anything.

"Dad?" I said, surprised. "Are you okay? Where's Mom?"

"She didn't come with me," he said. "I wanted to talk to you alone first."

"Why? What's going on?"

"I've been putting this off for a while until you would be well enough to understand what I'm about to tell you," he said.

He wouldn't sit down. He just stood there in the room, barely watching me. Whatever he was going to tell me was extremely serious.

"You need to break up with the Hayes girl."

"What?"

"I need you to, Dylan. You can't be with her. Not now, not ever. It's over. It *has* to be over and done with. Treasure your relationship until the mountain for all I care, but use the event as a means to an end to finish things with her."

"And why would I do that exactly?"

"Isn't that obvious? You nearly got her killed."

I couldn't believe what I was hearing.

"You're blaming *me* for this whole thing, when her parents

and Holly have already forgiven me?"

"They forgave you? Where did you get that idea?"

"Her mom came by last night."

Dad looked angry.

"She had no right to confuse you like that."

"In what way did she confuse me then, Dad? Is telling someone that you love them confusing? Is forgiveness so hard for you to understand?"

"She may have forgiven you now, but she won't do so again if this happens a second time. And it will. It'll happen twice, and a third time, and a fourth. Because that's how we live, Dylan. Are you going to leave her behind every time we get a warning?"

"I don't know yet," I admitted. "That will depend on her."

"She doesn't want to go. She told me so."

"We haven't talked about this yet," I said. "I'd like to form my own opinion if that's alright with you."

"Her opinion is quite clear. I checked."

"What gave you that right, Dad?"

"I'm your father. I raised you to be sensible. This whole relationship isn't sensible at all."

"There we go again," I said, sighing. "You are so adamant about hating her that you really don't care what I want, do you? Have you even tried having a grown-up conversation with her?"

He didn't say anything. He looked away.

"I'm not giving her up, Dad. I want this to count for something."

"Why, son? What is so special about her that you would risk your entire way of life for her?"

"She *is* my life now."

"More than your mother and me?"

I looked him square in the eye.

"Would you give up Mom if I asked you to?"

"No, of course not."

"What's the difference between her and Holly?"

"She's a natural-born prepper! She was born into this life. How difficult is it for you to understand that?"

"You know what, Dad?" I said. "I've had it with your manipulative behavior. You never wanted me to date Holly; you've made that abundantly clear from the start. But guess what? Now and then, lighting strikes. And when it does, you don't want to ignore that."

"So you insist on pursuing this relationship, despite my objections?"

"Yes, I am."

"Then you can't be my son anymore."

I was stunned. I looked at him in shock.

"Are you gaslighting me now?"

"I'm not doing anything. You've made it quite clear that what I want doesn't matter."

"Dad, are you serious right now?"

He took a deep breath, turning away from me. Then he stopped. His shoulders shook. He held his face between his hands. He was crying.

"Dad?"

He didn't say anything.

I waited for him to calm down. He wiped his face, shook his head, and turned around.

"It was all for nothing then," he said quietly.

That's when it hit me.

"You did it on purpose, didn't you? There never was an alarm. It was a test."

"I did it for your own good."

"Get out."

"Dylan…"

"Get the fuck out!"

"I didn't expect any of this to happen. I thought you would figure out on your own that it was a false alarm. I just wanted to scare the girl enough to drive her away, that's all."

"But you ignored all the earthquake signals too," I said angrily.

"We thought they were just tremors. How could I have anticipated this? I would never hurt you; you're my son!"

"Dad, are you seriously living on a different planet? Don't you know the police is coming down to talk to me today? They want to charge me for kidnapping."

"I'll talk to them. They should charge me instead. I'll fix it. They'll listen to me."

"Do you honestly believe everything can be fixed that easily, Dad?" I snapped. "You nearly got us both killed."

"I couldn't have known about the meningitis. Did you ignore the signs?"

"Yeah, Dad, I did," I said, sighing. "And you know why? I was too busy trying to deal with the anxiety *you* caused with your lies."

"That's not…"

"True? Save it, Dad. I don't want to hear it," I said. "Please go, before I say something you won't like."

His shoulders slumped again, but I knew it was all a game to him. He didn't feel an ounce of remorse. Who was this man?

"I didn't choose this life, Dylan," he murmured dejectedly.

"Neither did I," I said.

"We have to put this behind us. I want you to come home. Your mom and I need you."

"Fuck you, Dad."

My words shocked him.

"Don't speak to me like that."

"Why not? What respect do I have left for you, after you set this whole thing up on purpose? Maybe you *wanted* someone to get hurt so you'd have an excuse to get rid of her."

"I didn't want anyone to get hurt."

"Save it. Get out. You scare me, Dad."

He sat down and grabbed my head, but I refused to look at him.

"I won't leave. You're talking nonsense, kiddo. You have nothing to fear from me. Nothing has changed between us. You're coming home with us. We'll put this whole mess behind us and move on. Tomorrow will be another day, another situation to deal with."

"Another day, another disaster, right, Dad?"

"The world is one big mess, son. Nature pays us back in full for the way that we are overpopulating the planet and abusing its natural resources. But we, those who know this, will manage to survive. In the end, that's all that matters."

"Well, you're going to have to do it without me," I said. "If the world *would* end tomorrow, guess where I will be? It's not going to be in a bunker or that damned shelter. I will be holding Holly in my arms while we face our fate. From now on, I will choose love over fear."

Dad's face fell, but I didn't care. He hadn't apologized once for the mess he had caused, and I knew now that he never would.

"You know," I said, "I've been waiting for you to apologize, but I realize now that you aren't ready for that just yet. When that moment comes—if it ever does—I'm willing to sit down with you and talk about what happened on the mountain. But until that day, I'm afraid that we won't see each other again."

"Are you cutting off all ties with us?"

"Yes, I am."

"Your mother was not involved."

I smiled. "Of course she was, just as Lewis knew. He got instructions to allow us up the mountain and ignore us for the rest of the day, didn't he?"

Dad didn't deny it.

"I don't want to see her again either. Maybe someday, but not right now."

"What will you do?"

"I'll go back to Minnesota, hopefully get a scholarship and finish my medical degree. After that, the world will be there for me to explore."

Dad smiled lightly.

"You'll come back home, Dylan," he said. "No matter how you feel about this situation right now, one day you'll be a parent too, and you'll realize that the things we do are for our children's benefit alone."

"That's the thing, isn't it, Dad?" I said. "I'll never *ever* lie to my children the way you did to me. And I'll never *ever* question their choice of life partner, no matter who that may be."

"I never—" He stopped before he could finish his sentence. "I'll talk to you later, son."

He left me alone in that room. Maybe he thought I would be shocked or sad, but I wasn't. A tremendous weight was lifted from my shoulders.

I was free.

I slipped out of bed and walked with the IV pole in hand to

Holly's room on the same floor. Her mom had told me where to find her.

I walked in, and there she was, sitting on the side of her bed, looking like herself again. Emma sat in a chair by the window.

Holly was fine. She was just fine.

"Dyl?" she said, getting up.

"Please don't let me go," I pleaded.

It was enough for her to wrap me in her arms. We stood and cried for minutes, releasing everything we had ever held back.

I had chosen to love, and it was the best feeling ever.

Holly

The phone call came on an early Friday morning in the middle of December, around four a.m. It woke me up from a restless dream in which I was back at the shelter, but this time, Dylan wasn't there with me.

The cold loneliness stayed with me when I woke up from the sound of my phone ringing. An unknown number appeared on the screen, but I knew who it was. I had been expecting this call ever since we returned to college after the dramatic Thanksgiving weekend and its aftermath.

"Don't answer it," Dylan murmured sleepily next to me. His warmth was pressing into me; he still had his arm around my waist.

"I have to take this," I whispered. "It's Emma. She said she would call when she got back from London, remember?"

"Give her my love," he mumbled before turning around and falling asleep again.

I held back a sigh as the number flashed on my screen. Not Emma's number of course. His.

Since Thanksgiving, he was catching up on a lot of lost time, which included sleeping like a log for nights in a row. Dylan had started therapy two weeks ago, putting his trust into someone who didn't judge him for the events.

It had been eventful weeks. For the past six weeks, his dad had tried to call him several times a day. Day and night, he tried to contact Dylan. When he wouldn't pick up the phone, he sent him dozens of text messages. Dylan had blocked all of his dad's numbers on his regular phone and had thrown away the emergency phones, but that didn't stop him. He used all of his friends' phones, or had Dylan's cousins call him, pleading with him relentlessly to talk to his dad.

Dylan changed his number twice, but that didn't stop him either. Somehow, he always managed to get his hands on Dylan's numbers, proving the power he had over people close to him. It had reached the point that we didn't trust any of Dylan's friends or coworkers anymore. Anyone of them could be spying for his dad.

The only thing he had never done was contact me. Until now. I knew it was him. He had finally reached out to the one person he probably blamed for Dylan going no contact. Me.

I sat in the kitchen with the phone lying in front of me, debating what to do. These past six weeks I had contemplated several scenarios in case this would happen, but they were as unpredictable as he was.

He had even shown up at Dylan's dorm one night. Luckily, Harry had blown him off, telling him to go fuck himself. Knowing Harry, that was probably exactly what he had said. When Mr. Blair showed up on campus again the next day, Harry called campus security and told them this strange, old dude was wandering around flashing at girls. When I imagined it, I couldn't help but laugh. Mr. Blair was probably the last person in the world who would flash at college students. Still, he was arrested and restrained from ever returning to campus.

He tried to find my address, but he couldn't. The apartment was on my mom's maiden name. I did find myself driving around a couple more blocks every day, just in case anyone was following me. That didn't appear to be the case.

How could this situation have escalated to one where Dylan had to ghost his own dad and change his phone number regularly? I had always believed that Mr. Blair loved his son unconditionally, but now I couldn't help but wonder if he had only wanted an heir for his self-proclaimed throne.

We were finally getting in a good place. Dylan had just recently stopped checking all those morbid websites, like a drug addict kicking off a two-decade-long habit. It had taken him a lot of effort to stop gazing over his shoulder at every turn or staring at the skies in the morning, questioning if today would be Doomsday.

We had a discussion about his future here in Minnesota. After all, he had come here at his dad's request. He had never chosen for himself to become a medical doctor. He felt comfortable pursuing this career, but last week, he had decided to specialize in surgery instead of becoming a General Practitioner.

"If I am going to help people, I want to do it my way," he had said. "I've always wanted to be a surgeon, and it's not too late for that. It'll cost me an extra year, but that's fine. I really don't care."

I was so proud of him.

The call ended without me picking up. It began again. And again. Again. I debated switching it off. Ghosting that asshole would be the best thing I could do right now.

After eight attempts, he finally gave up. Then another number started calling. His mom's. The two of them were so pathetic.

Sitting there at my kitchen table in the middle of the night, with my phone lying in front of me, felt healing somehow. They were the assholes, not me. And certainly not Dylan.

I left my phone turned on and placed it upside down on the kitchen table. When I crawled back in bed, Dylan turned around. He was wide awake. A smile crept over his face.

"You survived their wrath," he said.

I smiled and curled myself against him, falling asleep against his even breathing.

Two days later, his mom showed up at the apartment. She stood in front of the building when I came home from work. It was late in the evening. Christmas was creeping up on us, which meant that we had a lot of extra work at the flower shop. What with work and our studies, these were pretty rough days.

Christmas lights were everywhere in the city, giving the streets extra flair and people somehow a faster pace. It was as if they had to become part of this joyful time of year, whether they liked it or not.

But Mrs. Hayes didn't act festive at all. Even under the strings of Christmas lights, I could see how pale she was. I'd seen her at the hospital twice, both times only in passing, but I remembered her as a proud woman. She had lost a lot of weight; her hair was long and unkempt. She looked sad.

I resisted the urge to feel sorry for her, remembering Dylan's warnings that she could turn from hot to cold and vice versa in the blink of an eye. She was a manipulator, and there was no doubt she would try to get under my skin.

"What are you doing here?" I said while digging out my keys. Dylan was upstairs working, which she fortunately did not know.

"I came to see you," she said, her voice hoarse.

"Me? Why?"

"Do I need a reason to talk to the woman who stole my son from me?"

"That's harsh," I said.

"It's the truth, isn't it?"

"Actually, it isn't. I never told him to do anything. You drove him away all on your own."

To her credit, she didn't deny it.

"His dad is sick."

"Oh? What's wrong with him?" I said.

"He's having problems with his heart."

"How serious is it?"

"Pretty serious."

"That's really sad to hear, Mrs. Hayes, but what does that have to do with me?"

"He needs his son. You need to convince Dylan to come home. His dad needs a reason to live."

"You could have texted Dylan. Or sent him an email," I said, not impressed by her claims. "Dylan's not a monster. He would have replied."

"He doesn't answer our calls anymore."

That was true.

"And I don't like sending emails. They're so impersonal."

"I'll tell him to contact you," I said, "but I'm not sure if he's going to take the bait."

She put her hand on my arm.

"It's not bait. It's true."

"Yeah. Sure. Can you please let go of my arm?"

She let go. I opened the door.

"He's inside, isn't he?" she said.

With one swift move, she stopped me before I could get in. If she was going to attempt to get in, I would knock her out. She tried. She pushed me and tried to enter the building. I pushed back while screaming.

Dylan almost flew down the stairs. He didn't even hesitate to push his mother backward. She tripped and almost fell. Her hostility was palpable.

"Dylan," she cried. "Come home."

"Never," he snarled, holding me against him. "Get out, or I'm calling the police."

"On your own mother?"

"Damn right. I'll file charges for stalking too."

All her bluster left her.

"When did you become such a cold man?" she whispered.

"Since your husband endangered the woman I love," he retorted. "Whatever you want from me, Mom, you're not going to get it, so please leave, okay? Forget I even exist. You no longer have a son."

Mrs. Hayes's face crumbled. Her reactions proved that she still didn't get why Dylan was so upset with her. She simply did not understand that her world was still the same, but his had changed forever.

"Goodbye, Mom."

Dylan shut the door in her face.

Dylan

Dad was on the local news the next day, while I was working at the diner. He had somehow managed to get himself noticed by our local press, probably for my benefit. I wondered how he had managed to do that.

When he appeared on the screen, he looked like this uber fanatic version of himself. He had lost a lot of weight and had grown a beard. He looked the part now.

Gone was the man who always took care of himself, who had been proud of his physical appearance. This was a new version of him that I didn't like. I felt guilt wash over me. This was on me, my responsibility.

I tried to keep my cool, but it was hard. I refused to show my colleagues and our customers how shocked and bothered I was by his television appearance. He tried to explain what doomsday prepping was all about, which resulted in a whole rant about nature and society.

"There are constant dangers out there," he said. "All we want to do is protect and preserve mankind. Believe me, someday soon, something will happen that will devastate our world. All the signs are there; we're just blind to them."

My colleagues didn't know he was my father, nor had they

ever found out what happened on the mountain during last Thanksgiving weekend. Everyone thought I had been in an accident. I had kept the real truth to myself.

I served coffee and hot chocolate while the interview finished. My dad got up and left. The journalist sat alone for a moment and shook his head with a pitiful glance in his eyes.

"Imagine living in fear all the time," the man said. "That must be such a terrible burden to bear."

He didn't know how right he was.

"Hey, that guy's name is Blair like yours, Dylan," a female colleague said, prodding me to look up at the TV, where a camera followed my dad behind the scenes.

"And half of the American population," I muttered.

She laughed. "True. Imagine being related to that crazy idiot, right?"

"Yeah," I said, glancing one last time at my dad. "Imagine that."

LIFE
AS
WE
KNOW
IT

EPILOGUE

DYLAN

F*uck.*

I'm running late. Like, seriously late. Forty minutes too late. Holly's never going to forgive me. I'm supposed to meet Holly and Emma at nine a.m. for a late breakfast with their parents, but things got hectic at work and I lost track of time.

She's probably wondering where the hell I am. Her dad will probably say, "Seriously, how is this guy going to be a doctor if he's always running late?" and her mom will shake her head as always and mutter, "This brilliant boyfriend of yours has an eidetic memory, but he sure as hell doesn't know how to read the time."

I take the electric step I bought last year, which brings me quickly across campus and to the hospital where I took up residency, and ride across the concrete paths to the south entrance, where the diner is located.

The sky is bright, as if the sun is making an extra effort on this beautiful October day. It hasn't rained in days. Colorful leaves seem to reflect the sun. This post-summer beauty is one I'd like to keep for a while.

I practically drop the step against the pavement and hurry

inside, where Holly, Emma, and her parents are waiting for me. Emma is now a medical student as well, but the two sisters don't share the apartment. Emma prefers to share a dorm with her friends, whereas Holly and I are now officially living together.

I asked her to marry me last Christmas after getting her parents' permission first. It was one of the best nights of my life. We would get married as soon as we both graduated, which would still take a while.

Cutting ties with my parents and the rest of my family has been the hardest thing I've ever had to do in my life, but it was also the best one. It changed everything. I can't even imagine going back there and living that life again. I'm done feeling scared all the time. I'm done chasing ghosts. It's been two years since that terrible Thanksgiving weekend. It has taken me fourteen months of therapy to come to terms with my past life. After finishing therapy, I found the courage to propose to Holly. It gave us all closure.

This life that I'm living right now is the best one I can possibly imagine, but it's been rough too. There's no denying that. I still feel so sad so many times. The loss of who I once was often weighs on me.

"Ah, there he is," Dan says, smirking while he gazes at his watch. "Partying late?"

"Working late, actually. Just pulled an all-nighter."

He gets up and pats me on the back.

"Good to see you, Dylan," Susan says, getting up so I can hug her. "How are things?"

"Pretty good."

"Hey, bro," Emma says, getting up to hug me. She's been calling me bro ever since Holly took me home after the Thanksgiving drama to recover. They welcomed me into their home, their lives, and their hearts, and they've been my support and family ever since.

"Hey, sis," I say, holding her tight.

We don't see each other much on campus as we're all living our lives our own way, but I'm close to her and treat her like the younger sister I never had. I can't imagine a life without these people in it anymore. They've been my lifelines in every way possible, and I love them more than words can say.

"Hey, sleepyhead," Holly says, kissing me gently. "Bad night, huh?"

"A couple of bad ones, but that's what you get when you have to pull your weight in an Emergency Room."

"You can catch some sleep later. What do you want to eat? We already ordered; Dad was starving."

"Just pancakes," I say, "thanks, and sorry for being late again."

"Don't worry about it," Dan said. "You're combining your studies with a residency, which is totally crazy."

"I know," I say. "Even having an eidetic memory doesn't always help. I have so much stuff to go through that it's mind-boggling."

"Maybe you should cut back on some of your classes?" Susan suggests.

I shake my head. "No, I want to get through this as quickly as possible so I can start earning some decent money." I look at Holly. "And give her the wedding of her dreams."

"I have a dream wedding?" she says.

"Everyone does," I comment.

"Oh yeah, we do," Emma retorts, laughing.

"You know you don't have to worry about that, son," Dan says. "We've got you covered. I told you that last year. We can afford it, and you deserve to get a fresh start in life."

"I know, Dan, and I really appreciate that, but I don't want to be financially dependent for too long. Paying for Emma's and Holly's educations will already cost you a fortune, and I want to stand on my own two feet."

"Which you're already doing," Susan says. "Our financial support is pretty unlimited, so it's really no problem. We love having you in our lives, you know that."

"And I love you for it," I say, thinking back on how her parents constantly offer to help me out in any way possible without wanting anything in return. These people are just amazing.

"I get you, Dyl," Dan says, "I really do. I've done everything myself too."

I shrug and reach for Holly's hand.

"It's a matter of pride, I guess, or a need not to be too much of a burden on anyone. I've been lucky getting the additional scholarship and grant for my studies to cover all expenses for this year, but it's still crazy. Fortunately, I'm getting paid for the residency, even if it's the minimal wage right now."

"But not for long," Holly says happily.

"Oh?" Susan says.

"Dyl has some amazing news to share. Go on, tell them already."

I smile. "Yeah, the thing is, I've been offered a position at the University Hospital, a surgical internship. Full expenses paid and all, and with plenty of time to focus on my studies. They've been really lenient and understanding about my situation, and I think I'm going to do it."

"That's wonderful, Dylan!" Susan says.

"It's amazing," Holly says, smiling radiantly.

I squeeze Holly's hand.

"It really is. It's a fantastic offer, so I'm going to do it. It will help me get into the world of cardiac surgery, which is what I really want to do," I say.

"But…?" Dan adds, feeling my hesitation.

"Even though I've cut ties with my parents, a part of me still thinks about their desire for me to become a GP, so I kind of feel guilty over it."

"Of course, and that's normal," Dan says. "They are your parents, despite everything that has happened between you."

"Have you considered talking to them? It's been two years. Maybe they've changed?" Susan asks.

I shake my head.

"They'll never change. The last time we spoke, they tried to reel me back in. My mom was all tears, and my dad kept saying he couldn't understand my decision to cut all ties with them. They put all the blame on Holly and me, and I don't want to go down that road again."

Holly squeezes my hand while my mind wanders off to those moments from my past. I tried to explain to Susan, Dan, and Emma what my life had been like. What it meant to check all the preppers' sites on a daily basis, morning, noon, evening, and often even at night.

Or what it was like to carry a phone with me at all times, too scared to miss a call. Or what it felt like to be in that constant state of panic, believing with my whole heart and without a single doubt that the world was coming to an end.

All of that is gone now. I've blocked all sites and apps and refuse to take a look at them ever again, but the anxiety still remains a part of me. My life is as normal as it can possibly be. For now, that's enough. If only I didn't carry this constant feeling with me that our world was being threatened by whatever was going on right now.

"Dyl?"

I look up to four worried faces and Holly's hand on my wrist. A stack of pancakes is standing in front of me, untouched. How long has it been there?

"I'm okay," I say.

A sigh of relief radiates through the diner, as if everyone was holding their breaths, waiting for my reaction.

"Really, I'm fine."

"Good, because I'm starving," Dan says.

HOLLY

"You're coming with us for Thanksgiving weekend, right?" I say when we get up while my dad pays for our breakfast.

"I am?" Dylan says, surprised.

I'll admit we haven't spoken about it yet, but I really want him to join us, even when he has a lot of work to deal with. I have loads of stuff to do too, but I don't want to miss out on this important family weekend. And I don't want him at the apartment by himself, especially not during this particular time of year.

"We can study at home if you'd like. There's plenty of space," I say, gently pushing the subject.

"I don't know, Hol."

He doesn't look at me, but I know why he doesn't want to come with us. To him, Thanksgiving weekend became this weird anniversary thing. Last year, he insisted on staying on campus and ordered me to go. When I came back, he had partially returned to the man he was before. I vowed I would never let that happen again.

"Dyl, I know you don't want to do this, but you need to. You need to be with the people that love you unconditionally."

He smiles when I say that. It's that beautiful, secret smile of his that appears more often these days. When he smiles, he brightens up my world. He's simply gorgeous.

"I love you," I whisper as I lean forward. "I want you with me."

"Oh yeah?" he says, looking me in the eye.

"Uh-huh."

"Just *with* you? Or *in* you?"

"Guys, get a room," Emma says, rolling her eyes. "We can hear everything."

I laugh, punching my sister playfully.

"Don't act so innocently. I know about you and what's-her-face."

Mom immediately turns her attention to my younger sister.

"Does what's-her-face also have a name?"

"No, she doesn't, and it's not serious, Mom. It's just some girl I'm seeing on and off, nothing more, nothing less."

"Girlfriends with benefits," I mutter under my breath. Mom frowns.

"Well, I hope you don't do it out in public like your sister at least?"

"Moooom!" Emma and I protest at the exact same time.

"What? Don't act as if you didn't have sex in the woods that day. People saw you, you know."

I don't know where to look. Dylan muffles his laughter.

"It's okay, Dylan," she says. "No one recognized you. You're off the hook. My daughter on the other hand… Now then, Emma, tell me all about this girl. What's her name?"

Susan walks out the door with Emma. Dylan laughs.

"That was a smart move," he says. "Clearing the air so your mom won't be shocked when Emma comes home with what's-her-face and announces she's ready to come out of the closet."

"Emma's already told Mom, but thank you for your compliment," I say.

Dad finishes paying for breakfast. The three of us walk outside, where Dylan picks up his electric step and looks at the skies, which are colored more brightly than usual. Clouds fill up the air in all shapes and sizes. It's a beautiful sight to behold. I love these autumn skies so much.

"Do you see that?" Dylan says, pointing at a faint blue line in the sky.

"Now that you mention it, what is that?"

"A plane's tail," Emma says. "What's so special about that?"

"Hm, that's not what that is," he says, which sends a chill down my spine. "Weird."

His words scare me, but I brush it off. Sometimes he still does that, mention things that are different from what most people would say. I know he's still on the mend, but it's still quite hard to get a grip on his thoughts and emotions.

When you free yourself from an abuser, you are often able to move on thanks to extensive therapy, medication, and help. The weird thing is that he wasn't abused at all, not mentally nor physically, and that his father had always been there for him. His mother loved him more than many mothers would love their children. It makes his decision to cut ties with them even more heartbreaking.

I still feel guilty over the whole thing, even if it was his decision to cut them loose. No matter how much I try to be there for him, I will never be able to replace that which he has lost. But I can focus on giving him new things to look forward to.

The last time he spoke to his mom was six months ago. It seems that every couple of months or so, he is willing to give their relationship another try, but it always results in heartbreak. This moment wasn't an exception to that rule. They always end up bashing him for having a change of heart.

First, there would be a rant about his choices, followed by a rant about me, followed by threats about the future. His mom was the worst of the two. Where his dad would try to use science to get through to him, his mom would go off the rails.

"One day you'll see that we were always right. Don't you get it, honey? One way or the other, the world as we know it is coming to an end. It's a matter of time, and we are prepared for it. But you will have no way back when Judgment Day comes."

"Okay, Mom. Whatever. Goodbye."

He says that rebuilding his life resembles the reboot of humanity after disaster struck. He calls it irony. I just call it sad.

We walk together to my dad's car, parked just a block away while Dylan holds his step with one hand and my hand with the other.

"Hey, guys?"

Emma is walking behind us with her phone in hand.

"What?" I say without turning around.

My parents don't even hear her talking. My dad's on the phone with someone while my mom stops in front of a crowded diner, walking inside without saying a word, just standing there watching television. Something's definitely wrong. My dad is talking busily on the phone, not paying attention to her.

I follow her inside the diner while Dylan is standing still, confused. He keeps his phone in his hand.

"Mom, are you okay? What's going on?" I say.

The television set is playing in the diner. The sound is turned up loud. Everyone is standing or sitting still, watching the broadcast. Our president is visible on all screens. Beneath him on the screen, there is a huge red banner that reads: *Special Worldwide Broadcast. Please stay tuned.*

The president isn't talking. He looks at the camera gravely, waiting for the sign to speak. Why the hell is he on the television, and why is everyone so quiet? Cold fear grips me.

"Mom?" I say, shaking her gently.

She is still standing motionless in the diner's doorway. My dad is still on his phone, but he has stopped talking. Dylan is next to me, holding me by the shoulders. He doesn't say a word. Neither does anyone else at the diner. The president looks into the camera and scrapes his throat audibly.

"Guys?" Emma repeats behind us.

"Not now, Em," I say sharply. "Something's wrong with Mom."

"Not just your mom," Dylan says in a hoarse voice.

That's the moment when I turn to Dylan and see how pale he has become.

DYLAN

This can't be happening.

This seriously *cannot* be happening. But it is. The presidential broadcast tells us so.

"I'm reaching out to everyone worldwide, with the help of fellow presidents, prime ministers, and monarchs, to share news with you that nobody ever wants to learn," our president starts.

Holly's fingers entwine with mine. *This is it*, I think, remembering my parents' predictions. *It's over.* The world as we know it is coming to an end. Even before the president says it, I know it's here—Doomsday.

"Unfortunately, I have to announce today that we are standing on the eve of what is called an *Extinction Level Event*."

He scrapes his throat again and pauses.

"We received devastating news that a mountain-sized asteroid is heading straight for Earth. We have known of its existence for many years, but since it was supposed to move past our planet without harming it as so many other asteroids do, we weren't worried about it. Until it swerved off course unexpectedly, just one week ago."

Another pause.

"An asteroid is not that extraordinary on its own," the president continued. "For millions of years, many have passed by our planet, sometimes, but only rarely, striking our planet with great impact. We continuously monitor them closely with all the technology that we have."

Pause. He drinks some water.

"Even a few years ago, NASA made history when they were able to crash a spacecraft into an asteroid the size of a pyramid and knocked it off course. This one, however, is too large to stop. None of the means we have at our disposal will stop the devastating impact this asteroid will have on our planet. It travels fast and is already appearing in the skies as we speak."

The faint blue line.

It is so quiet in the diner that you could hear a pin drop. No one is rushing outside like they do in a disaster movie. Everyone is staying put, listening in shock to what our president is saying.

"The impact of this asteroid will be comparable to the mass extinction in the Cretaceous-Paleogene extinction event that ultimately destroyed the dinosaurs. Meaning that all living things at ground zero, which will have a diameter of about three and a half miles—or roughly six kilometers—will be instantly killed."

I'm back in my parents' house, listening to my father's list of seven events that could lead to the end of the world. I remember them all by heart: a solar flare, geomagnetic reversals, an asteroid, the sea, volcanoes, global warming, or nuclear war. These are all E.L.E.'s, but Dad always said it's the fallout that will destroy humanity. That the real killers are floods, hurricanes, and earthquakes.

How could he have predicted this? Did he somehow sense that we were living in an era where an actual E.L.E. would take place? Is this what he was warning me about all this time?

"Unfortunately, that is not all," the president continues. "After the impact, many more will die from the shock wave that will be the direct result of the crash. In the hours, days, weeks, months, and years to follow, there will be a continuous array of earthquakes, tsunamis, and firestorms, causing worldwide havoc. Should you somehow be able to survive all of this, you will have to live in a world that will be forever changed, most likely without access to technology or modern equipment. In the upcoming years, our planet will also go through extreme changes, which will lead to mass extinction among humans and animals. It will take decades for our planet to recover, if not hundreds of years."

The president again scrapes his throat and looks into the camera as if he wants to talk to us individually.

"Unfortunately, this is not a movie. There is no magic solution. There are no missiles to be sent into space, no rockets that can hit the asteroid to obliterate it before it can get to us. Believe me when I say that from the moment of discovery, the brightest of the brightest have come together to find a way to save us all. We have failed. We cannot flee to a different planet and start all over again. We have no means to save us. Underground bunkers can only last so long. Those who survive, will have to exist in a new world, whatever that may be."

He looks away, whispering, "I'm sorry."

Cold fear grips my heart, and the first thing I want to do is reach out to my parents and beg them to protect Holly. Despite the president's message that it's nearly impossible to survive, they're going to attempt to do so anyway.

They've been preparing for this for years, and their parents and grandparents before them. Only, this E.L.E. will be much worse than they could have ever anticipated. No earthquake, no flood. This is beyond repair.

The president looks back into the camera. His voice suddenly changes.

"I am going to state this very plainly. There is no way out for anyone. In less than a week the asteroid will hit the heart of the Atlantic Ocean, impacting Europe and the United States immediately. The fallout will touch ground with every continent, every country, every life form. We are all in this together."

The diner remains eerily calm. It feels as if life has already come to a standstill. Behind us, people are standing quietly in the streets. Cars have stopped. Everyone is on their phones or trying to find a place that has a television.

"We have kept this under wraps worldwide with all of our governments to avoid drama, loitering and worldwide chaos. We will continue to maintain order. There will be a very strict policy for each individual. Let it be clear when we say that we will not tolerate misbehavior. Everyone who dares to harm his fellow man will face the end of the world behind bars. That is our global vow to you. No country will tolerate chaos. Let that be very clear."

I feel Holly's fingers twitch. She's crying.

"Instead, we implore you to say goodbye to your loved ones," the president continues, softer. "We ask you to use your final days to spend your time with those who are dear to you, who love you and whom you love. Do not waste time doing anything else. Whoever you are, whatever you've been doing with your life, whatever you may or may not have done, leave chaos behind you and focus on love and friendship. That's all that really matters right now."

Another silence, and then the president's wife appears next

to him, alongside his two young children.

"I am here with my family because I am a father first, and a president second. I will remain your chosen president until the moment I die, but I am going to spend my time with my family too. I'm going to tell them how much I love them, and we are going to have as many meals together as we possibly can. We are afraid, just like you, but we are also grateful for the time we still have together."

He looks into the camera while his wife hugs him with tears in her eyes. His children crawl onto his lap. They are young, but it's obvious that they know what is going on.

"I am so sorry," he tells the nation. "I am sorry that I can't give you the news that you all wanted to hear right now. I'm sorry that we don't have the technology to save our planet. I'm sorry that we are not able to tell you that many parts of this planet may or may not survive. We simply do not know. No science can predict the exact timeline of what is coming. We just know that it's going to be extremely hard for anyone to survive. I'm sorry that there are no guarantees that humanity will live through this, just like we don't know what will happen to all animal life. From now on, we leave our lives in the hands of nature and faith because that's all we can do. I wish each and every single living creature, whether it's animal or human, the best of luck. Goodbye."

The screen turns black.

I have to call my parents.

HOLLY

The television screen turns black; the worldwide broadcast is over. Normally, after a regular presidential announcement, the world would go back to normal immediately. Channels would resume their normal programming, people would move on.

But this is one of the few moments in human history, apart from tragic days like 9/11, when life comes to a standstill. This is the first time in human history that this is also literally the case.

A week from now, we will all be dead or heading there. People will suffer. Animals will perish. No one will escape. There is not an ounce of doubt in my mind that we will not make it. This is an E.L.E., and it is very real.

No heroism can save us. No knights in shining armor—space suits, in this case—will magically rescue the planet with an act of self-sacrifice. There are no secret spaceships to bring humans to other planets. There is no way out for anyone, including the most powerful men on the planet.

Perhaps there are some sort of secret shelters deep underground, where small groups of people will be able to survive, but what good will that do if the planet is going to change so drastically? If and when they would be able to organize such a rescue mission on such short notice, it will only benefit those who have something worth saving.

And then what? Imagine being cooped up in an underground shelter with tens, hundreds, or thousands of other people, having to survive on whatever had been foreseen, knowing that most people are dead and the world will be covered in ice for decades, if not longer? What good would that do?

I wouldn't want to be there as part of a group of survivors, knowing that it would come at the cost of my personal feelings, hope, and joy. I don't want to put myself through that just to be alive physically but dead mentally. Survival is only worthwhile when it means that there is light at the end of the tunnel. I'm not so sure that this scenario actually offers hope at all. If it even exists.

But it does exist, or at least partially so.

The shelters, hidden deep in the Montana mountains. The nuclear bunkers. The doomsday preppers. They have been preparing for this for ages, but would that even be enough to guarantee survival when one mountain tremor was enough to ruin a system of three solid generators?

And if they somehow miraculously survive years in those shelters, *then what?*

No, I can't do it.

I'm thrown back to those moments inside the shelter, remembering how cold and frightening it was in there, with only the sound of the generator buzzing to keep me company and the thought that, even if Dylan were to die at that moment, I would be able to survive on my own physically, but never mentally. The claustrophobia would drive me insane. I simply would not make it.

But what if I had to, for Dylan's sake? What if he wanted to go back there, leaving everything and everyone behind, under the condition that I would go with him? What if his life was dependent on my decision?

I remember listening to Dylan's frantic cries about how the world as we knew it was gone. How scared he was for *me*. His first thought had been for me; he had never cared about his own well-being. His decision to take me to that shelter had never been about his survival but mine. Does his survival now depend on my choice?

His parents will reach out for sure. They'll offer him a spot at the shelter. What if he would only go if I were to go with him? Or what if we could both go and I could take my parents and sister with me? I want them to be safe. If given this opportunity, should they not get the chance to grab it?

After the quiet shock, things finally start moving again at the diner, but not the way I expected. I believed that people would go crazy, that they would get up, pushing everyone aside on their way out. I expected them to head for the nearest store and start looting it.

That doesn't happen.

They do get up, grab their things, pay for their food and drinks, and walk outside after saying goodbye to each other. Some go to the waitresses and hug them. Others hug each other. There are tears everywhere. There is also shock.

Mom, Dad, Emma, Dylan and I walk outside too, looking at each other in complete bewilderment. The diner remains open, as if life goes on, but the seats are empty because everyone is heading home. It has never been so calm around campus. Not once.

Students are leaving, heading home. I hug classmates, say

goodbye to vague acquaintances. I know I won't see any of them again. The campus empties pretty quickly.

"Let's go," Dad says.

"Where to?" my mom asks.

"Home."

"My things are here," Dylan mutters. "I have a test tomorrow."

"Something tells me you won't have to take it anymore," Dad says. "Come on, son, let's go home."

Dylan leaves his step against the diner wall. I reach for his hand and pull him gently with me. As we walk toward Dad's car, Emma uses her phone to check what is going on online. I don't really want to see what is going on out there, but I still check too, if only to confirm that this is really happening.

Newspapers come out with shocking newsflashes within seconds, as if they had something prepared in case something like this would happen. Had they known, or were they just as surprised as us?

Dad unlocks his car; we all get in. I lean against Dylan, who wraps his arm around me as Dad starts the car and gets in the right lane. We don't bother going back to the flat to get our things. We just keep on driving, before the traffic clutters. It's just things—trinkets, clothes, my laptop, my books. They will never be used again.

We soon leave the University of Minneapolis behind us. I know we'll never see it again.

"Is this really happening?" Emma says after a while, sending text messages to her friends and *what's-her-face.*

"I'm afraid it is," Mom says.

"What do we do?"

"Nothing. There's nothing we can do," Dad says.

"That's not exactly true," Dylan softly says.

My dad glances at him through the rearview mirror. My mom turns around. Emma looks up from her phone. I feel my body freeze. We all know what he means. His phone buzzes, and I just know it's them before he even gazes at the screen. Yet another phone number. They've been keeping tabs on him.

"Mom," he says, picking up while I lean into him.

He lets go of me and sits upright, holding the phone close to his ear while he gazes outside the window. I don't hear what they're saying, but I'm convinced by the way Dylan's talking that it's both his parents on the phone.

"I'm fine," he says.

Silence.

"No, Mom."

Silence.

"Dad, I said no."

Silence.

"Mom, I'm serious."

Silence.

"Okay then, so what do you want me to do?"

Silence.

"Only if Holly and her family can come with me."

Silence.

"What do you mean, there's not enough space? There's plenty of room. There's just the four of them. They can share a bedroom. We can still gather plenty of food. Her dad's really handy; he can help."

It's quiet in my dad's car while Dylan furiously argues with his parents, who are obviously planning to head for the mountain shelter. Do they honestly believe they will be able to survive the asteroid impact? I want to laugh at the sheer ridiculousness of it until I see Dylan's expression.

He believes it too.

He genuinely feels there is a chance to survive inside one of their shelters, despite the fact it will probably take hundreds of years for our planet to recover. Meaning that they will spend their lives living in darkness until they run out of food, water, and electricity, hoping and praying that the world will have healed enough for them to survive. That's not going to happen.

"Mom, you can't be serious. I'm not going if she can't come with me. No, Mom. This is stupid. I won't come alone."

Silence.

"Oh."

Silence.

"Are you serious? You won't trick me?"

Silence.

"I know, Mom, but you've tried to trick me before."

Silence.

"Thank you for apologizing, Dad. It's okay. You did what you had to do."

Silence.

"Okay. That changes everything."

Silence.

"Okay, that sounds good. And you're sure about this?"

Silence.

"I'll tell them, Dad. I'll tell them. I'll call you back, okay?"

Silence.

"Love you, Dad. Love you too, Mom."

He hangs up the phone and looks at us with such hope in

his eyes that it breaks my heart. Right there, in the middle of the growing chaos on the streets of Minneapolis, while heading to the lake house in Beau, Dylan is offering us hope.

But is that what we want?

DYLAN

Holly and I are sharing a sun bed on the porch as we gaze up at the night sky. It's the night after we discovered that a massive asteroid is heading toward Earth. It still feels so unreal.

Perhaps I bumped my head. Or it's part of some terrible nightmare that I'm trapped in after the accident in the shelter. Maybe I've been in a coma all this time and I've dreamed these past two years.

Her parents are inside the house; Emma's gone to see a friend. Beau is just as calm and peaceful as Minnesota was when we left it. In fact, the controlled traffic on the way over here proved that it was calm everywhere. Holly used the word *subdued.*

"That speech was brilliant," she said when we drove to the lake house. "He said all the right things, didn't he?"

"He did," her dad said, "but it doesn't make it any less bittersweet."

We haven't spoken about my parents' offer yet. I know it's on the table, that her folks are discussing it right now. I know Holly is waiting for her parents to make their decision.

There are so many questions to be answered. What if Holly

wants to go, but her parents don't? Will she still go then? What if Emma wants to take up the offer, but she can't because of my parents' precondition that they can only come if I come too?

And what if Holly decides not to go, but Emma wants to? Do I sacrifice Holly to save her sister's life? It's all so mind-boggling.

And the thing is, I don't even know if I want to live like that. My parents automatically assumed I do, but I haven't made up my mind yet. I'm scared. I'm so damned scared for Holly, Dan, Susan, and Emma. They are my family now, and I'm holding their fate in my hands.

"We have to do it," I say.

Holly doesn't speak.

"We have to go. It's our only chance to survive."

No answer. She's looking up at the stars.

"Hol, why are we even contemplating this? It's the only thing we *can* do. It's what millions of others would."

I laugh, and even I can hear how bitter it sounds. I remember the shelter, the cold darkness of it. The threats that seemed to come from every corner. I remember Holly's anxiety, and mine. The fear, the hurt.

I cannot even imagine spending the rest of my life in there, trapped between those walls while fearing the inevitable ice age that will change our world into something unreal. But this is my one and only chance of saving Holly's life.

"I could never imagine the benefits of being a doomsday preppers' son," I continue softly. "I always felt like the odd one out, the misfit, the outcast. I was embarrassed so many times. I felt like they were taking my childhood hostage. That's what it felt like growing up with them. I didn't know what it was like to be hopelessly happy until you came into my life and showed me how simple it was. But now, with all of this, it's as if we've come full circle, you know? This is what it comes down to in the end: survival. This is what we have to do, now that it's real."

She still doesn't say anything, and suddenly fear takes hold of me. What if she doesn't want this?

"Holly? Talk to me."

"Let's go inside," she says. She sits up and looks at the starry sky with that one blue line crossing it, already larger than it was this morning. It's not even just blue anymore. It has this big array of colors that will only increase in the next days.

The asteroid is traveling at a speed that we can't even comprehend. A week, our president said, but it feels like it will hit us in a day. We don't have much time left. Yet the world seems to be at peace with it, or at least it does where we live. *Hug your loved ones.*

I saw this movie once called *Melancholia*, where two sisters anticipate the end of the world as a planet crashes into it. The ending of that movie stayed with me for a long time, as it was extremely powerful, dramatic, and touching at the same time.

The sisters and their family members knew there was nothing they could do about the crash and annihilation of our planet. I wonder now if they—or one of them—would be seeking shelter if they had been given the chance?

Inside, Holly's parents and Emma are sitting at the kitchen table. She just returned from seeing her friend. Tears stream down Emma's face, but Susan and Dan are strangely composed, just as Holly is. I am too because I can't afford to lose my focus.

"We have to do it," I say. "Take my parents' offer, I mean."

Dan smiles and pats the chair next to him.

"Sit down, Dylan."

"I can't."

"It's okay. Just take a seat."

I sit down and know what they're going to say. The answer is *no*.

When I glance at Holly and Emma, I know they agree with their parents.

God.

HOLLY

I can see the distress on Dylan's face. It's the kind of anxiety he has often shown in the past years when he had things to hide from me, like the truth about his parents or the fear and anxiety that washed over him after we returned from the shelter.

I reach for his hand.

"It's okay," I say. "It's our decision to make, and we made it together. You don't have to feel so guilty."

"Not guilty?!" he says. "I'm offering you a chance at survival! Why won't you take it?"

Gone is the composed man I'm engaged to. He's back to being that frightened young man who believed there is an answer for anything.

"I know that this might seem like a chance in a million to live through all this, Dylan," Dad says, "but we all know that this is unlikely to happen. We have to respectfully decline your parents' offer. We have talked things through, and we have decided to face our fate together, as a family."

"But why?" Dylan whispers.

"Because it's the only right thing to do," Mom says. "I know that it all makes sense to you, to go into the mountains and stay in that shelter for the following twenty years or so, because you were raised in that environment. Your parents have always meant well, and they are without a doubt wonderful people for thinking of you—and us—first. In the end, though, not even they will have prepared for this particular end-of-the-world scenario. It's different."

"Different how?" Dylan asks. "More serious? More extreme? Yes, but I'm sure they are still prepping for the worst-case scenario as we speak. We still have a week to get ready for the worst, so why not use that time?"

"It won't change how we feel about it," I say, adding my two cents. "I'd rather spend my last week with you, loving you all, reminiscing and remembering what our lives were like, than prepare for decades of cold winters and mayhem. It's not the quantity but the quality of life that matters."

"You make it sound like it's a terrible thing to survive," Dylan says, obviously confused.

"It's a chance, yes," Mom says, "but we are not willing nor prepared to do this. If this is the end of our life, then so be it. I'd rather spend my final days with my family than survive with strangers in a cave for God knows how long."

"It may not be as bad as it seems," Dylan mutters.

We all know that this is not true. The news reports have been very clear on this. The scientists have confirmed the situation all day long. Human life as we know it is over. Ironically enough, our ending is coming not by our own hand, but a disaster beyond anything our planet has ever seen. This asteroid is bigger than the one that ended the dinosaur reign over our world.

"What about you, Emma?" Dylan says. "You want to live, don't you?"

Emma wipes her tears away.

"Of course I do, but not at the cost of everything. If survival means suffering on a daily basis, I don't want it."

"My parents are offering us a chance at life," Dylan says desperately. "Isn't that worth trying?"

I draw Dylan's attention.

"But what if life after this event is not worth fighting for? I want to spend my final days living in joy as a farewell to an amazing life. This is what our president asked us to do, and I will hold on to that thought."

Tears flow freely down my face. Dylan starts crying too. He shakes his head. I hug him.

"Your parents are not crazy, Dylan. They never were. They are sensible, wise people, and maybe they stand a chance to live through this, so I think you should do too. Take that chance. Go to them. Be with them, as you were always intended to be."

Dylan struggles with our decision. It's pretty obvious that he doesn't know what to do. I don't want to lose him, but if he had never met me, he would be on his way to that shelter right now. I have taken that opportunity from him, and for that, I feel guilty.

"You have to forget about us," I say softly. "Please. Go home. You have to try."

He doesn't know what to say.

"I don't know," he says.

My dad smiles. "You don't have to decide now. You can take your time. There's plenty of time to drive up to the mountains. Whatever your decision is, I'll help you get back home."

"Thank you," Dylan whispers.

Dad gets up and pats his belly, smiling as he reaches for Mom's hand before leaning over and kissing her.

"Now then, I'm starving. What's for dinner? Let's make a

list of all the things that we love, okay? I don't want to spend my final days eating bread."

Mom laughs.

"Veggie burgers!" Emma and I shout at the same time.

DYLAN

The evening is surprisingly cheerful, something I could never have imagined this morning. We have an amazing dinner and sit out on the patio overlooking the lake. It's a gorgeous, star-filled night. How can this beautiful world of ours be shattered in just one week?

Holly and I share one sunbed, her parents the other one. Emma is on a rocking chair. Holly leans into me. I can hear and feel her breathing. The sense of peace is overwhelmingly beautiful.

I close my eyes and try to imagine living in the shelter with my parents, my uncle's family, some of their friends, and whoever else might be there. I'm sure that all over the world, a lot of people are trying to prepare for Doomsday, and that there will be thousands of them trying to survive the worst-case scenario. Perhaps, so journalists say on the radio, the impact won't be as grave as predicted and the survival rate will be much higher than foreseen. But we all know that this is just wishful thinking.

It has all been laid out before us, the timeline of what's to come. The floodings, the earthquakes, the fires, the cold, the famine. If you don't get killed immediately, that is.

A strange feeling of calm overwhelms me. My time has come, and I am strangely ready for it. I don't want to go away. I don't want to go back and leave these wonderful people behind, only to feel guilty for the rest of my existence while battling for survival. I don't want to be part of a post-apocalyptic world. I don't want to help put babies into this shattered world.

I want to stay here.

I touch Holly's face. She looks at me.

"Can we go to bed?" I whisper.

She smiles and gets up quickly.

"Goodnight," she says, pulling me with her.

"Night, guys," Susan says.

"Don't do anything we wouldn't do," Dan says.

"Don't be too loud," Emma adds.

Holly laughs. "Shut up, sis."

We go to her bedroom, where Holly shuts the door and the drapes and turns on the light. She is gorgeous like this. The light reflects the porcelain features of her face.

She's dressed in a light dress. I gently pull it over her arms and face. Her nipples are erect behind the lace pink bra that fits perfectly around her small breasts. She's still as slim as she has always been.

I unhook her bra and leave it on the bed. As she stands before me, dressed only in that tiny pink piece of underwear that covers up her private parts, I can't help but think how lucky I am to love this wonderful woman. Loving her has been the ultimate gift of life.

Sadness overwhelms me. This will be one of the last times we will be here together, and we both know it. But it makes it all the more special too.

"Stop thinking," she says, reaching for my T-shirt. "Take off your clothes. I want to see you."

She is already horny as hell; I can tell by the look on her face. Our lovemaking has only increased these past two years.

"You're perfect," she says.

"No, you are," I whisper.

I remove my shirt and jeans, and as I stand in front of her in my briefs, I realize once again that she is the only person in the world who knows me inside and out. I will never leave her. My decision has been made. She knows it too.

"It'll be alright," she whispers in that soft tone that she used when we were at the shelter, reassuring me that I had nothing to fear. "This will not be the end."

I want to hold on to her belief that there is more out there for us, a thought that I have never had while growing up. Now seems like the right time to start believing.

I stroke her breasts, tease her nipples softly before kissing them. They react to every touch. It turns me on to know that I can have this effect on someone as beautiful as her.

"Why did you fall in love with me that day on campus?" I said. "You could have picked anyone, but you chose me."

"I just knew," she says. "Like Jack and Rose knew."

I laugh. "That's so corny."

"But true."

"Show me what you've got," I say.

She smiles. "Gladly."

I lay her gently down on the bed and remove her panties. As she lies on top of the sheets, bared to me without any hesitation, waiting for me to take her, I'm amazed once again by her beauty. The small freckles on her inner thighs are like tiny little stars. The bigger one on her stomach, resting neatly near her belly button, has always fascinated me.

She is freckled all over, but I always feel this urge to kiss that one because it's near her flat stomach. She pants when I lean over her and kiss it. She groans softly.

"Please make love to me," she whispers.

"I will," I say. "Don't worry about that. Have some patience, for goodness' sake."

"Just fuck me already."

I laugh and do as I'm told. I feel complete, that's the only word that fits. We know each other so well. We move in a set rhythm that we define together, as if we are one person, coming together in a haze of happiness.

Everything feels perfect. *We* are perfect together. We stay entwined as she leans forward and kisses me so deeply that I'm in heaven again.

"I'm not done yet," I say.

She laughs. "Well, that's a first."

"But it won't be the last."

I set the pace this time, slowly but firmly bringing her to a new high. She's almost delirious.

Exhausted and spent, she rolls onto her side, staring at me with a satisfied, post-orgasmic smile.

"What the fuck was that," she whispers, panting. "That was amazing."

"The best ever," I say, stroking her face and hair. "I'm done. Seriously. I can't take it anymore."

"No, you're not," she says firmly.

"Excuse me?"

"You can rest now, but this is not over yet, mister."

"You're kidding me, right?"

"Nope."

"Are you telling me you want to pull an all-nighter?"

Holly touches my stubbled face.

"Oh yeah. You see, I've got all the time in the world and nowhere else to go."

"You've got a point there."

"But let's get some food first."

She pulls me out of bed. I groan.

"You are a horny, insatiable creature."

"Takes one to know one." She grins.

That is very true.

HOLLY

That night, the most beautiful, endless night we've ever had, felt like goodbye to me, but I didn't tell Dylan how I felt. He just couldn't get enough of me, so I figured this was his way of remembering me forever. I imagined him getting up in the morning, packing his bags, and saying goodbye.

I lost all track of time after a while and was so exhausted that I fell asleep beneath him, feeling his bare skin everywhere, as if he was one big naked blanket covering me from top to bottom. I fell asleep like a log, and when I woke up just now, he was gone.

I'm alone in bed. My first thought is: *he left without saying goodbye.* The loneliness is devastating. I imagine him sneaking out of the house and walking away, since all of his things are still in Minneapolis.

But as I reluctantly get up, dress, and head into the kitchen, he's right here, making breakfast alongside my mom. He showered—good thinking, or it would have been quite embarrassing—and he doesn't even seem exhausted after having fucked me for hours.

"Hey," he says, walking over to me with a cup of tea. "Made you this." He kisses me and sniffs. "You'd better shower first, or your sister will think we're living in a brothel."

"Thanks for that," I say. "How come you're so chirpy?"

"I got to do what I love the most," he says. "Love you. Go shower."

"Love you too, idiot."

I take my tea into the bathroom and sip it before and after my shower, feeling relaxed and content. But as I look out the window while drying my hair, a faint light blue streak, just like an airplane's tail, is clearly visible in the morning sky.

I sigh, get dressed, and head back to the kitchen, where Dylan and my mom are serving breakfast. Emma and Dad are sitting at the table. Dad compliments Dylan on the Eggs Benedict he prepared.

"You're an amazing chef," he says.

Dylan laughs. "It's just eggs."

"Perfect eggs."

We sit down and eat the copious breakfast while talking about everything and nothing, but always avoiding the sensitive topics.

When the doorbell rings, I volunteer to open. Our neighbors, Marie and Bernard, are standing in the doorway with a hamper filled to the brim with fruit and biscuits.

They've been here forever. Marie is best friends with my mom, while Bernard often goes golfing with Dad. In front of our house is their car, stacked with suitcases and boxes, as if they're moving away.

"Hey," I say, surprised, "is everything alright?"

"Yeah, well sort of," Marie says, offering me the hamper. "Are your parents here, Holly?"

"Yeah, come in."

They follow me into the kitchen, where my mom and dad

look up in surprise.

"Hey," Mom says, "what a nice surprise. Care for some breakfast?"

"No, thanks," Marie says. "I'm sorry we can't stay long. We're driving out to Los Angeles."

"To LA?" my dad repeats. "You're going to visit Alex?"

Their son, Alex, left eight years ago after a huge fight. He moved to LA and never came back. His absence has weighed hard on our neighbors, but never once have they admitted that it was their own fault that their son moved out after they voiced some racist comments about his girlfriend. As far as we know, they've never seen their grandchildren.

"Alex called last night. He wants to make things right between us before—well, you know. I'm guessing it's now or never."

The room grows very quiet. I see Dylan's expression change. I place the hamper on the table and smile.

"That's a good idea," I say. "Actually, Dylan and I are going to be visiting his parents too before our time is up. We're leaving today, so there's still time to say goodbye."

My dad and Emma look at me in shock, but Mom smiles and nods.

"We're all going," she says while she hugs Marie and Bernard. "We all should be with the ones we love in times like this, right?"

"Yeah," Marie says, her eyes glistering. "These are the moments that count, no matter what happened in the past."

Dylan takes a deep breath and looks at me.

"It's all that matters," he says.

DYLAN

Dan and Susan are singing to whatever song is coming up on Spotify as we make our way from Beau to Midstone, a journey that will take about fourteen hours.

We decided not to fly because we were unsure of the decisions around air traffic in the upcoming days. Rumor has it that the government is going to shut down all traffic in the next two days since they are already urging people to plan their last flights carefully and quickly.

We know that all traffic will come to a complete stop after the asteroid hits us. We also know that technology and electricity will diminish in a matter of minutes when the asteroid strikes.

Tsunamis caused by the crash will be miles high, and they will wipe out half of the country, as the water is expected to reach extremely far. None of the European countries will survive. The whole of the UK will be flooded, and the water will wash over Belgium, the Netherlands, France, Germany, up until the very south and north, hitting Portugal, Spain, Denmark and Sweden.

Those who survive that disaster will have to deal with a lack of food and water since all water supplies will turn toxic due to the asteroid shattering into pieces on impact. Toxic debris will pollute the air and make it impossible to breathe properly. Only if you don't get in touch with any of that, will you stand a chance of survival.

If you are able to live through the predicted new ice age, that is. The world will turn colder than ever. Temperatures will drop to a new all-time low.

All around the world, people are coming together in droves to pray. Rome and the Vatican are flooded with people who hope that God will somehow prevent this from happening.

Television reporters are showing footage from all over the world. Strangely enough, the president's call to use our last days usefully has been heard. There's barely any loitering. People of all color, religion, gender, and sexuality are coming together to talk, pray, and accept.

Countries have reconciled and governments have discussed all alternative options, concluding that there is nothing anyone can do. Armies are patrolling cities, but it has never been so peaceful and calm.

In our final hours, humanity's wars have been forgotten. Every fight has stopped. There won't be an exception to the unwritten rule of death. It's amazing to see. It's also quite eerie.

"Hey, I love that song," Dan protests when Emma leans forward to select another tune.

"I do too, Dad, but it's the twentieth time that you've played this damn song. Didn't you update your Spotify?"

"No, I like my little list."

"Then I'll add some more songs." She pokes Holly, who is leaning into me. "Come on, sis, let's drop some more songs on that boring old list."

Before long, we're all adding songs to the playlist, which is now a lot more varied. Holly's dad turns up the volume and opens the windows as we travel on the quiet highway to Montana, stopping in various small towns to eat.

It's almost perfect.

It's ten p.m. when we arrive at my dad's property. I can immediately spot the amount of work that he's been doing in the past few days, obviously preparing to leave for the mountain shelter.

There are a lot of cars parked on the terrain. I recognize my uncle's, my aunt's, my cousin's, and my mom's. The barn is open; supplies are being dragged out. It feels like the good old times, but with a sense of urgency added to it.

The front door is open. I walk toward it while Dan, Susan, and Emma are staring at the contents of the barn, slowly taking in what this former life of mine was about. Holly clutches my hand as I make my way through the house.

"Mom?" I call out when I hear noise in the pantry.

She's on her knees putting things in boxes, heaving and panting while she works.

"Dylan?"

She's on her feet in a split second and throws her arms around me.

"Dylan, you came home. God, I'm so happy. I didn't think you'd come back."

I pull Holly next to me.

"Holly and her family came with me."

"Hi, Holly," my mom says, hugging her fiercely. "Thank you for bringing my son home."

"Where's Dad?"

"He's out in the back. We don't have much time. We've got people driving back and forth to the big shelter. We've got plenty of room and supplies for about twenty-five people, for at least four years. The other shelters have been stacked too. We can save over a hundred people in total."

"That's a lot, Mom," I say, feeling a lump down my throat. "That's great. But is it going to be enough?"

"Enough? Of course it will be enough."

"It might be enough to survive a natural disaster, but is it enough for *this*?"

My mom is taken aback.

"I sure as hell hope so."

"Are you equipped for the ice age?"

Mom takes a deep breath.

"Not yet, but we'll figure it out once the time comes. Right now, immediate survival is more important. Come on, let me show you where you guys are going to be living."

I feel Holly's hand tighten around mine.

"Mom, I came to say goodbye," I say softly. "We're not going to go with you."

Mom freezes before laughing nervously. Her long, loose hair dangles in front of her eyes.

"Don't be silly, Dylan. Of course you're coming with us. You want to live, don't you?"

"Of course I do, Mom," I say. "I don't want to die. No one does. But this life that's waiting for us on the other side of tragedy is not what I want. I don't want to spend my days not knowing if there is a future for us. I can't. I just *can't.*"

She steps back.

"Then why the hell did you even bother coming here?"

"To see you one last time. To wish you all the luck in the world. To tell you that I love you and I understand now why I grew up the way that I did."

She laughs bitterly before shutting down the same way she always did when I was little and started asking questions about our way of life.

"You know what, Dylan? Go to hell, alright? All I ever did was for you. I've been a good mother to you. I've helped you in a world that was dangerous and revengeful. I've always done the right thing by you. And now you come here to tell me that you don't want the gift I'm offering? Get the hell out of here and stop wasting my time."

Every word she says is like a knife slicing through my heart. I had known upfront that she wouldn't understand, but a big part of me had prayed during the long ride over that she would understand my point of view.

She looks Holly up and down with such disdain it physically hurts.

"You'd rather die with *her* than stay alive with *me*?" she adds bitterly.

"I choose love," I say softly.

She obviously doesn't understand. How could she, when her entire family and husband have taught her that survival was always the only option?

"Goodbye, Dylan."

She turns around, kneels, and starts rummaging through the pantry cupboards again. I turn around, wrap my arm around Holly, and walk out the door, knowing that I'll never see her or hear from her again.

I never even got to see my dad.

HOLLY

We spend the night at a small motel on the outskirts of Midstone, where my dad has booked three rooms. Dylan is pretty upset, but not as much as I had expected. He had expected this, or so he told me when we showered together and made love on the bed after, followed by another shower.

In the morning, we have breakfast at the diner across the street before driving back home. Dylan looks expectantly out the window, even though he knows that his mom will not show up to reconcile. It's over, and we all know it.

"I don't want to go back home," my dad says. "I'm not sure about you guys, but there are so many beautiful things to see around here. Perhaps we should just take our time and enjoy this part of the world while we still can."

I think back on all of my friends who have been doing the same. Everyone has gone home to be with their loved ones, and we've all said our goodbyes on the phone or through text messages. We all agreed on what was important to us, and that was being with the people who matter the most.

There's nothing to go back to. Our house is still there, but it's empty now and locked up. A lot of people in our area are still at home with their families, but we have all that we need right here. What is there to go back to?

"You're right," Mom says, making the decision for all of us. "Let's hit the road."

We lay out a plan that will take us from Montana to Idaho, Wyoming, South Dakota, and back to Minnesota. If our calculations are correct, this will take us back home on the final day.

"I want to stand on top of a mountain when it happens," Dylan says. "Is there a beautiful area where we can go when—you know?"

"Yeah," Emma says. "Eagle Mountain. We can do that, right, Dad?"

"That sounds like a plan," Dad says. "Let's do this."

We all take turns driving in the next few days as we travel from state to state, taking in the most beautiful sceneries and routes.

We sleep in motels that have tons of empty rooms, enjoy dinners at fancy restaurants that are practically empty, where we are spoiled by the few people still working there.

We fill the car up with gas where we can, buy candy and sweets at gas stations, talk for hours about whatever comes to mind, sing along hundreds of songs, and repeat this day after day.

Every day, the blue line in the sky becomes more visible. Every night, it fills up the skies and paints them with color in a way we have never seen before.

We never speak of Dylan's parents again.

On the predicted doomsday, we end up back home. My mom and dad take the bags from the car. Mom starts filling up the washing machine while Dad mows the lawn. We have lunch by the lake and enjoy the scenery. But it's clear that there's a lot of uneasiness too.

The ducks aren't as cheerful and careless as usual. Birds fly restlessly through the skies. There are no more planes crossing the skies and barely any cars down the road. The lake is devoid of fishermen. All boats are lingering unused by the docks.

The asteroid is visible to the naked eye. It paints the skies in a threatening way. Television broadcasting is continuously tracking the asteroid, but that will cease soon, as the satellites that circulate around our planet are already being disrupted by the asteroid's arrival. Starlink is failing. The internet, Wi-Fi, and radio signals are constantly up and down.

Emma heads for her room while Dad walks inside with Mom and plays old vinyl records through the open living room windows. We know that all electricity will soon cease to function too. All that will remain is silence.

"Too bad we don't have Superman or Iron Man for real," Dylan says. "Where are those superheroes when you really need them?"

"I have my hero right here with me," I say.

I can feel him smile against my hair.

"Do you regret it?" he says.

"Not for a second."

"But?"

"I feel guilty," I confess. "You should not have had to choose."

"It was my choice to make," he says. "And I don't regret it for one moment."

I don't answer, because, what can I say?

After a while, he speaks again. His warm breath is comforting.

"Do you think it'll hurt?"

"I don't know," I say. "I'm hoping it'll be quick."

Dad leans out the window.

"If you want to go up the mountain, you should go now," he says. I look at my phone. It's five p.m.

"Come on," Dylan says, pulling me up. "Let's do this."

We walk inside the house, where Mom, Dad, and Emma wait for us.

"We're not going with you," Mom says. "Your dad and I will stay here, and Emma has chosen to do the same."

I burst into tears as I fling myself into my mom's arms. She holds me tight and uses her thumbs to wipe the tears off my face.

"Don't cry," she says. "You're stronger than that."

"I know," I say, "but I'm going to miss you so much."

"You won't have to for very long. We'll see each other again, I promise."

"I hope so," I say, desperately wanting to believe that this is not the end for us. "I love you so much, Mom."

"I love you too, honey. I'm so proud of you."

She lets go of me reluctantly and then hugs Dylan for a long time, wiping the tears from his face.

"You are a good man," she says. "Thank you for all you did for us. You have made us come alive again. You are an amazing human being. If I could have ever had a son, I would have wanted him to be like you."

Her words touch his heart. He smiles through his tears and hugs her tight.

"Thank you for being my second mom," he says. "I love you so much, Susan."

"I love you, Dylan."

Dad hugs and kisses me and smiles.

"You'll be forever in my heart," he says. "Don't you forget that. Think about us up on that mountain."

"I will," I say. "Thank you for everything, Dad."

"Love you, sweetheart."

He hugs Dylan and pats him on the back, whispering something in his ear that I can't understand. After a long embrace, we head to Emma, who is waiting for us by the door.

"Love you, sis," she says. "Thanks for being the best big sister there is."

"Thank you for being my favorite spoiled little brat." I smile through my tears.

"Just remember that in the afterlife."

She moves to Dylan, who hugs her tight. He's much taller than she is and has to lean forward to take her in his arms.

"You're the sister I've never had and always missed," he says. "Thanks for all the laughs."

"Love you, big brother," she says. "Take care of my sister for me, will you?"

"Always."

We open the door and head for my dad's car. I hesitate as I stand by the door, wondering if this is the right thing to do, but when Dylan touches my hand slightly, I know it is. We need to be up on that mountain together.

"Love you all," I say.

"We love you," my mom calls out.

I get in the car and start the engine.

DYLAN

The roads are empty as we drive through town on our way to Eagle Mountain, which isn't that far away. We can see its outline from the lake. This is one of the most beautiful areas in the state, and it just takes my breath away every time I see it.

We'll reach the mountain in one hour, and then we have to hike up the hill, which will take another two hours. We've got time. The radio is playing, but the sound is crackling and it's hard to understand now what people are saying. I check my phone.

"It's expected to hit our atmosphere within four hours," I say.

"Perfect timing," Holly reacts.

"It's weird, isn't it? That this is really happening?"

"Yeah, it is."

I wonder what it'll be like to stand up on that mountain. What it will feel like to see that damned asteroid hit our atmosphere before making its way downward at unmeasurable speed, leaving a worldwide path of devastation, mayhem, and death.

Holly parks the car at the bottom of the mountain in the empty parking lot. The tourist shop is closed. There is no one to stop us from going up the mountain.

It's deadly quiet, as are many places now. We barely crossed anyone's path on the roads either. Everyone's at home, waiting for the events to unfold.

Holly has been here many times before, and she knows where to go to hike up the mountain. It's a steep climb, but one that can be taken at a slow and even relaxing pace. Experienced hikers would take about an hour and a half, but we estimate it will take us a little over two hours.

We talk as we walk, eat along the way, and enjoy the view, even taking pictures on our phones, even though we have no more internet connection and mobile data is dysfunctional.

When we reach the top, it's already turning dark. In an hour or so, the sky will be filled with bright colors and stars, and of course the blue tail that the asteroid leaves in its wake. Holly gasps.

"It's beautiful. Dyl. I had no idea it was this gorgeous here. I forgot. Why didn't we come here sooner?"

"Because there was always something else to do," I say as I pull her close to me. Being here with her is the best moment of my life. This is our perfect ending.

HOLLY

I've never felt as much at peace in my life as at this very moment. It's hard to even describe all the feelings that are coursing through me right now, a mixture of sadness and joy and peace.

Please look out for us, I pray.

It's a warm evening, but up here on the mountain, it should be chilly. It's not. Even the climate has changed already.

I raise my head at the sky with its falling stars. The air is painted in bright colors, unlike anything I have ever seen before. The blues and reds were here before, but now they are so bright that it almost feels like someone has come by to paint the sky itself. There are more stars than I could ever count. It is absolutely gorgeous, even the asteroid's tail.

"It is stunning," Dylan says in awe, sharing my excitement. "I never thought the sky could be so amazing. Why did I never see this before?"

"Because this is the only time you *will* see the skies like this," I say. "This is pure perfection."

The asteroid speeds through the air, picking up speed. It's devastatingly big. I'm so scared.

Dylan turns me around. He kisses me while we hold hands. I feel calm again.

I have never felt this close to anyone in my life. It's the most stunning thing to feel so connected.

I know that this is not the end. I know that, no matter what, we will always be bound together. It's a soul thing. It goes beyond this life, beyond this planet, beyond anything.

"I choose to love," he whispers in my ear.

We kiss as the asteroid enters our atmosphere.

Printed in Great Britain
by Amazon

51793366R10236